Twinkle

A science fiction novel

SJ Parkinson

Edited by: Misti Wolanski (Red Adept Publishing)
Cover art by: Stephan Johnstone (SJDWORLD)
Formatted by: Polgarus Studio

DEDICATION

For Keith C. Blackmore

My longtime friend, fellow author,
and the man who encouraged me to
write out the many stories in my head.

NOTE

The dates referred to in this novel are centric to the United States for consistency. Due to the International Date Line, an issue occurs when dealing with Asia, as ten p.m. in New York City is ten a.m. the following day in Beijing. For simplicity and ease of continuity, please keep this in mind.

The Star by Jane Taylor
Published 1809 in *Rhymes for the Nursery*

Twinkle, twinkle, little star,
How I wonder what you are!
Up above the world so high,
Like a diamond in the sky.

When the blazing sun is gone,
When he nothing shines upon,
Then you show your little light,
Twinkle, twinkle, all the night.

Then the traveler in the dark
Thanks you for your tiny spark,
How could he see where to go,
If you did not twinkle so?

In the dark blue sky you keep,
Often through my curtains peep
For you never shut your eye,
Till the sun is in the sky.

As your bright and tiny spark
Lights the traveler in the dark,
Though I know not what you are,
Twinkle, twinkle, little star.

July 3rd

Chapter One
One for the Record Books

Sir Marcus Brandon, Knight Commander of the Victorian Order, sat in a fabric director's chair before a compact makeup table in a small windowless room. Normally used for storage, the space had been converted into an *ad hoc* dressing and makeup area for that night. Round white light bulbs, surrounding the large mirror before him, offset the harsh fluorescent lighting from above. The makeup artist standing to his right, a man named Philippe, tutted continuously as he applied more powder under Brandon's chin. While the noise was annoying, Brandon tolerated it. Philippe had been flown in from his home in Cannes for this one job.

A stringy youth came up to him on his left. He was no more than twenty, wore jeans and a black T-shirt, and had a pair of wireless padded headphones around his neck. He spoke respectfully. "Three minutes, Sir Marcus."

"Thank you," Brandon answered in his light English accent. He returned his attention to his reflection in the mirror above the makeup table. The mirror lights eliminated all shadows on his face. Tissue paper, tucked inside his collar, protected the white shirt from being stained with makeup. The bright paper contrasted with his fair skin and made the wrinkles at the corner of his eyes and mouth stand out all the more. *I'm getting old.*

1

Brandon's naturally red hair, parted in the middle and almost touching his shoulders, still had the untamed look of his university days. The only addition since graduating from MIT at seventeen had been a Van Dyke beard, which made him look somewhat sinister and old-fashioned, but he offset that with the natural white smile he always used publicly. Forty years old, Brandon was a multi-billionaire and acknowledged as the richest man in the world. He fully expected to be the first trillionaire within twenty years.

Brandon tried to swallow but couldn't. His mouth was dry, and he realized he was clutching the ends of the armrests of the director's chair. He was about to launch his most audacious and expensive business venture yet. He knew the tension would disappear once he was in front of the cameras, but that was little consolation for the moment.

Philippe stood back, dropped a triangular makeup sponge onto a side table, and crossed his arms. He looked down his long nose at Brandon for a moment then threw up his hands. "*Bon*, I can do no more."

Brandon shuffled forward on his chair to take a long look at the makeup. It looked comical to him, but knew it would look good on high-definition television, and that was all that mattered. He left the tissue paper tucked into the collar of his open-necked shirt. That would be taken away on set, moments before he went on the air.

Garbo, his lithe twenty-eight-year-old personal assistant, appeared at his elbow. He stole an appreciative glance at her in the mirror as he rose. Wearing a simple above-the-knee dark skirt and coral blouse, her only adornment, beyond the subtlest of makeup, was a double-strand choker of pearls. She carried her tablet and handed him a small bottle of water without prompting. They began walking toward the stage that had only been finished being built an hour before. Upon opening the makeup room door, muted strains of drum and bass dance music came to his ears.

Garbo walked with her tablet supported by her forearm, which was pressed against her chest. She tossed her long straight blond hair away from her face and spoke with the drawl of her native South Carolina. "All of the bureaus are standing by. The satellite feeds have all been validated. David reports no technical problems, and two backup circuits are standing by in case any issues develop at the last minute."

The pair stepped up onto a small raised stage behind a closed thick red curtain. A transparent lectern stood in front of a curved set. At the rear of the stage, eight large-format flat-screen displays were bolted to black aluminum stands in an arc. All the screens displayed the same slowly rotating logo of the Athena Group. Brandon looked at that logo with pride. The Athena Group owned over three hundred companies, and Sir Marcus Brandon was the majority shareholder.

Brandon stopped behind the lectern, finding Garbo had already placed a set of index cards on the surface. They contained his talking points printed in clear, inch-high black letters. He knew the script by heart, but billions of dollars were at stake.

Two men moved in toward him. One helped him slip into a navy blue blazer, before removing the makeup paper from his collar. The other fitted him with a pair of miniature wireless radio microphones. The wardrobe assistant used a lint roller to remove a few particles of dust that clung to the jacket before walking off set.

The sound man connected the radio microphone battery packs to the rear of Brandon's leather belt. "Sir Marcus, could you say a few words, please?"

"Testing, testing. One, two, three," Brandon replied in his normal speaking voice.

The sound technician looked off stage. "How's that, Bob?" He looked back at Brandon. "Thank you. That's fine." The sound technician left the stage.

Garbo pointed at the notes. "Do you want any changes?"

"No, the dress rehearsal went fine." Brandon nervously tugged his jacket lapels into place and shot his cuffs.

"Thirty seconds!" someone called out from the far side of the stage.

Garbo and Brandon left the stage and stood in the wings. Brandon closed his eyes, tipped his head back, took a cleansing breath, and blew it out slowly. The butterflies in his stomach kicked into a full-on frenzy.

"The social media campaign kicked off on schedule, and we have a full house," Garbo said. "All the major networks are represented. They still have no idea what we are announcing today. The bar's been open for an hour, so I suspect you'll get a decent reception." The last part of that sentence was accompanied with a toothed smile.

Brandon nodded once. His anxiety had peaked, and he didn't feel like saying anything at the moment. They waited the last few seconds in silence. Brandon repeatedly clenched and unclenched his fists.

Across the stage, the young man with the padded earphones began calling out with fingers raised. "Five, four, three." He silently counted "two" and "one" with his fingers.

After the count ended, the music began increasing in volume, and ten seconds later, the red curtain slid open, exposing bright and colorful spotlights sweeping swiftly through the crowd.

A confident feminine voice came over the in-house speaker system. "Ladies and gentlemen, welcome to the XVI rooftop lounge. High above New York's Times Square and in the heart of the theater district, we thank you for attending this Athena Group press conference."

The voice paused. Brandon shook his shoulders to get his jacket comfortable. He twisted his shoulders left then right to loosen up a little.

The voiceover continued, "And now, ladies and gentlemen, please join me in welcoming the chairman and chief executive officer for the Athena Group—Sir Marcus Brandon!"

The music peaked, and Brandon could hear loud applause. That would be his marketing staff salted through the crowd to generate buzz. He counted silently to three, forced a wide smile, and stepped forward into the bright spotlights. He waved his left hand up high as he stepped up to the lectern.

The lights half-blinded him, but he could see there were no free seats and several people stood around the periphery of the club. There were rows of faceless reporters, several cameramen, and in the back, the outline of the DJ at his mixing board. The lights of the New York City skyline backdropped the audience.

Playing the audience, Brandon pointed at the back corner of the room and waved while smiling broadly. He had no idea who was there. He waved purely for show.

The music faded as Brandon clasped the sides of the lectern. As the last of the applause faded, he began speaking. "Welcome. Welcome, everyone, and thank you. Thank you for your warm applause... Athena Group has traditionally held its press conferences in our London headquarters, but we thought we'd mix things up for this event. My staff initially planned to put me on the opposite side of the room, with the city behind me. However, given the choice of staring at my ugly mug or the grand New York skyline, I knew no one would pay me any attention."

Light laughter rippled through the room.

Thank God for the open bar. Brandon gripped the lectern even tighter but kept his face looking confident and relaxed. "Now, why are we here? I know the invitations we sent out were painfully vague, but we deliberately chose New York for this function because it's the city that never sleeps. The Athena Group's new venture will also never rest. Ladies and gentlemen, tonight I'm proud to announce the formation of Global News International."

Brandon half turned to his left, and the rotating Athena Group on the monitors slowly morphed into a graphic "GNI" logo. The news organizations present were not going to be pleased by him becoming a major competitor. He waited for the camera flashes to abate before continuing, "Global News International shall comprise of eight news bureaus around the world, with the corporate headquarters in Las Vegas, Nevada.

"Now, I know what several of you are thinking. With over a hundred international cable news channels already claiming worldwide coverage, how can Global News International lead the pack? Well, ladies and gentlemen, today we are not launching one news channel, but sixteen."

Behind Brandon, the left-hand monitor turned into an image of a Chinese newsreader sitting at a desk speaking soundlessly to the camera. "GNI Shanghai broadcasts the news of the world exclusively in Mandarin." The next monitor changed to a Caucasian newsreader. "GNI New York will broadcast in English." The rest of the monitors came on sequentially as Brandon said, "GNI Mumbai in Hindustani, GNI Madrid in Spanish, GNI Moscow in Russian, GNI Abu Dhabi in Arabic, GNI Lisbon in Portuguese, and last but certainly not least, GNI Paris in French. Those eight channels will deliver news impacting the global scene around the clock. Paired sister channels will report on the stock markets, currency trends, and other financial information in the same languages.

"With those bureaus, Global News International will speak the languages of more than half of the globe's population of seven billion. GNI will also broadcast through the Internet with subtitles and text feeds in several other languages. This will truly be the first global news service, and broadcasts will premiere tomorrow, July fourth."

During dress rehearsal, he hadn't worn makeup, and he was getting quite warm under the strong lights. The last thing he needed was to start sweating. Brandon took a quick sip of water from the mini-bottle. He could see several people talking animatedly to their neighbors. *Now for the coup de gras.* "Those of you who've interviewed me in the past know I enjoy getting my name in the record books, and I still hold a half dozen world records. With that in mind, and also acknowledging that tomorrow is the Fourth of July holiday, I wanted to do something spectacular to celebrate the launch of the GNI network. Later today, beginning over Shanghai at ten p.m. their time, pre-positioned satellites will drop fireworks from orbit. As the Earth rotates, each time zone will see the same show, beginning at ten p.m. I'm assured that the light show will be unlike anything ever seen before. We'll be setting three world records in the process. It'll be the largest and most expensive pyrotechnic show ever staged—and the first firework display staged from orbit."

Camera flashes kept going off. *Time to leave them wanting more.* "Thank you, and I hope to meet with each of you later in the evening."

Brandon raised his hand into the air and waved, cuing the music to come up, then he walked off with the rising trance music drowning out the many shouted questions.

Garbo met him in the wings with a full mini-bottle of chilled water. He took it from her and unscrewed the cap. "That seems to have gone well."

"The second phase of the social media blitz has begun on Facebook and Twitter. We're using hashtag 'GNI_Launch' as discussed."

The sound man came over to Brandon and removed the battery pack from his belt and the microphones from his lapel before leaving.

"Is Terry making the rounds?" Brandon asked before taking another sip of cold water.

Garbo checked her tablet. "Yes. He's reporting positive responses from two of the reporters in the room so far. I suspect he'll be able to hire at least six or eight of them tonight."

"Good. We need more people, and the press coverage will be friendlier if they know we are hiring reporters. Okay, let's get this makeup off, and I'll make the rounds. Has the last rocket launched?" He drank the rest of the mini-bottle as they walked away from the stage.

"No, should be in a few minutes. No problems have been reported." Garbo paused for a split second then said softly, "I want you."

Brandon stopped walking and, after making sure they were alone in the corridor, turned to look into her blue eyes. "Have the bed made up on the jet. It's a four-hour flight to Vegas."

"Certainly, Sir Marcus."

* * *

Air Force Colonel Alvin Smith hung up his telephone handset. As a NORAD[1] Watch Commander of the Cheyenne Mountain bunker, he made regular communication checks to headquarters at Peterson Air Force Base eight miles away[2]. The room he occupied had several large projection screens at the front, detailing information collected from around the globe. He had three computers of his own under his desk; he could call up real-time displays of any part of the world, if needed.

The largest screen to the left showed a grid map of North America overlaid with the positions of airborne fighter aircraft under his command. Smith logged the test call in the relevant binder and popped the last of his lunch, a tuna sandwich, into his mouth. Smith looked up as he chewed, trying to guess just how many millions of tons of granite were in the mountain above him. Smith and his small staff ran the backup facility, and they needed to be ready to take over at a moment's notice if NORAD headquarters was unable to fulfill its role.

Smith looked up. His staff—a mix of American and Canadian military officers, along with several civilians—went about their duties. Conversation was minimal—and, in fact, discouraged, unless it related to their duties. He looked up at the displays at the front of the room but saw nothing to concern him. Air Force One was still on its expected course. The president was returning from a four-day trip to England, and his aircraft was just north of Nova Scotia.

---

[1] North American Aerospace Defense Command. This organization monitors aerospace and maritime areas in the defense of North America.
[2] The Cheyenne Mountain bunker became operational in 1966 and had once been the center of North America's defenses. That role changed in 2008 when NORAD headquarters moved to facilities at Peterson AFB and Cheyenne Mountain became the NORAD Alternate Command Center.

The light board to the right of the screens showed DEFCON 4[3], the second lowest defense condition. NORAD had been at DEFCON 4 since just after the 9/11 attacks.

A loud buzzer sounded once, and multiple overhead speakers came to life. A female voice announced calmly, "This is Argus. We have a DSP launch detection."

The same message was broadcast to every NORAD command center.

Smith folded away his paperwork, clearing the space in front of him. An orbiting satellite had just detected the heat signature of a missile taking off somewhere in the world. He grabbed a white binder labeled "Defense Support Program Procedures" from a shelf above his station. Members of his staff did the same thing at their own desks. He opened the binder, grabbed the tab labeled "DSP Launch Detection," and pulled it open to that section.

NORAD headquarters, call sign "Argus," would deal with the situation, but Smith would read the checklist and be ready to take over at a moment's notice.

The loudspeakers spoke again almost immediately. "This is Argus, reporting an infrared bloom at nineteen degrees, thirty-nine minutes north; one hundred ten degrees, fifty-seven minutes east. This is consistent with the Wenchang Satellite Launch Center in Hainen, China."

Smith knew his people would be looking at the same data. They would not say anything to him unless they disagreed with the Argus analysis. One of the global maps projected on the front wall of the room added an arced missile track over eastern China.

"This is Argus. First stage separation and flight profile consistent with Long March 5 vehicle destined for low Earth

---

[3] DEFCON – is short for "Defense Readiness Condition." The scale has five graduated readiness states, where DEFCON 5 is the lowest state of readiness and DEFCON 1 means hostilities are imminent. During the 9/11 attacks, the nation was ordered to DEFCON 3. For a time during the Cuban Missile Crisis, the DEFCON level was 2.

orbit. We have 'yellow paper' for a commercial satellite launch."

Smith relaxed. A vehicle heading to orbit would not be a nuclear attack. "Yellow paper" was a code for signal intelligence. Thinking it would be a good time to test his people, he made sure he was on the internal channel for his staff only and keyed his headset switch. Major Palmer was on assignment to NORAD from the Canadian Armed Forces, and he was the duty threat assessment officer. "Palmer, what's the maximum payload for this Long March 5 vehicle?"

The answer came back almost immediately. "For low Earth orbit, payload could run between ten and twenty-five tons, sir."

A laminated chart on Smith's desk showed all operational Chinese missile systems. It showed one and a half tons to twenty-five tons for the LM-5. "Palmer, confirm that assessment. I show one and a half tons as minimum payload."

Palmer replied, "Sir, the vehicle in flight has an acceleration vector consistent with a 320, 504, or 522 model LM-5. It cannot be a 200 model, and therefore the lower end of the estimate must be adjusted to be consistent with the remaining models."

"Roger." Smith smiled. To work at NORAD, you had to be sharp, and Palmer certainly qualified. He looked up at a display that showed the arc of the launching missile. Several Long March 5 missiles had left Wenchang over the last few weeks. The Chinese had boosted a considerable amount of material into orbit. Smith wondered why they needed so much, so fast.

* * *

Captain Eric Reid stood on the conning tower of the *Virginia* class submarine, USS *John Warner*. He turned in a slow circle, scanning the relatively calm ocean surface with binoculars one last time. The last rays of the sun disappeared behind the distant black clouds on the horizon. If everything went to plan, his vessel would not be back on the surface for another hundred and twenty days.

Behind the submarine, a straight trail of white froth pointed back to Naval Base Point Loma near San Diego, California. The water disturbance was much less than what had been caused by older model submarines. Instead of a standard propeller, the USS *John Warner* used a shrouded pump-jet propulsor that made it much quieter and maneuverable. They had departed base an hour ago, and Reid looked forward to his submarine's first operational deployment.

The trip felt somewhat bittersweet. Reid had to leave his wife and two young sons behind. The teary, melancholy farewell he had received in the parking lot hours ago would be followed after the four-month deployment with a joyous reunion.

As captain of the boat, he could not think of those things, and he filed it away to focus on his duty.

"Lookouts below," Reid ordered without taking his eyes from the binoculars. He heard the other two enlisted men with him drop down through the metal hatchway. He heard the men descend on the built-in ladder. Reid took a long, slow breath of fresh sea air, knowing he wouldn't experience it again for months. He dropped the binoculars to his chest and pressed a rubberized intercom button. "Officer of the Deck, rig the boat for dive."

"Rig the boat for dive, aye, sir," came the expected response over the speaker. Reid heard a hydraulic hiss as the extended masts behind him began to collapse down into the hull.

Reid turned and slipped into the open hatchway at his feet. As he descended, he pulled the hatch closed over his head, then secured it. He slid down the ladder below the sail hatch, closing and securing that behind him. At the base of the ladder, Reid removed the binocular strap from around his neck before he walked back into the command center.

The Officer of the Deck—his name was MacLean—spoke as soon as he saw Reid. "Boat rigged for dive, Captain. We have a green board."

"Thank you, Mister MacLean. I have the conn," Reid said as he took his headset from a recess in the navigation table and placed it over his ears.

"Captain has the conn, aye," MacLean acknowledged.

Reid turned to the sonar station and keyed his headset. "Sonar, conn. Report all contacts."

"Conn, sonar. We have two convergence zone contacts, both heavy merchantmen, off the starboard quarter. Distance estimated between seventy and eighty nautical miles. No sub-surface contacts at this time."

"Pilot, dive the boat," Reid ordered calmly while placing his binoculars into their padded space under the navigation table.

"Dive the boat, pilot aye," repeated the officer manning the pilot station, acknowledging he had heard the order correctly. "Bleeding air… We have pressure in the boat,"

Everything sounded normal. The pressure test ensured no leaks or hull openings before the dive.

Reid decided to give MacLean some experience. "Mister MacLean, take over the dive. You have the conn."

MacLean seemed to grow a few inches as he straightened up. "I have the conn, aye. Pilot, open bow and main ballast vents."

"Open bow and main ballast vents, pilot aye," the pilot at the dive control station stated as he flipped the relevant switches.

"Five degrees down bubble," MacLean ordered.

The pilot pushed his joystick control forward. "Five degrees down bubble, pilot aye."

The submarine began tilting forward, descending below the surface. Reid leaned back against the navigation table to compensate for the inclined floor.

MacLean said, "Pilot, make your depth two hundred feet. Come to course two-eight-zero."

The pilot parroted the orders back to confirm them.

Reid's executive officer, Commander Harry Maddox, stepped into the command center. Maddox was much shorter than Reid, but in the tight confines of a sub, that was an advantage. He approached Reid and said quietly, "Galley supplies have been stowed, sir. I made sure Powell mixed up the cans this time, so we don't repeat what happened on the sea trials."

Reid chuckled. "Four days of beet soup was a bit much."

"Want me to take the first watch, sir?"

Reid considered that. "I have her for now, XO. I need to write MacLean's fitness report on this trip, so I want to observe him for a while. Relieve me in two hours."

"Aye, skipper."

* * *

Sir Marcus Brandon stepped out into the public area of the XVI club to be assailed by several reporters and the bright lights mounted on their video cameras. He was glad to see several of his staff step in to run interference. He preferred a one-on-one experience with the press to a rugby-style scrum.

The reporters likely to accept employment with GNI had been told to stand by in this area. They would get their interviews first. Brandon snagged a bottle of water from a waiter's tray as he passed. The bottle was cold and had just come from a refrigerator. He shook the water droplets off it. He wanted another sort of drink, but knew he needed his wits at their peak to succeed today.

Brandon turned to the closest reporters. "Evening, Carly, Peter... Let me talk to Pamela, and I'll be right with you. Good evening, Pamela."

Pamela raised her microphone to record their voices while her cameraman focused onto him. Brandon tried to stand so the rotating GNI logo would be in the background of the shot.

"Good evening, Sir Marcus. It sounds like tonight is a huge evening for you." Pamela placed the mic under his chin.

"Indeed, for both myself and the Athena Group, it's a landmark evening. Thank you for coming."

Pamela brought the mic back to her and referred to her notes. "A fireworks display from orbit. That's ambitious, to say the least. Where did that idea come from?"

Brandon forced a smile and gave his pre-rehearsed answer. "When we first had the idea for Global News International, we knew it would have to be launched in a spectacular manner. I happened to be in Shanghai three years ago for New Year's, and they put on an incredible show. Fireworks were a Chinese invention originally, so we asked several of their companies to put together proposals for a show here in New York. Lee Ernesto, my vice president of marketing at Athena, looked at their proposals, but he felt they were lacking imagination. Fireworks are launched from the ground, and as a result, relatively few people can see them. He later met several members of the China National Space Administration at a social affair and had the wild idea of staging pyrotechnics from orbit. With the much higher altitude, many more people could see them. The Chinese have been great partners throughout this project. After many months of hard work, we were able to get to this point."

Pamela said, "After your announcement tonight, one of your staff mentioned this undertaking would be costing the Athena Group one point four billion dollars. Isn't that an excessive amount of money to spend on, well, a marketing campaign for a new business?"

Brandon smiled more widely. His marketing people had seeded incorrect information through the crowd. Now he could take advantage of that for bigger effect. "Pamela, I need to correct you on a couple of points. First, the Athena Group is not paying for this display. I am, out of my own pocket. The stacked CPU cooling technology I invented is still selling well, and I'm using that royalty money to finance this venture. Further, the total cost will be just over two point eight billion dollars."

Pamela's eyebrows rose; she looked astonished. "That's a lot of money going overseas. Was there no interest from NASA or one of the private U.S. space companies? I'm sure they would have loved to participate."

Brandon paused to take a sip of cool water. "Of course there was. We asked all major space operators for quotes. However, either their pricing was unacceptable, or they were unable to meet our timeline. The China National Space Administration promised us they could do the work for the established budget and in the two-year timeline. The China Aerospace Corporation worked wonders in putting together the payloads. I just heard before coming out that the last missile launched successfully a few moments ago, so they certainly kept their word."

Pamela leaned into her mic again. "Why July 4th as the date?"

"That's an easy question to answer, Pamela. The United States has been my adopted country since I attended MIT as a teenager. It's a small way for me to repay the people of the United States for being so welcoming to a small lad from Bristol. Now if you'll forgive me, I need to go speak to some of your colleagues."

"Thank you, Sir Marcus."

* * *

James Calvin stepped down the ladder from Air Force One. He smiled then waved automatically for the distant pool of reporters behind the security perimeter. In theory, as President of the United States, Calvin could bar them from Andrews Air Force Base completely, but the negative press would far outweigh his peace of mind. The press had video cameras on him whenever he was in public. If someone took a shot at him, or if he fell down the steps from Air Force One, they would have a story.

For the cameras, he was always charm and smiles. In private, James Calvin had grown to loathe the office he occupied, and he counted the days to the end of his term.

Calvin looked off into the distance. A sharp white flash of lightning flickered briefly in the distance below black clouds. The unstable weather would soon roll in over Washington DC proper. *That's the bad weather the pilot warned us about. No ride in the Marine One helicopter today.*

He stepped into the back of his heavily armored limousine. Calvin always wondered how something so heavy could move so swiftly. The Secret Service referred to the limo as "The Beast." A sixteen-ton vehicle with five-inch armor-plated glass and multiple security systems. His oldest friend—and national security advisor—Keith Hurst waited for him in the rear seat.

"Morning, Keith. Step outside if you want your picture in the papers."

"I'll pass, Jim. You're the one who signed up for the glory," Hurst said gruffly before handing over a file folder. "Here are the latest DIA estimates for North Korea."

A Secret Service agent closed the thick rear door. Immediately, Calvin felt the change in pressure on his ears. He'd been told by his protection detail that the air pressure was kept higher in the limo than the outside to keep out gases and toxins.

Calvin opened the folder and cast a disinterested eye at the text within. "Has anything changed since I left London?"

"Nothing significant. No credible nuclear intelligence, but the potential is there. I still feel Iran is the larger threat."

The limo began moving forward. Calvin closed the folder and handed it back while sighing. "As do I. We're finally making progress in the region, and now Iran is using the negotiation process to delay action and work on their nuclear program in the background. It's only a matter of time before the Israelis act unilaterally and put a two thousand-pound smart bomb into the Bushehr reactor building."

"Short-term gain for them, but a crap storm for us to clean up," Hurst observed while shaking his head.

"If only we could move Israel to the Falklands and let them be Argentina's problem for a few decades," Calvin joked.

"Speaking of the Falklands, how was your U.K. trip?" Hurst put the briefing folder away in his valise.

"Good, once we got rid of the staff and could speak privately. Prime Minister Gladstone is like me, a straight talker, and never promises anything unless he knows it can happen. I'd love to see the house leadership with those traits. Things would go so much smoother. We had a couple of dinners together and hammered out a decent understanding. Tom will fill you in when we get back to the White House." Calvin looked out the bulletproof window. "Looks like a bad storm is coming our way."

Hurst tucked away the rest of the files and reports into his valise. "Rain tonight, but supposed to be gone by early tomorrow. Nice clear skies for the July Fourth celebrations. Did you hear what Marcus Brandon has planned?"

Calvin turned back to face his friend. "Launching fireworks from space? That must be costing him a fortune."

Hurst snorted. "He's paying the almost three billion dollars out of his own pocket. The Chinese space program will benefit greatly from the project."

Calvin shook his head. "Three billion for an exercise in vanity? He needs to run for congress."

"The pay cut would be unacceptable to him. The limey prick makes five billion a year just from his engineering royalties. The Athena Group adds another fifteen annually."

Calvin shook his head and looked back out the window. The flight from England had left his internal clock a little off, and the twenty-minute drive to the White House would be his only break until ten o'clock that evening. As a widower, he probably worked a lot more than he should. Replacing Carrie with someone else just didn't feel right to him. "I should've quit."

"What?" Hurst asked.

Calvin faced his friend. "I should've quit before taking office. Carrie died three weeks before I took the oath. I should've left then. Maybe if I had, I wouldn't be the sour and jaded son of a bitch I turned into."

"She supported your run for the presidency. She never failed to—"

"Carrie hid her cancer from me until she needed to be hospitalized, Keith. If I'd known sooner, I could've made her last few months comfortable instead of dragging her cross-country in that bus." Calvin slumped back into his seat.

Hurst animatedly pointed at Calvin. "I came to know Carrie quite well during the campaign. She was your most dedicated champion. She wanted you sitting there, in that job. I know little about life, but I do know you, and you're the best choice for the presidency. Unless, of course, you want Hamilton Kendall to take your job."

The last line felt like a verbal slap. Kendall, his vice president, was known for his personality and multiple connections in Congress, not his ability. "Yeah, there's always the obvious downside, isn't there."

* * *

Doctor Linda Krause looked into the mirror on her locker door. Her shoulder-length dirty blond hair had not been combed that morning. She grabbed a brush from the top shelf and spent a minute to make it presentable.

As she brushed her hair, she smiled subtly to herself. The Harborview Medical Center in Seattle had offered her a position just after her residency ended in Kansas City. Moving had been a royal pain and involved a painful breakup, but she had found Seattle to be a wonderfully relaxing city. Her new paycheck certainly helped, and her years of medical school, long hours as an intern, and sleepless nights became distant memories.

Satisfied with her hair, she replaced the brush and closed the locker door, placing her combination lock into the hasp. Krause walked up the hallway to the nurses' station while adjusting the collar of her lab coat.

"Evening, Doctor Krause," said the duty nurse.

"Evening, Carla. Can you pass me Mrs. Paulson's chart, please? How are you?"

Carla handed over the requested clipboard. "Great! I'm going to be a mom."

"Wow, that's wonderful news. When are you due?" Krause lost interest in the chart for the moment.

"February. It's my first, so I'm told he'll be late." Carla beamed.

"'He?' You're that sure this soon?" Krause asked.

"Must be. The big disruptions in my life are usually caused by men."

The two women chuckled at that. Krause looked at the chart in her hand. Several pages had been updated through the night. "Looks like we are 'go' for her Keratoprosthesis. Can you confirm the operating theater? I'll check in on Mister Herbert in the meantime."

"Of course, Doctor."

Krause walked down the hall, passing several hospital rooms. She read through the chart in detail. She knew the case very well, but reinforcing things in her own mind was part of her process. She entered the room with her patient. "Good evening, Mister Herbert. How are you feeling today?"

The older man in the bed turned to face her. The side of his head had a thick bandage taped in place. He smiled broadly. "Hey, Doc. I'm doin' good. I woke up without my double vision. Thought I was dreaming."

"Good to hear. I just need to check your eyes." Krause pulled the monocular direct ophthalmoscope from her coat pocket and switched on the small light. "Just lay back, look straight ahead, and relax." She moved in close and checked his eyes without the instrument. They looked normal. He'd been admitted with severe strabismus. His right eye always pointed to the right, causing double vision. Krause had performed a tenectomy early that morning to correct the condition.

Using the ophthalmoscope, she examined his eyes closely. No signs of bleeding, swelling, or other distress from the surgery, she was glad to see. She snapped off the light and stood, replacing the instrument in her pocket. "Well, it's looking good. I'll check in with you a couple more times, just to make sure everything is fine, and we should be able to release you tomorrow. You'll need to follow up with your own physician in about a week for a follow-up assessment, but as I said, I see nothing wrong at this point."

"Thanks, Doc."

Krause left the room, making notes on his chart. By the time she got back to the nurses' station, everything was updated, and she dropped it into the proper slot.

"Carla, I'm going for a coffee. Want one? My treat."

"I'm going to try and avoid caffeine, but I'll take an herbal tea if they have it."

"Of course. I'll be right back." Krause headed for the break room.

* * *

"Hey, Marv!" The voice echoed down the inside of the Boeing E-6 Mercury aircraft.

Dale Marvin poked his head up from behind the operator console he was inspecting. "There's no need to yell, Bill. I'm right here."

Over the console, he saw Bill Darber. Darber, his grimy white coveralls slightly too large, stood in the main entry doorway, holding up a cell phone. "Eddie's calling. He wants to know if the navy can start their acceptance checks tomorrow."

Marvin stood up and approached Bill, muttering under his breath. *If they would leave me alone to do my job instead of calling every damned hour, I would've had this aircraft ready last week.*

Darber handed him the cell phone, then waited there for the call to finish.

Marv took the phone outside before he began talking. The aircraft's shielding killed cell reception within the airframe. "Eddie?"

"Yeah. STRATCOM's been on the hooter all day. They want to get that airframe back to Tinker by the weekend. Is that doable?"

Surprise, surprise, Marvin thought while shaking his head. "We've been through this before, Eddie. Our contract says we have this bird for another week. We might—that is *might*—have it ready on time, but with the July Fourth holiday coming up tomorrow, there's no way we can do it early, unless you authorize triple time and a half for my people to work through the night."

"You know I can't do that, Marv. It's a fixed-price contract. Look, I'm stuck in the middle here. I just want to get them off my back."

The navy's "on his back" because Eddie's promised them an early delivery, just as he always does—trying to make everyone happy, while looking good to his bosses at the same time. His mouth starts flapping without engaging his brain, and my people pay the price. Marvin looked out over the hangar. Several of his crew worked on the leading edge of the wing, sealing it up. Each of them wore coveralls with "Raytheon Intelligence, Information, and Services" logos on their backs.

"Well, you can tell STRATCOM that it's the last-minute changes they wanted to the LFC that're slowing us down. That's the last internal system we need to validate. We can bring the navy guys in on the morning of the fifth to start their acceptance checks, but not before. That's what the contract says, anyway."

Eddie sighed over the phone. "There's no way you can do your magic and get it out earlier?"

"Not without your authorization for triple time and a half." Marvin turned to face Darber. He raised an eyebrow while shaking his head.

Darber smirked back. They both knew what a pain in the ass Eddie was.

"All right, Marv. I'll tell them to expect it on the fifth. Thanks, and enjoy your day off tomorrow."

"Right. Bye." Marvin hung up without waiting for a response. He tossed the phone back to Darber.

Darber chuckled. "We're all getting big fat raises?"

"Not funny, Bill. When will they be done on the leading edge?" He jerked his thumb over his shoulder, indicating the wing.

"An hour, then the sealant has to cure overnight. We're in good shape elsewhere."

"All right. When they're done, send them home." Marvin turned to go back inside.

Darber touched him on the shoulder, stopping him. "Hey Marv, we're firing up the grill at my house tomorrow. All the steak and beer you want, with fireworks after. The rest of the crew is coming."

Marvin paused. His first inclination was to say no, but he hadn't been to a crew function for some time. As their supervisor, he kept somewhat distant, but he still attended the odd party. "Sure. I'll swing by."

"Great. Bring the missus."

Marvin nodded and walked back into the aircraft. Once his inspection of the new wiring was completed and signed off, he, also, was done for the day

* * *

The Politburo Standing Committee of the Chinese Communist Party had only seven members, but those men effectively ruled over the one and a half billion Chinese citizens. Their word was law, and the few who dared to oppose them were expeditiously silenced.

General Secretary Gao had called for a meeting with little warning. The politburo members entered the small but elegantly furnished meeting chamber, far more similar than they were different. Each had black hair with varying degrees of gray streaking at the temples. They all wore a dark suit with a red or blue tie. Five of the seven wore glasses.

Each man had a pre-assigned seat. The general secretary took his place at the head of the table, with the others seated in order of seniority of their departments. He regarded each politburo member as they sat. Some poured ice water from decanters into cut glass tumblers. Others began making notes on the pads provided. There was little conversation; they all knew the reason for the meeting.

The last politburo member entered the room. Behind him, the double doors were closed by aides who remained outside. No external noise intruded into the heavily soundproofed room. More importantly, no one could listen in from the outside.

General Secretary Gao waited until everyone was seated before speaking. "The last Long March rocket ascended to low Earth orbit, as planned. All satellites are in position, and I see no reason not to enact activity six-eight-nine."

A long silence followed. The six other powerful men at the table seemed cowed by his statement. He said nothing, waiting for their reactions.

The first man to speak was the party secretary of the Standing Committee of the National People's Congress, Bohai Quishan. "General Secretary Gao, the initial discussion centered on using the technology developed by PLA Unit 63388 against Taiwan. This, as we all agreed, was a correct and elegant solution to the problem. However, the United States—"

"Must fall first," interrupted Wei Sun, Secretary of the Central Commission for Discipline Inspection.

My impatient ally and friend is speaking up early, Gao thought. *He must want to wrap things up quickly to visit one of his girlfriends before returning home. Maybe more than one girlfriend.*

Sun continued, "Neutralizing the defenses of Taiwan alone would come to nothing, as they are protected by a minimum of two American carrier battle groups and their imperialist submarines in the South China Sea. Our paratroop transports would be shot down, and our amphibious forces sunk easily.

"I have no issue with military losses to achieve the goal of liberating the province of Taiwan, but we need those same forces for occupation actions in other areas—the Philippines, Siberia, and Australia, primarily for their oil and resources. Nullifying the militaries of the United States, Russia, NATO, and other hostile nations, at the same time, will allow us to advance unfettered on all fronts." Wei took a cut glass tumbler from a serving tray.

Guoliang Jang, the Deputy Party Secretary of the State Council, spoke quietly. "What nations will not be affected, assuming we implement the full scope of the plan?"

"North and South Korea," Wei answered. "Taiwan, along with parts of southern Japan, are too close to major Chinese cities to risk exposing them. PLA Unit 63388 is currently developing tactical warheads we can use selectively against those countries in a few months' time. That should eliminate any opposition globally. Our disinformation campaigns in Xinjiang province and Tibet will ensure a minimum of casualties to *loyal* citizens in those areas."

Jang seemed to bridle against that response. "Why months? These should have been ready to be used now, for one fell swoop."

Wei shook his head. "The timeline was dictated by the British billionaire. The technology is bulky and will take additional time to reduce down to a size we can launch from mobile launchers. Any countries not affected will be isolated and contained by our navy and army. It's the American military that restricts our actions, to maintain their global hegemony. U.S. submarines are designed for hundred and twenty-day operational deployments. They shall be unaffected by the warheads. We only need to wait until their supplies run out and they are forced to return to port. By that time, the PLA[4] and PLAN[5] will have their home bases under control, and we can liquidate their crews easily. Once American subs

---

[4] Peoples Liberation Army.
[5] Peoples Liberation Army Navy.

pull back from the South China Sea, Taiwan will fall back under our control. At that point, we shall be able to operate as we see fit anywhere in the world, without any meaningful opposition."

Bohai Quishan began asking other questions concerning the proposed deployment of the Chinese military.

General Secretary Gao took stock of the men before him. Four of them supported his plan unconditionally. They recognized the need to remove the limits the Americans imposed on China's expansion. Jang and Shen were the two unknowns. Jang had always been reluctant, and Shen had sat silently all along, listening to the others with an emotionless visage.

The Standing Committee of the Politburo did not vote on issues. Instead, they made decisions by consensus.

General Secretary Gao waited until there was a natural lull in the conversation. He placed his left palm on the table before him and chose his words carefully. "With all that being considered, are there any objections to activity six-eight-nine commencing on schedule?"

Silence filled the room. The general secretary shifted his gaze from man to man. Jang and Shen exchanged a look. Wei and Bohai sipped water. No one spoke.

The general secretary began to inhale to conclude the meeting when Shen suddenly said, "Sun Tzu once said, 'To subdue the enemy without fighting is the supreme excellence.' As we execute this endeavor, we should keep this in mind. I find it amusing that this ignorant Englishman is not only providing us with a perfect cover for delivering our warheads, but also paying for the operation in its entirety."

There was laughter around the room.

After it faded, Shen momentarily held up a hand and continued solemnly, "However, we are, in effect, launching offensive action against every nation on Earth. While the gains are exorbitant, the scale of risk is staggering. We risk a grave loss of face internationally for many years. While I understand—and support—the driving reasons behind this operation, what we are attempting is unprecedented. All parts of this activity must work flawlessly. The importance of success should be made clear to all units involved. The penalties for individual failure need to be swift and merciless."

"Well spoken," said Jang, rapping his knuckles against the table.

Others in the room nodded. Several side conversations began.

The general secretary patted the table with his hand to regain their attention. "With no objections raised, we shall authorize action as laid out in the activity documentation immediately. Is there any other business?"

Bohai gestured with his hand. "I would speak with Wei and Yang before they leave. There is a timing issue with the railroads that needs to be addressed."

Gao stood up. "Then the orders to our forces shall be released, and the politburo stands in recess."

* * *

Lieutenant General Fang Lam walked through the corridors of the PLA 15th Airborne Corp headquarters on the way to lunch. A major from his communications staff intercepted him to deliver a note, which startled him. Typically, a lower-ranked officer would perform such a routine task.

The major saluted. Lam could not remember the major's name and couldn't be bothered to read his nametag. He simply nodded in return as he took the note. His stomach growled impatiently, anticipating the meal from his personal dim sum chef.

Lam opened the folded message paper. The faint text was typed in block characters, a characteristic of the encoding machine.

He frowned, his lips parting slightly as he read the three paragraphs. "Major, alert the commanding officers of the 43rd, 44th, and 45th divisions to assemble their men in their respective camps. Their senior officers are then to report here.

All corps leave is cancelled immediately, and all men are to return to their units. Coordinate with the People's Armed Police Force; any man on leave outside of Hubei or Henan province is to be collected and returned to their unit within twelve hours, without exception. Go!"

The major retreated quickly, leaving him alone in the corridor. Lieutenant General Lam reread the message. During the PLA invasion of Tibet, a single airborne division of ten thousand men had been transported to that country within forty-eight hours. He had just received orders activating all three of his airborne divisions for immediate deployment.

The message coding was clear. This was no exercise, and the scale of this mobilization was unprecedented. *We're going to war, and it's going to be a big one. There's no other answer. I need to call People's Liberation Army Air Force headquarters and speak to General Wen personally for more detail.*

Lam turned his back on lunch and hurried back up the corridor toward his office.

* * *

Known for its local beer and pretty women, the city of Qingdao lay on the coast of eastern China, with eight million inhabitants. The port at Qingdao moved over thirteen million containers a year, making it the eighth largest cargo container port in the world.

Faedong Li had been port operations manager at Qingdao for twelve years. Respected for his efficiency and evenhanded management, Li became a Communist soon after taking the job. He attended the requisite party meetings, but he did little else to promote communism. Indeed, he felt it ironic that his job centered on facilitating the massive capitalistic trade that provided his nation with hard currency.

He did ensure he displayed a party membership lapel pin on his suit jacket lapel. It made life easier when dealing with some local officials.

Li sat at his simple desk in the open-format office. Wanting constant involvement with his staff, Li allowed no walls or cubicles in the large second-floor office suite. His people worked hard to keep the port operational. Beyond the clacking of keyboards, sound of air conditioning, and the hum of an antiquated photocopier, there was little other noise.

Li knew the port had been quiet over the last week. Chinese-flagged ships had come into port and ordered to anchor. Some were held under customs regulations, while others were notified they were due for maritime safety inspections. No one seemed to be in a hurry to actually do anything about it, though, and the ships sat idle. Li thought it puzzling that there were so many ships sitting idle, but given his experience with the Communist bureaucracy, the situation was hardly unprecedented.

Several senior officers of the People's Armed Police Force pushed their way through the office doors and into the port office.

Li immediately knew something was seriously wrong. While the PAPF did come by infrequently for some reason or another, they had never done so in such numbers. Nor had they held such high ranks. Li saw no fewer than three generals walk through the door, along with at least ten men of lesser rank following behind with boxes and equipment in their arms.

Li stood, shocked and confused. He walked over, pulling on his suit jacket to appear as presentable as possible. He greeted the oldest uniformed police officer. "Good afternoon, Comrade General. I'm Li, the port manager."

"I'm Major General Po. This facility, its equipment, and personnel are now under my direct command. No activities of any type are to be conducted without PAPF oversight or prior permission, do you understand?"

Li didn't understand, but a person didn't object to senior authority in China without significant personal risk. He answered neutrally, "I serve the party."

Po simply nodded, turned to his staff, and began pointing around the office. "Communications go there. I want landlines and radio links operational in five minutes. Have all senior colonels report to me as soon as they arrive."

The general's staff moved quickly to follow his orders.

Po indicated a short and squat man to his left. "Comrade Li, this is Colonel Chio. He shall be your police escort and liaison. You shall do nothing outside of his presence. The following matters shall be attended to immediately.

"One, all foreign-flagged vessels are to depart the harbor at once. Tugs and ships of the People's Liberation Army Navy are standing by to assist. If any crews do not cooperate, they are to be boarded by PLAN and arrested. Their ships will be taken out by pilots, and their crews released when at sea.

"Two, any Chinese-flagged container ship with cargo aboard is to be offloaded. Empty containers are to be loaded and secured in their place. Those ships are to also have their fuel bunkers filled as expeditiously as possible.

"Three, Chinese flagged RoRo[6] ships are to be docked, unloaded, their bunkers filled, and boarding ramps left in place against the dock. Are my orders clear?"

Li heard the instructions but could only think of the myriad issues confronting him. *This will set the schedule of the port back weeks—no, months!* "General, you must understand, what you ask will require hundreds of workers and—"

Colonel Chio began drawing his service pistol out of his black leather holster while stepping toward Li. "You shall obey the major general immed—"

"Chio! Holster your weapon!" Major General Po commanded. He turned back to Li, tapping his party lapel pin. "Comrade, I see you are a party member and say this to make things easier. Several thousand PLA engineers are on their way by truck. Manpower will not be an issue. North Korea will be striking the harbor with missiles at some point in the near future. This threat cannot be ignored, and we act as part of a master plan that I cannot divulge. To safeguard the people, we

---

[6] Roll-on Roll-off. Ships designed with ramps to facilitate wheeled cars, trucks, or vehicle transport.

must ensure immediate obedience to our commands, and lethal force has been authorized to those who oppose us."

Li absorbed what Po had said. The North Korean mainland was only two hundred and forty miles away. They had missiles that could hit targets three times that distance, but why would North Korea attack the civilian port that they themselves traded with almost daily? Almost seventy percent of North Korean exports came through Qingdao. An attack there made no sense to him. They would be cutting off their own trade routes.

But Li's party membership would not stop him from being arrested or worse if he continued to object. He had a wife, daughter, with a grandchild on the way. He would not endanger their well-being. "I thank you for the clarification. I obey as the party commands, Comrade Major General."

Po simply nodded again and moved off, leaving an angry looking Colonel Chio behind. Li needed to get out and see his supervisors personally. He had some temperamental people working for him, and they needed to be warned of the dangers. "Comrade Colonel, I would speak to my staff to ensure the general's orders are carried out. Will you please accompany me?"

Chio, still red faced, gave a terse nod. Li moved toward the door. Several of his office staff looked at him questioningly as he passed. Each had the same look of shock on his face as more police entered the small office. Li said nothing and exited the room.

* * *

Colonel Alvin Smith could see a pair of civilian analysts having an unusually animated discussion over in what was informally called the "N" section of the operations room. He unplugged his headset and walked over to investigate. Smith came up on them from behind. Vinson worked for the National Security Agency, or NSA, and Noel was an analyst with the National Reconnaissance Office, or NRO. Their area had space for a third analyst, from the National Geospatial-Intelligence Agency, or NGA, who was away from his position.

Since 9/11, intelligence agencies had begun to share information more efficiently. Several major intelligence agencies had personnel assigned to NORAD. Any of the remaining U.S. intelligence agencies not on site could be contacted instantly from this room.

Vinson was saying to his colleague, "Maybe, but the whole area just lit up. It can't be a coincidence."

"What's up?" Smith inquired.

Vinson spun around in his chair, his usual colorful bow tie mixing with his dirty blond crew cut hair and thick black-rimmed glasses to make him look as if he'd come from the 1950s. "Colonel, in the last hour, we've had a twentyfold increase in chatter from several Chinese military units along the North Korean border. At the same time, we have activity at several large airports in the Hubei, Henan, and Jiangxi provinces. That's near where the 15th Airborne Corp is based. They are the strategic arm of the PLAAF[7] and one of their main first strike options. Last, the port at Qingdao just lit up. Several foreign-flagged ships are being forced to leave. One Canadian vessel had an engine issue and couldn't leave under her own power. Tugs put her out to sea escorted by gunboats of the PLAN. Qingdao's the closest port to the norks. The Chinese are obviously making a major play for North Korea."

Noel, the man Vinson spoke to, wore a conservative unpressed white shirt, a patternless red tie, and a short beard. He ran his fingers through his shaggy medium-length black hair to get it away from his face. "And I disagree, sir. I think the port and aircraft activity is unrelated. A lot of the traffic is on civilian or police bands. Overhead imagery does show a larger than average numbers of vessels, but with the global recession, idle ships in port are not unreasonable."

Smith absorbed that information. "Could it be a play for Taiwan?"

---

[7] People's Liberation Army Air Force.

Vinson pointed at one of the monitors on his desk, which showed a satellite image of the entire east coast of China, including North Korea and Taiwan. Vinson traced the east coast of China in a dogleg. "I thought of that. The distance from Qingdao to Taiwan is just under seven hundred nautical miles. There are several major military ports a lot closer for staging a Taiwan invasion. The North Korean angle makes a lot of sense. The Chinese can't make a play against Japan or the Philippines without us intervening. I highly doubt we would directly oppose China coming over the border to take on the norks unless South Korea was threatened."

Smith asked, "Have either of your organizations formed an opinion on this?"

Vinson crossed his arms. "No, this came down the pipe with the other traffic. No intentions have been firmed up."

"Okay, then let's let it sit for now. The DIA will analyze the traffic and give us their assessment in their next brief. Either way, it sounds like there is no North American threat." Smith's replacement came into operations. He excused himself to go turn the shift over.

* * *

After briefing his senior officers, Lieutenant General Lam dismissed them back to their units. In the next twelve hours, they were to assemble their men, two weeks' rations, light weapons, and ammo for deployment. He had not said where they were going. One of his officers brought up North Korea, but Lam didn't deny or confirm it.

No unit artillery, heavy weapons, or tanks were to be taken. The entire 15th Airborne Corp would deploy as light infantry.

Lam couldn't tell them where they were going, because he didn't know himself, even after speaking to his superior at PLAAF headquarters over a secure line. When asked what the target was, General Wen had refused to answer. *I wonder if General Wen knows himself. If not, then it's big. The Tibetans are under control—it can't be them. The Diaoyu or Nansha Islands[8] are a possibility, but three airborne divisions are enough to invade the Philippines, Japan, or even Australia. That level of force is well over what would be needed for a series of isolated islands of limited strategic value. Taiwan? Japan? Korea? Those make more sense, but the American carriers would step in and make life interesting for the troops. Interesting, and a lot shorter.*

Carrying two weeks' rations was unheard of. Normal operating doctrine dictated that no more than three days of food and water be carried. The two weeks' worth of food and ammo meant his men would not—or could not—be resupplied. It also meant they wouldn't be moving; they couldn't carry that amount of supplies and fight. Once deployed, they were staying put.

Lam clenched his fists in frustration. Without further information, all he could do was wait for further orders.

* * *

Faedong Li jumped into the driver's seat of his usual transport on the docks: a small, battery-powered golf cart with a faded roof of tan fabric and cracked fiberglass side panels from multiple collisions. The cart was practical for covering the large distances between the kilometer-long berths. Colonel Chio sat down beside him.

Li floored the accelerator. He needed to warn his people that the PAPF were deadly serious about having their orders followed. Turning the corner of the office building, Li could see at least a hundred police vehicles had parked down the row of ten berths. Each one could accommodate any size container ship. Massive overhead gantries, painted red and white, moved to shift containers on or off the vessels. Heavy mobile cranes

---

[8] The Diaoyu Islands are the name the Chinese use. They are called the Senkakus Islands by Japan. Both nations claim them. The Chinese named Nansha Islands are better known as the Spratly Islands and are claimed by China, Vietnam, and the Philippines.

lifted the shipping containers and stacked them up to six high on the larger ships.

As he drove, Li could see members of the People's Armed Police Force everywhere. Normally, the PAPF would carry holstered pistols. Today, each officer also had a machine gun. Each mobile crane had a PAPF officer beside the operator. He couldn't see into the gantry control cabins, but he wouldn't have been surprised to see them there, too.

A short, squat man in hard hat and reflective vest waved Li down. A nearby police officer started yelling at him to get back to work, but saw the colonel in the golf cart and quieted.

Li stopped beside the man, Kew, the superintendent who ran this part of the dock.

"Li, what's going on? I've been told to throw away my schedule and offload any cargo containers to replace them with empty ones."

He nodded. "Yes, that's correct. Follow those instructions."

"Am I also to continue emptying loaded containers into the bay?" Kew asked with an obvious edge in his voice.

Li turned to the colonel. "Why are we destroying cargo to make empty containers, Colonel?"

Chio looked irritated. "The plan calls for empty containers being loaded on all ships. That is all you need to know at this time."

Li felt complete frustration and bewilderment, but knowing the consequences of questioning authority, he forced himself not to say anything more. He turned back to Kew. "Carry on with your orders for now. Anyone impeding those orders may be shot. Tell your people."

Kew grabbed Li's forearm as he started to drive away. He jammed on the brakes, and Kew let go.

"Wait! What is this about North Korean missiles coming our way? Several of the men want to go home and be with their families."

Chio's presence dramatically limited what Li could say. "I don't know. I know very little. Do as they say, and hopefully things will return to normal soon." He pressed the accelerator pedal to get away from there.

Li went through the container stacks and drove along the fence line.

Two men wearing blue port coveralls—workers from the facility, but Li didn't know them—ran from behind a parked mobile crane. Several People's Armed Police shouted for them to stop, but they continued and clambered up the perimeter chain link fence. *They're trying to get out.*

Several dozen shots spat out, and the two men fell back onto the concrete border under the fencing. Before the bodies had stopped moving, several members of PAPF moved in, grabbed them, and began dragging them away. One of the fallen men left a wide blood trail on the ground.

Chio, his impatience obviously growing, ordered Li to drive on. He did, feeling disgust at the sight of his people being gunned down; he forced himself to look neutral and said nothing. Any disobedience would result in his own death.

After driving across the facility, they came to the RoRo loading docks. Four RoRo ships, typically used for carrying vehicles too wide to fit through the Panama Canal, were pulled up against the docks. They sat idle with their huge ramps resting on the dock. A fuel crew was topping up the bunkers. There was nothing Li could contribute there, so he drove past.

He turned up toward the front gates, to check on them. As the gates came into view, Li saw three rows of heavily armed People's Armed Police in full riot gear and shields, standing shoulder to shoulder across the four lane-wide entrance.

Chio suddenly ordered him to stop, and he complied, pulling off the side of the asphalt onto the gravel verge.

The line of men parted, and six-wheeled military trucks began rolling through. Each carried a dozen men in khaki uniform. The rear covers were off, letting Li see multiple tall pressure tanks with color markings in each truck bed. *Oxy-acetylene torches? They have hundreds of sets. Why so many?*

"The engineers have arrived," Chio commented. "Now the real work begins."

Li counted a hundred trucks pass, with many more behind. They kept rolling through, driving directly past him in his small golf cart.

He decided to try fishing for more information. "Do these engineers require any support from us, Colonel Chio?"

"I think not. They will ask if they do. Once they off-load their cargo, the trucks will refuel, move onto the RoRos, and park. I apologize for my earlier behavior, Comrade Li. I thought you were being obstructive, but I see now you are a supportive party member and wish us to succeed in our mission."

Li faced the colonel, who did look somewhat more relaxed than before. Li thought he could get more information if he cozied up to the colonel. "Thank you, Comrade Colonel. I accept your apology with gratitude. You must forgive me for my reaction, but this level of activity is unprecedented and is rather overwhelming to see."

"I understand. I, too, felt the same way. However, the party has given us our orders, and we shall carry them out."

"Indeed," Li said, turning back to the stream of military traffic. *But where are the party's orders taking us?*

Chapter Two
Léger de Main

The plain paper fax machine for the U.S. Federal Aviation Administration field office in Shanghai began spitting out a high number of pages. The duty clerk, Pat Lambert, scanned the content as it arrived. He'd been in China for three years and thought he'd seen it all. As he read the Mandarin text coming out of the fax, he was so shocked he had to sit down. He re-read the seven-page document twice before logging onto his computer and writing a concise translation to his supervisor in Washington DC.

Lambert made sure to scan the original fax and attach it to his assessment e-mail. No one was going to believe him without it.

* * *

Lieutenant General Lam received baffling follow-up orders from PLAAF headquarters by special messenger. The letter in his hand ordered his three airborne divisions to move by train to nine specified military and civilian airfields, "as soon as practicable." If the entire airlift capacity of the PLAAF were used, they could only load one division at a time. That meant two of the three divisions would be sitting idle until the aircraft returned—which, from a military point of view, was idiotic.

Dividing them up between nine airfields made no sense, either. They simply didn't have enough military transports to carry that many men, and flying out of civilian airfields would violate security. Civilians using the airports would see the troops. If only one of the civilians posted something on Weibo[9], any surprise would be lost.

"Am I the only sane man left?" he muttered, whacking the top edge of the letter with the back of his fingers.

Shaking his head from the lunacy of his orders, Lam stood to carry them out as best as he could. Being completely in the dark irritated him. He hoped whatever operation he was getting involved in was worth it.

* * *

The Federal Aviation Administration headquarters building in Washington, DC, was typically quiet after hours. Pat Lambert's fax arrived in the late evening, but the duty staff called the FAA Administrator at home.

The administrator, Frank Zinney, had just walked in his house from his nightly swim in his pool when the phone rang in his study. Zinney cringed at the distinctive ring tone of his work phone. No one ever called that line with good news. He walked in, pulled the towel from around his neck, and picked up the handset, wondering which airline had lost an aircraft. "Zinney."

"Good evening, sir. This is the duty officer. We have a priority message from Shanghai."

A two-minute conversation with the FAA duty officer ensued, during which the fax machine on his side table began spitting out pages. Zinney picked up each page out of the tray as it dropped out, scanning it for key words. Hanging up, he read each page of text completely.

Wasting no time, he called his deputy, Michael Bartholomew, on his cell phone. As the phone rang, he

---

[9] Weibo is the Chinese version of Twitter. Started in 2009, Weibo is very popular within the People's Republic of China. The Chinese government has ordered the removal of Weibo posts in the past, and ongoing official oversight and censorship continues to this day.

realized pool water was dripping from his swimming trunks onto the carpet. He patted his shorts down with the towel.

"Hello?" Michael sounded sleepy. Zinney checked the time on his desk clock. It was only eight p.m. *He's in bed already?*

"It's Frank. Something big is afoot," Zinney said.

"What's up?"

Zinney referenced the paper in his hands. "The Chinese Civil Aviation Administration has grounded all domestic airlines, effective immediately."

"What, all of them? That's twenty carriers!"

He sounds awake now. "Yes, all twenty. The translation of their official announcement reads, 'An internal investigation has revealed multiple violations with the use of non-standard replacement parts. All aircraft registered within the PRC are grounded until cleared by the inspecting authority.'" Zinney tossed the loose pages onto his desk.

"This is unprecedented, Frank. We always knew they had issues using cheap replacement parts, but they've never been this, well… public about it before. This is usually handled a lot quieter, and the scale of this is staggering. Do you think we need to look at the U.S. airlines that fly into the PRC?"

Zinney pushed his spectacles up onto his forehead and rubbed his eyes. "Absolutely, that's why I'm calling. We can't take the chance. If the Chinese took this step, then the issue must be huge. I'll want a review of Form 8120-11 submissions for the last six months on my desk when I get in at eight tomorrow. Let's see if there's any issues with unauthorized Chinese parts on U.S. carriers."

"All right, I'm on it. See you at eight."

"Thanks. Bye."

* * *

Li took his golf cart down to a long row of berths. Colonel Chio said he wanted to see if the engineers needed anything, but Li sensed that Chio was just as curious as he was, as to what was going on. Chio ordered him to pull over near a gangway.

After parking the golf cart near a ship that had already received a full load of empty containers, Chio slid off the bench seat. "Comrade Li, I need to go on board, talk to my officers, and make sure all is going smoothly."

Li suspected that was just an excuse to get a better look at what was going on, but he followed gladly. His own curiosity called to him.

On the main deck, Li could see into the lower level of containers, which had their doors wide open. Chio went inside, and Li followed hesitantly. In wonderment, Li observed hundreds of PLA engineers working their way through the container stacks, using oxyacetylene torches to cut meter-wide holes into the interior metal walls, floors, and ceilings. From the outside, the stacks of containers looked as they always did. However, internally, the holes allowed people to pass from one container to the next easily. The container stacks were becoming like Swiss cheese.

Large fans had been set up to vent the stench and smoke of burning metal. Ladders had been brought in and spot-welded in place. Li and Chio used them to easily ascend several levels. It got dark quickly. Li reached into his pocket and took out his car keys. A small keychain flashlight on the fob gave little illumination, but it was enough to navigate with. Engineers yelled between themselves as they worked, and the sound echoed through the dozens of empty metal spaces.

The two men had to exit back onto the deck to avoid choking on the thick fumes. There they found more engineers had arrived, uncoiling wire from spools. Several smaller holes were cut in the outside walls of the containers and ventilation hoses were fitted for fresh air.

Li couldn't stand anywhere for more than fifteen seconds before he had to move to get out of someone's way. The level of activity onboard was frantic.

Several military engineers, bordering on unconsciousness, were being carried out of the containers, supported by their colleagues, and taken to the small medical staff attending dockside and supervised by People's Armed Police Force officers. After a drink of water and a few minutes of compressed oxygen, they were escorted back into the warren of containers. Behind the medical team, three tarp-covered bodies were motionless on the dock. Given the conditions, Li was surprised there were so few.

"Colonel Chio, it would seem our presence is not required here. They have things well in hand." Li waved his hand to indicate the activity around them.

"Yes, I agree. I don't want to go back into those spaces again." Chio began to descend the gangway, dodging engineers coming up with more equipment.

Before following him, Li took one last look around the deck. What this had to do with protecting against a North Korean missile strike was beyond him.

July 4th

Chapter Three
Distraction

Doctor Edmund Wiater awoke in his Seattle apartment with nausea and abdominal cramps. He got up and moved rapidly for the *en suite* bathroom, taking short steps as he clenched to keep everything inside. His lower intestines gurgled, and it took all his self-control to get to the toilet in time. Watery diarrhea exploded from him as he sat. He doubled over, his guts cramping to get rid of as much as possible.

He moaned while cursing himself. The previous evening, Wiater had gone to a new Thai restaurant on a first date with someone he'd met through an online dating service. He'd thought the black chicken green curry he ordered looked undercooked, but he'd eaten it without complaint to impress her. He should have sent it back—she had made it quite clear later there was no need to call her again.

He sat on the toilet for five minutes, letting nature take its course. His windowless bathroom had an underpowered single light bulb in the ceiling. For the hundredth time, he promised himself to swap the bulb with a more powerful one. When done on the toilet, he wiped, flushed, and stepped directly into the shower.

Wiater turned up the water temperature as high as he could stand, soaping himself up thoroughly and rinsing off. Once done, he stepped out of the shower basin, toweled off, and put on his bathrobe. Feeling human again, he walked to the kitchen and drank two large glasses of water to offset any dehydration caused by the diarrhea.

Unable to swallow any more fluids, he went back into the bedroom to get dressed for work. His guts began groaning again, and he rushed for the toilet once more. Work that day would be impossible.

When finished in the bathroom, Wiater went into the living room and took his cell phone in hand. Even though it was a holiday, his staff would be in for a few hours. Data needed to be collected from the daily experiments. He called the extension of the senior graduate student in his research office at the Swedish Medical Center. The extension rang to voice mail.

"Steven, it's Doctor Wiater. I'll not feeling well and will not be in today. Continue with the chimeraplasty, and I'll review it tomorrow morning. Once you have the series data updated, take the rest of the day off, and enjoy the fireworks tonight." Wiater's guts began churning again. Another bathroom visit was non-negotiable. He hung up, tossed the cell onto the couch, and jogged to the toilet straight-legged.

* * *

James Calvin enjoyed the early mornings. When in the White House, he always came into the Oval Office at five a.m. The three hours he spent before the rest of Washington woke up was his most productive time of the day. An early morning shift of secretaries handled any work until his executive secretary, Margaret, took over at eight o'clock.

He was writing a personal note to a senator when a woman's voice from the door of the Oval Office interrupted him. "Mister President, Mister Hurst is here for your morning intelligence brief."

Calvin looked up, recognizing the woman, one of the early morning secretaries. "Thank you, Sally. Show him in."

Calvin stood and walked over to sit in the overstuffed arm chair near the pair of couches facing each other. He liked the informal seating for his briefings. After all, Hurst was his best friend. If he couldn't be informal with him, then what was the point?

"Good morning, Mister President," Hurst said as he crossed the threshold. He wore a gray suit and held several file folders in his left hand.

Hurst wasted no time. He laid his papers on the coffee table before him. "It's getting a little frayed, I'm afraid, Jim. North Korea is heating up." He sat on the end of the couch left of Calvin. He pulled two copies of the president's Daily Brief from his file folders and handed one to Calvin. He referenced his own copy. "China will be making a formal protest at the United Nations today for what it terms 'numerous incursions into the sovereign territory of the People's Republic of China.'"

Surprised, Calvin hurriedly opened the brief to the proper page to read it himself. "The norks are raiding China? Why? China's their only friend and major trading partner. Talk about yanking the dragon's tail."

Hurst leaned forward. "We're not sure. NSA did record a significant increase in SIGINT[10] from the PRC-North Korean border overnight, but only from the Chinese side. If there were incursions, we'd expect to see radio calls from both parties. NRO is conducting an imagery run this morning to look for any activity in that area. We'll have the results in tomorrow's brief. Best guess from the analysts is a border-wide alert to be on the lookout for North Korean troops. It appears the Chinese are mobilizing their 15th Airborne Corp to send to the region. That's thirty thousand-plus troops with the same capability as our 101st airborne. They might be contemplating an invasion and using this 'incursion' as an excuse to forward stage troops. However, if that's the case, we're not seeing any follow-on forces at this time. Just the airborne is on the move, so I would classify it as a defensive

---

[10] Signal Intelligence. Intercepted communications and/or electronic transmissions.

act for the moment. We'll know more when the PRC presents the U.N. with their statement later this morning."

Calvin crossed his legs and rested the briefing document on the side of his calf. "Have defense intelligence and state look this material over. If the Chinese are making a move on the Korean peninsula, we need to reassure Seoul with our support. What do we have in the area?"

Hurst flipped to the appendix at the back of the brief document. "Just under thirty thousand U.S. servicemen deployed in Korea itself, with another fifty thousand in Japan. We have two carrier battle groups, the *George Washington* and *Carl Vinson*, within two days of the Korean peninsula. Within four days, we can have a third carrier group there—the *Ronald Reagan* is currently on exercises near the Solomon Islands off Australia."

"Have PACOM[11] move the two closer carrier groups into the area. Nothing overt for the moment, just get them in the vicinity. I'll want to see contingency plans to reinforce the Korean peninsula in tomorrow's brief."

Hurst scribbled notes in the back of the briefing document. "No problem. Now, on to Iran…"

* * *

Sir Marcus Brandon's Bombardier Global 6000 private jet landed at the Henderson Executive Airport in Las Vegas with the morning sun still well below the horizon. There were faster executive jets with longer range, but Sir Marcus preferred the Bombardier. It had four hundred more square feet over the Gulfstream model, allowing him to have a separate bedroom with a large bed and private bathroom in the rear of the aircraft, yet still have seating for eight in the cabin.

Garbo had pulled Brandon into the aircraft bedroom before takeoff and kept him up for most of the four-hour

---

[11] PACOM - The United States Pacific Command is responsible for the military forces in the Pacific Ocean area. It is based in Honolulu, Hawaii.

flight. She had jumped into the shower after him and was still in the bathroom when the jet touched down lightly.

As the jet taxied to the terminal, he dressed as he always did. Dark suit jacket, comfortable blue jeans, and an open-collar white shirt. He'd just finished pulling on socks when a naked Garbo strode shamelessly out of the small bathroom. She wrapped her arms around his neck, pressed her breasts and hips against him, and kissed him passionately.

Brandon pulled back slightly. "That's the way every man should begin his day. Now, hurry up and get dressed. We don't have a lot of time."

She ran her hands down his back and gave his backside a slight squeeze. She grinned. "Certainly, Sir Marcus."

Brandon slipped on his loafers, left her to dress, and walked out the bedroom door. His steward waited for him near the front of the aircraft with a crystal glass of pineapple juice. Apart from the flight crew, he was the only other person aboard. Brandon took the drink with an appreciative nod. "Thank you, Benson. Call ahead, have breakfast for two waiting at the penthouse. French toast, bacon, fried tomato, coffee."

"Yes, sir. The car is waiting for you at the terminal," Benson replied.

The jet still taxied, so Brandon sat down in one of the white leather chairs to sip his juice. The jet glided to a halt, and the engines died moments later.

Garbo stepped out of the bedroom, wearing a dark skirt, heels, and a white blouse with her pearl choker. She carried her tablet, as usual. The entry door opened, and she walked past him without saying a word, to get to the ladder first. Brandon followed closely behind, and they got into the backseat of the stretch limousine together.

Garbo began making calls on the car phone while updating her tablet, leaving Brandon to look out the window, his thoughts wandering. Garbo had been with him for two years, and they had been lovers for eighteen months. She made his life so easy on the road, and he was away from home nine months of the year. Everything was arranged ahead of time, appointments were lined up efficiently, and the other benefits of having Garbo around were obvious. He wished his wife could be like her.

* * *

Oscar Blake made sure he was up bright and early. Shingling his bungalow's roof would take all day, and it promised to be hot later in the afternoon. He'd recently inherited the home from his deceased father, and the property hadn't been maintained properly for the last five years. The roof was three years past when it should have been replaced.

By climbing up the aluminum ladder on the outside of the single-story home, he got onto the shallow pitch roof to see the bundled shingles waiting for him. His neighbor and close friend, Eddy, had helped remove the old shingles and bring the new ones up the previous evening. Blake considered himself to be in good shape. As a U.S. Park Ranger, he needed to be. His average workday involved being a trail guide on the steep trails of Olympic National Park, but carrying the ninety-pound shingle bundles up the ladder had challenged even his stamina.

Blake looked north. From his rooftop, over the Strait of Juan de Fuca, he could see the southern tip of Vancouver Island. The usual morning mist was just clearing off, and it promised to be a clear day.

Around him, the surrounding houses of the rural neighborhood showed no movement. The twenty thousand people of the town of Port Angeles, Washington, lived quiet lives. In the other direction, he could see the Olympic mountain range. Living between the forest and sea, Blake felt at home.

He chided himself for wasting time and descended the ladder to get his tools. Eddy would be by as soon as he got off the midnight shift from the Coast Guard station, and Blake wanted everything ready by the time he arrived.

* * *

"Mister President, the car is ready," a secretary said from the door.

"Thank you, Joyce." James Calvin rose from his Oval Office desk and left the room. His Secret Service detail enveloped him as he walked out.

Calvin overheard one of the agents speaking into his wrist microphone. "Rook is mobile."

"Rook" came from the many chess games he played, usually with Hurst. The Secret Service agents guided him through the Roosevelt Room, then into the lobby. Not the usual route.

"Avoiding the front door today, Mike?" Calvin asked a nearby agent.

"Yes, sir. Just mixing things up."

He stepped outside into sunshine and clear skies. The rain of the previous evening had blown off overnight. His heavily armored limo waited for him with door open. He stepped into the rear, and an agent closed it behind him with a solid *thump*. The young Special Advisor to the president Barbara Morgan waited for him inside. The limousine accelerated away from the West Wing.

"Morning, Barbara. Where are we off to today?"

She tossed her brown hair over her shoulder. As part of her job, she coordinated the speechwriters. "Good morning, Mister President. We have two speeches this morning, followed by lunch at the Pentagon with the joint chiefs, a meeting with the Speaker of the House, and then back here for dinner and fireworks tonight. Here's the speech notes. It's what we discussed. We want to push the education agenda." She handed over a three-page document.

He glanced over the notes quickly. "What's the first stop?"

"American Legion. Should be a friendly crowd. Second speech is with the Arlington Chamber of Commerce. Same speech with three lines added to push the small-business funding initiative."

Calvin dropped the notes beside him. The changes were inconsequential, and he would have a teleprompter to guide him at both locations. "How are Fernando and the kids?"

She smiled warmly. "They're doing fine. Fernando just got promoted to regional sales director. Rebecca starts kindergarten in the fall, and Veronica is off to summer camp next week. They're really looking forward to the fireworks tonight. Fernando didn't want them up that late, but fireworks from space? That's something they have to see."

"You should bring them to the White House. We've invited the ambassadors and members of both houses," Calvin suggested.

She shook her head. "Too much bother getting through security. No, once I get home, I'm kicking off my shoes and staying there. I'll have a nice glass of wine and relax while Fernando barbecues dinner and handles the kids."

"I can't better that offer, I'm afraid," Calvin said good-naturedly.

He looked out of the window as the car moved through the city. After the holiday, he would try to get up to Camp David for a long weekend. He couldn't relax in the city—at least, not in *this* city.

* * *

Sir Marcus Brandon stood on the small dance floor, surrounded by a vocal, enthusiastic group. Primal, throbbing drum and bass began to beat. In his booth, the DJ grabbed his microphone. "Ladies and gentlemen, welcome to the VooDoo Rooftop Nightclub on the fifty-first floor of the Rio All-Suite Las Vegas Hotel and Casino!"

The wall-to-wall crowd cheered and screamed, waving their free drinks in the air. Brandon lifted his hands, urging them to make more noise. They were easy to motivate, as most were members of the local marketing firm he had hired, along with their spouses.

The DJ continued, "It's a beautiful sunny day in Las Vegas. I'm DJ Roper, and I'll be with you all day and into the night as we celebrate the first transmission of the Global News Network!"

Everyone applauded and screamed again. DJ Roper ramped up the volume and faded in a heavy bass dance track that vibrated the room for a couple of minutes.

He lowered the volume slightly and finished with, "GNI will begin broadcasting worldwide in exactly one hour from now, but until then, let's get this party *started*!"

The crowd screamed, and several people began dancing. Aware he was the target of several photographers, Brandon gave out high fives to the people around him and then raised his glass. He danced for a few minutes and then casually walked down the carpeted stairs to the restaurant below. He'd reserved the space for his use, and GNI tech staff had set up a remote broadcast station for the press.

Brandon dropped his drink glass onto a table, grabbed a bottle of water, and then sat down for the first of many press interviews.

A makeup artist began preparing him for broadcast in high definition. Garbo appeared and gave him a subtle thumbs-up against her black tablet case. *Everything is ready and good to go.* He nodded back at her, and she vanished. The GNI logos looked right on the monitors behind him, so he returned his attention to the room.

His first interviewer, Denise Cartwright, moved to the seat across from him. She was currently working for SKY News in the UK, but she had tentatively accepted a position with the New York GNI bureau. She would be putting in her two weeks' notice later that day.

"Good morning, Sir Marcus. Sounds like a royal party upstairs." Cartwright sat down and wiggled to get comfortable. Her English accent dripped with sophistication. Her father, the Duke of Clarence, was one of the largest landowners in England. Technically, he should call her Lady Denise, but she hated using the title in her job as a reporter.

"Good morning. Yes, we hired the top two floors of the Rio hotel for the next day. If you're going to celebrate, then do it in style. Please feel free to have a drink after. Your press pass is good for the entire celebration."

Cartwright pressed her hand against her ear for a moment. "We'll be going live in ten seconds."

Brandon got comfortable, dropping his water bottle into the side pocket of his director's chair.

Cartwright nodded her head once, pressed her finger against an audio earpiece, then looked over at Brandon. "Thank you, James. Yes, I'm here with Sir Marcus Brandon in Las Vegas for the premiere of his Global News International channels. Sir Marcus, good morning."

Brandon smiled widely. "Good morning, Denise, and welcome."

"Sir Marcus, social media is overwhelmingly in favor of your plans to launch a fireworks show from orbit. Anticipation is building, and it seems your desired world records are close to becoming reality. Tell me, how do you plan to top this next time?"

Brandon laughed heartily at the unexpected question, throwing his head back in genuine enjoyment. But he needed to stay on message. "Well, Denise, there's nothing I like more than challenging myself. Honestly, I don't know how I'll top this, but for the moment, I'm focusing on getting GNI off the ground with a bang."

Cartwright continued, "Launching multiple news bureaus and a total of sixteen channels in several countries seems quite a daunting challenge. Do you have any fallback plans if anything goes wrong with the initial broadcast?"

"Actually, GNI has already been broadcasting for six weeks." Brandon reached for his water bottle.

"What?" She rapidly flipped through the press release paperwork on her lap.

Brandon held up his hand. "I didn't mean to confuse you. We've been broadcasting for six weeks internally. The signal hasn't gone out publically. We wanted to work out the kinks ahead of time, as a sort of dress rehearsal. The bureaus have been broadcasting in closed circuit, testing links, lighting, and getting the mistakes sorted before they go to air. When we go live later this morning, the news teams should be well practiced and professional."

"I see. Thank you for clarifying. Will Lady Brandon be joining you for the premiere?"

"No, I'm afraid not. She's back in England, working with projects for her charitable foundation, and couldn't make it out." Brandon did a quick time zone calculation. *Late afternoon in the UK, so Cilla should just be opening her second bottle of gin for the day.*

"Thank you, Sir Marcus. James, back to you in the studio."

A moment later, she stood and shook his hand. "Nice to see you again, Sir Marcus."

"I hope to see more of you in the near future, Denise." He winked, and she blushed visibly.

Cartwright left, and another reporter took her seat. Brandon took a swig of water and steeled himself for the second of eight scheduled interviews.

* * *

Beijing, a city of over twenty million people, waited impatiently for the upcoming show. Young and old, men and women, boys and girls—all gazed into the night sky waiting for the announced ten p.m. start time. All local radio and television stations had been broadcasting the story for hours. The morning city newspapers all had dedicated their front pages to the GNI launch and fireworks show.

GNI crews had set up several cameras in and around the city. Escorted by members of the People's Armed Police Force, they had no issues getting where they needed to be.

Carl Waverly, a former unit producer for CNN, had worked in China for a decade and had never seen this level of cooperation from Chinese authorities. Now working for GNI, he was responsible for getting shots of the first overhead show, to record its impact on the people around him. Not an easy task for a city that ranged over ten thousand square miles.

The success of the launch rested on his shoulders. His visuals would be seen on televisions around the world. The various GNI bureaus would provide commentary in their own languages then rebroadcast the footage on their respective channels. He wasn't worried—he loved the pressure. Waverly lived for the stress, and the only thing that could make things better would be a war breaking out halfway through for him to film.

He would have preferred the war, to be honest. It would be better than covering a silly fireworks demonstration, even if it was a large one from space. *Whoop-de-doo...*

Up above him, a light flashed. Waverly looked skyward but saw nothing. His watch said ten p.m., so he pulled his headset over his ears and pressed the transmission stud. His voice went over a radio to the three dozen camera crews he had employed. "Heads up, people."

The words had just left his mouth when the night flashed into day, casting long shadows. He had to turn his face away from the brilliance. Across the city, millions of voices screamed together in appreciation. It faded back to black, and he looked skyward once more. A bright green spider web of fluorescent trails appeared and diminished before the ends of the trails exploded all at once, covering the sky above with huge explosions of color. Yellow, blue, and red patterns appeared in quick succession.

Waverly realized immediately that his assumption had been wrong. These were not typical fireworks. These pyrotechnics were expansive, covering the night sky in a long band. He tried to calculate the size of them, but without a reference point, that was futile. The explosions were so high up that they were without sound. The radiance of the display dropped his mouth open, and he felt six years old again.

More colorful blasts covered the night sky from one horizon to the other in a rippling wave. Waverly had been warned they would not last long, only a few minutes.

The last explosion was the strangest and most exotic. During his youth, Waverly had a black light illuminating a psychedelic poster. The last pyrotechnic had that same color. It hung in the air—shimmering, undulating, and seeming to shift the colors of everything around him. Reds became blue. Blues became green. Greens faded to black. He blinked, and in the short time his eyes were closed, the scintillating light vanished.

The undisturbed night sky returned, and Carl Waverly joined millions of Chinese citizens in screaming and wild applause.

Forgetting his job for a moment, he pulled out his android phone and opened his Twitter app. He thumb typed rapidly for several seconds and then paused. Waverly used hashtags to find tweets after they'd been posted. With only eight characters left, he added the first one to occur to him. His mother had read him a nursery rhyme when he was much younger, and that memory came to the fore.

He hit send, and his tweet went out to his three thousand followers.

Once in a lifetime orbital firework display
over Beijing. Must see! Best!Lightshow!Ever!
Majestic, tremendous, colorful, brilliant!
#Twinkle

* * *

Colonel Alvin Smith walked into the NORAD bunker under Cheyenne Mountain. As he passed the inner blast doors, he powered off his cell phone. No radio signal could hope to penetrate the bunker shielding and the granite mountain. He walked up to the console and nodded to Colonel Holmes, who had been on duty for the previous eight hours. "Colonel."

"Colonel." Smith smiled. It was the same greeting they'd used for seven months. "Is the world still turning?"

"It got quite exciting an hour ago. The first of Brandon's space launched fireworks went off over eastern China. They were so bright, they set off DSP satellite alerts. You can expect the same thing every hour, on the hour, as it works its way west. They're being dropped from low Earth orbit, so no danger to any of our birds. Vandenberg will be streaming us live video from the International Space Station for the next display. Everything else is in the log." Colonel Holmes stood and gave a formal salute.

Smith returned the gesture. "Sir, I relieve you."

Colonel Holmes finished the salute and responded, "I stand relieved, sir. Have a good day, Alvin."

Smith sat at the console, stowed his briefcase under the desk, and opened the log to review the previous shift's activities as Holmes walked out of the chamber.

On the wall in front of him, a large-format display turned blue for a few moments before a NASA logo appeared on a white background. The logo stayed on the screen for several minutes. Smith began a series of calls to check communication lines and recorded the successful results in the log binder. As he finished, video of the inside of the International Space Station replaced the logo. There was no sound, but the people in light blue coveralls on screen floated in mid-air. They appeared to be setting up a large-format camera in a view port.

"Excuse me, sir." An airman appeared at Smith's elbow with a clipboard of forms.

He took it and worked his way through the routine paperwork, signing where necessary. When done, he handed the clipboard back.

After the camera had been secured, the video image changed to an external view. Smith assumed the feed came from the camera he'd just watched being set up. He easily recognized the Himalaya mountain range. The ISS, currently over Africa, was on an arced course that would take it over India in a few minutes.

Smith looked at the large wall clock. The second hand was five seconds away from the top of the hour. The screen flashed a brilliant white without warning, stunning Smith.

Overhead speakers came to life. "This is Argus. We have a DSP detonation alert."

Smith saw the staff opening their binders to follow procedure. He did also, but admittedly a lot slower than usual. The light show had grabbed his attention. With the planet Earth in the background of the video, the true scale of the explosions was staggering. A wide band of multicolored lights appeared. *That must be along the path of the satellite dropping the pyrotechnics.* It looked impressive from his vantage point. From the ground, it must be awe inspiring.

"This is Argus reporting an extra-atmospheric detonation at thirty-one degrees, nineteen minutes north; eighty-nine degrees, twenty-four minutes east; at an altitude of three hundred and nine kilometers. Detonation is non-nuclear—repeat, non-nuclear. No follow-up action required at this time."

As spectacular as the light show was, Smith still had a job to do. With that scale of explosion, it could easily mask a missile launch. He needed to brief his staff to be vigilant.

* * *

The command center of the USS *John Warner* was deathly silent except for the muted sounds of air conditioning. Captain Eric Reid's OOD—Officer of the Deck—made his approach to the simulated surface target. Reid had a clipboard in his hand to make notes. The XO was in the torpedo room to ensure no actual weapons were launched during the drill. ADCAP[12] torpedoes cost several million dollars each and were not used haphazardly.

The Officer of the Deck, Lieutenant Kaplan, cuff the sweat from his brow. Reid smiled slightly at the sight. He himself

---

[12] MK-48 Advanced Capability Torpedo.

had been in the same position when he was a lieutenant, and he remembered the pressure.

Kaplan spoke into his headset. "Sonar, conn. Any change in bearing or speed of Sierra One?"

"Conn, sonar. No change in bearing. Still making turns for sixteen knots," came the immediate response.

Kaplan nodded. "Raise photonics mast."

Virginia-class submarines did not have periscopes. Instead Kaplan stood near a large-format flat-screen monitor that showed the output of a state-of-the-art photonics closed-circuit system. He moved the view using a handheld device with a thumb controller.

Kaplan used the controller to circle the camera, to view all around, and then stopped on the target. The Q-70 computer had overlaid a crude ship-shaped object on the display for Kaplan to see. Reid saw him press the stud on the control to send the bearing to the fire control system. "Bearing, mark. Range, mark."

A naval rating at the fire control board called out, "Set."

The next command would fire the torpedo. Reid had told sonar to throw the young officer a curve to see how Kaplan would handle it.

Sonar came over the headset before Kaplan gave the order. "Conn, sonar. Aspect change on target—turns increasing. He's zigging, sir."

Kaplan looked downcast but immediately ordered, "Lower photonics mast. Sonar, conn. Keep me updated on Sierra One aspect change."

"Conn, sonar. Sierra One turning to port and increasing turns to twenty knots."

"Sonar, conn. Is Sierra One's bearing passing zero-four-five degrees?"

"Conn, sonar. Stand by."

A minute passed. Reid thought Kaplan looked seriously worried. A "zig" was a turn of up to ninety degrees. Ships turned like that to throw a submarine's targeting off. The target had been on a course of one-three-five degrees before the turn, so if zigging to port, the ship would settle on a new course of no more than zero-four-five. That would place the sub in a bad position for an attack.

"Conn, sonar. Sierra One passing zero-four-zero degrees. Aspect change is constant, sir."

Kaplan smiled and said out loud, "He's not zigging, he's coming about. Firing party, assume Sierra One is coming to a new course of three-one-five degrees. Pilot, come to course two-niner-zero."

"Course two-niner-zero, pilot aye."

The sub began leaning as it turned. Reid made notes, impressed that Kaplan hadn't fallen for the deception.

"Conn, sonar. Sierra One is steady on course three-one-five. Speed is back to sixteen knots, sir."

"Final bearing and range. Raise photonics mast," Kaplan said formally.

The monitor displayed the surface and the computer-overlaid target. Once again Kaplan scanned all around and settled on the target.

"Standby forward," a member of the fire control team announced on his headset.

Kaplan spoke while pressing a stud on the photonics controller. "Bearing, mark. Range, mark."

A naval rating at the fire control board responded, "Set."

"Shoot," Kaplan ordered.

"Fire one," said the petty officer at the FCS board. "One fired, sir. Clock is running. Impact in two minutes, three seconds."

"Bring the ADCAP up to maximum speed and cut the wires," Kaplan ordered.

"ADCAP to max speed; wires cut, sir. Impact now sixty-one seconds."

"Pilot, come to course zero-zero-five. Make your depth four hundred feet. Increase speed to one-third." Kaplan said calmly.

"Come to course zero-zero-five, depth four hundred feet, speed increase to two-thirds; pilot aye."

The next minute passed slowly.

The petty officer at the fire control board said, "Torpedo detonation should be... now. We will hear the impact... now."

Nothing was heard, but no torpedo had actually been fired.

"Conn, sonar. I have breakup noise from the target."

"Pilot, make your speed ten knots. Descend to two-zero-zero feet and turn to course three-one-five," Kaplan ordered.

Reid stepped forward. "Belay that order. Pilot, maintain depth, ahead one third, come to course two-eight-zero."

"Maintain depth, ahead one third, come to course two-eight-zero; pilot aye."

Reid continued, "Exercise is terminated. Mister Lamberth, you have the conn."

Lamberth walked toward the tactical navigation table. "I have the conn, Captain."

Reid toggled the 1MC handset; his voice would now be heard throughout the boat. "This is the captain. The exercise is terminated. Stand down from General Quarters. XO, report to the command center. That is all." He hung up the 1MC while saying, "Mister Kaplan, please join me in the wardroom for your debrief. Chief of the Boat, have the XO join us there."

"Aye, Captain," replied Chief of the Boat Duggan.

Reid let Kaplan go down the corridor first. He'd made errors, but nothing major, and his performance was good overall. They needed to discuss the exercise and have Kaplan explain his reasoning behind the path he had taken.

Reid had been satisfied with crew performance to this point. They would have many more exercises over their deployment to keep their alertness up.

* * *

"Welcome back to the continuing Global News International coverage of the orbital fireworks display. I'm Kaliram Singh, and I'm standing in the National Park of Uzbekistan within the capital city of Tashkent. It's almost ten o'clock here, and anticipation is building. Word of the upcoming light show has spread through social media, and the park is packed with over two hundred thousand people. Many more people—some estimate up to a million—are spread out in the city on rooftops, gardens, and balconies, waiting for what has been hailed as the most spectacular pyrotechnic display ever. Around me in the park, people are spread out on blankets and portable chairs. The mood is festive, and I can hear several bands playing. There are jugglers and vendors circulating around, entertaining the crowd."

"Immediately after the display we will be joined by..." The night sky vanished in a pulse of pure white light. "Mahrood, are you getting this on the camera? Ladies and gentlemen, let me tell you, the brilliance of this is staggering. I see the—Ooooooh! My, this is a phenomenal sight. The colors cover almost the entire sky! The colors are crawling across the sky in wonderful patterns, I'm sorry, but I simply don't have the words to convey the majesty and scale of this... this... magnificent spectacle."

Sir Marcus Brandon turned away from the flat-screen television in his suite. "So far it seems to be going well. Garbo, how's the social media campaign going?"

Garbo slid her fingers across her tablet. "We did hit a bump. No one save our marketing firm is using the recommended 'GNI_Launch' hashtag. Instead, 'Twinkle' has caught on. You know, like the poem. It's recognized internationally, is currently trending in the top ten, and is moving up rapidly. I suggest we jump on the wagon."

Brandon never paused. He recognized the advantages of social media, and swimming with the current was much easier. "Do it. Have Terry switch the campaign over to 'Twinkle' right away. I'll want to see the ratings first thing tomorrow morning. We need to see how well we have penetrated the market and then review steps to improve."

"Yes, Sir Marcus."

* * *

A call came in while President Calvin was in the backseat of the limousine as they traveled between speeches. "Hello?"

"Jim, it's Keith."

Calvin had several minutes to talk before the car arrived. "What's up?"

"Just keeping you in the loop. Our orbiting DSP satellites are going off whenever Brandon's fireworks go off every hour on the hour," Hurst called out.

Calvin had heard that term before, but couldn't remember from where. "Sorry—remind me, what is DSP?"

"Defense Support Program. A series of satellites in orbit with infrared sensors that can detect heat blooms from launching missiles and nuclear detections. Brandon's shows are so large, they're setting alarms off at NORAD. Some of the White House staff has been approached by the press, looking for confirmation, so you may be asked about it."

"Is there any danger?" Calvin's attention was caught momentarily by a placard-wielding man on a street corner. The haggard man looked homeless, and his sign read in large dark red letters, "REPENT, for the end of the world is nigh."

"As of now, none. NORAD tells me the detonations could cover a missile launch, but we would eventually pick the boosters up. Besides, the display has moved west, and all Russian and Chinese missile sites are to the east. I don't think there'll be an issue. On other matters, the Chinese formally delivered a protest to the UN over incursions into their territory by North Korea. They claim to have ambushed three North Korean company-sized patrols well past the border and taken several prisoners. There's no response from the norks, but that's their standard response to most things."

Calvin snorted. "That's true enough. Anything else?"

"Chess tonight?"

"No, I can't. With the July Fourth celebrations, I doubt I'll have the time. Put yourself down for a thrashing tomorrow night. Oh and I'm heading up to Camp David this weekend. Feel free to invite yourself. I have to go—we're pulling in now."

"Right. Bye."

* * *

"Doctor Krause, to the nurses' station. Doctor Krause, to the nurses' station, please," came over the overhead speakers.

Linda Krause jerked to consciousness and got up from the worn couch in the staff break room. She had caught an hour's nap after her surgery. The announcement hadn't used a color code, so there was no rush. She walked down the short corridor to the nurse on duty. "Yes, Carla?"

"These were just delivered for you." Carla pointed at a bright bouquet of flowers at the end of the desk. They were beautiful. She saw lavender daisy poms, purple butterfly asters, and pink mini-carnations, plus a few other flowers she didn't recognize. *They're lovely. A patient sent them, I expect.* A small envelope was held by a plastic stick. She opened the card.

Am in town. Want to get a drink and catch up?
—Donovan
Cell: 287-1452

Krause immediately scrunched the card up into a ball. Her first inclination was to throw it away, but she pocketed it. She would toss it later, where no one would see. She looked at the nurse and pointed to the blooms. "Carla, can you take these over to the terminal care wing and give them to someone deserving?"

"Why not keep them? Who are they from?" Carla stood up.

Krause didn't want to talk about it. The memories were still painful, and while she knew Carla fairly well, they were not close enough to discuss Donovan. "No one. Give them to someone who'll appreciate them."

Krause walked back to the break room, closed the door behind her, threw the card deep in the trash bin, and sat down on the couch she'd left minutes before. She placed her face in her palms and wept quietly.

* * *

Blake had the first row of roof shingles in place when a familiar rusting red pickup truck with a bright yellow driver's door pulled into the driveway and parked behind his station wagon. Eddy jumped out of the truck, wearing work clothes and carrying a twenty-four case of beer. Blake put his compressed air nail gun down and walked to the edge. He looked at his watch. Just after eight in the morning.

"Bit early for beer, isn't it?" Blake called down.

"Gimme a break. I just got off work. I'll put these in the fridge. You want one?"

The July heat was already making its presence known that morning. "Yeah, what the hell."

Minutes later, Eddy climbed the ladder, tossed over an ice-cold beer can, opened his own, and looked at the roof. "You've got a nice first row down."

"Thanks. It's supposed to be a hot day, and I wanted to get it over as soon as possible." Blake cracked open the tab on his can.

"Yeah, too bad you installed them wrong."

Blake had been about to take a drink but stopped with the can halfway to his mouth. He looked at the shingles he'd nailed down. They looked fine to him. "What?"

Eddy pointed. "You're supposed to put the first row on upside down so the slots in the shingles point up the roof. Look, you can see the ice shield below through the cracks."

Blake saw what he was talking about but was still unsure that it was wrong.

Eddy grabbed a loose shingle and placed it on the edge, with the slots pointing up toward the peak. He placed a second tile on top with the slots down. "There, see? This way you have a solid asphalt base all the way along the bottom."

Blake closed his eyes and rubbed his temple with his free hand. "Damn it. You're right. I wasted my morning."

"Well, you did invite me over for my roofing expertise, remember?" Eddy slapped him in the shoulder. "Come on. It's not that bad. We can have this fixed in fifteen minutes."

Together, they pulled up the first row of tiles and reversed them. Blake grabbed one of the compressed air nail guns and began nailing them down.

Eddy took the second gun with obvious trepidation. "I've never used these before."

Blake showed him the one in his hand. "I rented them yesterday. They're simple to use. Press the tip down and squeeze the trigger." Blake demonstrated by setting two flat-head roofing nails into opposite ends of a shingle.

He stood back and let Eddy try his. He pressed the gun down and squeezed his trigger, but nothing happened. Eddy pulled it up and turned it sideways to look at it.

Blake took a half step forward. "There's a safety switch on the handle. Both the tip and safety need to be depressed for it to fire."

Blake saw Eddy press the safety. The gun was pointed right at him, but it wouldn't fire unless the tip was also pressed dow—

The gun fired. Something struck Blake near the bridge of his nose. His hand instinctively slapped against the left side of his face. He backpedaled down the roof, fell over the edge, and landed heavily on his shoulders. His head smacked into the grass, stunning him.

Blake lay there in a daze, trying to comprehend what had happened. He pulled his hand away and saw no blood, but what concerned him most was his fuzzy vision. He couldn't see his hand properly. *Did my head hit the ground that hard?*

Eddy appeared at his side. "Don't touch your face—don't move. Oh man, I'm sorry. It went off in my hand. Lay still. Don't move. I'll call an ambulance."

Blake moved his hand in front of his face. It looked warped and out of focus. There was a dark area in his left eye. He reached to touch it, but Eddy grabbed his hand and pushed it back down. "Don't move, Oscar!"

Eddy dialed a short number. "This is Petty Officer Gainsbridge, U.S. Coast Guard. I need an ambulance to fourteen eleven South Coyote Run Lane. I have a man with a nail in his eye and a possible concussion."

Nail in my eye? Blake tried to reach up again, but Eddy grabbed his wrist to keep his hands away from his face. Eddy held Blake's arm to his chest. "Stay still! The nail went into your left eye. Try not to move. The ambulance is on its way."

Blake lay back and tried to relax, but a sense of doom flooded over him. *Jesus, Mary, and Joseph, not my eye. Please, don't let me lose my sight.*

Chapter Four
De Integro

The overhead speakers announced, "This is Argus. We have a DSP detonation alert."

Colonel Smith grabbed his procedures binder for the third time in three hours. The hourly blasts of high-intensity light had started out being good from an exercise perspective, but the repetition could actually hurt responsiveness. His people were getting used to nothing bad happening. If something did, it might not be caught for several seconds or even minutes later. Not a good thing when nuclear-tipped missiles could be involved. He needed to make sure no one slacked off. After making sure only the internal staff would hear him, he keyed his headset microphone. "All right, people, no complacency. Remember to follow all procedures and report anything out of place. We're going to have several more of these today, and we need to stay alert."

From the speakers came a disinterested female voice. "This is Argus, reporting an extra-atmospheric detonation forty-six degrees, fifty-eight minutes north; ten degrees, fifty-four minutes east; at an altitude of three hundred and twelve kilometers. Detonation is non-nuclear—repeat, non-nuclear. No follow-up action required at this time."

Smith checked the coordinates on the room displays. *That show is centered over Lichtenstein and will cover Europe from Finland through Germany to Italy, then south over Africa.* He shook his head, trying to imagine the scale of the thing.

After several minutes, no more information arrived. Smith adjusted his seat cushion and tried to relax, but he couldn't. He had no idea why he was feeling anxious. The feeling took him back to growing up on his stepfather's farm in Nebraska. Once he felt the same anxiety two days before a twister ripped through the adjoining town, killing three people. He had no idea why he felt the same sense of foreboding while sitting under a granite mountain, perfectly safe. *Or am I?*

* * *

Doctor Phùng Vinh just happened to be at the E.R. desk of the Olympic Medical Center when the ambulance call came in. As a Level III trauma facility, they were well equipped to handle most severe issues.

Doctor Vinh had his people standing by when the ambulance attendants rolled the male victim in through the doors.

"What do we have?" Vinh asked as he pulled the stethoscope from his shoulders.

"Single nail fired from a compressed air gun into the left eye. He fell off a roof after the injury and may have a concussion. He's stable otherwise," said the senior paramedic.

Vinh checked the patient's heart. It sounded strong but rapid. Not surprising, in this situation. Vinh turned to the head nurse as he returned the stethoscope around his neck. "Okay, let's get a cranial X-ray, front and left side." Vinh leaned down over the injured man. "Sir, my name is Doctor Vinh. What's yours?"

"Oscar Blake."

"Mister Blake, you've suffered a penetrating injury to your left eye. It's important you minimize any movement of your eyes to stop further damage. Are you in any pain?"

"No, not really. I'm just…" His voice cracked.

Vinh placed his hand on Blake's chest. "That's all right, Mister Blake. Just relax, we'll take care of you. You'll be fine. Are you on any medications?"

"No."

Vinh turned back to a nurse. "Ophthalmoscope." Then to Blake. "Do you have any allergies?"

"No."

The nurse handed him an instrument. Vinh came close and used it to examine his eye. "The nail's embedded in the sclera directly beside the caruncula of the left eye. I can't see much as it has such a broad head."

The head nurse returned with portable X-ray equipment and a technician. Both wore lead aprons. Vinh left the room to give her room to work.

Outside the exam room, he was intercepted by a man dressed in a tartan lumberjack shirt, baseball hat, and jeans. "Doc, how's Oscar?"

"Are you related to Mister Blake?" Vinh returned his stethoscope to lie around the back of his neck.

"No, he's my friend. My nail gun caused…"—the man pointed at Blake—"that."

"Look, Mister…?"

"Gainsbridge."

"He's going to be fine, Mister Gainsbridge." Vinh said. "After we stabilize him, we'll airlift him to Seattle. We don't have an ophthalmologist on staff. Does he have a wife, or any family you can contact?"

"No, he's single. His parents are both dead. He hit his head when he fell. You should check that, too."

"We're taking X-rays now. If you go down to the waiting room, and I'll come down with an update as soon as I can." Vinh turned to leave.

"Thanks, Doc."

* * *

Garbo ran into Brandon's hotel suite, shouting, "Twitter is down! Twitter is down!"

Startled, Brandon turned from watching the television. "What?"

She was wearing a broad smile. "The fireworks just went off over Europe! There were so many tweets using the 'Twinkle' hashtag, the indexing servers at Twitter couldn't keep up and crashed. All of them! San Francisco, New York, San Antonio, Boston—all their data centers are down. This is great news! Every news agency on the planet will report this and the reason why! We'll boost awareness across every demographic. This is huge—free publicity, Marcus. More than we could've ever dreamed of!"

He considered the situation for a moment. "All right, let's get the editorial staff on it. I'll need a statement—no, wait, an apology! Issue an apology, say that the popularity of the GNI launch has been much larger than we expected, and I'm sorry that the fireworks show has caused this Twitter disruption."

"Perfect. We'll get a lot more traction with that," Garbo said gleefully.

Brandon shooed her away with the back of his hands. "Go! Get it out, quickly."

She rushed out of the room. Brandon walked over to a side table, filled with trays of snacks, sliced meats, and rolls. He pulled a bottle of *Taittinger Comtes de Champagne* from the silver ice bucket at the end and regarded the label. The champagne, bottled in 2000, had a reputation of being the best in the world. He had been saving it for later, but the present moment could not pass uncelebrated. He undid the foil and wire before popping the cork across the room.

After pouring himself a tall fluted glass, he raised it to the city of Las Vegas outside the floor-to-ceiling windows and simply said, "Cheers," before taking a sip.

* * *

Oscar Blake felt helpless and miserable as he lay in the gurney waiting. After his X-rays, Doctor Vinh had returned, told him there was no concussion, taped a hard curved patch over his injured eye, then told him he'd be airlifted to Seattle for further treatment. That was twenty minutes ago, according to his watch. Blake couldn't help thinking the longer he sat here, the greater the chance he would lose the vision in his eye. A nurse was off to his blind side. He could see her when he turned his head, but otherwise, no one else was visible. He was thirsty, but the nurse had refused to give him any water.

Doctor Vinh appeared at his elbow. "Mister Blake, we've had a slight delay in the airlift. The helicopter aircrew exceeded their flight hours and is on a mandatory rest cycle. We're looking for alternate transport now."

"I can call the Coast Guard station for assistance." Eddy's voice came in from the hallway. "We have a chopper on standby."

Vinh replied, "The Coast Guard typically doesn't do that for us."

"You leave that to me, Doc. Oscar, hang in there, buddy. I'll call them right now."

* * *

Eddy Gainsbridge stepped outside of the E.R. entrance and dialed the number from memory on his cell phone. "Come on... Come on, answer!"

"Coast Guard Air Station Port Angeles. How can I direct your call?"

"Martha, it's Eddy. Can you track down the XO? It's an emergency."

"One moment, Eddy."

Soft on-hold music began playing in Eddy's ear. It played for twenty seconds before a man's voice answered, "Commander Mitchell."

"Sir, it's Petty Officer Gainsbridge. I'm at the Olympic Medical Center. There's a man here with a nail through his eye that needs immediate surgery. The air ambulance is down and he needs transport to Seattle."

"That's not part of our mission, P.O. You know that." Mitchell said seriously.

"Yes, sir, but the man's a friend of mine. It's Oscar Blake."

"I'm sorry P.O., but I can't make an exception for your friend. Our helicopter is on standby for maritime search and rescue callouts."

Eddy looked around, but no one was nearby. He still lowered his voice so he couldn't be overheard. "Sir, you know him. Oscar's the ranger who carried you down from the west peak of Mount Olympus last year when you dislocated your knee. I wouldn't be asking if it wasn't critically important, but he could lose his eye over this."

There was a long pause. Finally, Mitchell said, "For anyone else, under any other circumstances, I would say no, but he carried me down seven miles of horrific trail. Let me talk to the C.O. and see if we can run a training flight into the city. I'll support you, but it's his decision for a go or no-go."

"Thank you, sir."

* * *

Another Argus alert came and went with the fireworks over the UK. Smith still felt anxious but forced it into the back of his mind until some sort of empirical evidence came his way to substantiate his feelings. Instead, he finished up his paperwork in anticipation of the shift change. With eighteen hours off, he could catch some sleep, then watch the fireworks from his balcony as it passed over Colorado later that evening.

The desk phone rang. He answered, "Watch Officer Colonel Smith."

"Alvin, it's Mike Palmer."

Colonel Palmer would be relieving him in fifteen minutes. "Hey, Mike."

"Sorry to do this, but can you cover my shift? A school bus backed over my son, Billy, and he's in the E.R. with some pretty serious injuries."

Smith stiffened. "Will he be okay?"

"Not sure. He just went into surgery. I'll call the general, but I needed to know if you can cover for me first."

"No problem, Mike. You take care of your son. I'll take the shift."

"Thanks, man. I owe you. Gotta run. Bye."

Smith hung up the phone. *Well, it looks like my only fireworks experience will be over remote satellite video. Now I'll get to see it sixteen times instead of just eight.*

He began the process for coming on shift, validating comm channels and testing the phones. He'd just finished logging the results when Vinson and Noel walked up to his station.

"Colonel, do you have a moment?" Vinson asked.

"Of course. What do you need?" Smith twisted around in his chair to face them.

"China—specifically the port of Qingdao. We're getting indications of a lot of military activity in the docks. Not only do we have three regiments of engineers assigned there, but indicators point to two entire army corps of PLA being sent there."

"Two army corps?" Smith asked incredulously. "That can't be right."

Troop movements of that scale were extremely rare and never without serious implications. Smith knew a U.S. army corps had two or three divisions of roughly ten to fifteen thousand men each. He was unsure what comprised a Chinese PLA corps, but it had to be comparable.

Vinson continued, "We have SIGINT and overhead imagery from multiple sources. Plus we got lucky. A Chinese merchant marine cargo vessel is tied up across from the container port with serious electrical issues. One of their Philippine crew posted cell phone pics we intercepted. It shows the docks covered in heavy trucks unloading troops, lots of them."

"So what's your assessment?" he asked both men.

Noel pointed at a map of the Korean peninsula and the Chinese east coast. "The Chinese are protesting at the U.N. about North Korean patrols coming over their border. The nearest port to the norks is spooling up with two army corps, and airborne and engineer support. Foreign-flagged vessels were escorted out of the harbor. My only issue is this is a civilian container port. There's no way to carry that many men on board container ships. Space below deck is minimal, and the imagery shows that the ships are fully loaded with containers."

Smith nodded at Vinson. "And you?"

"I've got the same reservations, but I'm sure they're making a play for North Korea. They're using the incident with the U.N. as justification. They have several major RoRo ships, which can carry a good amount of troops and equipment. If they make several trips, two corps can be landed in under a week. It's possible the army equipment is in the containers, but the norks don't have any decent port facilities for unloading them quickly. That aside, they're going to invade. Nothing else fits the information."

Smith folded his arms. "Assuming you're correct, you must have queried your agency superiors. What did they say?" He already knew the answer. They wouldn't come to him if their own organizations were pushing it up the chain of command on their end.

Vinson sighed. "NSA says it's under review by senior analysts."

Noel nodded. "NRO is waiting on the NSA and DIA assessments before forming an opinion."

Smith pointed to the red phone on his desk. "Gents, if you want me to pick that phone up and call the president, I need a lot more than that. We are responsible for North American security, not North Korea's. If your own people aren't supporting you, then what can I do?"

Vinson rubbed his temples with his fingers. "Nothing, I suppose."

Smith agreed with their assessment of the situation. The number of coincidences far exceeded what he considered to be average. Picking up the red phone would result in his being placed in contact with the president, but unless there was an imminent attack about to strike the U.S., he would be instantly relieved of duty and potentially arrested. "All right, this is what you do: cover your butts. Get all your ducks in a row, and document your observations. Make sure you get acknowledgement from your superiors and their responses. If the crap does hit the fan, you'll be covered."

Vinson nodded subtly. Before he moved back to his station, he commented, "You really have to wonder if the signs for Pearl Harbor and 9/11 were like this."

* * *

Blake was on the edge of falling asleep when several people appeared around his gurney. Doctor Vinh entered his sight line. "Good news, Mister Blake. We have a Coast Guard helicopter *en route* to take you into the city. I'm going to cover your injury. Just hold still, please..." Blake felt the doctor place a thick gauze bandage over the patch and tie it around the back of his head. "There, you're all set. We'll be moving you outside in a few minutes. Sorry for the delay."

Coast Guard? Looks like Eddy came through. "Thanks, Doc."

Eddy came in the room and shook Blake's hand. "Don't worry about anything. I'll grab a couple of guys from the station and have your roof done by day's end. It's the least I can do. When you get there, have them call me if you need anything. I'm sorry again, Oscar."

"Take a look at that air gun and make sure you get the safety fixed. I don't want this happening to anyone else," Blake said.

"I will."

A couple of attendants began rolling the gurney outside, leaving Eddy behind.

Blake looked up to see several fluorescent lights passing by above. Then he was through a pair of double doors and could hear the rotor of an approaching helicopter. It landed nearby, and the downwash buffeted him. The gurney was stopped under the whirling blades near a door.

A woman in a Coast Guard flight suit came over in a flight helmet. She yelled to the attendants, "If he's only got an eye injury, we can use the copter's seat and leave your gurney here."

Blake was helped off the gurney and into the copter by several pairs of hands. Once aboard, he was strapped in.

The woman reappeared. Her flight suit nametag said DONOVAN. "Just relax, sir. We'll be there in twenty minutes."

Blake felt his gut contract as the helicopter lifted off in a hurry. They tilted forward almost immediately and applied a lot of power. They did not seem to be wasting any time.

He turned to Donovan and waved her closer. She pulled her helmet away from her ear to hear him. She had no ring on her finger. "No need to rush, miss. I have a reservation."

She smiled—which was reassuring, he thought. "This chopper is the fast response bird for maritime search and rescue. We need to get back to the station as soon as possible, once we drop you off."

"Okay, thanks." Donovan returned to a nearby jump seat. Blake closed his good eye and tried to relax. His injured eye itched, but he resisted the need to scratch it.

Before he knew it, the helicopter was landing. Donovan pulled the sliding side door open and then helped him up.

Hospital staff waited for him with a large wheeled hospital gurney. He sat down before being assisted to lay back. They rolled him straight into the building. More fluorescent lights passed until he ended up in an elevator, which was going down several floors.

The doors opened, and Blake was pushed out.

A woman in a white lab coat intercepted him as he left the elevator cab. She had shoulder-length dirty blond hair and intense green eyes. She held the railing of the gurney and walked alongside him as he traveled down the corridor. "Mister Blake, I'm Doctor Krause. I'm an ophthalmologist, and I'll be handling your case. How did this happen?"

"I was shingling my roof when a nail gun misfired," Blake said.

"Are you currently on any medications?" she asked.

"No."

"Any allergies I need to know about?" Krause checked his pulse.

"No, Doctor."

They rolled him into an exam room. "Let's put him in curtain three."

A woman on his blind side said, "Here's his X-rays."

They were slapped up on a lit panel beside him.

He could hear Doctor Krause clearly talking to what Blake thought looked like another doctor—except he was too young, so Blake assumed he was an intern. "The good news is it's a short roofing nail. The broad flat head probably helped stop it from penetrating deeper. Bad news, it looks like the tip has embedded itself into the choroid. It's very close to the fovea. I can't tell from these. All right, Mister Blake. Let's take a look at your eye." She removed the gauge and protective patch over his injury, took an instrument, and shined it into his eye.

Krause said, "Looking good. None of the major tissues were hit. The lens and sack are intact, which is very good news, Mister Blake. We do need to operate, though, to remove the nail properly and make sure there's no lasting damage." She turned off the light. "If you have no objection, we can prep you for surgery right away."

"Thanks." He grabbed her sleeve as she backed away. "Be straight with me, Doc. What are the chances I'll lose my sight in that eye?"

She moved closer, leaned in, and spoke reassuringly. "Without knowing how badly the back of the eye is damaged, I can't say with certainty. I do know that I've had patients with worse damage come out fine. We'll do our best; you can be assured of that."

He let her sleeve go. "Thanks, Doc. Big bunch of roses coming your way if you succeed."

"I only like pink ones." Her full white-toothed smile displayed confidence, which Blake appreciated. She turned to a nurse. "Please prep Mister Blake for surgery. Bethany, can you run him through the forms?"

* * *

Hour after hour, the Argus alerts came and went as the pyrotechnic display moved across the time zones over the Atlantic. Colonel Smith eventually ignored the light display on the screens. They were the same each time. His inability to leave the command bunker to see them for himself and the repetition of the alerts combined into disinterest on his part.

The next show would be visible along the entire U.S. East Coast, and he promised himself to be alert. If anything different was going to happen, this was the time. The East Coast had the densest population centers and would make the largest target.

Smith ate the roast beef sandwich from out of his supplied box lunch. The beef could have been better, but as he was working through his second shift, he didn't complain. He was looking forward to the cellophane-wrapped chocolate chip cookies, however.

Colonel Smith returned his mind to the issue of the Chinese military buildup as he chewed. Vinson and Noel were both professional, seasoned analysts in their own right. They wouldn't be assigned to NORAD otherwise. If they were concerned, then he needed to be as well. The assumption that China was going to invade North Korea simply didn't add up—they would stage out of ports controlled by the People's Liberation Army Navy and not a civilian container port. Containers were designed for bulk cargo, not troops. When a container was sealed, there was no airflow or any way to get out. Troops sealed inside would suffocate after only a few hours. The RoRos could take a division's worth of vehicles at a time, but—and it was a huge but—North Korea had sixty diesel electric submarines. In shallow coastal waters, they would be horrifically effective against defenseless civilian bulk carriers. China shared a long land border with North Korea. Attacking from there dramatically simplified things and neutralized the sub threat. *Could they be trying to bluff the norks into thinking they are landing by sea to pull troops away from the northern border? A possibility, but why dedicate two entire corps for a diversion?*

Unable to come up with a resolution, Smith decided to use his time more productively and eat his chocolate chip cookies. He'd just pulled open the cellophane packaging when he heard, "This is Argus. We have a DSP detonation alert."

Smith dropped the cookies back in the box lunch and reached for his DSP procedures binder.

* * *

The double doors closed on the soundproof room containing the seven men of the Politburo Standing Committee of the Chinese Communist Party. They all sat down at the table in a somber mood.

General Secretary Gao said without preamble, "Gentlemen, as I speak, fireworks are going off over the east coast of the United States. Our embassy staff report there's been no alert, alarm, or attempt to avoid them. The foreign press is promoting the event, and everyone is expected to see the show. The U.S. President has been seen on television only moments ago and is doing nothing untoward.

"As we agreed, we would only proceed with the activity if the element of surprise were achieved. I believe this has been accomplished. Do we have any dissenting opinions?"

There was silence around the table.

"Very well. We shall proceed on this worthy endeavor," Gao said.

* * *

President Calvin stood just outside the Rose Garden on the lawn of the White House. Several senior members of the cabinet, representatives of the House and Senate, plus their families were around him. A cordon of Secret Service agents formed a series of protective rings around the president. The children stared up at the sky, agog with wonder as the lights overhead completely transfixed them.

Calvin, too, could not tear his eyes away from the spectacle. He regretted his earlier mocking of Brandon's idea and found himself truly impressed.

A black light shifted the color spectrum. He'd been told that would be the final part of the display. Everyone applauded and screamed in delight.

Soon after, the Speaker of the House came up to him to shake his hand. "An impressive evening, Mister President. I doubt tonight will be surpassed for some time. Thank you for the invitation."

"You're very welcome, Mister Speaker. I would hope we could spend more informal time together."

"True, but my party majority leader would not like that, I suspect," the speaker said with a wry smile.

"I see your point. He'll be my main opponent in the next election. At least your family got to enjoy the White House grounds."

An aide made his way through the layers of Secret Service agents and came up beside Calvin. "Excuse me, Mister President. Your call is ready in the residence."

"Thank you. Please excuse me."

"Good night, Mister President," the speaker answered.

Calvin walked inside, followed by his protective detail. There was no call scheduled. He'd asked the aide to give him that message to get away from the crowd. With the speeches and busy appointment schedule that day, he needed an early night.

Calvin stepped into the Executive Residence and ascended up the stairs to his bedroom. Several Secret service agents standing post acknowledged him as he passed.

With the door of his bedroom closed behind him, Calvin slipped out of his suit, brushed his teeth, and slipped into bed.

* * *

Faedong Li was having the longest and most stressful day of his life. His port had metaphorically been turned upside down and shaken, hard. After spending many hours with Colonel Chio at his side, the policeman had become quite chummy and talkative. Li found he preferred the man sullen and obstinate, because then he hadn't had to talk to the buffoon. *No, buffoon is incorrect. This animal is a thug, pure and simple.* Since Li had witnessed the gunning down of two men, Chio had not only tried to make light of the situation, but he actually joked about the way the bodies hit the concrete. He went on to regale Li with stories of other people he had killed. Some died in interrogations, others under orders from the party, for being a "hindrance to the state."

Chio told him, while laughing, that the cost of the bullet used to execute criminals was typically charged to the family. The thought of such insensitivity revolted Li.

Li forced himself to nod politely through the tales, though repulsed by the mindless killer in uniform sitting beside him. Chio did not talk much when traveling, so Li made sure to use the golf cart often for "regular inspection tours." Normally, Li seldom made more than one trip a day, but if it shut Chio up, then driving around the docks was a small price to pay.

Li began to turn a corner at an intersection between warehouses. Cross traffic had stop signs, giving him right of way.

A PLA truck ran one of the signs and came within inches of hitting the cart. Li pulled over to the side of the intersection while the truck driver frantically hammered his horn. A policeman, standing on the running board of the passenger side, withdrew his pistol and began to point at Li, but then he saw Colonel Chio, stopped, and saluted instead as the vehicle went by.

A long line of trucks came along soon after—dozens, from what Li could see. As they passed, he spotted stacks of thin mattresses under the canvas cover of the truck beds. Essentially little more than wooden boards wrapped in a cover, there were several dozen per stack, with each truck carrying four stacks each.

Li waited by the side of the road as the many trucks passed.

Chio lightly tapped his shoulder to get his attention over the road noise. "It makes my heart soar to see so many beds. It means a significant force is being assembled. I hope we see success in the field, Comrade Li."

He gave a slight nod in answer. Still unsure what was going on, Li had no idea what lots of troops could do to offset the threat of a missile strike. The story he'd been told simply didn't add up. Li could not say that, obviously, so he kept his response positive. "China's military has seldom lost on the field of battle, Comrade Colonel."

Li saw Chio beam at his response before he turned away to continue watching the line of trucks rolling by. Strangely, several tanker trucks, marked as carrying aviation fuel, passed in a small group.

Ten minutes later, the last truck went by. Li, acting purely on impulse, followed. They made their way to the container berths. There, several PLA trucks unloaded their beds onto the backs of engineers. Like army ants, they carried their burdens up the long sea stairs and onto the container deck. There, more hands pulled the mattresses inside the container warrens. Li assumed they would be pulled through the interior holes made earlier and spread out inside the containers for troops. He made a quick estimate, based on the average number of containers on each ship. With only ten men per container, there could be ten thousand troops per ship. There were a dozen container vessels all outfitted the same way. *A hundred and twenty thousand men to invade and occupy North Korea?*

"What a sight," Chio said quietly.

Li watched additional trucks arrive as the empty mattress trucks left the dock. Hundreds of sacks of rice, containers of water, and other food items were unloaded. Heavily guarded trucks laden with ammunition came next. Li could only shake his head at the scale of the operation.

Further down the dock, a mobile crane came into view. It lifted one of the aviation fuel trucks he had seen arrive earlier up on top of the containers. Once the truck was in place, the crane drove down the dock, parked, and raised a second tanker truck farther back onto the same vessel.

* * *

Linda Krause waited patiently in the operating theater with her nurses. She wore a light green set of scrubs, blue nitrile gloves, surgical face mask, and hair cover. Her gloved hands were suspended in the air, waiting for the anesthesiologist, Doctor Claire Gooding, to confirm that the patient was stable. Gooding was focusing on the patient's heartbeat monitor, blood pressure readout, and temperature. Gooding made eye contact with Krause and nodded once.

Krause moved to the patient as her nursing staff slid several stainless steel trays of instruments in around her. "Dorothy, music please."

One of the nurses moved to the side of the room and activated a rheostat wall switch with her forearm. The first strains of Pink Floyd's *Division Bell* album came over the overhead speakers. All surgeons could choose music when working, as long as it was tasteful and none of the nursing staff objected to it. Krause loved the band but only listened to their music in the surgical theater. When operating on the intricate and delicate human eye, the music let her relax. The music volume was low, so everyone could easily speak.

Once she had everything she needed, she looked up at the wall clock. "Operation started at nine forty-two p.m. Speculum."

A nurse handed her the instrument, and she leaned forward over his face.

She placed metal tabs under the eyelid and turned the thumbwheel to open his eye wide. The patient—she would not think of him as anything but that until she finished—had his head held in position by a series of padded braces and straps so his head couldn't move. Krause moved closer and surveyed the area around the injury. She realized that all of the surgical staff in the O.R. were women. That was a rare event. "Okay ladies, let's get to work."

* * *

Sir Marcus Brandon stood out on the 52nd floor balcony of the VooDoo Lounge at the Rio Hotel and Casino. A thump-thump-thump noise came from inside as the DJ played on in the bar, even though most of the party attendees had moved outside. The light show was supposed to start at ten p.m. Champagne had been circulated to all guests a few moments before. Brandon swapped which hand held his champagne so he could check his watch. *Just a minute or so to go.* Off in the distance, the many other hotels on the Strip were plainly visible. Caesars Palace, Cosmopolitan, and Paris. The pyramid-shaped Luxor to the right had a brilliant beam of white light lancing from its apex up into the sky.

Garbo came up beside him, fingering her tablet. "Twitter is back up, but they are filtering the hashtag Twinkle for the next hour or so to be safe. I spoke to their operations manager. He said they've never seen such a deluge of tweets in his time at the company. We completely overwhelmed their data servers. He wanted to thank us for the stress test, believe it or not. He's been pushing for larger capacity hardware for three months, and no one paid any attention. He says they are now."

Brandon laughed. "Next time you talk to him, say 'No charge.' Cheers." He held up his champagne, even though she had none.

Garbo snagged a fluted champagne glass from the tray of a passing waitress. She raised it toward him, and they clinked in toast. Without warning, night turned to day as the sky above them pulsed with an intense white light. Brandon had seen the video of the earlier shows on television, but seeing it in person transfixed him. The crowd around him erupted into screams of appreciation and applause. The sky darkened again before a dance of color hundreds of miles wide began.

All doubts he had about hiring the Chinese vanished. They had been the lowest bidder by a long shot, met all of their deadlines, and now the result spoke for itself. *What a show! A spectacular life-changing experience that will be remembered by everyone.*

Garbo took his hand in hers and pressed up against him. Though typically reluctant to show intimacy in public, he didn't object. All eyes were skyward, including theirs—and besides, it just felt right. Her hand was so soft and warm. He squeezed her fingers as a wave of light moved from one horizon to the other. She countered by moving closer, pressing her breasts against his upper arm.

The color spectrum shifted for the final effect for the show. The noise of the people around them intensified. He leaned down and said near her ear, "Cancel the rest of my appointments for the evening. Let's go back to the suite and celebrate properly."

She pulled away from him and looked up into his eyes. She had to speak loudly to say, "Certainly, Sir Marcus."

Chapter Five
The End of the Beginning

"Conn, sonar. Broadband contact, close aboard, bearing three-zero-zero. Definitely subsurface."

Captain Eric Reid immediately pulled down the 1MC handset. "Rig for ultra-quiet." Replacing the handset, Reid turned to the sonar operators, lowered his voice, and asked, "Sonar, conn. Do you have a range?"

"Conn, sonar. Negative. As a guess, I would think no further than two thousand feet."

Reid turned to the Ship Control Station. "Pilot, maintain depth, reduce speed down to four knots, and do it slowly. Stand by to maneuver."

The officer manning the diving station repeated the orders back as Reid walked the short distance to the sonar station. The sonar area was called a "compartment" by tradition. On older sub models, the sonar operators typically occupied their own dedicated space. However, to make things more efficient, *Virginia*-class subs had the sonar stations in the open-concept command center proper. The captain only had to take four steps to talk to the lead operator. He tapped him on the shoulder. "What do we have, Tolly?"

Petty Officer Second Class "Tolly" Toledo never moved his sight from the screens. He held up an index finger and carefully adjusted the signal gain controls.

Reid said nothing further. He gave the sonar operators a lot of leeway, especially Tolly. On shore, Tolly would be seen as loud, brash, and vulgar. On the boat, he focused himself on his duties like a laser beam and, while on a duty shift, never made a sound unless necessary. Tolly was currently listening to the multiple hydrophones along the sides of—and trailing behind—the submarine. He reached up and tapped the large center screen, where a small line showed from the noise. "That's a sub, sir. Our courses are a few degrees from being parallel. He's doing no more than ten knots and—"

Tolly pressed the headphones against his head. "Sir, the Q-70 can't get a firm I.D. profile, but I'd bet serious money that's a Russian Akula with a high-speed screw. I'm sure of it. He'll pass under us to port in a few minutes."

Reid nodded, even though the sonar operators would not see it. "Right. We'll shadow him as long as he's in our patrol area. Send your best estimate of his course to the navigator. Let me know if there are any changes to his profile. Designate contact as Akula One."

"Aye, skipper."

Reid went back to the navigation table. Lieutenant Morrison, the duty navigator, and Commander Maddox, the XO, were already there.

Maddox saw him approach. "Captain, if the track for the Akula stays constant, he'll parallel the South American coast."

Reid looked at the wax pencil mark on the chart. "You think he's rounding the cape?"

The XO said, "We did get intel on the upcoming Russian-Venezuelan naval exercises, and he's unlikely to use the Panama Canal to get there."

Reid considered that. "On his current course, he'll be at the edge of our patrol area in fourteen hours. Let's keep the boat at ultra-quiet and follow him. It's good training. Prepare a SLOT buoy and keep it updated with his profile and our log to date. We'll launch it four hours before he departs our area. Hopefully, someone else can take over shadowing him."

"Aye, sir."

* * *

Doctor Krause bent closer to examine the patient's eye, illuminated by multiple bright lights over the surgical bed. "Okay, it looks like the damage to the back of the eye is minimal. That's excellent. Helen, can you retract the upper lid a little more?"

Helen Overt, her favorite surgical nurse, turned a small knob on the speculum holding Oscar's upper eyelid open.

"Perfect—right there, thanks. I just need to make a few cuts in the surrounding tissue to loosen the nail."

Overt had the micro scalpel waiting for Krause before she asked for it. "Do you know what he does for a living?"

Bethany Shore, the other operating room nurse, said, "Park ranger, according to his admission forms. Why?"

Overt pointed at Oscar's lower body. "I haven't seen legs that nice in a long time. He's in good shape."

Shore said, "I thought you were seeing that fireman—you know, what's-his-name."

"Eric? No, we broke up a week ago. His attitude was right from the eighteenth century. We only had three dates, and he started talking about how if we got married, I'd have to give up nursing to stay home with his kids."

"Ugh, why is finding a good man so hard?" Shore asked, shaking her head.

Krause would have loved to dive into the conversation, but she needed to focus on the surgery. "Bethany, can you grab the top of the nail with a pair of Kelly forceps?"

Shore leaned forward and locked the forceps around the flat head of the nail. "Got it."

"Hold it steady. Almost got it free." Krause focused on the job at hand.

The next few minutes passed with no one saying anything. Krause made a series of small perpendicular incisions in the surface of the eye around the nail shaft.

"All set. Ready for the tricky part?" Krause stretched momentarily. Standing in the same position for a long period locked up the muscles in her lower back.

"Ready," Shore acknowledged.

Krause leaned forward and looked at the eye through her magnifier eyepiece. "Go ahead. Slowly, pull it out."

Shore carefully began bringing the nail shaft out of his eye.

"Stop! There's a small piece of metal protruding on the side. Give me a moment." Krause made a tiny notch with her micro scalpel. "Okay, keep going."

Seconds later, the nail came free. It clanged in the stainless steel kidney-shaped bowl Shore dropped it in.

With the broad head of the roofing nail out of the way, Krause could see the damage to the eye. The iris was a dark green, one of her favorite colors, with irregular flecks of gold. "Good news—the damage to the cornea isn't as bad as I thought. We should be able to sew everything up easily. Reverse cut compound needle and some ten-oh suture please, Helen. I'll need Vannas scissors next."

Overt handed her the pair of locked tweezers that held a small curved needle with gossamer thread. Krause carefully began to sew up the eye.

"I heard that global fireworks show is pretty amazing. Too bad we're going to miss it, stuck down here in the basement," Overt said.

"We need to get you a decent guy, Helen. The right one will make you see stars and explosions every night," Shore quipped.

Female laughter filled the operating theater.

* * *

"I stand relieved, sir," Colonel Smith said formally before moving aside to let the incoming shift commander sit down. His shift had officially ended.

He'd pulled double shifts before, and usually, they were relatively easy on him. Performing the same repetitive drill, every hour on the hour, had drained him, leaving him unusually wrung out. Although once the fireworks had orbited west, past the continental United States, he had been able to relax somewhat.

Smith picked up his briefcase and walked to the entrance tunnel. He closed his eyes, rubbing his temples. He wanted a beer, a steak, and his bed, but the order was negotiable.

He wanted something else, but he was between girlfriends at the moment. He'd looked up Colorado demographic information when he was posted to NORAD. Black people made up only four percent of the state population, which created a diluted dating pool for him. Not that he was against being with a white woman, but he found black women to be more appealing.

Smith sighed and moved his thoughts to more practical issues. He felt so tired; did he *really* need to stop at the grocery store on his way home?

The fresh air and long walk out of the granite and concrete tunnel began to wake him up. He emerged under the stars feeling like a new man. He looked up, regretting not seeing the light show for himself. But if it proved to be popular, surely it wouldn't be long before someone else repeated it.

Smith saluted the airmen guarding the entry gate as he walked past and out into the parking lot. He unlocked his car and slipped into the driver's seat.

He decided he would go to the store. The grocery store was open until midnight, and his desire for steak had faded somewhat, but not the need for a six-pack.

* * *

Doctor Krause stood over Blake, making a post-surgical assessment in the recovery room. Several wires connected to monitoring instruments displayed his respiration, heart rate, blood pressure, and other relevant information. All his life signs were positive, nothing that concerned her. His wounded eye had been covered with a thick white padded bandage to protect it.

His good eye popped open suddenly, surprising her. People usually took more time to come out of anesthesia.

"Hello, Mister Blake. Can you hear me?"

His lips parted and moved slightly as he exhaled, but no words emerged.

She smiled down on him. "Just relax. You're in the recovery room. Everything went well in surgery. We got the nail out, and I was able to repair the surface damage to your eye. I doubt you'll have any long-term issues."

"My eye... Can't see..." His voice rasped, and his hand slowly moved toward his face.

She easily intercepted his arm and pressed it back down. "Yes, we bandaged the eye to keep the micro-sutures clean. You should recover all of your sight. There was no damage to the back, and your prognosis looks excellent. Let it heal, and we'll take the bandage off in a few days. Until then, you just need to relax and spend some time with us to recover."

He closed his eye and said quietly, "Yay, hospital food."

She grinned, amazed that he could still joke even when heavily drugged. "We have really good cooks here. I think you'll be happy with the meals. I'll drop in on you in a few hours. Get some sleep."

Krause stood to leave but found his hand holding hers gently.

"Thanks, Doc." He squeezed her hand lightly before it fell to the bed.

His breathing became slower, and she moved off to let him rest. *He seems like a decent man. When we get the bandages off, I'll be able to look into both of those beautiful dark green* — She stopped, turning back to look at him on the hospital bed. *Why did I think that?*

She rebuked herself for the unprofessional thoughts, filled in his chart, and left the room.

* * *

Sir Marcus Brandon lay diagonally across the king-sized bed in his Vegas suite. The floor-to-ceiling windows let the lights of the distant Las Vegas Strip in the darkened room. Garbo, naked, straddled him and slowly grinded against him. She liked showing off her lithe body while she pleasured him. Her flat muscular stomach tensed and released in time to the soft music playing in the background. She pulled his hands up to her breasts and leaned forward into them. Brandon squeezed firmly, the way he knew she liked it.

Garbo's moans got louder. Her head went back, and her breathing increased.

Brandon looked to the flat-screen television opposite the bed. His news channel showed live video coming from Alaska and Hawaii as the orbital fireworks tracked west. The volume was muted, and he had seen the display himself a few hours earlier, but the video still grabbed his attention. Close-ups of the Juneau crowd showed wonderment and smiles everywhere.

The success of the promotion exhilarated Brandon, exceeding his highest expectations. The coverage of the orbital pyrotechnics on every cable news outlet network would ensure huge exposure for the launch. Brandon absentmindedly ran a hand across Garbo's naked back, and she sighed in appreciation.

Garbo stopped moving and slapped his chest with an open hand. "You're watching TV?! Seriously?"

"Just making sure the quality of the coverage on GNI is maintained." He turned back to look up at her.

"That's my job," she protested.

"It would be, but you're a little busy shagging me at the moment." He smiled to let her know he was joking.

She propped herself up on her hands. "I didn't hear any complaints earlier."

"Have you ever heard me complain when you're in that position?"

The faintest hint of a smile appeared on her lips. "Never, but you need to pay me a little more attention when I am."

She slid up and grabbed the remote control off the nightstand. She shut off the TV and threw the remote over the side of the bed where Brandon couldn't reach it.

"Now pay attention to me. You can watch TV later," she said before beginning to kiss him again.

* * *

Li rose from the small couch in the break room and rubbed his eyes. He checked his watch. *Only two hours' sleep.*

Why is the ground vibrating? His staff had not been allowed to go home, and the People's Armed Police were still doing their jobs, but everyone was relatively quiet. Li could feel a low rumble through his feet and that confused him.

Colonel Chio was looking out a side window. Li approached him, and one of his office staff standing by the break room handed him a porcelain cup of hot tea as he passed. He accepted the gift graciously with a bow and smile. Li looked over at Chio and asked for a second cup of tea, which he held out to Chio once he reached him. "Tea, Comrade Colonel?"

Chio faced him, and a slight grin emerged. He bowed slightly in appreciation and took the offered drink. "Behold the might of the PLA, Comrade Li." He indicated out the window.

Li looked to see three parallel lines of trucks extending two kilometers down the dock. The parked vehicles turned out of sight down an access road. Each vehicle carried at least a dozen men and their gear. The men were dressed in combat fatigues, large backpacks, and rifles. The trucks inched forward, and their engines were what was causing the floor to vibrate.

So that's what woke me. Li decided to see how much info he could get, as Chio appeared in a good mood. "There must be hundreds of trucks." He took a sip of tea as nonchalantly as possible.

"No, comrade. There are almost two thousand trucks out there. Can you imagine? Once they drop off the men and equipment they carry, they will return to make at least two more trips each. Other troops are coming in on trains and marching here. Twelve divisions of our best troops. Such assembled combat power has not been seen since the days of Chairman Mao. His heart would swell with pride at their presence. What a day! To be here, to witness this… this history in the making. Isn't it wonderful?" Chio smiled broadly, still watching out the window.

"Memorable, certainly, Colonel. The North Koreans will not know what hit them."

Chio spun on him before looking around wildly. "Between us, that information is safe, but you should not mention that to anyone else, comrade."

Li agreed immediately. "Of course, Comrade Colonel. I understand completely."

Chio nodded once, took another look around the room, then returned his gaze to the outside world. He took his first sip of tea.

Twelve PLA divisions hidden inside container ships? Why so many? Why not just cross the China-North Korean border? The North Koreans are puny compared to our military. Going in there by sea makes no sense at all.

* * *

"This is Michael Willis reporting live in Sydney, Australia, for GNI. Ladies and gentlemen, from the reaction of the crowds here, the last scheduled overhead light show has proven to be a huge success. The light show has now faded, but the sound of the applause and screams of joy continue as everyone here celebrates the conclusion of GNI's premiere broadcast day. I've covered wars and all sorts of natural disasters in my reporting career, but I cannot recall any event coming close to the scale of this wondrous spectacle.

"The largest sporting event is the World Cup, held every four years. It reaches three billion people. Over the last twenty-four hours, almost every person on the face of the Earth—seven billion souls worldwide—have witnessed this epic light show. All human beings, regardless of location, social standing, religious beliefs, or political leanings, have been equally amazed by this display. This unifying spectacle will go down in history as the first truly global entertainment experience.

"I wish you a pleasant evening. Good night, and we now go back to the studio…"

July 5th

Chapter Six
Something's Wrong with the World

Diran Kouyoumjian was halfway through his midnight shift as a civilian air traffic controller at Heydar Aliyev International Airport in Baku. There was little traffic at this time of night, and none coming into the airport itself for several more hours. Most of his job was to monitor transient aircraft that came through this sector of Azerbaijan airspace. He drained the last of the strong coffee in his mug and began to rise to get another.

A voice crackled over his headset. "Baku Center, Indair two-two-niner heavy, three-five thousand."

Diran sat and ran down the list of flight plans for aircraft expected that evening. *There he is. India Air flight number 229. Boeing Dreamliner 787 out of Mumbai, heading to London. Flight plan is filed, and there are 231 souls on board.* Diran checked his radar plot and saw the transponder signal marked on his screen. "IA229" had an indicated altitude of thirty-five thousand feet. Everything appeared correct, so he toggled his microphone. "Indair two-two-niner heavy, Baku Center."

Diran filled in the log indicating the aircraft's details and then relaxed. He should have no further communication with that flight until just before they left his airspace. He went over to the coffee machine, located right beside his workstation. He didn't even have to remove his headset to pour a new cup.

The door slammed shut behind him. Diran turned. The other shift controller, Saro Burian, returned to his desk. Older than Diran, Saro had gray hair, was balding, and wore silver-rimmed glasses that sat crookedly on his bulbous nose.

Saro dropped the rolled-up newspaper onto the desk. "Diran?"

Diran pulled the left cup of his padded headset clear of his ear. "Yes?"

Even though they were both from Azerbaijan, English was always spoken when on shift to ensure no confusion of languages.

"Avoid the bathroom for the next while. Blame the wife's Chykhyrtma."

Diran groaned and shook his head. "Oh, not again. Did you at least open the window?"

"Yes, and I lit the candle. Give it an hour." Saro wore a smug expression.

"The last time you said that, I went in there and almost had my eyebrows singed off. Why do you eat that stuff?"

Saro pulled a bottle of hand sanitizer out from a desk drawer. "She would be insulted if I didn't! You know what she's like. I volunteer for the midnight shift to get away from her all night. Then I can go home to sleep all day. Those extra eight hours of silence are bliss, I tell you."

Diran had a sip of coffee. "Still, you really should—"

A long burst of static came through his headset. He thought he heard something sounding like a high-pitched man's voice near the end, but it was cut short, and the language was neither English nor Arminian—nor French, which Diran spoke a little of. Diran held up a hand to his headset and tried to listen as hard as he could.

Saro came up beside him and put on his headset. "What did you hear?"

Diran sat down at his workstation and answered Saro on his hot mic, over the internal communications. He pulled the earpiece back into place. "A voice, and a lot of static. It sounded strange." He looked up at the radar screen. There were half a dozen jets in his airspace, and he waited for the radar to do a full rotation to refresh the plot. An aircraft radio, when used, automatically broadcast on the radar transponder for ten seconds to highlight who was talking. The only jet indicated on his screen was "IA229," so the static had to have come from them.

Diran was about to dismiss the static as a mis-keyed microphone when he noticed IA229 had dropped four thousand feet in altitude without authorization. They were just over thirty-one thousand feet and still descending. That serious breach of their flight plan was a danger to all flights near them.

Diran keyed his headset. "Indair two-two-niner heavy, Baku Center."

There was no response.

Saro asked, "Did they check in?"

Diran tapped the log. "Yes, routine check-in, no issues."

The aircraft's altitude dropped below thirty thousand feet on the radar scope.

Once more he keyed his radio. "Indair two-two-niner heavy, Baku Center. You are descending below thirty thousand without clearance. Respond."

Again, he waited in vain for a response.

Saro pointed at Diran's screen. "Two-twenty-nine is all over the place. He isn't coming down in a smooth spiral. He's jinking left then right. Look, there—another jink left. You think this is a hijack?"

Diran sat bolt upright when the word "hijack" was mentioned. He keyed his mic again. "Indair two-two-niner heavy, Baku Center, respond immediately." The word "immediately" was not used lightly in aviation.

Three seconds of silence followed.

Saro reached for a telephone. "I'm calling it in. We're going to need a military intercept if he goes below ten thousand."

A scared, panicked man's voice came over the radio. "I have control… I'm the captain; I shall fly the aircraft… Sanjay! Stop fighting me! Release the contro—"

Diran assumed the captain had triggered the wrong switch and broadcast on his radio. IA229 was now passing fifteen thousand feet. He tried his luck again. "Indair two-two-niner heavy, Baku Center. Respond immediately."

Saro chimed in. "The military's scrambling a pair of MIG-29s out of Dollyar. Seven minutes to intercept."

Diran could only nod. *Ten thousand feet in altitude, they're dropping faster.* "Indair two-two-niner heavy, Baku Center. You are descending below ten thousand feet and are in violation of your flight plan. If you do not respond, you will be intercepted by military aircraft. Respond immediately."

The radio came alive. "We cannot see. Baku Center, we cannot see!"

Diran responded, "Indair two-two-niner heavy, understand you cannot see. Use your instruments and level out. You are at eight thousand, five hundred feet and descending."

Saro handed him the weather outlook. "No clouds or weather within a hundred and fifty miles of flight two twenty-nine. No turbulence or strong winds. It's a beautiful night out there."

Still no response. The aircraft was at seven thousand, five hundred feet and still descending. "Indair two-two-niner heavy, Baku Center."

Six thousand feet. "Indair two-two-niner heavy, Baku Center."

Four thousand feet. "Indair two-two-niner heavy, Baku Center. Respond immediately."

At two thousand feet, the radar blip faded from his screen.

"Indair two-two-niner heavy, Baku Center... Indair two-two-niner heavy, Baku Center."

Saro asked, "Anything?"

Diran shook his head. "No. They're off the scope. Get onto the Dollyar airbase and give them their last position."

"Right." Saro rolled his chair back to his desk and picked up the phone.

"Indair two-two-niner heavy, Baku Center."

"Baku Center, Virgin one-seven-three heavy." This man sounded Scottish, different from the previous speaker. "We see flames on the surface of the Caspian Sea. It's northeast of the Baku peninsula, roughly fifty nautical miles from the coast."

A quick check of the map on the wall sent a chill through Diran. The position of the fire was six miles west of the aircraft's last seen radar position. Two hundred and thirty-one people gone, just like that? He was under no illusion of their surviving at that rate of descent into water.

No one had ever died during his shift before. "Virgin one-seven-three heavy, Baku Center… Roger," was all he could say, and his training forced him to say it completely without emotion. Diran reached for his phone to initiate a search and rescue callout.

* * *

In a rather dreary government building in Rail Bhavan, New Delhi, India, Ajay Sharma, the Minister of Railroads, sat down to begin another day. Several stacks of file folders waited on his desk. Maintenance files, requisition reports, project plans, amendments, rail line site studies, budget projections, and various other bureaucratic paperwork awaited his attention. Sharma paused, looking at the stacks, wondering where to begin. He was certain the piles got higher every day. He pulled a file folder down from the highest pile. He estimated it would take him three or four hours of continuous reading to get through the paperwork.

"Minister Sharma?" The mild voice came from his office doorway.

Sharma looked over the pile of paperwork on his desk and squinted to see Tanvi, one of his senior engineers, half over the threshold. *Another interruption? How am I to get through this never-ending paperwork, with people wanting to consult with me?* "Yes. Come in."

Tanvi entered, looking down at a pink message form in his hand. "I bring bad news, sir. We've had a report of a train derailment outside of Jodhpur. Seventeen carriages and fourteen freight cars went off a shallow embankment. It appears the train was traveling too fast for the curve. Emergency services are responding, but they report issues in contacting fire stations in the area."

"What issues?" Sharma demanded. A train crash would generate even more damned paperwork.

Tanvi looked fuzzy.

He still had his reading glasses on. Sharma pulled them off and tossed them aside.

"Sir, we don't know. Several fire stations didn't acknowledge the order to attend the scene."

"That's unacceptable. I shall contact the Ministry of Home Affairs immediately and have them involve the police to assist." Sharma lifted his phone receiver and pressed 0 for the operator.

Another voice came from near the door. "Minister, I have a report of a train accident."

Sharma slammed the phone down. It was unacceptable for everyone to come barging into his office to repeat what he already knew. "I'm already dealing with the Jodhpur incident, damn you."

Sharma normally addressed people by name, so they would know that he knew them. However, the person in the doorway was blurry. The man at the door meekly replied, "Minister, I know nothing of Jodhpur. I'm sorry, but my report involves a collision between two commuter trains in Hyderabad."

"Hyderabad? What are you talking about, man?" Sharma went to remove his reading glasses, which usually solved the problem of his fuzzy sight, but his fingers brushed his bare temple, and he realized his glasses were already on his desk. Sharma squeezed his eyes closed for a moment, but it didn't help. He had stayed up the previous evening to see the fireworks, but was in bed at his usual time so lack of sleep was not the issue.

"Sir, a commuter train struck another that was loading passengers in the central station. He ignored all signals to stop. There are many dead, and a large fire has broken out."

Sharma looked out his window. It had promised to be a sunny day earlier, but he thought it looked darker than normal. There were no clouds in the skies above, which baffled him. He rubbed his eyes.

The voice of Sharma, his male secretary, came over the intercom. "Minister, you have calls waiting from Vadodara, Chennai, and Mumbai. There have been severe rail accidents in those cities."

Five accidents in one day! Sharma couldn't remember having five serious accidents in a three-month period.

Sharma stood and walked out the door to his balcony. The news of major train accidents was tragic, but his sight was getting worse by the second, and that concerned him more. The skies were so dark, he was expecting to see an eclipse in progress. As he looked over the low jagged silhouette of the New Delhi skyline, Sharma's sight went completely black.

* * *

Kandahar, Afghanistan. What a crap hole. Even the sunrise looks filthy, thought Major Edward Palmer, USAF, as he looked out over the American-run airbase. Beyond the tall concrete barriers and sandbags around the perimeter, he saw a desperate, dirty, and ignorant country. Last night's light show had perked things up for a few minutes, but after the pretty colors had vanished, the dusty sandy nightmare he lived in had returned.

Behind him, his C-5B cargo aircraft, the largest airframe in the world, was being refueled and loaded with cargo for the trip back to Dover Air Force Base in Delaware. He ran the profile through his mind as he continued his pre-flight walk around of the airframe. The first leg of the trip would be north, with their first air-to-air refueling in Romanian air space. Then on to the UK, with another refueling over the North Sea. Greenland would see them meeting their last tanker, and then straight home to Dover from there. Total flight time would be around fifteen hours and just over seven thousand miles' distance.

Palmer was glad to be going home. Afghanistan was a dump. While Delaware was not the most exciting state, it had the advantage of being in the U.S., and that suited him just fine.

One of his loadmasters, Master Sergeant Kennedy, came up beside him. "Everything's loaded, sir. Fuelling is complete, and cargo is secure. Weight and balance figures are waiting for you in the cockpit."

"Thank you, Master Sergeant."

Kennedy walked back to the aircraft, and Palmer continued his walk around, checking for obvious cracks or fluid leaks. With a length of almost two hundred and fifty feet and a wingspan nearly as wide, it took a long time to inspect. As he progressed around the airframe, he pulled the locking pins from the landing gear.

He entered the aircraft by way of the portside access hatch, counted the pins, and stowed them. Palmer went to the cockpit, slid into the pilot's seat, and grabbed his headset. His copilot, Captain Francesca Willem, was already on the right-hand side of the cockpit, running through her thick laminated checklist. He pulled his headset over his ears and spoke through his hot-mic headset. "How we doing, Frankie?"

"Good, sir. Pre-flight is done. Ready for engine start on your word."

"I'm going to let you handle the air-to-air refueling. I know we usually land in Germany, but you need the experience, so I requested tankers all the way home."

"Yes, sir. Thanks!" Frankie said eagerly.

Palmer looked behind him and saw the flight engineer station was unmanned. "Where's Dom?"

"Toilet. He said he'd be back in two minutes," Frankie said without looking at him.

Palmer opened the aircraft flight log binder and began to double-check the weight and balance figures. Once satisfied they were accurate, he signed to acknowledge that he had accepted them. The cockpit door closed behind him. Palmer turned.

Technical Sergeant Dominic "Dom" Pezzino nodded to him as he sat down at his console behind the pilots. He pulled on his headset. "Morning, sir. We're good to go. Hatches and ramp secure, with everyone strapped in. I had to top up the oil in number three. It's got a slow leak, but due for an engine change when we get back home."

"Morning, tech sergeant. Okay, everyone, let's get the show on the road. Engine start checklist."

Palmer read the checklist, while Dom and Frankie checked the systems. In two minutes, engine one was idling. The crew repeated the same start sequence for engines four, three, and two.

Frankie stated, "All engines at idle, sir. Chocks are away; ground crew is clear. We're good to taxi."

"Very well." Palmer contacted the local tower on the radio and asked for permission to taxi. Once given, Palmer advanced the throttle, and the large aircraft began to roll forward. In a few minutes, Palmer keyed his radio. "Kandahar Tower, Hagar four-seven heavy ready for takeoff, runway two-three."

A bored voice came over the radio. "Hagar four-seven heavy, Kandahar Tower. Clear to take off, runway two-three."

"Hagar four-seven heavy, roger." Palmer turned off the radio and spoke into his hot mic. "Throttle, forty percent, N-one."

Frankie said, "Check."

Palmer pushed the four engine throttles forward. Frankie kept her hand behind his, ready to take over if anything happened. The sound of the large engines overwhelmed almost everything else. Each of the four TF-39 engines on the aircraft pushed out forty-three thousand pounds of thrust.

"Brakes coming off." Palmer pressed his toes against the top of the pedals, and the brakes disengaged. The airframe began to roll forward, at first slowly as inertia held it back. As the speed picked up, Palmer had to make subtle corrections with the rudder pedals to steer the aircraft and keep it straight on the runway.

Frankie said, "V-one."

They reached a hundred and twenty-five knots. Palmer kept the throttles forward.

Soon after, Frankie repeated, "V-R."

They were at one hundred and thirty-five knots. Palmer counted to three mentally before saying "Rotate."

He pulled back on the stick, and the C-5B Galaxy pulled up into the sky. The end of the runway disappeared underneath them.

"Gear up," Palmer ordered.

Frankie pulled up the landing gear lever. The hydraulic motors started up with an audible thump. "Gear up."

Palmer began to relax. Nothing had gone wrong on takeoff. "Frankie, take control."

"I have control."

Palmer released the control stick before him and pulled off his gloves. As long as none of the locals took a pot shot at them with an RPG, they would be fine.

Dom's voice came over the intercom. "Major, is there something wrong with the lighting?"

Palmer scanned the light panel. Any errors or system malfunctions would be displayed there first. All looked good to him. "No, why?"

"Everything looks darker, for some reason," Dom said.

"It's funny you say that, tech sergeant. It does look darker. I thought it was just me," Frankie said.

Palmer didn't know what to say. Everything looked right to him. *Are they trying to play some sort of joke?* He didn't mind horseplay on the ground, but not in the air, and they knew that.

He looked out the window. Below, the sands of Afghanistan looked as they usually did. "Are you two kidding around?"

"No, sir," Dom protested.

"No, sir. Things look, well, strange. Fuzzy, even," Frankie added.

Food poisoning happened rarely, as the military had high standards, but it was possible. Palmer felt fine. If his flight deck crew were affected by illness, then they needed to be relieved and get some rack time in the back. Fortunately the Galaxy carried a complete backup crew in the rear crew compartment, since they flew such long distances.

"Sir, everything's getting darker," Dom said, sounding panicked. "Oh God! No! I can't see!"

Frankie began sobbing. "I'm losing my sight too, sir. It's going black. Oh Jesus, no... no... no..."

He placed his hands on the flight controls. "Frankie, I have the aircraft. You and Dom get into a rack, and the relief crew will take over."

Palmer toggled the internal speakers. "Relief crew to the flight deck. Relief crew to the flight deck immediately!"

Frankie was able to stand with the help of the built-in overhead handgrips, and she used them as a guide to move aft. Palmer checked over his shoulder and saw Dom moving with her through the rear door of the cockpit.

He'd expected to see the relief crew within seconds, but none arrived. "Relief crew to the flight deck, immediately," he repeated over the internal comm system.

Palmer had no choice but to return to Kandahar. He began turning back toward the airbase and pressed his radio. "Kandahar Tower, Hagar four-seven heavy. Pan-pan, pan-pan, pan-pan. We have multiple crew members with an unknown affliction. Request immediate clearance to land on runway zero five."

No response.

He waited thirty seconds before trying again. "Kandahar Tower, Hagar four-seven heavy. Pan-pan, pan-pan, pan-pan. We have an onboard medical emergency."

Nothing. He changed to an alternate radio in case of a hardware problem and repeated his call for assistance, but he again heard nothing. With no communication to the ground, he decided to escalate things.

He turned his transponder code to "7700," which would broadcast an emergency signal that sounded alerts on all of the Kandahar ATC workstations. *That should wake the lazy bastards up.*

"Kandahar Tower, Hagar four-seven heavy declaring an emergency. Mayday, mayday, mayday. I'm coming around for an emergency approach on runway zero-five. I'll need ambulances on arrival."

Only a brief pulse of static came to his ears.

Palmer became aware that even though he was facing almost directly into the sun, it was getting dark in the cabin. He triggered the internal P.A. system. "Any available crew member, report to the flight deck immediately."

He would normally be able to see to the horizon on such a clear day. Everything was getting fuzzy, like a camera lens being slowly turned out of focus. He squinted, then blinked, to no avail. Palmer hurriedly adjusted the flaps and ran through the pre-landing checklist, beginning to feel a little panicked.

"Kandahar Tower, Hagar four-seven heavy. Mayday, mayday, mayday. I'm on an emergency approach to runway zero five. I do not—repeat, *do not*—have radio communication with you. Several flight crew members cannot see, and my sight is failing. Will attempt to get her down before..." He released the microphone button, as he was unwilling to voice the consequences of not making it.

Wanting to get there as fast as possible, Palmer waited until the last possible moment before pulling back the throttles. He had over three thousand hours operating Galaxy's. He could land the airframe as long as he got to the runway. He would be landing overweight due to the load, but he couldn't take the time to dump fuel.

He could see the end of the Kandahar runway and began to prepare the C-5B for landing. Palmer recited the landing checklist to himself as the aircraft descended. "Landing lights, on. Landing gear, down. Flaps down, full. Autopilot, off.

Auto-throttle, off. Reduce speed to one hundred fifty-five knots."

He struck thoughts of his wife from his head the moment they arose. He needed to focus on getting the aircraft down safely if he wanted to see her again.

Palmer's vision had turned to gray, and it was getting darker with each passing moment. No one appeared to help him, which was worrying.

A hand slapped down on his shoulder. He jumped and turned. It was Kennedy, one of the loadmasters.

"Sir, everyone in the back is blind. They're all calling for help."

"Can you see?" Palmer shouted over the noise of the hydraulic motor.

"No, sir. I heard your call for help, but I got turned around in the cargo bay."

"Get everyone strapped in. We're making an emergency landing."

Kennedy disappeared through the cabin door.

Palmer could barely see anything. The end of the runway was almost upon him. He focused on his instruments for the approach. His airspeed was bleeding off, so he nudged the throttles slightly to compensate. The twenty-eight tires of the landing gear hit the ground, but the overweight Galaxy bounced back up into the air.

At that instant, Palmer lost the last of his sight.

He had no choice but to pull the throttles back hard, to get the aircraft down. It struck the ground, but this time he felt the impact on the left side wheels. As the right side came down, there was a horrible noise from the starboard side of the aircraft.

Palmer felt the airframe tumble completely out of control. Inertia flung his limbs around as metal tore around him.

* * *

Keith Hurst's secure telephone rang, waking him from a sound sleep. He opened his eyes and looked at the LED clock on his nightstand. It said 3:12. As national security advisor to the president of the United States, middle-of-the-night calls were common. His staff did their best to filter out the less important matters until his morning brief, but there were times when an emergency forced sleep into second place.

Hurst grabbed the handset by the second ring. He had to wait for the encryption to handshake before he could say, "Hurst."

"Good morning, sir. This is the night watch officer. We have several NSA intercepts from the following countries: India, Pakistan, Uzbekistan, Turkmenistan, Tajikistan, Kazakhstan, and Russia all placing their militaries on high alert. We've had sporadic reports of multiple air, car, and rail accidents, resulting in thousands of deaths. Many radio and television stations have gone off the air in those countries."

Hurst snapped on his bedside light and sat up. "Accidents? Do we know the cause?"

"No, sir. The strange thing is, NSA claims many of the foreign military units that were signaled never acknowledged the alert. There also appears to be a major communication disruption with U.S. CENTCOM units in Afghanistan and our embassies in the aforementioned countries."

"Are the comms being hacked, or is there some sort of natural phenomenon like sunspot interference?" Concerned about the call, Hurst looked at the empty space beside him. His wife had left him several years before, directly because of the election campaign and the late-night calls.

"No, sir. Not that we can see. The circuits are up, and the phones are ringing, but no one is answering."

Hurst swung his legs out of bed. *Has someone come up with a way to simultaneously disrupt communications with American bases, embassies, and headquarters, or is this some sort of terrorist attack?* "Does NRO have anything on overhead imagery?"

"No, sir. No major troop movements in the CENTCOM area. In fact, NRO reports minimal movement overall."

"I'll be in the office in thirty-five minutes. I'll want everyone in for an early brief for the president. Get the joint chiefs and SECDEF up to speed. Warn the Secret Service that we may be moving POTUS with short notice. If this is an attack, I want to stay ahead of it. See if we can get drone surveillance of any U.S. bases in Afghanistan ASAP. We need answers."

"Yes, sir."

Hurst hung up and hit the bedside crash button to summon his protection detail. This was no time for subtlety. He needed to be in the White House as soon as humanly possible.

* * *

Colonel Smith looked up at the wall clock. He'd been back on duty for two hours, and there had been no alerts from Argus. He smiled to himself. Things were back the way they should be.

The rest of the world was suffering, though. Smith kept getting reports of strange NSA intercepts through Vinson, and they were increasing. Lots of communication disruptions; many aircraft, train, and ship disasters, including several American military units in the Middle East. No one knew what was going on. A massive solar storm had disrupted satellite communications years before, but there had been no related accidents. Someone tried joking the Rapture had arrived, but he was quickly shouted down.

A loud buzzer sounded once, and overhead speakers announced, "This is Argus. We have a possible DSP launch detection."

Smith silently cursed himself for thinking positively. He grabbed his DSP procedures manual and began running down the checklist.

"This is Argus reporting an infrared bloom, twenty-seven degrees, three minutes north; forty-nine degrees, thirty-four minutes east. There is no ascending missile track."

Excellent news. It couldn't be a missile launch—not a successful one, at any rate. He typed the coordinates into his computer, and an overhead image appeared, showing the location on the global map. The map displayed the east coast of Saudi Arabia, a place called Ras Tanura. He'd heard of it— Ras Tanura was the home of the Saudi Aramco oil refinery, one of the largest in the world. They produced over a half million barrels of oil a day, and the facility was massive— several square miles of distillation towers, pipes, and fuel storage tanks. He checked the time. It would be just after nine in the morning in Saudi Arabia.

Smith sat back in his chair. If a heat bloom sufficient to set off an Argus alert had occurred inside a refinery, then it must be an explosion. NORAD detected large explosions on occasion. Their satellites *were* designed to detect heat from rocket motors.

Over his headset, Smith heard Noel say, "We have live imagery from GEO-2 on the center screen."

Looking up, Smith saw the images broadcast from halfway around the world as the GEO-2 satellite came up to the site of the incident. GEO-2 satellites had high-resolution infrared cameras that could zoom onto the area as it passed. The infrared spectrum filtered out the smoke and only showed hot spots. Half the refinery was ablaze. Smith glanced at the on-screen scale showing the size of the picture presented. Four square miles of metal supports, twisted pipes, and tons of fuel oil combined into an inferno. *It looks like someone really screwed up.*

He had no idea how many people worked in the refinery. Hundreds, certainly.

Smith turned his attention away from the screen. Tragic as the accident was, it was no threat to the security of the United States. The price of gas would certainly go up because of this accident, but NORAD was not tasked to safeguard against that.

A voice crackled over his headset. "Colonel Smith, there's a tanker coming up on the refinery dock."

Smith looked up to see a large crude carrier approaching the blaze at the water's edge. The hi-res cameras on the GEO-2 let him see it clearly. The vessel was gargantuan.

Vinson's voice came over his headset. "Sir, I have an ID on the ship from AIS data. It's the *TI Oceania*. She's an ultra large crude carrier, twelve hundred and two feet long, carrying over three million barrels of oil at max capacity."

"Roger." There was nothing else to say.

The rapidly moving tanker looked to be a half-mile away from the dock. The ship rode high in the water, which meant it was probably empty and approaching the dock to take on a load of fuel. He looked on helplessly, unable to do anything. *The crew must be able to see the fire. Why don't they just reverse engines and stop?*

The tanker maintained speed and course. Orbital motion of the satellite soon had him looking down at the ship from a thirty-degree angle. The ship approached closer and closer, until finally, in what looked like slow motion to Smith, the bow of the tanker rammed into the massive concrete dock at speed. The nose crumpled slightly on impact before the ship's momentum drove it forward, up, then over the wide concrete and steel jetty jutting out into the Persian Gulf.

There was no noise, but Smith could imagine the sound of inch-thick hardened steel plates being torn asunder as irresistible force met an immovable object. The front of the *TI Oceanic* jutted into the air.

The front third of the tanker snapped like a twig and fell into the water on the opposite side, like ash dropping off a cigar. The only saving grace was the bunker tanks were empty and there was no subsequent explosion. At the stern, the propellers still moved, churning up water and sediment, but the tanker sat, still and broken, as the GEO-2 satellite passed over the horizon and lost visual.

Smith realized his fists were clenched. He released them and saw fingernail marks in his palms. *What the hell is going on?*

Chapter Seven
Realizations

Major Konstantin Valerievich Derzhavin sat in the pilot seat of his Mikoyan MiG-29, cruising at thirty-two thousand feet in level flight. His position was northwest of the Moscow Oblast. Around him, in an inverted "V" formation, were seven other members of his unit, the 234th Guards Fighter Regiment. They were returning to base after early morning aerial defense exercises, and his heart felt as if it would burst with pride. Not only had his pilots won the scheduled exercise engagement by killing all eight of the opposing fighters, but they had done so with only one "kill" against them. The pilot who had been "killed," an officer named Vasily, would receive no end of ribbing once they landed. There would be more taunts than normal, as Vasily was a braggart who thought himself superior to the others and had few friends in the squadron.

Derzhavin checked his air speed and referenced the map on his center screen. They would be landing back at the Kubinka air base in under twenty minutes.

"Donets two-one, Ampere." The new voice came through over Derzhavin's flight helmet without preamble on a scrambled UHF sideband frequency.

From his morning briefing, "Ampere" was the call sign of a Beriev A-50U AWACS aircraft. He had no idea why they were calling him. "Ampere, Donets two-one."

"Donets two-one, Ampere. Alert condition potato. Expedite return to base."

He frowned reflexively. "Potato" was the day's code indicating they needed to go to Defense Condition Two. Before they had taken off, the Russian air force was at Defense Condition Four, the lowest possible. Going from Four to Two in one jump was unprecedented. The next level up, Defense Condition One, meant they were at war. *What's going on? Another attempted coup? Or is someone actually about to attack us?*

"Donets two-one, Ampere. Alert condition potato," the AWACS repeated. "Confirm receipt of order."

Derzhavin realized he hadn't said anything. "Ampere, Donets two-one. Potato confirmed. Returning to base." He keyed the VHF radio to speak to his pilots. "Donets flight, we are accelerating to Mach one point five." He pushed his two engine throttles forward with his left hand, and his airspeed began to increase.

Over his flight helmet, one of his pilots said, "The major wants to get back early so Vasily can buy us all drinks."

"Quiet on the frequency! Use proper radio procedure. Alert condition potato," Derzhavin ordered.

The alert code word shut them up. Derzhavin's speed passed Mach one without any indication other than the Mach gauge. A quick look over his shoulder showed his flight still in formation. *At this speed, we'll be back to base in seven minutes, and then what? Load up with missiles and start war patrols? I hope someone has solid intelligence when we land.*

"Donets two-one, Donets two-five. I'm having a problem."

That was Vasily's call sign. Derzhavin looked over his shoulder. Vasily's fighter looked to be operational, without smoke or any other external condition that looked out of place. "Donets two-five, what's the issue?"

"Sir, everything is going dark," Vasily said.

"Donets two-five, check your circuit breakers for your instrument backlighting," Derzhavin said patiently.

"It isn't my lights; it's my eyes. My vision is getting darker. Everything's going black, fuzzy, and dark. If this continues, I won't be able to see to land."

Derzhavin retarded his speed a little and slid back until he was even with Vasily's aircraft. Vasily had his visor up and appeared to be staring at his fingers. "Donets two-five, reduce speed and stay on my wing. We'll land together. Descend slowly and start a turn to port. We'll land at the emergency field at Volokolamsk. Everybody else, make your way back to base. Donets two-two, take flight lead."

Sergei, his senior pilot, said, "Donets two-two, affirmative. Donets flight, form on me."

Derzhavin had to maneuver to stay clear of Vasily, who was coming dangerously close to him. "Donets two-five, level out. Your right wing is dropping!"

"I can't see sir. I'm completely blind. I have no idea which way is up or down. Mother of God, help me!"

Vasily's nose dropped suddenly. *If he's unable to see, then there's no way he can land the aircraft.*

Derzhavin keyed the UHF frequency. "Ampere, Donets two-one declaring an emergency. One of my pilots is having issues with his vision and may need to eject. He will require medical services. We are currently twenty-seven kilometers west of Volokolamsk. Will stay in the area as long as I can."

"Donets two-one, Ampere. Affirmative."

Vasily's jet was pointed directly down. Derzhavin pulled his fighter around hard to keep him in sight. Given the speed of descent, there was no way the pilot could recover from that angle.

"Eject, Vasily. Vasily, eject now!"

Vasily's Perspex cockpit separated from the aircraft, and Vasily's ejection seat fired him out of the cabin. He tumbled for a moment before the drogue chute deployed. A moment later, Vasily's main parachute opened, he separated from his seat, and he floated toward the earth. Derzhavin glanced back toward Vasily's MiG-29. He hoped it would avoid hitting anyone. The aircraft continued to accelerate toward a large field. He returned his attention back to Vasily. "Ampere, Donets two-one, my pilot has ejected just north of Shakhovskaya. He will need assistance on the ground and an ambulance."

"Donets two-one, Ampere. Affirmative."

Derzhavin looked down just in time to see the MiG strike a farmer's field at speed and explode. He deployed his speed brakes and slowed as much as he dared, to keep Vasily in sight.

The VHF radio came alive. "Donets two-one, Donets two-two. I'm having issues with my sight also. It's like I'm in shadow all of a sudden."

Before Derzhavin could respond, "Donets two-six. My vision is fading."

"Donets two-eight, what the hell is happening to my eyes?"

"Donets two-three. I can't see colors anymore."

Derzhavin felt bewildered. His own sight was fine, but most of his pilots were suffering the same strange malady. "Ampere, Donets two-one. Many of my pilots are reporting issues with their vision. What's going on? Over."

"Donets two-one, Ampere. We have several aircraft, both civilian and military, reporting the same problem. Potato is in response to that threat. There's a theory it may be tied to the fireworks last night."

Derzhavin had missed the light show, having spent the previous evening in his brother's basement apartment, tasting his latest batch of homemade vodka. They'd heard about the show, of course, but hadn't made it up the stairs until the fireworks had already ended.

He was very glad he'd stopped to take a piss before going up.

The fireworks had been sent up by a British millionaire, so it could be an attack by the West. He keyed his microphone. "Donets flight, land immediately at the closest available airfield. Land now, wherever you can!"

Vasily finally landed on the ground. The canopy of his parachute collapsed near his body. Derzhavin made a single orbit of his position before turning back toward Kubinka. If this were an attack by the West, he promised they would pay.

* * *

"Thank you for seeing us before our usual time, Mister President." Keith Hurst walked into the Oval Office with several members of his staff behind him—the others in the room being why he used his friend's formal title.

His staff carried a foldable chart stand and several maps, which they began to set up. Calvin already had a copy of the daily brief in his hand. Today's copy was twice the usual thickness.

"Sit down, gentlemen. Keith, maybe you can explain why the world is going into the crapper at the moment." He tapped the thick report in his hand. "Is this accurate?"

"Yes, sir. We've confirmed thousands of alarming incidents, originating in India and working their way westward."

Calvin sat. Hurst walked over to the stand that his staff had just finished setting up. A large map of Asia waited for him, clearly marked with various time zones.

He pulled an extendable pointer from a pocket and began his brief. "The first incidents began here, six hours ago, in India and Siberia. Reports of multiple train accidents, fires, and collisions, plus innumerable road fatalities. Since then, we've lost contact with most of our embassies and military units in those areas, and we've had civilian radio and television stations go off the air."

"You said 'most of our embassies,'" the president cut in. "Were we able to get through to one?"

"Yes, sir. Fifteen minutes ago, I spoke with the deputy ambassador in Tbilisi, Georgia. He reports the entire staff and marine security detachment are blind. He went across the street to the..."—Hurst looked at his notes—"the Jo Ann Medical Center to get assistance and found it filled with locals who lost their sight. The few hospital staff that retained their vision are overwhelmed with caring for blind members of the public. They were getting reports from several other cities—everyone in the country of Georgia seems to be affected.

"We also have this footage taken from a Reaper drone flying over Kandahar." An aide activated a television built into a wall. The video showed a dusty-looking airfield, surrounded by tall concrete walls and sandbags. A thick column of black smoke rose from the runway. The camera turned and zoomed in to show several men in U.S. combat uniform. They were walking around like Frankenstein, their outstretched hands flailing.

The president asked, "If the base personnel are blind, who's controlling the drone?"

As the aide turned off the television, Hurst answered, "The Reaper drones are piloted via satellite link from Creech Air Force Base in Nevada, Mister President. As the men in Afghanistan are also blinded, we can infer that this is the cause of all the air and ground disasters in other nations."

"This is definitely spreading across the globe?"

"Yes, sir." Hurst was hesitant to give the rest of his information, but he had to as part of his job. "The prevalent opinion amongst my staff is this is directly tied to Marcus Brandon's fireworks last night. Symptoms appeared in those countries almost exactly twenty-two hours after exposure."

"I saw those last night." Calvin looked horrified.

"As did I, along with the vast majority of people in the United States," Hurst said.

There was a long silence. Everyone in the room appeared shocked.

"How does a light show in space result in blindness?" Calvin asked.

Hurst sat down on the couch beside the president. "A member of my staff spoke to the senior ophthalmologist at Walter Reed. The human eye can be affected by intense bursts of light, resulting in temporary or even permanent damage. Lasers, arc welding, or a highly focused beam of light can destroy the optic nerve with enough exposure. He had no opinion on how something like that could be weaponized, though. Such intense light would have immediate results, and he couldn't explain why it took almost a day to manifest symptoms... Which brings up another possibility."

"Yes?" Calvin tossed the brief aside onto a table.

Hurst indicated toward the map with his pointer. "All of these incidents could be the result of an unrelated pathogen or virus. The light show may have nothing to do with it, or it may have simply acted as a catalyst."

"You must have a reason for saying that," Calvin said.

"Yes, Mister President. The fireworks began over eastern China, but we've had no reports of anything untoward in that nation, save the continuing drumbeating and intercepts over North Korea. A virus present in India and the 'Stans' countries could have been mutated by the light. If China does not have that virus, then they would not suffer any aftereffects."

President Calvin turned to an aide. "Get onto the Attorney General. I want Marcus Brandon located and questioned immediately. Find out what he knows. Call for the Secretary of Defense—"

"He's waiting outside, sir, along with the Secretary of State and the head of Homeland Security," Hurst said. "I thought it would be prudent to bring them in."

"Excellent. Get them in here," the president ordered. His aide went to get them, but Calvin didn't wait. "Where's the vice president?"

"On his way back from California on Air Force Two." Hurst knew where all senior staff was at all times. He had to know.

"Find out if he saw the fireworks. Also, question the remainder of the cabinet, Speaker of the House, and the President pro tempore of the Senate. I want to know if anyone in the line of succession for the presidency didn't see the pyrotechnics last night."

The 25th Amendment to the U.S. Constitution allows the president to step down temporarily if "unable to discharge the powers and duties of his office." Losing his sight would probably qualify for that, so he needs to see who hasn't been exposed.

Hurst watched the Secretaries of Defense and State enter side by side, followed by the Secretary of Homeland Security. They all sat on the couches. Their aides also entered and stood behind, in close proximity.

The president wasted no time. "Ladies and gentlemen, there is a wave of blindness spreading from India and coming westward. It may or may not be related to the orbital fireworks last night. Until I get evidence to the contrary, we have to assume it does. Ewen, what's the DEFCON level?"

Ewen Blackburn was the Defense Secretary. An Alabama native, his voice had a southern drawl. "Sir, we're at DEFCON Four."

"Raise it to DEFCON Three immediately. All military leave is cancelled indefinitely, and units are to assemble in their home bases. Find out who in the military was not exposed to the fireworks last night. I need to know how many troops we can depend on. Begin examinations of as many service members as possible. See if we can identify the cause of this malady and give the highest priority we have to solving it. Kenneth…"

Secretary of State Kenneth Donovan looked regal in a bespoke charcoal gray Michael Andrews suit. His head came up and tilted back slightly, so he was looking down his long nose as he answered, "Yes, Mister President."

"Reach out to our allies for anything on this. Make it clear we don't have a cause, nor do we know with certainty who's responsible or even why this is happening. It's my position that we share any and all information about this threat freely. If the world is going blind, we have limited time. Madeleine and Keith, if you would stay behind. Thank you, everyone."

The others left the room, leaving the Secretary of Homeland Security and Hurst with President Calvin. The door closed.

"Madeleine, if this hits us, we're going to have a lot of people helpless. What's your opinion?"

Hurst regarded Madeleine Carver with unease. She was a little too hawkish for his tastes. "Mister President, it's possible there'll be panic in the streets when news of this hits. I would think a call-up of the entire National Guard would be needed to keep control. If so, we can't wait. We need to do this now.

"Further, it's possible there will be someone trying to take advantage of this situation. We should evacuate you to Mount Weather and get Congress into their bunker at Fort McNair. With such extreme circumstances, martial law may also be needed."

Hurst wouldn't voice an opinion unless asked, but he didn't like the introduction of martial law at all.

The president seemed to consider Carver's suggestion. He leaned back into his chair and crossed his legs. "The National Guard will probably be needed on the streets to stop food and water supplies from being plundered, but most will probably lose their sight. Let me think on that. I need to know how many troops will be affected first. We can start spooling up the emergency response plan, but I'll be staying in Washington for the moment. As for suspending the Constitution and imposing martial law, I think we're still a long way from that. Please look into contingencies for safeguarding as many lives as possible. Thank you, Madeleine. That's all."

Whew, Hurst thought as she rose and left the Oval Office. No martial law. He doubted Calvin would ever go for it, but desperate times…

As soon as the door closed behind her, leaving Hurst and Calvin alone, Calvin said, "Keith, I want you to work on two questions. How is this… affliction, for lack of a better word, caused, and how do we cure it? We have a lot of scientists and doctors on the government payroll. Let's get them working on a solution. I know time is against us, but I refuse to be the last President of the United States."

Hurst nodded, "I've had my staff touch base with as many research and medical experts as we can find. Another question in my mind, Jim, is how China escaped without effect. If the fireworks did have something to do with this, then how did over a billion people who saw the same display not be affected?"

"On your way out, ask Barbara Morgan to come in. I need to work on one hell of a speech to reassure everyone."

Hurst rose to leave. He was having a hard time reconciling what was happening. "Will do. Make it a good one, Jim. Some of us need that reassurance right about now."

* * *

The loud buzzer sounded again, and overhead speakers announced, "This is Argus, We have a DSP launch detection."

Colonel Smith grabbed his DSP procedures manual. In the last two days, he had grabbed that binder more often than he had in all the rest of his duty time combined.

"This is Argus reporting an infrared bloom, fifty degrees, eighteen minutes north; twenty-six degrees, thirty-eight minutes east. There is no ascending missile track."

Smith looked up at the global map. The indicated spot was in the northwest portion of the Ukraine. He keyed his microphone. "Can we get an overhead shot of that area?"

Seconds later, what looked like a large industrial complex surrounded by forest appeared on the screen. The date stamp on the lower right of the image told him the photo had been taken four months earlier.

"What are we looking at?" Smith asked the room at large.

Vinson said, "Colonel, that's the Khmelnitsky nuclear power plant operated by Energoatom. It produces two thousand megawatts of power from two reactors. Two additional reactors are under construction."

Smith momentarily considered asking how a nuclear power station could produce enough heat to set off a DSP satellite, but he already knew the answer. The Chernobyl reactor was only two hundred or so miles away. "Any real-time coverage?"

Noel, the NRO representative on duty, responded, "Negative, Colonel. We have no assets nearby."

Several minutes went past. Announcements from NORAD confirmed everything his staff had told him.

Vinson's voice came over his headset. "Colonel, I did a web search and found a webcam located in the nearby city of Netishyn. Appears to be on a tall building, and it's facing the reactors."

"Put it up on the main display," Smith ordered.

The blue screen to the right of the main display flickered momentarily before the side image of four reactor towers appeared.

"The two towers on the left are operational," Vinson said. "The two on the right are under construction. The webcam is refreshing every sixty seconds."

The image looked grainy, as the reactors were a good distance away from the camera, but the reactor buildings looked intact and uniform. There were no obvious deficiencies in the structures or issues he could see. *Everything looks normal.*

The image refreshed, and the external wall on the second reactor building was frozen mid-exploding up and over the roof of the third reactor. The thick steel pressure vessel constraining the nuclear material had obviously failed, exposing raw nuclear fuel to the outside air. Smith had no idea how something like that could happen. *I thought there were all sorts of procedures and fail-safes on those things.*

No matter what the cause, people needed to know about it in a hurry. "Vinson, send a screenshot of that image over to NORAD headquarters."

Smith watched the image and waited for the next refresh. The picture updated, and half the building was now a twisted pile of steel and concrete. The roof had collapsed, and an exterior wall had disintegrated. Dense gray smoke rose into the sky at a sharp angle.

Rotating red lights began turning in the corners of the room—the lock-down signal. It meant the large metal doors protecting the mountain bunker were closing, sealing them in. A series of colored numbers in the right corner of the view screen changed from "4" to "3," and a loud tone sounded as it did so.

Before Smith could discover why the DEFCON rating had changed, loudspeakers built into the ceiling sounded. "This is Lieutenant General Wachowsky." Smith knew Wachowsky was the officer in charge of NORAD, and he had never addressed his command directly over the speakers before. "I've just received a message from Space Command headquarters. There's been a series of serious accidents worldwide resulting in the deaths of thousands. The cause appears to be a blindness pandemic. People began losing their sight in several Asian countries, and this has equally affected both civilian and military populations. The affliction is rapidly moving west and has spread as far as Eastern Europe at this time. American military units on duty in Afghanistan and the Middle East have already been affected by this phenomenon. The cause is unknown, but it is suspected to be linked to the recent orbital light display. All military personnel are to report to their supervisors and let them know if they directly observed the pyrotechnics launched from space.

"I want to repeat, we do not know that the lights are the cause of the blindness. Nor do we know if we will be affected in this country. Space Command is working on a solution. Until further notice, all leave and off-base passes are cancelled. NORAD headquarters and the Cheyenne bunker are now locked down. We are now at DEFCON Three. That is all."

Several people simultaneously stood at their stations and began asking questions of their neighbors.

It didn't take long to gauge the mood of the room. Everyone in the room knew family or friends that could be affected by the pandemic. Children, husbands, and wives were outside, without a million tons of mountain overhead to protect them. Everyone's first instinct was to be with those loved ones.

Smith understood that urge, but the nation needed protection. He keyed his microphone and stood. "Everyone settle down."

He waited for everyone to stop talking and look at him. "We still have a job to do, people. We're here to protect the nation. Every citizen of this country needs us here, focused, and ready to deal with any threats regardless of what they are or where they come from. Supervisors, poll your people and get a list to me ASAP of who saw the light show. If we're going to get through this, we need to be professional."

Smith released his microphone button. The atmosphere in the room immediately calmed down, and the men and women got back to work.

An Air Force Technical Sergeant came over to Smith and handed him a pistol in a belted holster plus two extra clips of 9mm ammo. "There you go, sir. Sign here, indicating receipt, please."

Standard procedure. At any DEFCON level above 4, Beretta M9 9MM pistols were issued to all NORAD officers.

Smith signed for the weapon and then stared at it. He hoped it wouldn't be needed.

* * *

A GNI logo with an animated "Breaking News" banner appeared on Sir Marcus's flat-screen television, grabbing his attention. A pre-recorded voice-over said, "We interrupt regular GNI programming for breaking news."

The logo faded away to be replaced by a dapper middle-aged reporter in a light gray suit. "This is François Bergeron at the GNI Paris Bureau with a special report. The last few hours have seen a massive number of accidents from India to Eastern Europe on both the small and large scale. A number of aircraft have crashed, trains have derailed, and there have been numerous industrial incidents. The estimate of the dead so far is over a hundred thousand and climbing rapidly. Communications in affected areas have been disrupted, and until now, we had little idea what was causing this wave of destruction.

"Our sister news bureau in Abu Dhabi has gone silent and is off the air, but our engineers here in Paris have been able to access the cameras in their studio. This is what we saw."

A news studio appeared. The camera was pointing down, but a good portion of the news desk and the bottom half of a GNI logo could still be seen. In front of the logo, two people were feeling their way along the wall. "Several staff members of GNI look to have been struck blind. We were able to access an external building surveillance camera looking down on Corniche Road West in downtown Abu Dhabi, and here is the live feed."

"Garbo!" Sir Marcus Brandon cried out, his eyes riveted to the screen.

The camera switched to an external shot, showing the public road from a high angle. Several cars were parked mid-road at strange angles, while even more vehicles were off to the side, up against concrete dividers. Two cars, which had suffered front-end collisions, had smoke coming from under the hoods. The fender of a station wagon had wrapped around a decorative pole near a small park.

Among the chaos of the errant vehicles, a dozen people could be seen. Some sat against concrete dividers or cars. Two women had their backs against a white van, clutching each other. Others were moving slowly, feeling their way along as best as they could. "As you can see, the people in the street also seem to be unable to see. GNI has tried to contact other news organizations in the affected areas without success. From what we can determine, the effects are widespread, and the phenomenon is spreading its way westward."

Brandon screamed again, this time as loud as he could. "*Garbo!*"

"GNI will continue to offer coverage of this tragedy as it spreads. In a few moments, we'll be joined by Professor Helmut Lang of the *Institut Pasteur* for expert analysis. Meanwhile…"

Garbo came out of the suite bathroom, pulling on a long white robe. "What? Why are you yelling? I was in the shower."

"GNI is reporting a mass series of accidents, starting in India and working their way west. Thousands are dead, and it looks like people are being struck blind. My God, what if it is the fireworks?" Brandon felt as if he were drowning.

"Wait a minute—you think our light display is causing people to go blind? You can't be serious."

Brandon pointed to the screen. "You think it's random chance that something like this breaks out less than a day after we set off powerful explosions in the atmosphere?"

"Wait a second. Let me make a call." Garbo finished closing her robe and grabbed her cell phone.

She walked away, leaving Brandon alone with the television. The news reporter was repeating himself, leaving Brandon with his own thoughts. He'd been assured by the Chinese scientists that formulated the pyrotechnics that there would be no negative effects. He'd been adamant from the first day of planning about that. They had said the fireworks would be no different than the ones a person could buy over the counter. The size of the charges was the only difference. The demos they had showed him proved to be harmless, but a lingering doubt haunted him.

Garbo returned pocketing her cell phone. "I just called the GNI Shanghai Bureau. There have been no incidents in China, and that's where we started. Whatever's happening in India and elsewhere must be unrelated. Some sort of strange infection, a mutated bird flu virus, I don't know."

The news made him feel better, but apprehension lingered.

A loud knock at the door sounded. Garbo went to answer it as Brandon turned to watch more coverage.

"Sir Marcus Brandon?"

Brandon turned back to see three men and a woman in suits approaching him. The man in the lead opened a black leather wallet to show off a gold shield. "I'm Special Agent Peter Wendell of the FBI. We need to ask you some questions, sir."

Chapter Eight
Grounded

Marvin pulled into the parking lot across from the Raytheon hangar. The door hinges on his old four-door Buick creaked loudly as he got out. He stopped and stood, stretching his back. As he got older, his flexibility suffered. *My back is getting just as squeaky as that door. It needs oil, too*, he thought as he slammed and locked the car door.

Though Marvin worked at Centennial Airport in Centennial, Colorado, he lived in Englewood, which lay just south of Denver. The drive to work each day was no more than a dozen miles, but every time he left home, he felt the tension return. He'd worked in aviation for almost thirty years and saw his job as more of a burden than employment. He used to be able to get things done, but now his role as a manager was subject to distant committees, accountants, and bureaucrats who thought their entire world existed within three thick corporate policy binders. Marvin's direct supervisor worked out of Garland, Texas, and he only put in a rare appearance if there were major issues.

Marvin stopped and stared up at the early morning sky. *I should retire. We have the money saved. The kids are off to school, and I know Catherine would love to travel more. If we sold our place, we could downsize and move to South Carolina. She'd love to be closer to her brother, and he does have that huge lake full of bass outside his front door.*

Christmas was five months away. He decided he'd retire just before those holidays and start the New Year retired, relaxed, and happy.

Marvin walked through the security checkpoint, wordlessly showing his laminated credentials to the security guard at the door, who waved him through. Within minutes, he'd slipped on his coveralls and walked out of the locker room into the hangar proper. The E-6B airframe always struck him as majestic. It even had a decent name, *Mercury*. The fact that this converted Boeing 707 could do six hundred miles an hour while coordinating a nuclear battlefield made him proud to be an American.

He'd felt the same way the night before, at Darber's BBQ. The overhead fireworks that lit up the sky were incredible to behold.

Bill Darber walked up. Beside him was a naval officer in a service khaki uniform with his hat folded, the end of it under his belt. "Marv, this is Lieutenant Short. He'll be heading up the acceptance team for the E-6."

Short stuck out his hand. "Good morning, sir, Nice to meet you."

Marvin looked the officer over. *Damn, but they look younger every year. This one looks like he shaves once a week.* "Lieutenant, if your people are ready, we can start with the interior systems. We have to do a final inspection of the exterior surface sealant before we sign that off."

"That works," Short said. "My crew is inside, setting up now. The pilots are scheduled for the test flight first thing in the morning."

Marvin frowned. "We typically schedule that after everything else has been signed off. We do find problems on occasion during the checkouts. Why the rush?"

"We're at DEFCON Three and need all the Mercury birds back in service because of the blindness epidemic."

"Huh? The what?" Marvin asked, lost.

"Didn't you see the news this morning?"

"No, I read the newspaper during the morning coffee break."

Short began explaining the situation.

* * *

"Mister President, Prime Minister Gladstone would like to speak to you. He said it was of critical importance."

"Thank you, Mary. Put it through, please, and ask Keith to step in. Thank you, gentlemen. We'll have to discuss this later." The White House staff rose and began to filter out of the Oval Office. Calvin stood from the comfortable easy chair and walked back to his desk. The phone began ringing as he sat down in the high-backed chair.

Calvin turned on the speakerphone. "Morning, Harry. What can I do for you?"

Usually a genial man, Gladstone sounded deathly serious. "Jim, I'm not sure what you've been told about this wave of blindness sweeping its way west, but it's bad. I've been watching the GNI coverage. Their Paris office's reporters lost their sight while on television. They stayed on the air live as it happened. We've had communications open with our embassies in Berlin, Paris, Copenhagen, Rome, and Zurich. All of them went blind at the same time. The entire European Union has been affected. If the current trend continues, I'm expecting the same thing to happen to us in the next fifteen minutes or so."

Keith Hurst walked into the room from his personal entrance into the Oval Office. He carried a yellow legal pad and pen.

Calvin waved him into a nearby chair. "My national security advisor has just joined the call, Harry. What can we do?"

Gladstone's voice sounded muffled for a moment, as if he was talking to someone with the mouthpiece covered. "Sorry, Jim. My staff are handing me more updates. Several flights originating in Europe are down. I just ordered all U.K. aviation grounded, rail traffic suspended, and a full call-up of military and police. Any inbound flights are being told to turn around or land at the nearest airport. Everyone just got into work or school, and they'll all want to get home. Jim, do you have any idea as to the cause of this?"

Calvin looked over the phone at Hurst. "We have some working theories that it might be indirectly linked to Marcus Brandon's light show last night. He's in Las Vegas, and I have the FBI questioning him now."

Gladstone said, "We have a military research facility at Porton Down near Salisbury. One of their scientists recorded the light emissions from last night's pyrotechnics. He concluded the levels of visible light emitted, while intense in the UV range at times, were within safe levels. I'm having the data sent to the White House, along with anything else we can pull together."

Calvin raised an eyebrow. "Really? Then either the lights were a catalyst for something else, or it is a viral pandemic."

"If it were a virus, it would be spreading in all directions, not just westward across the time zones. The lights have to be involved, but we have no bloody idea what mechanism is causing this. Jim, listen. You won't be affected by this for several hours. Use that time to make a difference. I'm remaining at Number Ten if you need to talk— Give me a minute, something's happening." The line muffled again.

Calvin looked over at Hurst. "I want the entire cabinet here as soon as humanly possible. We need to start preparing things."

Hurst went and spoke with one of the president's secretaries through the door. That left Calvin alone with his thoughts for a minute.

Gladstone's voice came back on the line, interrupting his considerations about what actions would be necessary. "Jim?"

"We're here, Harry."

Hurst sat back down beside him.

"It's happening. Everything's getting, blurry… Like heavy clouds rolling in, making everything incrementally darker. Colors are fading. The rubber plant in the corner looks gray, not green. Jim, I want you to find out what's happening and who's responsible."

"I will. Count on it."

"I have to go, Jim. I need to be with my wife. If this is happening to her, then…"

"I understand, Harry. Good luck."

* * *

Lieutenant General Lam's staff car slid to the curb outside of the international terminal of the Hangzhou Xiaoshan International Airport. An aide waited for him and had his door open before the vehicle stopped. Lam stepped out, returned the salute from his aide, and then paused to look down the terminal sidewalk. Normally the tenth busiest airport in China, all he could see in either direction were hundreds of his airborne troops in khaki uniforms, frantically unloading trucks or carrying equipment. Several supervising NCOs screamed for everyone to hurry.

Lam checked his uniform. He also wore field khakis, but his were pressed with knife-edge creases, and his boots had a high shine. He made a minor adjustment to his shirt then walked inside the terminal. His aide would follow with his bags.

Soldiers milled around inside. Some stood; others sat on available seats or on their backpacks. More NCOs were yelling, which echoed off the hard surfaces.

The airport design was open concept. Exposed metal roof trusses were suspended on tall concrete columns forty feet high. Both were painted white, which significantly brightened up the interior. Pink counters were contrasted by a waxed off-white marble floor.

He saw no civilians within the terminal. The few men behind the check-in counters were members of the People's Armed Police Force.

Lam looked up to see several monitors, displaying lists of several dozen departing flights. Each had "Cancelled" beside the flight number. He turned to his aide, who was hurrying to catch up with a pair of large bags. "Where do I go?"

The aide stopped and braced to attention. "Through security, then to Gate A06, Comrade Lieutenant General."

Lam strode that way. He'd been through the airport before and knew where security was. Many men were heading in the same direction, but they moved out of his way when they saw him coming.

There were PAPF officers present at the security checkpoint when he arrived, but they were simply waving the troops through. With the airborne soldiers openly carrying automatic weapons, ammunition, and grenades, the metal detectors were superfluous.

Lam cut to the head of the line and walked through. Several officers, NCOs, and PAPF personnel saluted him as he passed, but he simply nodded in return. Too many soldiers were saluting to return them all. On the secure side of airport, he spotted a sign for gates A01–A08 and went in the direction of the arrow.

The civilians staffing stores and kiosks off the wide corridor were busy selling snacks, food, books, and magazines to the military men. He wondered why they were allowed to be there until he remembered the PAPF. They would not let anyone leave the airport until the airborne soldiers had landed at their destination. He was the senior airborne officer and still didn't know where they were going, so he doubted there would be any serious security breach from having a soldier buy a bowl of noodles.

Upon reaching gate A06, Lam looked through the tall glass windows to see a large Airbus waiting on the tarmac. The fuselage and wing tip lights were on. Movement in the cockpit caught his attention as a pilot in a white shirt sat down. More large aircraft sat at adjoining gates and featured the names of three different Chinese airlines.

"Comrade Lieutenant General Lam."

He turned to find a Chief Sergeant Class 1 saluting him. He returned this salute, for Chief Sergeant Class 1 was the highest NCO rank in the PLAAF. His cloth name tag said CHENG.

"General Wen sends his compliments and orders you to attend him immediately. If you'll follow me, sir."

Lam nodded once. Cheng turned and marched off; Lam followed and indicated for his aide to remain behind at the gate with his luggage.

Cheng led him down several walkways, passing thousands of airborne troops at their gates. He turned into a restaurant and walked to the back. Several PAPF officers stood guard inside the door with machine guns across their chests.

Cheng stepped out of Lam's way and used an open palm to point. Lam saw a table beside a large window overlooking the airport runways.

Sitting there, enjoying a bowl of noodles, was General Wen.

Lam came up to the table and saluted. "Lieutenant General Lam, reporting as ordered, Comrade General."

Wen didn't look up. He dropped his chopsticks, reached down into a bag by his feet, and withdrew a thick brown paper envelope. He double-checked the tape over the seal and handed it over. "These are your orders. Do not open them until you are airborne and over the Pacific." Wen raised his head and stared at Lam. "Know that failure will result in the harshest consequences. Dismissed."

He retrieved his chopsticks and resumed eating.

This was not the way to brief the senior field commander going into what looked like a major battle. What if I have questions or discover problems? Shocked by the treatment, Lam examined the thick blank envelope in his hand. Every join and flap had been sealed with two-inch transparent tape.

A glance at Wen told him he would not receive any more answers there. Lam saluted, turned on his heel, and left the restaurant. He was so distracted by the envelope in his hand that he didn't notice a pair of PAPF officers following him until he was well on his way back to his gate.

He turned and faced them. They stopped and braced to attention but said nothing.

They're escorts. Making sure no one takes the orders from me… Or are they to make sure I don't open my orders until I'm in the air? Lam looked at the envelope once more. It felt much heavier all of a sudden. *Where on Earth are they sending us?*

* * *

The cabinet meeting began without formality. Hurst took his position beside the president. *How he bottles up the anger at our situation is beyond me. I'd want to nuke someone.*

Calvin said, "You've all seen the news reports. In less than four hours, we have to assume that the east coast of the United States will suffer the same malady that's affected Europe and mainland Asia. Within eight hours, the entire mainland of the United States will be affected. We need to do three things. First, ensure the U.S. government still functions. Second, safeguard as many lives as possible. Last, but most importantly, we need to prevent this or find a cure.

"I'm issuing orders covering the following points. SCATANA[13] will be executed immediately. All air traffic within the territorial borders of the United States is to land within two hours. If they cannot get to their destination within that time, then they're to land at the closest airport. Any inbound international flights are to turn around. All public transportation is to halt in three hours' time, and any travel by car is to be discouraged. Citizens are to stay at home.

"The armed services shall establish shelters for those military personnel that go blind. The few who retain their sight will have to care for those without. All National Guard units will be activated under the same conditions. DEFCON Three

---

[13] Plan for the Security Control of Air Traffic and Air Navigation Aids. A joint plan that dictates how the Department of Defense, the FAA, and the FCC shall control air traffic and navigation aids during an emergency. This was last used during the 9/11 attacks.

has been activated, and it's my intention to go to DEFCON Two in two hours.

"Congress shall assemble at Fort McNair, the vice president shall go to Raven Rock, and I'll be at Mount Weather with all of you. The Emergency Alert System[14] is to be activated, and I shall address the nation in one hour's time. Does anyone have any questions?"

Everyone began talking at once, so forcefully that Hurst was momentarily shocked. He stood up and pounded the table with his hand. "Quiet! One at a time."

The Secretary of Energy, Damien Cox, a bookish man with thick spectacles, spoke first. "Mister President, if what you say is true, then we need to bring the nation's nuclear reactors into an idle state. I've seen reports that at least three reactors in Asia and Africa have had problems. If we can dial down power output, we reduce any issues. The same should be done for other energy infrastructures. Pipelines, oil rigs, refineries, and power generating stations will also need to be addressed."

Calvin nodded at once. "Agreed, if you need manpower to assist, coordinate with the defense secretary."

"That will result in brownouts and even blackouts nationwide, sir," Cox said.

The president quickly answered, "I understand, but given the circumstances, to minimize the potential for disasters, we've got little choice. Hospitals and the emergency services will have generators. Anything else?"

Defense Secretary Donovan leaned forward. "The initial numbers are in for the survey of military personnel. Over ninety-five percent saw the fireworks. Obvious exceptions are submariners, missile silo crews, and duty personnel in the various bunkers around the world. However, I think it's fair to say that the vast majority of our armed forces will be rendered combat ineffective in short order. NASA tells me the International Space Station crew is also affected."

---

[14] Formerly known as the Emergency Broadcast System until 1997.

More murmurs erupted around the table. Housing and Urban Development Secretary Denise Carlyle pushed herself away from the table and stood. "Mister President, please accept my immediate resignation. I'm leaving." She began to walk away.

Calvin rose. She'd taught at the same university Calvin attended, and the president had picked her personally for the post. "Denise, we need you. I can't accept your resignation. Not now."

She stopped and turned, bringing herself up to her full height. Her eyes were raw. "I quit. There's no way I'm going into a hole in the ground while my family and friends lose their sight. I'm going to go home to be with my son and daughters. They'll be terrified when it happens. Besides, I saw the lights with them. I'll be unable to do my job regardless. I'm sorry, but my mind is made up. My family comes first." She wiped her eyes and left the room.

Calvin sat down and immediately leaned into Hurst's shoulder to whisper, "Have the Secret Service make sure she gets home safely."

Hurst waved over a female aide and passed on the message to her. She chased after the former secretary.

"If anyone else wants out, now's the time," Calvin announced.

No one moved or said anything for several seconds.

"Mister President…" said Secretary of Defense Evan Blackburn while tapping the end of his pen on the blotter before him. Hurst thought Blackburn's brown toupee looked ridiculous under the harsh fluorescent lighting, but he kept that to himself. "There comes a time when you need to put the needs of the nation first. This is one of them. I intend to stay and serve to the best of my ability."

Everyone else around the table nodded, and no one dissented.

Calvin glanced down at the table before scanning the faces in the room. "Thank you, ladies and gentlemen. In the rush to get everyone here, we never found out... Did any of you not see the lights? If you didn't see them, please raise your hand."

He slowly counted to five.

No one moved.

"All right. Let's keep going. What's next?

* * *

In the reflection from the television studio monitor, Michael Alvarez could see his tie was slightly askew. He took the opportunity to adjust it.

When done, Alvarez looked up to see the floor manager standing beside camera one begin his countdown on five fingers. "Five... Four... Three..." For "Two" and "One," the floor manager indicated only with his fingers and said nothing.

He finished and pointed at Alvarez. *We are on the air.*

"This is Michael Alvarez on the GNI news desk in New York. I'm joined by Mary Lewis, senior political reporter for the *Washington Herald* newspaper, coming to us by video link... Mary, good morning, and thank you for making it in so early. Many Americans are just waking up to find air travel is being suspended across the country. Additionally, trains and public transport are to be closed within hours. What's your first impression of this?"

"Morning, James. Nice to be here. This appears to be an attempt by the Calvin White House to limit damage when this supposed blindness pandemic reaches the United States. It's hard to judge at the moment, simply because the amount of information coming from the affected areas is minimal."

"Sorry. You said 'supposed'? Am I to assume you are having doubts about the cause of this?" *What is she doing?*

"Of course, nothing like this has ever happened before. We do know there's a communications disruption to Europe and points east, but there are a series of perfectly logical explanations why that would happen without resorting to some fantasy story—"

Huh? "One moment. Are you suggesting the president of the United States has been taken in by some sort of hoax?"

"Well, I won't go that far—not yet, anyway. I do have doubts about this story, though."

Alvarez shook his head. "It sounded incredible to me, until I saw the GNI Paris bureau affected just over an hour ago while they were on the air."

"Yes, but… Well, there's just no easy way to say this. It's possible that Sir Marcus Brandon is cooking up another sensational story to get attention for the launch of the GNI network, just like Orson Wells convincing the nation in 1938 that they were under attack by Martians."

Alvarez was shocked. He'd known Lewis to be a bit of a shrew at times—that was why they had her on. She was always good for an over-the-top sound bite, but was she suggesting a professional news organization had deliberately pretended to go blind to mislead the public? "No, it isn't possible. As our viewers should already know, Sir Marcus is the owner of GNI. He made it clear in a written memo on the day of the company's formation that he would not participate in any editorial capacity, nor censor the stories we aired. GNI is an independent news agency with no editorial oversight from our parent corporation, the Athena Group."

Lewis smiled. "Then why is the FBI currently questioning Sir Marcus in Las Vegas?"

What! "I hadn't heard that."

Lewis's smile widened. "A source tells me the Las Vegas office of the FBI is currently questioning Sir Marcus and his senior staff. You really have to wonder why. Now, I'm not going to suggest GNI is 'in on it,' but you have to wonder at the timing."

Alvarez wondered about that and almost immediately discounted it. Marcus Brandon was an egotistical show-off, but he'd never known the man to lie or use either his employees or companies in an unscrupulous way. The director came over his earpiece and told him to expect a commercial in fifteen seconds. "We'll have to disagree there. It's time for a commercial break. Please stay tuned for the presidential address to the nation. We'll be right back."

The floor manager signaled, making the "cut" sign.

"We're clear," Alvarez said.

"Well, that was fun." Lewis commented over the video link. She was still grinning over her little surprise.

Screw you and your showboating. Alvarez stood, disconnected his clip-on microphone, and walked off the set without saying anything. He needed a bathroom.

* * *

"Ladies and gentlemen, the president of the United States." Press Secretary Lisa Morton announced from the podium in the James S. Brady Press Briefing Room of the White House.

She walked away from the podium as everyone in the room rose to their feet. She placed her back to the wall in time to see President Calvin enter the room. He wore a charcoal gray business suit and red tie. He always looked his best in dark clothes. Lisa had warm feelings for the man, but she kept them to herself. It would be inappropriate, on so many levels, for her to carry on a relationship with the president.

Calvin strode up to the podium. He carried no notes or papers. Everything he would say had already been preloaded into the teleprompter by the speech writing team.

He faced the press corps, placed his hands on the sides of the podium, and indicated for everyone to sit. "Good morning. Thank you for coming on such short notice. Today, our proud nation—indeed, the entire globe—faces a challenge of unimaginable scale. In the last twelve hours, a third of the population of the Earth has been stricken by an unknown ailment. From India to the United Kingdom, from Russia to South Africa, billions can no longer see."

The press corps in the theater seats covered wars, famine, and political intrigue on a daily basis. They typically covered those events with a blasé attitude.

They all looked shocked. Some appeared horrified.

Calvin continued, "The cause of the blindness is unknown, but it is relentlessly approaching our shores. There's no reason to think that this epidemic will not affect us. I pray it doesn't, but we must take precautions to protect the lives of our citizens. In addition to the enforced landing of all aircraft and cessation of public transport, I've ordered all power generation facilities to reduce output. Nuclear reactors shall be placed in a safe condition while refineries and pipelines shall be shut down. I've just spoken with Canadian Prime Minister MacDonald and Mexican President Vega, who are taking similar measures. We shall be coordinating efforts. It's hoped that the terrible accidents seen in Europe, Africa, and Asia can be avoided, should our populations be affected.

"To the citizens of the United States, I ask you to remain at home and be with your families. Turn off as many appliances and electrical devices in your home as possible. The Emergency Alert System has been activated, and will be used for updates. We shall work unceasingly toward a solution and an eventual cure for this malady.

"I'm declaring a national state of emergency. I've ordered a call-up of the National Guard in every state. I wish to emphasize that contrary to rumor, martial law is not—repeat, *not*—being enacted. I and the cabinet feel that this is not necessary at this time. The military of the nation is on heightened alert and shall be on watch against anyone trying to take advantage of this situation. Our resolve is steadfast, and we shall prevail through these difficult times with God's blessing. Thank you."

The president left the podium as the mass of reporters surged forward, demanding answers to shouted questions. Secret Service agents had to physically restrain them as Calvin left the room, and Lisa had never seen that before.

They would be after her in short order, with a thousand questions. She would handle their predictable questions while deflecting the difficult ones. The turmoil kept her occupied and meant she'd be busy—too busy to think of her empty bed, lonely apartment, and annoying cats.

A group of Secret Service agents stayed in the doorway to stop the reporters from following the president. While they were distracted, Lisa angled toward the back door to avoid the ruckus and made her way down the hall toward her office. She could see the Secret Service agents escort the president outside into the Rose Garden.

An agent near her spoke into the radio microphones on his cuff. "Rook, en route to Site MW."

* * *

Doctor Edmund Wiater awoke feeling human again. The cycle of getting into bed for fifteen minutes then rushing for the bathroom had ceased around two a.m. Apart from being coated in dried sweat from the night before, he felt fine.

He looked at the alarm clock on his night table and saw he still had two hours to go until his alarm went off. The feeling of being covered by clammy perspiration annoyed him, and he would be unable to sleep again. He got up, grabbed a razor and can of shaving cream from the bathroom sink, and stepped into the shower stall. Wiater seldom shaved in the shower, but today he would make an exception. He turned up the heat and enjoyed the feeling of the hot water. He generously applied a full handful of shaving cream to his cheeks and neck before shaving. After shampooing, he rubbed his body with a bar of soap and finally emerged ready to begin his day. The long shower had rejuvenated him and washed away the last vestiges of his illness.

He toweled himself off, then combed his thinning hair into place before walking into his bedroom.

July in Seattle got quite hot, and several people he knew went to work in shorts. Wiater chose to wear tan slacks. In his lab, he preached safety, and long pants made sense when dealing with corrosive acids and bases. He put on a light green long-sleeved shirt, added a black belt, and slipped on his thick-rimmed black glasses. Wiater looked at his balding head in the mirror. For the thousandth time, he considered getting hair plugs, then just as quickly dismissed the idea. *I am what I am.* He went into the kitchen to make a light breakfast.

An irritated squawk from the large cage in the corner got his attention as he passed through his living room. With his illness, he'd completely forgotten about his pet parrot, Petey. He pulled off the blanket covering the cage to discover a desperate bird pecking at an empty seed bowl. He spoke soothingly to the bird as he worked in the cage. "Good morning, Petey. How'd you sleep? It looks like you have quite the appetite. No. No biting! I was ill. Yes, I know. I'm sorry, I forgot to feed you. Here's some popcorn, now I know you like that." Wiater filled up the seed bowl, then added a handful of popcorn from a nearby plastic bag and dropped it onto a side dish in the cage. The bird leaned down and took a kernel in its beak. He held it with his foot while his sharp beak broke off pieces. "I'm glad you forgive me."

Wiater went to the kitchen and put together a simple meal of a bagel and instant coffee. While waiting for the kettle to boil, he began planning his day. Getting in early would work out nicely, he decided. He could get caught up from his missed day before the interns got in.

When he was done with breakfast, his plate and mug went into the dishwasher. He snagged his car keys and left the apartment.

Once in the car, he popped in an '80s hits CD, and his fingers tapped against the steering wheel in time with the Thompson Twins. The drive into work was quick, which struck him as a pleasant surprise. *I need to come into work this early all the time. There's no traffic at all at this time of morning, apart from those army trucks traveling on the road opposite. Some sort of exercise or parade, I suppose?*

He turned into his reserved parking spot at the Swedish Medical Center. The parking lot was almost empty. The white painted sign stated, "Dr. E. Wiater – Genetics." Wiater locked his car then strode toward the entry doors. Upon entering the building, he turned up the stairwell to get to his office on the third floor. His key card got him through the security door. He dropped his keys into a convenient bowl by the door and took a white lab coat off a hook. He made sure his laminated security pass was clipped to the lab coat pocket before putting it on.

Wiater's office was only three paces from the entry door. He turned on his computer and began scanning the e-mails that had arrived during his absence. Seeing nothing of import, he began reviewing the notes his grad students had left on his desk the previous day.

* * *

The distance from the helipad, where the Marine One helicopter had just landed, to the east portal entrance of the Mount Weather Emergency Operations Center was just over three hundred feet. Even so, a motorcade of armored SUVs was used to transport the president.

Sitting beside Calvin, Hurst could see the increased security. A lot of troops were in sight with rifles cradled in their arms. Technically a FEMA site, Mount Weather—or more specifically, the bunker underneath the mountain—had been in operation since 1959. Mount Weather, or Site MW as it was colloquially known, was the designated emergency bunker for the executive branch of the United States government.

Hurst had been thoroughly briefed on Mount Weather when he took office. It had remained a closely guarded secret until December 1974 when TWA Flight 514 had flown into the side of the mountain. That accident resulted in the secret facility being revealed to the public by the press, but it still housed the president and his cabinet in times of crisis.

The line of vehicles left the helipad and soon approached the open large garage door leading into the building. They entered without slowing. The bright daylight swapped with orange-colored fluorescent lighting, on the top of an arched and downward-sloping tunnel.

Hurst looked over at the president. Calvin was hunched over briefing papers and letting the world pass him by unnoticed.

After driving fifteen hundred feet into the tunnel, the column of vehicles halted at a guard post. The large outer blast door—made by Mosler—was open to admit them. Each of the eleven locking cylinders of the thick stainless steel was as thick around as a man's thigh. Secret Service agents opened the rear door to let the president alight before escorting him inside. The group passed through a second equally massive blast door then turned down a side corridor.

Hurst followed with his valise in hand.

Paul Sampson, the senior Secret Service agent in charge of the presidential protection detail, approached from the side. "It took me some time, but I found two agents for you. They were on duty in the joint operations center in the White House during the fireworks."

Hurst nodded. "Excellent. They can look after him, then. Thanks, Paul."

Sampson just nodded and moved away.

Stacked pallets of cellophane wrapped food were against the left wall of the long entry tunnel. Hurst estimated they had enough supplies to last ninety days sealed off from the outside world.

A series of turns through smaller steel hatches brought them to the presidential suite. The rooms had been carefully decorated to appear like the president's rooms in the White House. Hurst had to remind himself that there were thirteen hundred feet of rock over his head.

James Calvin sat down in an armchair, took one last look at the briefing papers in his hand, sighed deeply, and handed them off to a nearby aide. "I need the room, please. Keith, stay a moment?"

The rest of the staff departed, and the last one out closed the door.

"Keith, no one in the line of succession avoided seeing the fireworks. If they are the cause of the blindness, then the U.S. government is well and truly screwed."

Hurst sat down beside him on a couch. "Maybe in the long term. Short term, we still have you."

"Not if I go blind as well, dammit!"

Was this fear or frustration, what Hurst saw in his friend? *Either way, he needs a kick in the pants to get him out of his funk.* "Blind or not, you're still president. We have to keep positive there'll be a cure for this eventually. If you don't think that's possible, then resign and walk out of here. We need a leader to get through this, not someone who feels sorry for themselves."

Calvin glared at him for several seconds. The rosy cheeks on his face told Hurst just how close he was to losing his temper.

Calvin looked away, closed his eyes, and took a deep breath. "You're the only person who can talk to me that way and get away with it... Sorry."

"No apologies needed, ever. I'm just as concerned as you and everyone else out there who saw those damned lights. We face this problem together."

A polite knock on the door was followed by the face of an aide. "Mister President, I have the latest reports from the nuclear reactor shutdowns."

"Come in. Thank you, Keith. We'll talk later."

* * *

Doctor Edmund Wiater finished reviewing the previous day's notes and began setting up a series of experiments that would run over the next seventy-two hours. He took his portable music player out of his desk drawer and began listening to some classic '80s through the headphones. He would normally let one of the grad students or post docs do the work, but he still enjoyed getting his hands dirty with real science.

Besides, he felt truly excited by his latest project of enhancing the human immune system to fight genetic maladies. His work had only reached the experimental level, but the results had been encouraging to date. If he could make it work, then a trip to Stockholm would be in his future.

Thoughts of a Nobel Prize made Wiater smile all the more as he began powering up the sensitive scientific instruments.

The fluorescent lights above him flickered. He looked up, but it didn't worry him unduly. His instruments were on protected circuits, supplied by the medical center's own generators and battery backup systems. The overhead lighting was still directly connected to the main grid, however. They would not be brought over to the protected wiring until the next phase of infrastructure improvements scheduled for the spring.

If the lights did go out, it would be mildly inconvenient, but his experiments would continue uninterrupted.

* * *

"Mister Hurst, the president would like to see you," a female aide said, jolting him awake from his brief nap.

He rubbed his eyes, sat up on the small couch, and straightened his tie. "Thanks, Jennifer." She left the small office designated for his use. He stood, pushed his fingers through his hair, and walked to the presidential suite.

Two Secret Service agents stood post outside the door. As he passed, Hurst nodded to the older agent, assuming he was the senior. On entering the suite, Hurst saw his friend sitting in the easy chair, his hands on his knees. He was alone. One of the agents closed the door behind him.

"Yes, Jim?"

"I lost my sight a couple of minutes ago." Calvin's voice cracked. "Everything faded to gray then went totally black. I can't see anything."

Hurst checked his watch. "It's the predicted time. I slept longer than I thought." He sat down on a couch near his friend. He looked up and saw a muted television, tuned to a cable news station. It took him a moment to realize that his own sight was growing dimmer by the second. "It's happening to me, as well."

The sound of a gun firing came from the corridor.

Hurst stood and ran to the threshold, ripping open the door. A male Air Force officer was lying on the corridor floor. He looked to have fallen, but the pistol in his hand and blood on his temple contradicted that. *A suicide?*

One of the Secret Service agents guarding the doorway made his way to the body and took possession of the pistol before checking for a pulse. "He's dead."

Another pair of Air Force officers appeared from a side corridor. They grabbed the body and carried it out of sight.

Hurst turned to the senior agent. "The president has been affected, and I'm losing my sight now."

"Neither of us saw the fireworks, sir. We'll be able to assist you. I'm Agent Carter, and that's my partner, Agent Nance. There might be a few others in the bunker who should keep their sight as well. Not many, but…"

"Do either of you have family?" Hurst squinted down the corridor. Things were getting blurry.

"No, sir. We're both single. We'll take care of you as best as we can."

"Thank you." Unable to think of anything else to say, Hurst shut the door. He walked back to the couch. The last few feet, he had to feel his way along the back edge to find his spot. The last vestige of sight left him as he sat down. Panic gripped him. He began breathing rapidly while clawing at the couch.

"Relax, Keith. It'll pass. I had the same reaction," Calvin said.

Hurst felt his friend's hand on his arm, which helped.

He closed his eyes firmly then opened them again, but he saw nothing at all. In total darkness, the silent tears were unstoppable.

Chapter Nine
Party Crashers

The telephone on Colonel Alvin Smith's desk seldom rang. As senior officer on watch, he typically placed the calls. So when the trill from his desk phone sounded loudly, it did surprise him somewhat.

"Watch Officer, Colonel Smith."

"Smith, it's General Wachowsky."

Smith picked up a pen to make notes. The senior officer of NORAD had never called him directly before. "Yes, sir?"

"I've reviewed the reports. Your staff has the highest incidence of people who've not seen the pyrotechnics. Most of them were on duty with you in the bunker during the shift last night. I'm therefore tasking you to take over from NORAD headquarters on the hour."

Smith looked at the wall clocks. That would be in seven minutes. "Yes, sir, I understand."

"I'm sending you additional personnel. None of them should lose their sight, but it's only a handful. Your people will have to remain on duty until we resolve this. There is no relief crew. I hate to pile on the bad news, but the vast majority of our armed forces could be affected by this, according to the estimates."

"Wow, it's that bad?" He looked around the room. Had anyone overheard his exclamation?

"It gets worse. The president, his entire cabinet, and the joint chiefs have all been stricken by this, this... affliction. We're wide open, and that brings me to the real point of this conversation."

"Yes, sir?"

After a brief pause, Wachowsky continued, "I watched the light show last night with my family. From what I can determine, you're the most senior officer who didn't. Effective immediately, you'll be taking over as commanding officer of NORAD for the duration of this emergency. Assuming this does affect me, you'll be running everything. One of my staff is coming over with a briefing packet. She'll get you up to speed on the latest intel and brief you on some of the command protocols you're not aware of. Clear?"

Smith's mind reeled. *I'm going to be the man responsible for the security of North America? That's a three-level jump in rank responsibility!* "Yes, sir. How do I reach you?

"All that info will be in the brief. If you have any questions after that, give me a call."

"Yes, sir. Thank you, sir."

Wachowsky hung up the phone. Smith stared at the handset before replacing the receiver. It felt surreal to him, to be promoted to be NORAD's commanding officer.

He had a lot to do and very little time to do it.

Smith keyed his desk microphone to address his staff. "Attention. This is Colonel Smith. We'll be taking over responsibilities from NORAD Headquarters in five minutes. All staff are expected to be at their posts at that time. That is all."

A few people made a dash for the bathrooms.

Smith understood why they needed a nervous pee. He would wait until they were done before going himself.

* * *

Faedong Li sat on the padded seat of his golf cart at the northeast end of the concrete dock. His hands grasped the wheel as he regarded Qingdao harbor. A dozen massive Chinese container ships prepared for sea. Thick anchor chains inched upwards noisily, driven by hydraulic winches.

The ships sat low in the water, heavily laden with men, weapons, and supplies all hidden inside the interconnected containers. Five pilot boats ran around at high speed. Each with a large People's Armed Police Force contingent visible onboard. They seemed eager to get the vessels out of the channel.

A deep bass horn sounded nearby, startling Li. He turned to see a RoRo, loaded with green PLA trucks, heading out of the harbor. Troops lined the rails on all levels. He guessed there were over a thousand men visible, possibly more.

Li's gaze followed the line of ships as they headed out to the shipping lanes, and he felt confusion.

Colonel Chio returned. He had excused himself minutes before to go behind a container and relieve himself. Chio sat down on the passenger side of the cart. "A glorious and inspirational sight indeed. We're lucky to see this event. It's something we can boast of to our grandchildren."

Li mentally filtered what he wanted to say before ending on something acceptable. "Yes, North Korea will certainly be unable to stand against such might."

He decided to push his luck with the colonel, who was now acting like his best friend rather than the bully Li had observed earlier. "Colonel, these ships are destined for North Korea, you said?"

"I did, yes. This was made quite clear to us in the initial briefing we received along with the secrecy of the operation. Why do you ask?"

Li pointed seaward. "I ask because I'm confused. Once clear of the mouth of the harbor, North Korean-bound ships typically turn northeast. All departing ships seem to be traveling southeast, directly out to the Pacific, as you can see."

Colonel Chio looked and appeared startled. "Well... I can... Perhaps it is a deception. Yes, a cunning deception to keep their defense forces confused and off-balance for the assault."

That was highly improbable. The farther out to sea the ships were, the longer they had to travel and easier they would be to attack. The only explanation he could imagine was they were not heading for North Korea at all. *They just told the People's Armed Police that for security. Chio just isn't bright enough to realize it. The target is Taiwan. It has to be. Now that will be something to tell the grandchildren about!*

A series of helicopters, mounted with torpedoes, appeared overhead and headed out to sea, toward the departing convoy. Li counted two dozen aircraft.

* * *

Sir Marcus Brandon sat on the overstuffed couch in his Las Vegas penthouse suite. The FBI agents left only a minute ago, and even though the penthouse had powerful air conditioning, a rivulet of sweat ran down his back between his shoulder blades. The aggressive two-hour questioning session had wrung him out emotionally.

Garbo returned from escorting the FBI agents out of their suite. She had wept several times as the agents questioned her. She stopped in front of him, fists clenched at her side.

"They think we're responsible for what's happening!" she said, uncharacteristically shrill.

"You know damned well we're not, Garbo! You've been in every planning meeting, written every memo, sent every e-mail concerning this project! When did I ever say 'Let's blind the world'?"

She pointed at the closed double doors to their suite. "Then why were those agents here? Our fireworks went off last night, and today everyone is going blind? That can't be coincidence! What have we done?"

"Yes, it looks bad, but it's a coincidence. It *has* to be! As you said, China's unaffected, and the light shows began there. Explain to me how over a billion Chinese saw the same thing and nothing happened to them?" Brandon had been truthful and taken the same line with the FBI. He'd arranged for a global pyrotechnic display from space and nothing more.

"I can't, obviously..." She collapsed on the couch at the opposite end, away from him. Her face dropped into her hands. "Thousands dead, they said. Maybe hundreds of thousands; what a nightmare!"

Her sobs shook the couch. Occupied with his own thoughts, Brandon stood to fix himself a straight scotch. He didn't care that it was early. He needed a drink. He skipped the ice cubes and poured half a glass of Glenfiddich single malt into a crystal tumbler.

He took the tumbler and walked over to a floor-to-ceiling window. Brandon took his first sip as he looked out toward the black mountains in the distance. *That's strange. The mountains look dim. Are rain clouds moving in?* He leaned forward slightly to check for clouds up in the sky, but there were none.

The sky should have been a deep blue, but instead he saw a strange grayish color. *It has to be the glass in the windows, filtering the light.* He grabbed the door handle to the balcony and tugged it open. Warm air flooded into the suite, but the color remained unchanged. *What's happening?*

Realization hit him.

He dropped the tumbler. It shattered on the aluminum threshold of the sliding balcony door.

"Marcus, what was that noise? Why's it so dark? Did you close the curtains? Marcus... Marcus?"

The reality of his sight slipping away rendered Brandon speechless. He grasped the side of the sliding balcony door and looked toward the mountains as the last of his sight faded to black.

"Marcus! Where are you?" Her flailing hands suddenly touched his back. She latched onto his arm so hard that her nails dug into his skin. She moved toward him until she had him in a firm embrace. "Hold me. I can't see!"

"Neither can I. Whatever's happening, it's affecting us as well."

"What do we do? How do we fix this?"

His own frustration came out. "*I don't know!*"

Garbo began sobbing again. He pushed his way onto the balcony to get away from her.

She clutched at him. "Please Marcus, hold me."

"Do you think a hug will fix this? The entire world is going blind and I... I caused it." His own words hit home. This *had* to be his fault. He couldn't deny it any longer. Something in the fireworks, whether by accident or by design, had caused this epic tragedy. Billions of people unable to see, flailing their way along streets and in their homes, calling for help that would never come. And he was responsible.

I've singlehandedly doomed the human race to a slow, inevitable, and dark demise.

Brandon walked forward, hearing the crunch of broken glass under the sole of his shoe. Feeling the air at waist height, he moved ahead until he felt the warm metal balcony railing. Garbo refused to let go of him. *Even if a miracle cure is discovered, I'll still be responsible for the deaths. Thousands... Hundreds of thousands... Or more... I'll be the worst mass murderer in history. No...*

Brandon stepped over the railing. He felt the gravel verge with his bare feet.

Garbo kept a firm grip on him, shifting her hands so she held him around his neck. "Marcus, what are you doing? Marcus?"

He leaned out from the rail and let go. He presumed Garbo would release him, but she clutched him desperately. His fall paused, but he was heavier than she was.

He pulled her over the railing and instinctively grabbed her.

Brandon tumbled the fifty stories to his death, surrounded by Garbo's scream.

* * *

The aide General Wachowsky had promised turned out to be an attractive Air Force captain named Tyler. She was tall, only three inches shorter than him, slender, and carried herself with confidence. Captain Erica Tyler was also black, and he thought her brown eyes were incredible. Tyler had arrived with three thick-ring binders and a series of loose file folders all stamped with various security classifications. Smith escorted her to a briefing room that had a clear glass wall facing the operations center, letting him keep an eye on the room and listen to the chatter coming over the ceiling speakers while they spoke. There was much less than normal. All civilian aircraft had landed, and only the odd high-priority military flight still remained airborne.

She'd methodically and professionally taken him through most of the material she'd brought, bringing him up to speed on recent intelligence and procedures he needed to know as the acting commanding officer of NORAD. There was a lot to digest. Smith had already used half of a notepad taking notes, and his pen moving continuously.

"Per the continuity of government plan, the president and cabinet are at Site MW, while the vice president is with the joint chiefs at Site R. Most members of Congress were in their home states due to the Independence Day holiday. Those in DC have assembled at Site E, but some congressional members from the western states elected to go to Site D, as it's closer."

Smith nodded. That was straightforward and exactly how they had planned it. The leadership of the United States was safe and secure in several underground bunkers. Smith glanced at the briefing agenda she had given him earlier. "All right. What's next, strategic assets?"

"Yes, Colonel. No navy ballistic missile submarines currently deployed have any issues with their sight. They've been ordered to remain at sea as long as possible and should be able to carry out their mission for up to four months in some cases. Minuteman ballistic missile silos are also being crewed by the same men who were on duty at the time of the light show. Carrier groups at sea report many of their people saw the fireworks. Those who didn't were either below decks at duty stations or sleeping. However, most of their deck crew, pilots, and senior bridge officers were affected. Their combat effectiveness is rated at between ten to twenty percent of normal. The aircraft carrier *Theodore Roosevelt* is off the Libyan coast and is currently being captained by a lieutenant, as she's the only officer who can see."

Smith rubbed his temple. "Damn, any good news?"

"I'm sorry sir, but that *was* the good news. If you turn the page in your briefing notes, you'll see our military units report between ninety-three to ninety-eight percent of their personnel to be combat ineffective. Most fighter squadrons are down from twenty-four planes to one or two at best, with bare bones maintenance crews. Several bomber wings of B-1s, B-2s and B-52s are completely blind. The army and special forces are essentially useless."

Smith shook his head and tapped his finger on the report. "When I attended the Air Command and Staff College at Maxwell, we calculated casualties for a surprise nuclear attack. They were half what I see in front of me."

Tyler placed her hands in front of her, intertwining her fingers. "It isn't the best situation, sir. However, we can't give up hope of a cure."

Smith asked before thinking, "How did you avoid seeing the fireworks?"

"My best friend is getting married, and I went to her bachelorette the night of the third. I wasn't feeling well and went to bed early on the fourth. I regretted missing the show when I woke up, but now..." She shrugged slightly.

Smith realized he had drifted into personal territory, and that might be misunderstood. The Air Force took a hard line against harassment. He decided to return to the matter at hand. "I see Tinker is reporting only fifteen E-6Bs active..."

"You have a good eye for detail, sir. That's correct. One's in the Raytheon depot in Centennial, Colorado, finishing up an upgrade to its avionics. It is scheduled to return to duty later in the week, but—"

"Colonel Smith, report to operations immediately," came over the speakers.

Smith didn't hesitate and jogged out of the conference room. On the way to his desk, he could see several red inverted "V" shapes appear near over the ocean off the coast of Alaska.

"AOC, what do we have?" Smith asked.

The duty air operations controller said, "Sir, we have ninety-plus large airborne targets approaching the outer edge of the Alaskan ADIZ in formation. They'll pass into the interdiction zone in two minutes."

"Identification?" Smith asked.

"No transponders active, and specific airframe type can't be identified at this distance, but they're large. Given their speed, they could be bombers, commercial jets, or transport aircraft. Their current track will take them just to the north of Antones Island. There are no DVFR or IFR flight plans filed for that route."

The U.S. military was crippled, and now more than ninety aircraft were approaching Alaskan airspace. One unidentified aircraft without a flight plan could be a clerical error; ninety was an attack. As commanding officer of NORAD, it was his responsibility to stop it.

"What assets do we have to intercept?" Smith asked.

"Elmendorf reports three squadrons of F-22s aircraft serviceable. However, they're all grounded, as they're expecting to start losing their sight in twelve minutes."

This can't be coincidence. Smith looked over his shoulder and locked eyes with Captain Tyler, who remained looking out of the conference room he had just left. He pointed directly at Tyler and beckoned her with his index finger. He turned back to the room. "Get onto the Elmendorf CO. If he has any pilots that didn't see the fireworks last night, get them in the air, ASAP. I want those aircraft intercepted, identified, and turned around. Make sure their F-22s are carrying warshots."

"Yes, sir," the AOC responded.

Tyler appeared beside Smith. "Yes, Colonel?"

Smith pointed at the unoccupied desk beside him. "That's your spot. You're now my aide. I want you in on all communications. I'm not fully up to speed on the background details and need your input. Let me know if I miss anything relevant as we go along. You're going to be my conscience, sanity check, and devil's advocate for the near future, so get comfortable."

The AOC announced, "Aircraft have just entered the Alaskan Air Defense Interdiction Zone. They are not responding to radio calls on any frequency, including guard channels[15]."

Smith picked up the red phone handset on his desk. It was the first time he had ever used it beyond daily tests. He had the emergency code of the day memorized, but still looked it up to ensure no mistakes. There was too much riding on this call.

The phone was answered immediately. "Alert operator."

"Indigo. Indigo. Indigo. Get me the president."

* * *

Hurst was getting annoyed by the white noise hiss of the bunker air conditioning system when one of the phones on the president's desk rang with a distinctive descending trilling sound.

That was the hotline, used only in cases of crisis.

The president made it there in three rings. Hurst followed as quickly as he could, but he banged his knee on a coffee table. Hurst heard something crash to the floor. Hurst cursed under his breath at not being able to see as Calvin activated the speakerphone. "President Calvin."

"Sir, this is Colonel Smith. I'm the Watch Commander at NORAD. We have ninety-plus unidentified aircraft entering the Alaskan ADIZ. They are on course for Alaska."

Calvin asked, "Bombers?"

---

[15] Guard is short form for "Aircraft emergency frequency." Civilians use International Air Distress (IAD) or VHF Guard on 121.5 MHz. The military uses Military Air Distress (MAD) or UHF Guard on 243.0 MHz.

"It's possible, sir. Excuse me a moment; I'm being handed more information... Mister President, after analyzing their speed, altitude, flight, and radar profiles, we feel most of them are a mix of Boeing 747 and Airbus 303 airframes. We've detected two additional aircraft using radar frequencies consistent with KJ-2000 aircraft. Those are Chinese military aircraft, similar in size and capability to our own AWACS. We're also starting to see some slower aircraft coming into range. Roughly twenty additional aircraft lagging behind, slower and at a much lower altitude. We assess those as heavy military transports."

Something concerned Hurst. "Colonel Smith, this is National Security Advisor Keith Hurst. Two questions: are we sure these are Chinese forces, and what do we have in Alaska to stop them?"

"Sir, the radar signatures are unique to the KJ-2000, and only China has those airframes. They are high-value military aircraft. We're launching three F-22s from Elmendorf. They're fully loaded with six AMRAAM and two sidewinder missiles each."

Hurst thought that number was unusually low. "Only three fighters?"

"Yes, sir. They're the only pilots who did not see the fireworks. The rest of the aircrews at Elmendorf are going to lose their sight within the next five to ten minutes. Even if we launch additional aircraft, they'd be blind well before encountering the incoming force. Sir, this has to be an invasion. The route, timing, and numbers of aircraft suggest a strong military force, plus they're arriving minutes after the blindness is taking effect in that area."

"I concur," Calvin said. "Send whatever forces you can to intercept the incoming aircraft and warn them off. Shoot them down if they do not comply. I'm also ordering DEFCON Two nationwide. If this is an invasion, you need to make them pay for every inch, Colonel Smith."

"Yes, sir."

Hurst said, "Colonel Smith, keep this line open. Feed us additional information as it arrives."

"Understood, sir."

* * *

Major Pheobe Lemmon looked down at the deep blue waters of Bristol Bay, just off the Alaskan coast, from forty thousand feet altitude. Her speed held constant at one and a half times the speed of sound. The efficient design of her F-22, a pair of powerful Pratt & Whitney engines, and internal weapon bays for minimal air resistance meant she could travel that fast without using afterburners. She glanced left and right, making sure the two other F-22 Raptor fighters were still with her. Of the two regular and one reserve F-22 squadrons at Elmendorf, they were the only three pilots who didn't see the fireworks last evening. They had all been on duty in the base operations bunker the previous evening, as squadron liaisons. The rest of the squadron pilots were either on duty or raving it up in a huge party at the officers' mess, celebrating Independence Day.

Of the three, Lemmon, from the 90th fighter squadron, was the senior officer and put in charge of the interception force. Captain Richard "Beans" Douglas of the 525th fighter squadron flew to her right, while First Lieutenant Tom "Scar" Agar of the 477th reserve fighter group was to her left.

Lemmon had initially regretted not being able to attend the July Fourth party at the mess. She had worked hard to get her wings and win respect from the male majority of pilots in her squadron. She liked to be part of squadron events and have a good time on her time off. However, that regret had changed quickly when the fireworks were blamed as the cause of the blindness wave sweeping the globe. If she'd partied with the rest, she'd be in the base gym lying on a cot with the rest of her squadron mates, waiting for the darkness to descend. Instead, she was leading the first strike against what was briefed as a Chinese invasion force.

The last time the United States was invaded, in 1814, English troops burned down the White House. Lemmon assured herself nothing like that would happen on her watch.

A voice came over her headset. Lemmon was in charge, so they used her squadron call sign, Dice. "Dice zero-one, Top Rock. Niner-zero plus heavy bogies, flight level three-two, distance one-two-zero, speed four-eight-five. Intercept course two-six-five."

Top Rock was the call sign for the Elmendorf NORAD intercept controller. Lemmon didn't acknowledge the instructions. Transmitting would reveal her location. Her F-22 was in stealth mode; any electronic system on her aircraft that could transmit was on standby.

She could still receive information, though. On a square screen in front of her, a plot of the incoming aircraft updated. A satellite receiver downloaded almost real-time information, updated by the Top Rock controller. Ninety "heavy" aircraft—over 255,000 pounds apiece—were flying at thirty-two thousand feet. Her optimum intercept course was 265 degrees.

She nudged her stick slightly to the right to put the heading on her heads-up display onto "265." She smiled behind the O_2 mask covering her lower face. She had no problem shooting down unarmed transports. They were foreign invaders and—

Lemmon's electronic warfare suite generated a warning tone and flashing light on the instrument panel. One of the KJ-2000 AWACS phased array radars had just swept her aircraft.

She was unconcerned. In exercises, even American AWACS could not see the stealthy F-22s outside of a forty-mile radius, and they were still a hundred and ten miles away from the Chinese.

A second beep came over her headphones. Lemmon wiggled her butt and shoulders into her seat and tightened her harness straps even tighter. She gave a hand sign to her wingmen to activate weapons. *Time to go hunting.*

A solid tone sounded in her headphones indicating the enemy AWACS had locked radar onto her. Wide-eyed in astonishment, she keyed his radio, "Dice flight—"

An orange fireball caught her attention off her left wing. Captain Douglas's F-22 came apart and fell in a long black arc. There was no chute. Lemmon hit her transmit button and jerked her flight controls hard to maneuver out of the path of any weapons coming her way. She checked Agar's aircraft. "Scar, take evasive—"

A fireball erupted under Agar's dual engine exhaust, causing the aircraft to tumble. A wing cracked off as the back end came up, just before Agar's F-22 exploded.

A white cylinder passed within inches of Lemmon's canopy as she continued to fly her fighter in random directions. She activated her AN/APG-77 radar to scan the skies around her. A fast-moving shape caught her peripheral vision. She turned toward it and spotted a gray shape against a white cloud above her. The silhouette looked just like her own F-22.

There's not supposed to be any other U.S. aircraft out here. Who the hell is that?

The fighter turned, and she saw the single red star on the aircraft's vertical stabilizer. *The Chinese have a stealth fighter in development, the Chengdu J-20, but there were only supposed to be two in existence.* She pulled back on her flight stick and brought up her weapon display. *Time for payback.*

Without warning, several large bullet holes peppered Lemmon's Perspex canopy. Her eyes registered the damage for the briefest of moments before the material shattered and the right side of her canopy blew off into the sky. Even with her helmet visor down, the wind buffeted her.

Several alarm tones sounded in her ears. Both engine fire lights were lit, main hydraulic pressure was falling quickly, and her flight controls were getting sluggish.

The aircraft was doomed. Lemmon needed to eject, but not before she warned people. She deployed air brakes to slow the aircraft speed. That would give her a chance to survive ejection. "Top Rock, Dice zero-one. Flight was ambushed by

Chinese stealth fighters. Chinese AWAC radar locked onto us at one-one-zero miles. All Dice aircraft are lost. Ejecting, ejecting, ejecting."

Lemmon pulled the ejection handle. Her harness yanked her body and legs back against the seat a millisecond before the seat exploded upwards.

The various alarm tones stopped, and all she could hear was the sound of air rushing around her.

A massive jerk took her by surprise. *Dammit, that hurts.* The seat fell away, and she found herself floating under a canopy of nylon. Still wearing her O_2 mask, Lemmon looked down at the white-capped waves below. She had a small raft and survival gear, but she knew she was already dead. The water temperature would be forty-five degrees Fahrenheit, and the Coast Guard was just as affected by the blindness as the military. She looked up to see four J-20 fighters forming up and flying east. Her hands clenched into angry fists. *Bastards.*

* * *

Smith sat up straight when he heard "Crystal Palace, Top Rock" come over the room speakers.

Colonel Smith keyed his desk microphone. "Top Rock, this is Crystal Palace."

"Crystal Palace, Top Rock. Be advised we have no other air assets available to intercept the bogies. Our surface-to-air missile crews are all blind. Army ground troops are deployed, but there are very few who can fight. Better start praying for us. The first aircraft will be here in fifteen minutes. We'll keep this channel open as long as possible."

"Roger, Top Rock." Smith released the microphone key and turned to update Keith Hurst, who was waiting on the other end of the hotline for updates. When done, he turned to Captain Tyler. "What's their play?"

"Sir?" She looked puzzled.

Smith pointed to the map on the displays at the front of the room. "The Chinese—what's their goal? A hundred twenty aircraft sounds like a lot, but even a 747 can only carry five or six hundred troops. Simple arithmetic tells me that's two or three divisions of soldiers."

Tyler thought that over. "China is hungry for fuel just like any developing nation. Alaska has rich oil and gas reserves, plus gold, silver, zinc and copper. If everyone is blind, then three divisions are more than enough to hold that territory."

Smith frowned. "If everyone is blind, a single division could secure all of Alaska. Why are they bringing three? I'm getting the feeling this is just the opening act. The Chinese think strategically and long term, so what's their end game? If we can understand what they're after, we can deny it to them, or at least try." Smith sat bolt upright and shouted, "Noel, what's the latest on the ships in Qingdao?"

"One moment, Colonel. I need to access the latest imagery in the database," Noel responded.

While waiting, Smith continued where he left off with Tyler. "If Alaska is their goal, then they'll stop there. If they keep coming further east then we know they have grander schemes."

Noel came over with some overhead images. He laid them out on the desk in front of Smith. "They're at sea. The last pass by one of our IKON satellites shows Qingdao harbor is empty. This photo shows a large group of container ships and RoRos here, about sixty nautical miles out, on course for the Pacific. Looks like they are traveling together. Convoy formation, making roughly twenty knots."

"Bound for the west coast of the U.S.?" asked Smith.

"Possibly. They're certainly heading east, with a rough course that will end up somewhere between Seattle and Los Angeles at the moment. Ships can change direction, though, sir. They could be heading to the east side of North Korea."

"No, that was a bluff. If North Korea was their goal, there's no need to attack us. We're blind, and they know it—because they caused this, and they think we're helpless. It has to be them. Their rockets launched the fireworks. The Chinese planned and timed these ships leaving port around us going blind. Logically, those ships are part of their plan. We just need to figure out where they're going and why."

* * *

Major Lemmon had never been this cold in her life. She lay in an inflatable one-person raft, her flight suit dripping wet. She still wore her flight helmet to keep warm but had detached the O_2 mask.

She'd almost drowned after landing in the water. Cutting away tangled parachute cord had taken a lot more effort than it had in training. She supposed that was because the training was done in a calm, heated base pool with lifeguards, not bobbing up and down in frigid five-foot waves in the Pacific Ocean.

Now she drifted more than seventy miles away from the nearest point of land, with little hope of rescue. Above, she could see the contrails of dozens of large aircraft as they passed eastwards. She closed her eyes, letting the feeling of failure seep into her soul.

Lemmon cursed the Chinese and their sneak attack, knowing she could do nothing to change it. She'd been given the opportunity to stop them and failed. *They've developed some sort of radar system that can see past our stealth defenses.*

With her clothing soaking wet, she wouldn't last more than a couple of hours. Her teeth began to chatter, and shivers rippled through her.

"Ahoy!" came a man's distant voice. Lemmon sat up and looked over her shoulder. A large crab boat with fish pots all stacked on the main deck hove into view. Lemmon was speechless. "Ahoy! You all right?" cried a man standing at the rail.

Lemmon waved. "Yes, my fighter was shot down!"

"One moment! We'll get you aboard."

Lemmon could barely believe she was saved. The boat slowed and came up beside her.

She could smell the vessel as it approached. Years of fishing left it with a nose curling stench of diesel and rotting fish. One of the crew, dressed in yellow rain gear, thrust out a gaff, and Lemmon caught hold of it. Two men pulled her closer, while a third grabbed the rope around her raft. She was able to step up and several pairs of hands grabbed her arms to make sure she made it. They took her inside without hesitation and walked her down to the mess. The heat inside the boat hit her like a blast furnace. Her teeth seemed to chatter more in reaction.

The interior of the boat looked like something from the seventies. The faux dark wood paneling was warped and had suffered from years of abuse. Faded and creased centerfold models covered the walls behind the dining table.

Lemmon pulled off her flight helmet. Her damp red hair fell in front of her face. She flipped her head to get it up and off her eyes. It whacked against her back.

"Better strip off. We have a change of clothes for you. Here's a towel. I'm Bob, chief engineer. That's Mike, and the guy making you coffee is Wheezer. We saw your jet hit the water, then Wheezer saw your chute. Did you say you were shot down?"

She hesitated. Being surrounded by burly fishermen didn't encourage her to take her clothes off.

Bob seemed to realize the same thing. "Turn around lads, give her some privacy."

The men turned their backs on her. Lemmon unzipped her g-harness and flight suit, her chattering teeth affecting her speech. "I'm M-m-major Lemmon. Yes. I w-w-was shot down by a Chinese stealth f-f-fighter. There's a huge number of aircraft heading for Alaska."

"Don't take this the wrong way, but did you hit your head when you ejected?" Bob asked calmly.

Lemmon dropped her flight suit in a pile on the floor and began toweling off. "Look, I know this is hard to b-b-believe, but— Wait a sec. You guys can see. Did you see the fireworks last night?"

"No, the captain told us about them when we woke up. He said it was a huge show. We were in bed after fishing cod for thirty-two hours straight. Why?" Bob handed back some spare clothes. A white T-shirt, flannel shirt, and gray track pants.

Lemmon pulled on the track pants. They were three sizes too big, but she didn't care. She was feeling warmer already. "The fireworks are c-c-causing everyone to go blind around the world."

The three seamen all exchanged looks.

She pulled on the T-shirt. "You can turn around. Thanks."

Bob turned around to face her, looking worried. "The captain lost his sight about an hour ago. He's in his bunk. The first mate's in the wheelhouse. We're heading to Unalaska to get the captain to a hospital. We called the Coast Guard, but they didn't respond."

Lemmon pulled on the flannel shirt. Colin handed her a mug of coffee and she sat down at the round table. "Then you're lucky. The Chinese are taking advantage of this to invade Alaska. I was one of three pilots left that could still see. They blew us out of the sky, and now we're wide open." She took a sip of the strong brew.

"What can we do to help?" Bob asked.

She knew there were few citizens as patriotic as Alaskan fishermen. "Do you have a satellite phone? I need to call Elmendorf." Lemmon finished the hot coffee in three large gulps.

"Up in the wheelhouse. This way."

* * *

Inside the Cheyenne Mountain bunker, Colonel Smith spoke with Noel and Vinson at his desk. Captain Tyler sat beside him, looking through a stack of files. "I need you to reassess all intelligence received over the last forty-eight hours. The Chinese convinced us they were making moves into North Korea, and we know that is false. We're the targets, and everything has to be looked at again in that light."

Noel began saying something, but Captain Tyler suddenly spoke over him, "Colonel, when will Hawaii lose their sight?"

Smith turned to look at a world map before looking back. "Same time as Elmendorf. They're on the same latitude. Why?"

"I would bet there are Chinese aircraft heading there also."

Smith swiveled his chair to face her. "What's your reasoning behind that conclusion?"

"Elmendorf and Hawaii are midpoints. They'll be needed for refueling the shorter range aircraft. The 747s can make it to the continental U.S. in one hop, but the slower transports and AirBus airframes can't. They'll need to stop off and refuel. Hawaii is a lot further away from China than Alaska, so they just don't see them yet."

Smith looked back up at the world map. What she said made sense. Taking Elmendorf and the Hawaiian Islands would certainly make sense for follow-on forces. If they could set up a relay of aircraft, fifteen to twenty thousand additional troops could arrive in the U.S. every day.

He didn't have to think about that long before keying his microphone. "Top Rock, this is Crystal Palace. It's essential you blow up any fuel tanks, pipelines, and any support infrastructure for aircraft operations. It appears their intentions are to use your base to stage in more troops."

"Crystal Palace, Top Rock. The troops from Fort Richardson have already planted the charges, sir. All aircraft, transports, and runways are set to go at the same time. We're just waiting for them to land so we can give them a warm welcome."

Smith had to smile at Top Rock's bravado. "Good. The warmer the better." He turned to Tyler. "Call Hawaii and have them do the same. Whatever they can do to deny use of our facilities is to be given their highest priority."

"Yes, sir."

Smith unmuted the hot line. "Mister Hurst?"

"I'm here, Colonel. The president is listening, as well."

"We're getting a handle on their intentions. Chinese forces are inbound to Elmendorf AFB in Alaska. We strongly suspect that another group is heading to Hawaii, but that's currently unconfirmed. They can use those locations for refueling their shorter range aircraft and transports. We're also tracking a convoy of container ships heading to the west coast. Their intentions are unknown at this time—"

Tyler handed him a handwritten note as she held a telephone handset to her ear. It said simply, "Radar on Oahu sees eighteen-plus inbound aircraft. Landing in thirty minutes. No air intercept capability remains. Prepping explosives on all flight infrastructure now."

Smith nodded at her before returning his attention back to the call. "Sir, at least eighteen unidentified aircraft are moving toward our military bases on Oahu. They have no air defenses remaining. Ground forces are sabotaging any refueling capability—"

A worried voice came over the room speakers interrupting him. "Crystal Palace, Top Rock with an update. Chinese forces are on the ground. We blew the runway as they came in, but only one set of charges went off. Two thirds of runway 6/24 is still usable, roughly six thousand feet. Runway 16/34 is completely cratered and unusable. Two jets crashed on landing. I'm told they are AirBus airframes with China Air markings. Eight landed successfully. Their troops are moving this way. Our defenses are crumbling, sir. We're secure in the ops bunker, but we can't hold for long. Stand by, more reports coming in…"

Tyler hung up her phone and said quietly, "They've done everything they can do in Hawaii. Same situation as Elmendorf, limited defenses, and most people are blind—"

"Crystal Palace, Top Rock. Chinese troops have entered the base gym. They are bayoneting the blind we put in there. There's at least a thousand sightless military personnel in there being cared for by a half-dozen people who could see. They tried to surrender and were cut down. I could hear their screams over the phone."

Smith couldn't believe his ears. *Killing defenseless people for no reason?* "Top Rock, you've done what you can. Get out of there. Find a way to communicate back to us and get clear. We'll make sure they get payback for this."

"Crystal Palace, no can do, sir. We only have two people in the bunker who can see. Besides, they're all around us. It's too late. Be advised, the majority of the aircraft continued eastward. They're moving toward Canada and the U.S. with—" A loud explosion sounded over the radio link followed soon after by rapid machine gun fire. "Ops bunker has been breached! I can— I can hear Chinese voices yelling orders. They're getting in! No... No! I'm sorry, Crys— Uggghhh!" The radio link broke off.

Horrified at what he had heard, Smith had no idea what to say.

Moments passed.

"Colonel Smith, this is President Calvin."

"Yes, Mister President?"

"We heard everything. Pass on what just happened to all commands. Make sure they know the kind of enemy we are fighting and have everyone do what is necessary to protect the lives of our men and women in uniform. This is obviously a premeditated attack. They will pay for these atrocities, and we shall fight them at every step of the way."

* * *

<MSG START>
MSID:
05e8cfc05f4e58cbae731ae4a14b3f03d5dae12abe89651a43
eb9d61e30e24cb
TO: 21A, 22A, 23A2, 23C, 24A, 24D, 24G, 26B3,
28, 29N, 29Q, 32DD, CNO, FB13
PRI: FLASH (Z)
FROM: COMSUBPAC
SUBJ: COMSUBPAC HQ Violation

Global blindness pandemic continues to spread. All branches of American military degraded between ninety-three to ninety-five percent.

Troops of the People's Republic of China have landed in Alaska and Oahu. They are currently assaulting Pearl Harbor-Hickam, Wheeler AFB, MCBH, and COMSUBPAC HQ. Further communications from COMSUBPAC HQ to be disregarded. Crypto being destroyed on completion of this message. Units to remain at sea as long as practicable and await tasking from NCA[16].

We shall resist as long as possible.

May God bless you and keep you safe.

Jenkins, P.F. - Rear Adm. COMSUBPAC
<MSG ENDS>

Captain Eric Reid stood at the OOD station near the photonics station. He read the message through twice, searching desperately for the word "Exercise."

He looked up at his XO, who had just handed him the message form. "This sounds surreal."

Commander Harry Maddox nodded. "Another Pearl Harbor. It sounds like this blindness thing is rampant. Do we tell the crew?"

Normally, Reid would share details from the outside world, but this was much more complicated than an army versus navy football score. A lot of men on board had families. "Tell them about the Chinese attack but not the blindness. The submarine force is probably one of the few combat elements unaffected by this. I need them focused on their jobs. Fill in the Chief of the Boat, and he can break it to the crew. Tell him

---

[16] National Command Authority is the term used by the American military to collectively describe the legal authority of the president as commander-in-chief of the armed forces and the Secretary of Defense.

COMSUBPAC has gone dark due to a surprise Chinese assault. Knowing we're being attacked will motivate them, but we keep the rest between ourselves."

"Yes, sir." Maddox left to follow the orders.

Reid looked over the chart showing the patrol area he was to defend, but his thoughts were on his family, his own wife and children. Reid's first inclination was to drive the sub to the nearest piece of American shoreline, abandon ship, and get to them as fast as possible.

He couldn't imagine them blind, alone, and struggling to survive. *My family or my country? Which do I choose? If I choose my family and abandon ship, then the Chinese win. How long will we have together after that? Not long, I bet. No, the only way to protect them and everyone else's family is to stay here and do my duty.*

Reid hated to do it, but he shut them out of his mind. He had to; otherwise he wouldn't be capable of doing his job.

His patrol had only been at sea a few days. With proper rationing of food, they could stay out four months, maybe even five if they really cut back. Then what? He realized he was frowning deeply. With COMSUBPAC going dark due to the Chinese assault, who could he turn to for orders?

Chapter Ten
Orders from on High

Deep inside the Mount Weather bunker, while the phone to NORAD was momentarily muted, Keith Hurst said to President Calvin, "I don't see why you're hesitating, Jim. We're under attack, if we don't do something soon, we could be overrun."

"If the only option open to me is nuclear attack, then you should be glad I'm hesitant. Let's assume I give the order and launch nukes. What will the Chinese do?"

"Retaliate, more than likely. They'll send their own ballistic missiles our way," Hurst said immediately.

"Then we'll be blind and irradiated. How does that help?" Calvin asked simply.

Hurst had to feel for the edge of the couch to pull himself forward. "Jim, they've already hit us with weapons of mass destruction, and they're using the blindness to their advantage. Alaska and Hawaii have fallen, and their forces continue coming deeper into North America. Our troops are helpless and being killed. Today, it's in the hundreds. If we don't stop this, it'll be up in the thousands."

"I know, Keith, but I'm not willing to plunge the world into a nuclear winter at this time. It's possible we can find a cure, and then we hit back. Until then, we need to roll with the punches. Once I begin tossing nukes around, everyone loses. We're not completely out of options yet. At the moment things look desperate, I'll admit that. However, launching missiles sets the country back fifty to a hundred years."

"Are you considering surrender?"

"Never!" Carter responded immediately. "As long as I hold this office, we'll fight them. I'm surprised you'd think that of me."

Hurst closed his eyes and sighed deeply. "Sorry Jim. Really, I am. I just want this nightmare to end."

"We both do. Any word from Congress?"

"They're bickering amongst themselves. Not being able to see isn't hampering their abilities to argue. The house leaders are trying to assign blame and arguing in circles."

"No difference in their behavior, then," Calvin said sardonically.

* * *

Oscar Blake lay in his bed and waited until Doctor Krause replaced the bandage back on his eye. He thought she looked tired. Blake heard several people's voices coming from down the hall. They sounded upset and somewhat agitated.

"How's it looking, Doc?"

"You'll be fine, Mister Blake. Are you experiencing any headaches or pain?"

"No, I slept like a baby last night, and I could run a marathon now. What's with all the noise?"

"There's been some sort of… I don't know what to call it… phenomena? People began showing up unable to see. I've no idea why so many would be affected. The hospital's full, but more people keep arriving. We're running out of places to put them."

Blake sat up higher. "Wow, that sounds bad. Any idea what's causing it?"

"I've examined a few people, but I'll need to run some tests before I can make any conclusions. None of this is making any sense. Anyway, that's not your concern. You just rest, and you'll be out of here in a day or two. Try not to rub your eye in the meantime."

"Sure. Thanks, Doc."

* * *

Doctor Wiater stretched and took a brief break from his experiment preparation. He checked his wristwatch and was surprised to see it was after nine thirty, but none of his lab staff or interns had shown up for work. That was unprecedented. The four people who worked with him were young, but all had proven to be conscientious and reliable.

He tugged the ear buds from his ears, and the music disappeared. He was sure he would have heard the phone ring, even with the music player, but checked if anyone had left voicemail. The message light was unlit. Concerned, he picked up the telephone handset and dialed the home number of Charlie Moran, one of his post-docs. Wiater immediately heard an ascending three-note tone, followed by an uninterested female voice saying, "Your call cannot be completed, please try again later."

He dialed again and heard the same thing. Wiater looked up the number of Gwen Illis, a grad student who worked with him. Again, the three-tone message. *This is strange.* He stared at the receiver in his hand.

He shook his head. There had to be a logical reason why he couldn't place any calls, and he would simply have to wait until someone showed up. He replaced the handset, put the ear buds back in, and continued his experiment preparations.

* * *

At the Cheyenne Mountain NORAD bunker, things were quiet. Smith had already ordered the various communications links to Elmendorf cut and their crypto codes nullified. He didn't want the Chinese troops to have any insight into their operations. *Not that they need it. They are walking through a defense system that was once regarded as impassable without severe losses.* On the big screen in front of him, the travel arcs of several aircraft groups, plotted on the screen, looked like a curved fan.

The planes were spreading out to hit multiple targets across North America.

"Crystal Palace, Sleekness."

Sleekness was the call sign for the NORAD air controller for the western Canada region. Smith keyed his microphone. "Sleekness, Crystal Palace. Go ahead."

"One of our F-18s out of Cold Lake scored two hits on incoming heavies. Both aircraft were seen going down in flames."

Smith smiled. That was the first bit of good news in recent memory. Two felled aircraft meant a thousand fewer enemy troops to worry about. "Excellent news, Sleekness. Pass on congratulations to the pilot."

"Crystal Palace, the pilot was shot down. She mentioned fighters with no radar signature before she went off air. No word on her status at this time, and we have no more air assets to deploy."

That sobering news destroyed Smith's initial happiness. "Roger."

That was all he could say.

Captain Tyler handed him a file folder. "This is what we have on the J-20 Chinese stealth fighter, sir. It's a fifth-generation stealth fighter with an estimated range of twenty-one hundred miles. Performance is considered to be inferior to the F-22 Raptor, but it's also significantly cheaper. The Chinese can make five J-20s for the same price as one F-22 Raptor. They must be using tanker support to bring them this far."

Smith flipped through the file. "If we had a decent fighter screen, we could hit those tankers and remove their advantage... But we don't." He tossed the file onto his desk with exasperation and jutted his chin at the center screen. "Looks like I was wrong. They're not using the aircraft to secure west coast ports. Their tracks are taking them much further inland. So what's their plan? Where are they going? I know, I'm repeating myself. I'm sorry."

He rubbed his eyes. It had been a long day.

"Here, Colonel. I made you coffee. One of the airmen told me how you liked it." She handed him a porcelain mug.

"Thank you. That wasn't necessary, but I appreciate it." He took a sip, regarding her face. *One sugar with cream. Perfect.* The Air Force had strong policies against harassment, and he could face charges if he pursued Tyler and she objected. That didn't stop him from finding her attractive. Besides, even if he did want to get her attention, he needed to be careful—good-looking women had well-developed defenses from being hit on all the time. If he wanted to be successful, he'd need to do the unexpected and—

The Chinese are doing the unexpected. Smith sat bolt upright, spilling some coffee on his trousers, but he ignored the hot liquid and put the mug down. "Air Intercept Officer, can you project the tracks of the inbound aircraft? I want to see where they're heading."

"Yes, sir." On the front screen, the solid line tracks of where the aircraft had been extended with dotted lines showing their predicted paths.

He was right. Smith pointed to the screen, thinking out loud. "The different groups are going to North Bay, Washington DC, and Denver. Others are heading for U.S. Air Force bases: McChord, Peterson, Tinker, and Travis. They're doing an end run. Elmendorf had the NORAD bunker, while Hawaii coordinated the Pacific fleet. All the places they're heading to are command and control facilities. They're not attacking our military bases to fight us. They are trying to decapitate us by hitting command and control facilities."

Tyler said, "Some of those tracks are heading to DC—Andrews, specifically. The government will be in direct danger. Bunkers can't protect you if there are no troops keeping people away. They blew into the Elmendorf command bunker easily enough."

"You're right." Smith unmuted the red phone. "Mister President?"

"Yes, Colonel?" Calvin responded after a few seconds.

"Sir, we've analyzed their intentions. It appears they're trying to interdict our command and control. Their flight paths are taking them to all of the major bases relating to North American Defense and the execution of OPLAN 8044[17]. We feel anyone in sites D, E, MW, and R will be in danger."

"Are you certain, Colonel? These bunkers have been the backbone of our Continuity of Government plan for over fifty years. Now you're saying we need to abandon them, and I'm supposed to run away?"

Smith took a deep breath and steeled himself. "Sir, the sites were always supposed to be at the center of a multilayered defense. Aircraft interdiction zones, air force, and army units were supposed to stop or degrade any attacker well before they got to you. With the blindness pandemic, all those have been brushed aside. The ops bunker in Alaska lasted roughly twelve minutes after the Chinese landed. Site MW has heavier defenses. It might resist a day at most before it's breached. If we lose you, sir, we lose hope. They want us leaderless and uncoordinated for when their naval convoy arrives in twelve days."

Silence followed. Smith wondered if he had gone too far, but it was his job to speak his mind.

"Give us a moment to talk this over, colonel," the president said before the phone went silent again.

* * *

Keith Hurst muted the hot line to NORAD. "So Jim, what are you thinking?"

Calvin was silent for a long time.

---

[17] OPLAN 8044, formerly known as SIOP (Single Integrated Operational Plan) is the blueprint of various attack strategies for nuclear weapons. It would be the "playbook" used by the president to select an appropriate nuclear strike from a preset list of options.

While waiting for an answer, Hurst held his hand up in front of his face and tried to see his fingers. He urged himself to see, but his vision remained completely black. Something touched his nose. He jerked back in surprise before realizing it was his own thumb.

Calvin said, "We invested a lot of money in these bunkers to bring all of the communications together to run the country. If we leave, we'll have nothing."

"That's not true, Jim. Yes, we have all these high-tech electronics, but this country was run for sixty years before the telegraph was invented. We'll adapt. Hell, we'll set up a pony express if we have to. Colonel Smith was correct. If they're trying to topple the government, then we need to get you out of here to ride this storm out."

"Fine. Where do we go?"

"One moment. Agent Carter!" Hurst yelled toward the door.

He heard it open, and Carter asked, "Yes, sir?"

"Come in a moment. Shut the door. We need your input." Hurst heard his soft footsteps approach, amazed at how quickly he was adapting to the eternal blackness. "Agent Carter, Chinese troops are approaching the area, and we suspect they are going to try to capture the government. We need a place to hide the president. It has to be out of the way, secure, but reasonably close. They'll be searching for him, so he'll have to be out of sight and off the radar. We can't use any operational base or bunker.

"I actually know of a good location, sir. An old abandoned bunker in my hometown. I used to explore it when I was a teen. It still had power and lights, the last time I was in there. It's about a hundred and forty miles away in Pottstown. Given clear roads, we could get there in three hours or so."

Hurst thought that sounded fine. "Mister President, any objections?"

"I trust my protection detail. That sounds fine to me," Calvin said.

"Very well. Agent Carter, we'll need a car. We can't take the Beast. The limo would stand out too much."

"We have some plain black SUVs here we can use. We'll take two in case of trouble along the way. Then we'll have a backup."

Hurst agreed. "We'll need food, supplies, and water for at least a week. A cell phone, as well. I don't need to tell you that this information goes no further than you and your partner. No one needs to know where we are heading."

"Of course, sir. Is anyone else coming?"

There were a few others who could see, but in Hurst's opinion, the fewer people involved, the better. "No, just the four of us. We'll send those who can still see out in small groups. Maybe we can form a guerilla army in time."

"I'll make the arrangements and be back in a few minutes."

Hurst waited until Carter left. He stood to stretch his legs. "If Smith turns out to be wrong, we can always come back. We should warn the vice president and congressional bunker staff. Give them the chance to disperse, as well."

"Agreed. I'll call the V.P.," Calvin said.

"Okay, I need to find a bathroom, then I'll get onto the phone. Be right back."

* * *

Doctor Wiater finished his experiment setup. Once he double-checked everything was set correctly, he turned on the main initiator and walked away while checking his watch.

It was almost eleven o'clock.

He stopped in his tracks. None of his employees had shown up. Mystified, he peeled off his lab jacket and hung it on the peg near the door. He would grab an early lunch and while out, try to determine why no one had come into work.

Wiater went into the hall and locked the door to his lab behind him. He took the stairs and exited out of the stairwell at street level. The inch-thick metal fire door slammed closed behind him, and he stopped. The door slam was the only noise. East Jefferson should've been a busy street with traffic, buses, taxis, pedestrians, and the occasional horn toot from an impatient or frustrated driver.

He saw no moving cars or any people at all. A single piece of newspaper blew down the center of the road. Nothing else moved.

Where is everyone? This looks like the opening scene of a zombie movie. Why are there no cars?

He began walking toward 16th Avenue. A light breeze was rustling the trees by the road, but other than that, everything was still. Off in the distance, a dog barked once. That was the only sound he could discern. His foot touched the asphalt on 16th Street when he heard a heavy thud close behind him. He whipped around to see a body at the base of the medical center he had just left. He ran over and checked for a pulse, even though he knew there was nothing he could do.

The woman's light blue scrubs and clip-on ID card told him she was a nurse. He found no pulse and looked up. *She must have come off the roof, nine or ten stories up. A suicide or accident?* Wiater dialed 911 on his cell, but got a three-tone "All circuits are busy" response. He needed to find a policeman, and the Seattle Police Headquarters was just over the highway to the west. He could report the death and also get answers to his many questions. It would be less than a mile, and he was an avid walker, so he strode down East Jefferson.

Wiater looked up and down each block at every intersection. The few people moving were off in the distance, well north and south of him. They moved slowly, as if drunk. The faint, but obvious sound of a car alarm went off well behind him, he ignored it.

After walking four blocks and crossing 12th Avenue, he saw someone nearby—a teenager, no more than thirteen or fourteen years old, leaning up against a red brick wall. She had the look of living rough, which was not uncommon. A lot of homeless people lived in the area.

"Hello," he said gently.

"Who's that? Stay away!" Her voice sounded brittle. She warded him off with her left arm while looking to the left and right of him. Her other hand was tucked into her jean jacket pocket.

Is she drunk or high? She's not focusing on me, her pupils are dilated, and she's not acting right. Substance abuse or withdrawal symptoms? "My name is Edmund Wiater. I'm a doctor. What's wrong?" He moved closer.

"You're a doctor?" she asked.

"Yes." He moved right up to her to hear what she said better.

The fingertips of her left hand brushed his shirt. Her right fist came out of her jacket and thrust toward him. The tip of a stubby knife jabbed into his left bicep.

"Ow!" He backpedaled and easily avoided her subsequent attacks.

She wailed incoherently, slashing the air wildly. Wiater retreated to a safe distance to watch her. She didn't move toward him but kept swinging the knife wildly, making high-pitched noises with each stroke.

Wiater looked at his arm. He was bleeding—not badly, but he definitely needed stitches. Harborview Medical Center had an ER, and that was only two blocks away. He applied pressure to the wound with his palm, skirted the wild-eyed girl with the knife, and continued on.

* * *

Colonel Smith of NORAD was signing off another in an endless stream of update reports when Keith Hurst's voice came over the red phone. "Colonel Smith, am I on speakerphone?"

Smith dropped his pen onto the desk before leaning forward. "Yes, sir."

"I need to talk to you privately. Pick up the handset, please."

Smith lifted the red phone handset, which automatically cancelled the speakerphone function. He waved the people around him away. When they were clear, he said, "All right, it's just me on the line, and I'm alone."

"The president and I are heading to an undisclosed location. I'm going to give you a cell phone number we can be reached at. We'll turn it on every three hours for fifteen minutes starting at three PM, Eastern Time. This number is to be used for emergencies only, and you alone should know it. We're going to lay low until some sort of cure can be found. If the Chinese occupy us, your orders are to resist them to the best of your ability."

The president's voice quickly followed. "Colonel Smith, things are going to get much worse before they get better. As NORAD commanding officer, you are tasked to defend the North American continent. You'll need to conserve resources, be patient, and strike when only you have a strong advantage. Organize whatever opposition forces you can, and hopefully, we can emerge on the other side of this crisis."

Smith nodded. "I understand, Mister President. Mister Hurst, as you are leaving official communication channels, we'll need some form of authentication to know your orders are valid. At the start of any phone call, use a baseball reference. If your call does not start with that, I'll know you are compromised."

"Excellent idea, Colonel. You can use any star constellation. We'll be leaving here in a few minutes." Hurst finished the call by passing on the cell number.

Smith removed his watch, took a black permanent marker, and wrote the cell number on his skin. When he replaced the watch, the number was hidden under the band.

An incoming radio transmission came over the room speakers. "Crystal Palace, Ringmaster."

Ringmaster was the call sign for the Canadian NORAD headquarters in North Bay, Ontario. Smith keyed his microphone. "Ringmaster, Crystal Palace, go ahead."

"Crystal Palace, we have ten incoming hostile aircraft on final approach to the base. We have less than a dozen defenders who can see. I suspect we'll not be on the air for too much longer, so I have a favor to ask. When you get around to hitting back, kick 'em in the balls for us, eh?"

Smith chuckled. He normally wouldn't, as Ringmaster shouldn't use such language over the official Blue channels, but North Bay was probably about to suffer the same fate as Elmendorf. Smith responded, "Roger, Ringmaster, with pleasure."

"Crystal Palace, when they're on the ground, we'll be destroying all radios and crypto."

Smith recalled the president's orders. "Ringmaster, destroy the gear now. Take those people who can see and bug out with as many weapons and supplies as you can. Resist to the best of your ability, but do so only when you have the advantage. It may be weeks or even months before we can fight back effectively. Protect your people, and prepare to fight them in the long term."

"Understood, Crystal Palace. Ringmaster, signing off."

Smith swiveled around to face Captain Tyler at her desk. "Make sure the North Bay codes are invalidated immediately."

"Yes, sir." She picked up her telephone to follow the order. "Colonel?"

Smith turned to see the NRO analyst approaching. "Yes, Noel? What do you need?"

"I'm actually looking for permission to hack the NORAD network, sir."

Smith experienced a moment of incredulity, unsure he'd heard him properly. He indicated an empty chair nearby. "Come again?"

Noel sat. "I want to set up remote access into the NORAD network so we can get in from the outside world. I heard your bug out order to Ringmaster. If you intend to do the same when the Chinese get here, then having remote access to the systems will give us an advantage. I'll be able to access selected global resources, maybe the satellites, and even some low-grade communications, if necessary."

"What happens when they do get here and blow everything up?" Smith asked.

"I doubt they would destroy the systems. They want as much intelligence and technology as they can get their hands on. However, let's assume you're right, and they do blow it all up. We have a small server room in the back of the air conditioning plant, in a wiring closet. It's used for redundant data backups. Unless you know it's there, it's almost impossible to find. Each of those backup servers has access to all others. I want to put remote access software on those servers and punch a hole in the firewall so I can access it. I usually wouldn't even consider it, but..." He shrugged.

Smith hadn't had a lot of time to think ahead, and Noel was correct. They needed every advantage they could get. "All right. Get on it."

Noel left, leaving Smith to consider his future plans. *Unless we want to get slaughtered, we need to get away and hide somewhere off-site until we can find some sort of solution to the blindness.* Smith then ran his eyes over the people in the room. There were not that many, but the entire defense and subsequent future of the United States rested on their shoulders. *We should break up into smaller groups, to minimize detection and casualties. Of the twenty people in here, we can divide up into five groups of four each.* He checked the radar image showing the inbound aircraft. He had maybe an hour before the Chinese arrived. *Time to get organized.*

* * *

Doctor Wiater needed his free hand to maintain pressure on his wound so he used his shoulder to press through the outer frosted glass doors of the emergency room. Its spring hinges let him pass easily, and it swung closed as he passed.

Inside, he found at least eighty people quietly huddled on seats, sitting in corners on side tables, and on the floor against walls. Many were wrapped in blankets.

The room was deathly quiet. No one spoke or moved.

His first impression was they were all dead, but he quickly realized some were moving slightly. He made his way to the reception desk, stepping carefully over the various limbs in his way. There was no one behind the counter, so he turned and made his way into the treatment area. That section was almost as crowded.

A woman dressed in a white lab coat had her back to him. She had a stethoscope around her neck, below disheveled dirty blond shoulder-length hair. She was examining the eyes of an elderly woman, so doubtless either a doctor or nurse. He saw no other people working and made his way over to her.

He quietly waited behind her for her to finish the exam.

"Okay, Mrs. Gunderson. If you wait here a few minutes, I'll take you back to your daughter," the woman said.

She turned and did a double-take as she saw him. "Morning. Looks like you're having a bad day."

"Certainly a strange one," Wiater replied.

She moved her index finger in front of his face, and he tracked the motion with his eyes. "You can see? Then it looks like you're having a better day than most." Her eyes moved to his injury. "You're bleeding. Come over here and sit down."

"Thanks. A young girl stabbed me on the street and got me in the bicep. The bleeding is minimal, so I doubt she hit the brachial artery." Wiater stated.

She peeled back his sleeve to examine the wound. "Yes, it's a minor laceration, but you'll need a couple of stitches. Do you have medical training?" She pulled a nearby tray of instruments closer.

"Yes, I'm a geneticist from the Swedish Medical Center. My name's Edmund Wiater."

She rolled up his sleeve, exposing the injured area. "I've heard of you. I'm Linda Krause. Until this mess hit, I was an ophthalmologist."

"I saw everyone in the waiting room. There's almost no one in the streets. What's happening?"

Krause glanced at him and started cleaning the wound. "You mean you don't know? They say the fireworks last night caused some sort of blindness. The effects are being felt globally. The president addressed the nation and told everyone to stay home. They've cancelled all flights, public transport, and… Hold still. I'm going to apply a topical anesthetic. They're closing down the nuclear plants and all power infrastructure."

She cleaned the injured area of his arm thoroughly with what looked like an alcohol pad. It stung for a few seconds. Krause then misted the area with a small aerosol can before grabbing a suture needle.

Wiater hated needles. He looked away as she worked. "I missed the show. I was ill and went to bed early last night. That explains why my staff didn't come in this morning. Except for the girl who stabbed me, the only other person I saw up close was a nurse who jumped—or fell—off a rooftop."

Krause began stitching his wound. "The suicide rate has skyrocketed. We have half a dozen bodies in the morgue from this morning alone. There's another dozen upstairs we haven't had time to bring to the basement. Some people just can't handle being sightless. I suspect more people would kill themselves if they could find a way to do it. At least losing their sight makes it harder. This morning one of the women outside told me she'd swallowed a full bottle of pills. We pumped her stomach, but luckily, they were just laxatives."

He chuckled despite the pressure he felt on his arm. "So what's the cause?"

Krause shook her head. "I've examined quite a few victims, but it makes no sense."

"What did you find?" Wiater leaned forward, his curiosity piqued.

"It looks to be acute retinoblastoma."

The diagnosis surprised him, "That's typically a children's disease, and quite rare. Only one in fifteen thousand get it normally."

Krause picked up a pair of surgical scissors and snipped the knotted suture end off close to his skin. "I know, and it's baffling. Why would the world's population suddenly develop retinoblastoma from a fireworks show? There, all done. The stitches will dissolve in two weeks or so. Just keep the area clean."

"Thanks. Are you here alone?" The stitches looked to be even and professionally done. Wiater pulled his sleeve down.

"No, I was in surgery during the firework show with an anesthesiologist and three nurses. They're spread out around the hospital, doing what they can for existing patients and the blind. I should be trying to nail down the cause of this affliction, but I'm just too busy taking care of the day-to-day of keeping them alive and healthy."

Wiater stood. "Maybe I can help. You said you had a lot of suicides. Statistically, some have to be organ donors. I'll start by inspecting the inside of their retinas and confirm your retinoblastoma suspicion. Then I'll see if I can determine the cause."

Krause pushed the tray of instruments back out of the way. "That sounds great. We have labs in the basement, adjacent to the morgue, that you can use."

"I'll get started right away."

* * *

Hurst sat in the wide rear seat of a Chevrolet Suburban SUV. He knew they were out of the long tunnel when he felt a slight increase of temperature on his face. *That must be the sun.* Keith Hurst had to imagine the trees going by at the side of the road as they left the Mount Weather bunker complex. He felt guilty, leaving people behind that he had known and worked with to probably die, but he convinced himself he was doing the right thing.

Before departing, he had talked to several blind staff members and told them the president, in danger of being captured by the Chinese, was being taken to the Greenbrier

Resort Hotel[18] in West Virginia to hide. Hurst hated the lie, but they would be questioned. Some would eventually talk under duress.

He considered it a cruel trick to use the people staying behind. However, telling them the truth would not help, and telling them nothing would only result in more abuse from their captors. *At least they'll all tell the Chinese occupiers the same story, which should make it all the more believable.*

The president sat beside him but said nothing for most of the trip. The plan was for Agent Carter to drive them, following an identical SUV driven by his partner, Agent Nance. Carter told them the tinted windows would not allow anyone to see them. Hurst had to take his word for it.

"In some ways, I'm glad I can't see what's happening, Keith," President Calvin said suddenly. "If I never see again, then I'll remember the country when it was great, instead of seeing it in decline and ruin."

Hurst turned in the president's direction. "You'll see again. It's just a matter of time."

After a pause, Calvin said, "Agent Carter? We seem to be doing a lot of zigzagging."

From the front seat, Carter responded. "Yes, sir. There are a lot of abandoned cars and trucks on the road here. We're picking our way through the mess. It looks like the road opens up in about a hundred feet or so. We'll be on the highway in five minutes."

"Thank you," the president said.

* * *

Smith addressed the small crowd of Air Force personnel and civilian contractors gathered in the NORAD ops room. "All right, any more questions?" No one said anything. "Good, you

---

[18] One of the nation's premier resorts, an emergency Cold War fallout shelter for Congress was built under the west wing of the hotel in 1960. Called "Project Greek Island," it remained in use until 1992, when the *Washington Post* newspaper revealed the secret location.

all know the plan and what's at stake. Destroy any classified material before leaving. The Chinese landed at Peterson five minutes ago, so they'll be here soon. Dismissed, and good luck."

The group broke up into their designated teams. Noel, Vinson, and Captain Tyler remained with Smith. He had chosen them to go with him.

Smith didn't want to leave. He felt that he was abandoning his post, but he was in an untenable position. Besides, the president had ordered him to leave, so unless he wanted to surrender to the Chinese, he had to move. Peterson AFB was only eleven miles away. He was running out of time.

"Noel and Vinson will carry the food and water. I've got the laptop, map, and crypto codes. Captain Tyler will carry the reference files we'll need. We'll meet up at the main entrance in two minutes." They began to disperse. "Noel, did you get your special project done?"

Noel faced him. "Yes, Colonel. Everything's in place."

Smith simply nodded, and Noel walked off. Smith went into the men's bathroom and used the urinal. After washing his hands, he pressed his hands on either side of the washbasin and looked in the mirror. "I've looked better."

The faint sound of automatic weapons fire came to his ears. Smith ran for the main entrance. A small group of people milled about, looking confused and scared. Noel, Vinson, and Tyler were among them.

A small explosion sounded, reverberating on the hard surfaces of the chiseled granite and hurting his ears. The large twenty-five-ton outer and inner blast doors were closing.

A technical sergeant, standing at the controls, yelled out, "Stand back, sir. Chinese troops in the tunnel outside are shooting at anything that moves."

That quickly? They must have been tasked specifically to take this bunker and come straight here. There was a loud thump as the thick door closed, followed by the sound of hydraulic motors driving the eleven locking pistons into the surrounding walls.

Those doors would not stand forever. The inner blast door also closed completely and locked into place.

"How many got away, Tech Sergeant?" Smith asked the man operating the door controls.

"The shooting started a minute after the first group left, Colonel, so it's hard to say. The gunfire came from the north end of the tunnel, and that's the way most people went."

With the main entry tunnel compromised, there was only one other option. "Okay, we need to leave through the escape hatch. Tech sergeant, lead the way."

The technical sergeant walked down a series of steps leading to the engineering section. The rest followed. They had to pass through a series of metal hatches and maintenance areas. The noise of heavy pumps grated on his unprotected ears. Eventually they came to a gray concrete wall with a large red metal cover protruding high up the wall. A bright red steel platform and four-rung ladder stood just under the hatch.

The technical sergeant climbed the short ladder and unbolted the cover. While he waited, Smith did a head count. He came up short by a half-dozen people.

The tech sergeant removed the cover, reached in the hole, and flipped a switch. The inside of the tunnel lit up. He then looked inside and gave Smith a thumbs-up. "All clear, sir."

Smith ascended the ladder. He'd never seen the inside of the escape tunnel before. Several hundred feet long and only four feet in diameter with a level concrete bottom, it would require him to exit on his hands and knees.

He addressed the group. "I'll go first. Tech Sergeant, you'll be the last one in. Seal the hatch behind us as best as you can."

"Yes, sir. I have some wire I can use to hold it in place."

Smith entered the escape tunnel and began working his way to the other end.

Chapter Eleven
New Homes

Hurst felt the vehicle slow before the Suburban SUV began bouncing up and down slightly.

Agent Carter said from the driver's seat, "We're here, Mister President. I just need to get around the gate. Hold on. It's going to get a little bumpy."

"How does the city look?" Hurst asked.

"Like a ghost town, sir. I've only seen five people moving since we hit the city limits. None of them could see. There are lots of vehicles parked haphazardly in the streets. I can see smoke columns from a dozen fires over Pottstown. A couple of them look quite big. One sec—we're almost through."

Hurst felt a large bump, then smooth driving returned. The SUV parked soon after.

"We're here. Stay inside for a few minutes, please. We'll do a quick sweep of the area," Carter said before Hurst heard the driver door open then close.

Hurst turned to his friend. "Well Jim, I don't really like the look of the place, but I hear the schools are decent around here."

He was rewarded with a laugh. "Glad to see losing your sight hasn't dulled your brilliant wit."

"Nice to hear you laughing again. See, you're not such a miserable bastard after all." Hurst hoped he could keep Calvin's spirits raised. "How are you doing?"

"I'm actually feeling pretty good. Getting away from the job seems to be agreeing with me. The presidency looked so appealing when I was asked to run, but if I had only known…"

Hurst knew what he was referring to but wanted to keep him talking. "Known about what?"

"The constant demands on my time, the complete lack of any privacy, the politics of compromise, the endless criticism no matter what I do or don't do—that sort of thing. You know what I'm talking about. You get less sleep than me each night, keeping up with the state of the world." Calvin sighed. "If Vice President Kendall hadn't gone blind, I would've resigned without any reservations just to get away from the Oval Office."

Hurst twisted in his seat to face Calvin, placing his back against the inside of the door. "You're not a quitter and never have been, Jim, so forgive me if I find that hard to believe. I know you're the right president to lead us through this crisis, and we *will* get through it."

"Only time will tell. History—"

The driver's door opened, and Agent Carter said, "We're all set. The entry shaft to the bunker was unlocked. Mister Hurst, Agent Nance will take you, and I'll escort the president down the steps."

Hurst exited the vehicle. He heard the doors close, followed by the door locks engaging. The scent of grass and distant flowers seemed sharper than usual. Hurst held Agent Nance's elbow and walked a short distance. The warmth of the sun disappeared, and he knew he was inside. The feel of rough metal came through the soles of his shoes. Nance took his hand and placed it on a cool metal railing, then led him downstairs slowly while giving aural prompts. The temperature dropped at least twenty degrees as he descended. The fresh air of the outside world disappeared, and a musty, dank odor replaced it.

"Two more steps. Right turn, then more steps. Okay sir, you're down. We're going to go straight ahead," Nance said.

The floor sounded like gritty concrete to Hurst's ears. Each step echoed, and suggesting the space was quite large. "It sounds like a big room, Agent Nance."

"It is. I would guess this open area to be at least a hundred and twenty square feet. There are multiple columns and quite a bit of trash on the floor. That's why we're going so slowly. There are a few lights on, but most of the area is in shadow. Here we are. There's a chair in front of you. I'm going to leave you here a few seconds and scout out the surrounding rooms. The president's coming now."

Hurst felt ahead of him and found the plastic back of a chair. He sat down, hearing other footsteps approaching.

Agent Carter said, "Here's a chair, Mister President."

Chair legs scraping on the ground sounded. "Thank you," Calvin said.

Hurst was about to make a comment about the cool temperature when the sound of a door being forced open came to his ears.

Nance's voice echoed harshly off the walls. "Freeze! Federal Agent! Let me see your hands! Don't move!"

Scuffling noises followed.

"What's going on?" Calvin asked.

"Not sure, sir, but I have you covered." Carter replied before calling out, "Nance, talk to me!"

"I have a man in custody. Looks like he's been living here," Nance called back.

What the hell? This place is supposed to be abandoned.

"Take me over there, Agent Carter," Calvin said.

"Sir, we need to wait—"

"Take me over there—actually, bring both of us," he insisted.

A hand took Hurst by the arm, so he stood. The three men walked toward the area where the noise had come from.

Hurst felt himself getting warmer. "What do you have, Agent Nance?"

A strange man's voice sounded from ground level. "Why you harassing me? I ain't done anything."

Nance answered, "I went to check out the rooms and found him in here. He's got a stack of mattresses, some bookshelves, a small electric space heater, and even a laptop."

"Let him up, please," Calvin requested.

Hurst heard him being picked up.

Calvin softly asked, "What's your name?"

"David Ogden."

"Mister Ogden, my name is James Calvin."

Hurst heard Ogden take a sharp intake of breath. "It can't be. You're the president."

"Yes, sir, I am. Do you know what's happening to the rest of the country?"

"No, I was sleeping when he jumped me. You sort of lose track of time when you're down here."

Calvin filled Ogden in on what had been happening over the last twenty-four hours.

Ogden swore when he learned about the blindness. "Is that why you can't see?"

"Yes. This is Keith Hurst. He's my national security adviser. He's also blind. The two other men with me are Secret Service agents. Most of the nation's military is sightless, and Chinese troops are moving in to take over."

Agent Carter suddenly asked, "Where did you go to high school?"

"Pottstown High, just down the road. Why?"

"You were a year ahead of me. I remember you now. You did all the audiovisual work for the school theater group and football games."

"Yeah, I was always good with that stuff. Too bad I couldn't make a living at it. I've been out of work for a long time. I lost my house in a fire a year ago. No insurance, so I was homeless for a month before I moved down here. I thought being forced to live here was hard luck until you arrived. Now it looks like it's the best thing that could've possibly happened."

"Why come down here?" Calvin asked.

"I found this place by accident when wandering around town one day." Ogden sounded proud of himself. "I got curious and found a way in through the secondary entrance. Oh, that reminds me—don't go up the stairs into the main building. There's a big-ass alarm set that will wake all of Montgomery County if you go up there. Anyway, when I lost my house, I had nowhere to go, so I came here. Luckily, the electricity was on, and I hooked up a few things to get comfortable. Look, I don't have much, but I'm happy to share."

"Thanks. Agent Carter, can I have a word?" Calvin asked.

Hurst heard them move off, so he took over the conversation. "That space heater is a good idea, Mister Ogden. It's pretty dank out in the main part of the bunker."

"This is the upper level. The lower level has a foot or so of fetid water, so there's a lot of mold. When the door to my room is closed, the heater keeps most of it away. The rest I was able to wash off the walls with some bleach. It's a constant sixty Fahrenheit in the bunker, summer or winter. That heater takes the edge off. It gets pretty boring down here, but I do have my books, music on the laptop, and the Internet."

That surprised Hurst. "How do you get Internet in the middle of a concrete bunker?"

"It wasn't easy. I had to drop some cable down one of the vent stacks, and then put a wireless router inside one of the vents outside so it couldn't be seen. I pick up the free hospital wireless network next door pretty well."

Calvin returned, saying, "Mister Ogden, Agent Carter is willing to vouch for you, so if you don't mind sharing as you said, we'd be happy to join you."

"Sure. Can you take the handcuffs off now?"

The president said, "I'm sorry, sir. I can't see. I didn't realize you were wearing them. Agent Nance, would you release him, please?"

* * *

It took some time for Colonel Smith to get the thick exterior door at the other end of the escape tunnel open. The door locking mechanism had been greased, but it hadn't been used for some time, and it was stiff. Smith ended up kicking the release latch with his heel.

Green forest and fresh air appeared. Smith was the first out. He slowly poked his head over the doorsill, expecting a rifle round at any time, but he heard only the sounds of the forest.

He exited and waved the others out. He counted eleven people before the tech sergeant appeared. "I'm the last one, Colonel."

"Help me close the door." The door weighed several hundred pounds and took considerable effort to move. Together, Smith and the enlisted man forced the spring-hinged door closed with a deep *thunk*. Painted a dark gray color, the door blended into the granite mountainside. There was no exterior handle and no going back.

Smith had hunted deer and knew sound carried a long way in the forest. He lowered his voice. "Okay, everyone, you know the plan. Split up, and good luck. Noel, Tyler, and Vinson, you're with me."

"Sir?" a voice asked quietly.

Smith turned to see the technical sergeant.

He raised his palms skyward. "Sir, I don't know where to go."

Smith checked his name tag. "Okay, you're with us, Folsom. The other teams are moving away from this area. We're going to skirt north then turn to get in a position to view Peterson air base. We need to establish how many troops they have on the ground and get a handle on their intentions. It'll be dark in a few hours, so I want to be out of the forest before then. How well do you know the area?"

"Very well, sir. I helped engineers do some survey work when I was first assigned here, and we walked all the trails up here. I can lead the way," Folsom said confidently.

"You're on point. Everyone else, follow as quietly as you can. No talking," Smith ordered. "Sound carries a long way in the woods."

Folsom turned onto an uphill trail, and the rest followed. A typical July day presented them with sunshine and hot temperatures. Before long, Smith was perspiring freely. He'd left his uniform jacket hanging on the back of his chair in the ops room, so his dress shirt stuck to his sweaty torso. He undid his tie and pocketed it. Folsom led the group into a grove of trees. The shade helped cool him off.

The group's clothing stood out in the green forest. The civilians wore light shirts and ties with long trousers, while only Folsom wore camouflage fatigues. Smith heard something behind him—Captain Tyler was stripping off her blue dress uniform jacket. She gave him a brief closed-lip smile and he nodded in response before turning back to the trail.

After an hour of travel, Folsom crouched down and waved Smith forward. He edged carefully to the head of the column, then he knelt down beside Folsom to look at what he was pointing at.

The vantage point looked down on the main tunnel entrance of the NORAD bunker, a half mile away. A dozen Chinese troops in plain green uniforms guarded the perimeter as another dozen or so worked inside the fence line.

They were bringing bodies out of the tunnel and stacking them outside.

Smith felt disgust at the sight. He'd worked beside those people every day, and to see them treated in such a manner turned his stomach. One of the troops piling them up suddenly jumped back. Another soldier with a rifle ran over and drove his bayonet into the body pile.

They found someone alive. Smith flushed with anger as Folsom whispered between clenched teeth, "We're going to get the bastards for that, I hope, sir."

"Count on it, Tech Sergeant. Count on it," Smith said in a low voice meant for Folsom alone.

"Okay, let's keep moving. Stay low." Smith waved the small group forward while signaling that they needed to stay down.

The ground rumbled, and a sharp explosion came to his ears from the direction of the tunnel entrance. He looked back to see debris and smoke coming from the tunnel mouth. *They're trying to blast their way into the bunker.*

* * *

After the dust had cleared, Lieutenant General Lam walked into the tunnel mouth leading to the Cheyenne bunker entrance. He was keen to get into the bunker and establish his headquarters there.

He was amazed to see how little damage their explosives had caused to the granite. He screamed for the officer in charge of the engineers. "Major Poh!"

The short, squat man ran up to him and saluted. "Comrade Lieuten—"

Lam had no time for niceties. "We need to get in that bunker as soon as possible. You are holding up the entire operation!"

Poh stammered, "Sir, the shaped charges we planned to use were on an aircraft that was shot down. We are forced to use regular plastic explosive, which—"

"You shall not fail me. If you're not inside that bunker within an hour, I will have you shot. Go!"

Poh saluted, then ran from Lam with absolute desperation on his face.

Lam looked up the long tunnel. When he had opened his orders on the aircraft, his eyes had doubled in size. He had been expecting North Korea or Taiwan. Attacking the United States had seemed like a dream; the blindness warheads, fantasy. But the unopposed landing at the Peterson air base verified the truth of the matter.

His orders were to capture all command and control centers of the U.S. military, and this bunker needed to be occupied whether they had the right explosives or not. General

Wen had warned him about failure. Lam would not be one of the ones put up against the wall for not achieving his objectives.

* * *

Captain Eric Reid liked to walk the entire length of the submarine daily. Not only did he have a chance to make sure everything was shipshape, it allowed him to interact with the crew briefly. Chief of the Boat Duggan followed closely behind with a clipboard, to make notes on any issues. As they made their way through the compartments, he could feel the tension in the submarine.

During the workups and sea trials prior to this first deployment, he always received a smile or at least a genial nod from crew as he passed. Now, they looked at him with blank stares, if they looked at him at all. News of the Chinese assault on Pearl Harbor had been met with a mix of disbelief and anger.

Reid and Duggan made their way to the rear of the engine room. The motor drives and heavy equipment all rested on thick vibration-absorbing material to keep noise to a minimum. Reid pointed out a minor oil spot on the floor to Duggan, then moved forward into the maneuvering room. After entering the compartment, he let Duggan secure the heavy water-tight hatch behind them.

This section of the sub held several duty personnel monitoring the reactor and drive systems. Focused on their duties, they didn't look up when he entered. Kaplan, the lieutenant on duty, glanced up as Reid approached. Kaplan came closer to Reid. "Afternoon, Captain. May I have a word in private?"

Reid assumed he wanted to discuss his performance during the earlier torpedo drill and nodded. The two officers went to a corner while Chief Duggan carried on inspecting the area.

Kaplan darted nervous glances over his shoulder as he spoke. "Sir, I'm sorry about this, but I'm hearing some wild rumors circulating among the crew. They're saying that in addition to the Chinese invasion of Hawaii…"

"Yes, Mister Kaplan?"

"Well sir, it's said a wave of blindness is spreading globally, and they are worried about their families back home," Kaplan said quietly.

Reid should have been surprised, but submarines had a close-knit community, and secrets seldom lasted long. "And what did you tell them?"

Kaplan stiffened. "I told them to stop speculating and get back to their duties, sir."

"That's a good response. If you hear any further rumors of that type, repeat it," Reid said, trying to maintain a confident demeanor. *I should have known word would get out eventually.*

Kaplan looked as if he was about to say something further, but instead said, "Yes, sir."

Reid left Kaplan standing in the corner and, seeing nothing out of place in the compartment, moved his way forward.

* * *

Doctor Krause entered while making notes on a chart. "How are you feeling today, Mister Blake?"

She stopped and looked up to realize she was talking to an empty bed. She checked through the open door of the bathroom and didn't see him. Concerned, she went up the crowded hallway, looking for him.

She found him three rooms down. He had changed out of his gown and back into his street clothes, jeans and a red long-sleeved lumberjack shirt. He was giving a middle-aged woman in the corner a box of raisins. As he turned, she saw he had a cardboard flat of raisins, holding a dozen small boxes.

"Mister Blake, what are you doing?"

Blake faced her. She was glad to see he had not touched his bandage. "Helping as best as I can. Some of these people have not eaten in a day. I went down to the kitchen and grabbed some snacks."

"The staff can—"

"Doc, the staff is overwhelmed. Apart from you, I've only seen two others who can see. If I can take the load for them here, then they can focus on others who need the help most."

She tried to press her point. "You need to rest."

"I will, when these folks are taken care of. My eye is hurt, but I still have use of my hands and feet. I'm not doing much. When's the last time you slept?"

Krause took a half step back. She wasn't used to her patients inquiring after her well-being. "I'm fine. I had a couple of hours last night, but that's not the point. You need to go back to—"

"I *need* to help. Look, I'm a park ranger. When in the wilderness, you use whatever resources you have to survive. Right now, you need every able body who can see to keep these people going." He lowered his voice and moved closer. He was a good six inches taller than her, so she had to tilt her head up to maintain eye contact. She focused on his visible green eye. "This is a survival situation, Doc, and it's only going to get worse with time. There isn't a lot of food downstairs, and we're on the backup generators. They won't last forever."

Krause didn't have the strength to argue. If this had been a usual workday, she would order him back to bed and be fully justified in doing so. However, today was hardly typical. God had seemingly picked up the world, turned it over, and shaken hard. Everything was topsy-turvy, and she could see Blake wasn't straining himself. He was only carrying raisins to people who needed them. She thought that was, well, noble. Looking up into his good eye, she also thought his take-charge attitude to be quite appealing. "When you're done, you need to rest in your bed. Your eye needs time to heal."

"No problem, Doc." He smiled at her. Feeling a blush developing, she nodded and hurried away.

* * *

Colonel Smith thought having Folsom along to be a blessing as they descended the mountain. For the last hour in the forest, Smith had no idea where he was. There were no landmarks or references, and it looked like the same trail for miles. The only unnatural feature they passed was a chain link fence they had to climb over.

Folsom confidently led the group down the slope. Smith worried that the sun would set before they got out of the trees and that they'd have to overnight in the bush. Just as the sun was setting, Smith sighted a paved road beyond a grove of pine trees. The asphalt appeared relatively new, dark black with bright yellow road surface markings.

Folsom pointed out a large home across the paved road with a smile. "We're at the intersection of Willow Stone Heights and Broadlake View, sir. There's a gated community up to the left. We should be able to find a car there."

"Good job, Folsom. Lead on. Everyone, stay to the side of the road. If you hear anything approaching, run into the trees," Smith ordered.

They easily made their way up the road. Smith's issue oxford shoes were killing his feet and toes. The smooth soles were not designed for long hikes in the woods. As he turned the corner toward the gated community, he saw Folsom indicating a dark blue van parked crookedly outside the gate.

Folsom checked the vehicle. "It's open, and the keys are in it, sir."

The sun went down, plunging the area into dusk.

Folsom had jumped in and started the van up before Smith got there. The headlights came on, with the engine illuminating the gates and asphalt road.

"Kill the lights!" Smith ordered.

Folsom turned off the engine, and the van became quiet again.

Smith came up beside the driver's door, which Folsom had left open. "We can't drive with lights. They'll be seen for miles. See what you can do about keeping them off, Tech Sergeant."

"Yes, sir. Let me get the fuse box open." Folsom stepped out and reached under the dash.

Captain Tyler came up to him while slipping on her jacket. It had already started getting cooler. "Colonel, what's the plan? Where are we heading?"

Smith had a lot of time on the hill to think that far ahead. "About eight months ago, the landing gear of an air force trainer clipped the roof of a building on a turf farm just off the edge of the runway at the Peterson air base. I went out there as part of the accident inquiry. It's just outside the base fence line, and you can see most of the operational part of the airfield from there. It'll give us a good view to assess what they are up to."

The van started up, lights off, and Folsom was still smiling as he tapped the brake pedal. He'd even turned off the interior lights. "All set, sir. I think I know the place you're referring to. That's the turf farm on East Pikes Peak Avenue?"

Smith nodded. "That's right. You can drive. Take it slow, and if you see anything coming, just pull off the road, and we'll try to hide. How much fuel do you have?"

Folsom looked at the dash instruments. "Three quarters. Enough for three or four hundred miles if we take it easy, sir."

Smith opened the two side doors to the passenger compartment, then turned to the group. "Everyone get in."

Once inside, he slammed the doors and got into the passenger seat beside Folsom. The van began moving slowly down the hill, toward the main road.

* * *

The van entered the turf farm at a crawl. Smith felt tense. Had the Chinese seen them? He had seen how cruelly they treated the wounded and was sure prisoners would be treated the same way.

The van pulled up to the small single-story home, and Smith cracked open the door to alight.

Folsom stopped him. "One sec, sir. Let me turn the van around for a quick getaway. I'll park it by the Quonset hut so it's out of sight of the road as well."

Smith waited for him to do that and shut off the engine. "Keep quiet, everyone. Remember: no lights." He got out and closed his door as quietly as possible.

The others joined him and walked to the house. The front door was open. A quick search revealed no one was home.

The master bedroom and kitchen at the rear of the home faced the airfield, which was plainly visible over South Powers Boulevard. A living room, bathroom, and children's bedroom with twin beds were at the front. Smith found a trap door in the kitchen floor and descended on wooden steps into a small root cellar to find shelf after shelf of preserves and bottled fruits. There were also potatoes, onions, and several shelves of canned goods. There was enough food to feed them well for a month, at least.

On his way back up the stairs, he spotted a rectangular case hanging on a nail that looked familiar. He opened it to find a pair of field binoculars and a small guide to birds. He left the book but took the binoculars.

Smith reached the top of the stairs and closed the trap door behind him.

Folsom approached him. "Water is running, and we have power. Captain Tyler said she was taking a shower. I'll put the van inside the barn so it's out of sight."

Smith nodded. "Do it."

Noel walked into the kitchen from the living room.

"Noel, you and Vinson go around the house and unscrew the lights. Don't forget the outside bulbs. I don't want anyone turning on a light by accident. When you're done, get some rest. Folsom and I will take the first watch. You and Vinson take the kids' room, and Captain Tyler can have the couch. I'll wake you at four."

"Yes, Colonel. Mind if I check the television, sir? There might be something on the news." Noel pointed to the corner of the living room.

Smith looked at the large-screen TV resting on a wide black set of shelves. "Not until we get some garbage bags or blankets over the windows. We can't have any light revealing our position."

"Roger. I'll do that. There must be a linen cupboard around here somewhere," Noel said.

"I'll be in the kitchen." Smith sat at the kitchen table, facing the window. Placing his elbows on the table for stability, Smith peered through the binoculars at the distant airfield. Smoke columns rose in at least two dozen areas. Some of the largest were over the fuel tanks and flight line. Several buckled airframes still had visible flames. The few defenders had successfully torched any serviceable aircraft.

On the flight line was an eclectic mix of Chinese aircraft. There were two AWACs-style aircraft painted light gray, each with a large flat radome mounted above the fuselage. Nearby were six sleek fighter aircraft. They looked like the U.S. Air Force's F-22s, but they were slightly smaller and had red stars on the tail fins. *Chinese J-20 stealth fighters.*

Further down the flight line, three 747s with Chinese airline logos were parked in a line in front of the maintenance hangars. Their yellow inflatable emergency exit ramps had been deployed, probably to get the troops out of the aircraft, but the bright yellow rubber now flapped limply in the breeze.

Assuming five hundred troops per aircraft means fifteen hundred soldiers on the ground. He couldn't see any soldiers moving, but given the distance and time of night, that wasn't surprising. They were there; he was sure of that.

His gaze returned to the 747s. *Why are they not refueling them for a return trip?* That didn't made sense to him. *They look abandoned. No crew, the doors are wide open, and those exit ramps should have been stowed. Even if they're not going to fly back to China for more men, they should still be prepped for takeoff to be used inside the United States.* For a military mind, that was plain common sense.

He scanned the area again and noticed the black smoke columns... realized the defenders had also destroyed the airbase fuel supplies. *The aircraft had been abandoned because they couldn't be refueled. They're not going anywhere until the base facilities are repaired and new jet fuel is trucked in.*

A soft rustling behind him caught his attention. He turned to see Captain Tyler drying her hair with a towel on the kitchen threshold. The long pink bathrobe tied around her slender body contrasted wonderfully against her dark skin. "After that shower, I feel almost human again. Hiking through the woods in a uniform skirt and heels is not what I call a good time."

Smith smiled automatically. Realizing his smile might be misconstrued—she was a fellow air force officer, after all— Smith turned back to the binoculars. "The airbase is a mess. There are roughly fifteen hundred troops out there. I have the men unscrewing light bulbs and covering the windows to stop any light from showing. If you want to take the couch, I'll wake you at four to take over."

"No problem, Colonel."

A moving pair of lights caught his attention and he focused his binoculars on that area. "I see movement. Looks like a Humvee. There's someone standing in the back with a handheld spotlight scanning the fence line."

"That's strange. You'd think they'd be using night vision." Tyler came closer and placed her hand on his shoulder.

Smith assumed she did that to see out the window. He could smell her lilac-scented shampoo. He didn't want to face her. "They probably are, but a metal fence at night would be hard to see unless you were right beside it. The spotlight lets them check it a lot quicker, I bet. Wait— Someone's running."

The spotlight illuminated a figure on the inside of the fence line. He saw the flashes of automatic weapons fire coming from the Humvee before he heard it. The figure fell.

"They just shot someone?" Tyler asked.

"Looks like it. One of the defenders trying to get away." Smith watched the Humvee stop. The headlights blinded him and didn't let him see that area anymore. He dropped the binoculars and rubbed his eyes.

"I've never seen anyone— Why would they—" she stammered.

Smith looked up at her. "This is war, Captain. People are going to be killed. It's unfortunate, but unavoidable."

Smith returned his attention to the airfield. The Humvee drove back to one of the larger hangars and disappeared on the far side.

July 6th

Chapter Twelve
Disappointments

Doctor Krause got up after a two-hour rest on the break room couch. Even though she'd felt utterly exhausted, sleep would not come. Oscar Blake's words haunted her. What would they do when the food ran out and the generators died from lack of fuel? How would the people in the hospital—or, indeed, humanity—survive? Would this be a return to another dark age of ignorance and lawlessness, or just the end?

She got up and went into the adjoining bathroom. She settled for washing her face instead of taking a shower. When done, she checked that she looked presentable and headed for the stairwell. She needed to see how Doctor Wiater was progressing on his research.

After descending down the stairs into the basement, she turned up the hall to the laboratories. There she found Wiater hunched over a stereomicroscope, moving the focus knob in minute increments.

"Any luck?" she asked as she entered the room.

Wiater pulled away from the eyepieces and rubbed his face with his palms. "Yes. I'm just not sure if it's good or bad."

"What did you find?" Krause moved closer.

Wiater stood and indicated she should take his place on the stool. "Take a look." He went over to the coffee maker that was around the corner in the glass-enclosed room.

She sat and looked through the microscope. She recognized the tissue sample as a dissected retina. "Is this from one of the suicides?"

"Yes. A twenty-two-year-old, otherwise healthy woman," Wiater called back.

She examined the tissue through the microscope. "That's definitely retinoblastoma, but for that amount to grow this quickly... It's unprecedented." She looked up at him.

Wiater walked back from the coffee maker with two white mugs in his hands. "I concur. I've seen the same thing on samples from four other people. I work with cancer cells daily, but I've never seen such uncontrolled growth."

He handed her a mug before pulling up a stool and sitting beside her.

"You told me yesterday you were a geneticist, but what's your research specifically?" Krause asked before sipping the hot drink. Her nose wrinkled at the bitterness. It had to be the worst coffee she'd ever had.

Wiater sat up slightly. "Are you familiar with purple sea urchins?"

"I've heard of them, but nothing in depth," Krause replied.

"Sea urchin embryos are easy to work with in a lab environment. They have no shells, are almost transparent, and grow rapidly in simple seawater. If exogenous DNA is injected into urchin egg cytoplasm, it is taken up and expressed during future development."

Krause knew the words, but she had gone without sleep for too long and didn't quite get what he was saying. She restated what he said in simpler terms to reinforce it in her own mind. "Okay, so you can inject DNA from other species into urchins and they will use that foreign DNA in future developing cells."

Wiater nodded. "Correct. The second reason we use them is the purple sea urchin is the closest non-chordate animal relating to human DNA. We can use them to mirror experiments to our own genes."

"I follow you." She took another sip and almost shuddered. The coffee was horribly bitter, but she needed the caffeine.

"The urchin species has a resilient immune system," Wiater continued. "The innate immune gene repertoire for the purple sea urchin is about ten times more complex than that of humans. This may be why we seldom see cancerous growth in urchins, but that's pure speculation. I hope to utilize those immunity defenses to buoy up human resistance to disease and potentially retard cancer development."

"A cure for cancer? That's big if you can get it to work." She put the mug down, deciding she didn't need caffeine *that* badly.

Wiater shook his head. "I've been working on this for seven years, and while promising, there's still a long way to go."

Something occurred to her. She pointed at the tissue sample. "Wait, can this be used to fight the retinoblastoma? That's a type of cancer."

"No, we're still mired in the preclinical stage, running experiments to understand the process. We're nowhere near a cure today. If lucky, I might see it in my lifetime, but I doubt it. However, given my background, I may be able to identify the cause. Cancers are characterized by out-of-control cell growth. The reason people are losing their sight is the retinoblastoma is growing over their rods and cones like a blanket, blocking the light. Find the cause of that, and we might have a chance at stopping this."

Krause pointed up. "What about reversing it? We have a lot of people upstairs who need a cure."

"I know the stakes we're playing for, Doctor. I just need to make sure we don't make things worse." Wiater took a gulp from his coffee mug. "Mmm, perfect."

* * *

Keith Hurst slept remarkably well his first night in the bunker. Ogden and the two secret service agents had brought down sleeping bags and inflatable mattresses from the SUVs. They made space on the floor in Ogden's room for three beds. One for Hurst, one for Calvin, and the last for whichever secret service agent was not on duty at the time. Hurst's mattress was no more than an inch and a half thick when inflated, but its insulation was excellent. Even when directly on cool concrete, it made for a comfortable bed. The small space heater in the corner threw off enough heat to offset the coolness of the rest of the bunker. Last, no exterior noise penetrated, and he slept soundly.

On waking, the darkness and absolute quiet disoriented him. He felt a little panicked until he remembered he couldn't see. He lay back, closed his eyes, and took in several deep breaths to calm himself.

"You awake, Keith?" Calvin asked from beside him.

Hurst took a deep breath. "Yes, how'd you sleep?"

"Great until you started snoring. Agent Carter ran in with his weapon drawn. He thought you were trying to bring the bunker down on top of us."

Hurst twisted up on his elbow. "I'm sure I wasn't that bad."

"I had to kick you to get you to stop. I was afraid Chinese seismographs would detect us."

Hurst heard Calvin getting up. "Funny. You should be headlining in Vegas." He heard movement. "Where are you going?"

"This headliner needs to piss," Calvin said.

"I'll take you, sir," Agent Carter said from the opposite side of the room. Hurst heard him move over toward Calvin, and the pair left through the door.

A few moments later, a voice startled him. "Mister Hurst?"

"Who is that?" Hurst wasn't sure if that was Agent Nance. He hadn't heard Nance speak a lot and was not sure if that was his voice.

"David Ogden."

Hurst relaxed. "I'm sorry, Mister Ogden. I didn't realize you were here."

"You may as well call me David. Everyone does."

Hurst smiled. The time for formalities was well past. "I'm Keith. How can I help you?"

"Just wondered if you wanted some breakfast. I was going to make some oatmeal."

"That does sound good, thank you." Hurst sat up and felt his chin. He had quite a bit of stubble present. He decided to ignore it for now. He couldn't see to shave even if he wanted too. Unzipping himself from the sleeping bag, he stood up and felt around for his trousers. He eventually located them by touch on a wall.

Ogden said, "I need to get to the grocery store later today. I doubt there'll be a crowd, from what you were saying."

"The agents brought food. We're happy to share." Hurst slid on his pants.

"I need orange juice and vitamins. Living underground in these conditions, I need to keep my vitamin C and D levels up. Plus, we'll need some more toilet paper if there's going to be five of us."

"I can't argue with that," Hurst agreed while zipping his trousers. He recognized the aroma of brewing coffee.

From the sound of things, Ogden had started making the oatmeal. "Can I ask you something? If it's classified or something, I understand."

"Of course." Hurst began feeling his way to the opposite side of the room, where a table waited.

"What's the plan to get rid of the Chinese? Are we planning some sort of offensive or what?"

Hurst considered what he could say. He doubted Ogden was a Chinese spy, but the fewer things he knew, the less he could betray. "The Chinese have taken our military out of the fight. We still have subs at sea and a few other things, but we can't order them, as the Chinese have taken over our command and control. We can't talk—"

"You missed the chair back," Ogden said. "It's to your left."

Hurst felt the chair. He sat down. "Thanks. The first thing we need to do is find a cure for the blindness. With the majority of our combat forces and civilian population helpless, there's not a lot we can do."

"So without a cure, most people are basically screwed."

Hurst paused. His first inclination was to disagree, but newly blind people without someone to look after them were going to have issues. "It depends. Not everyone will be affected. Some people did retain their sight. We can only hope for the 'milk of human kindness' and hope the sighted take care of the blind in the short term."

"Hmmm," Ogden said, noncommittally.

"You disagree?" The smell of the coffee reminded Hurst of his own kitchen.

"I've been homeless for six months and see very little compassion, day to day. The vast majority of people walk by, pretending not to see me. There are a few—precious few— who stop to even talk. If this does go on for some time, then I expect to see as much bad as good among those left unaffected. Here's some coffee. There's a spoon inside. It has powdered creamer added, and there are sugar packets at the center of the table."

Hurst felt ahead of him and grabbed a packet. He carefully tore it open and, holding the rim of the mug, tipped it in. He stirred his coffee with the spoon.

Ogden asked, "Have you ever read *Macbeth*?"

"Years ago. Why do you ask?" Hurst placed the spoon on the table and took a sip. He thought it to be a reasonable cup of coffee, considering the conditions.

"We studied it in high school English class, and it always stuck with me. It's a violent play. Lots of murder, deceit, and war. Many of the characters end up dead by the end."

"Yes? Sorry, I don't follow your meaning," Hurst replied.

"As I recall, that's where the term 'milk of human kindness' originated. Here's your oatmeal. I put some strawberry jam on top for flavor."

* * *

Smith awoke suddenly, half-sitting up in alarm as someone shook his shoulder.

"Sorry, Colonel. You said you wanted to be woken at noon," Noel said.

Smith rolled onto his side and rubbed his eyes with the fingers of one hand. "Yes... Yes. Thanks."

Noel continued, "I found a bag of disposable razors in the bathroom cabinet. I'll leave some for you on the dresser."

Smith brought his fingers away from his face to see Noel had already left. It felt as if he had just fallen asleep seconds ago. He'd been so tired that he hadn't even bothered to get between the sheets and had lain on the comforter wearing his uniform.

He looked out the master bedroom window to find an overcast day. Low gray clouds with black bottoms threatened rain. Smith rolled out of bed, his feet landing on the cool wood floor. The house had a shower, and he intended to take one. He took one of the razors from the dresser.

The scent of brewed coffee came to his nose, and thoughts of a shower retreated slightly. He grabbed his oxfords and tied the shoes on, then he headed for the kitchen. He found Captain Tyler standing by the stove wearing a floral apron, placing bacon strips into a hot skillet. Noel and Folsom sat at the kitchen table. Folsom had the binoculars to his eyes and was scanning the airfield.

Smith poured himself some coffee from the coffee maker. "Any movement?"

Folsom answered. "There's irregular foot and vehicle patrols running on the inside of the fence line, but no air traffic at all. We think they're using the hangar on the end for their headquarters. Most of the traffic is centered there. We've heard distant explosions as well. The last was roughly forty-five minutes ago. No idea what that was. Nothing we could see, anyway."

"Where is Vinson? Sleeping?"

"No, Colonel. He's in the living room, accessing NORAD through my back door. He's trying to access the internal camera system at Cheyenne Mountain."

The toaster popped up, and Smith stepped over to Tyler.

"Morning, sir. Hungry?" she asked with a slight smile.

"Very. Is this for me?"

"Yes. Will be ready in five minutes." She pulled the two pieces of toast out and buttered them.

"Thanks. I appreciate it. I'll check in with Vinson and be right back." Smith took his coffee and walked into the living room.

Vinson sat on the couch with a laptop on the coffee table. He looked up as Smith entered. "Hey, Colonel. Just in time. I got access to the internal security cameras fifteen minutes ago."

Smith sat down beside him, setting his coffee mug on the table. On the screen were sixteen mini-videos with various camera angles, arranged in a grid and showing the bunker they had left the day before.

"Can you bring up the main ops room?" Smith requested.

Vinson pressed a few keys. "Sure. There you go."

The small image grew to full screen. The high-resolution image let Smith see the room in detail. "There's no one there!"

"They haven't been able to get in yet." Vinson had a broad smile.

Smith raised his eyebrows. "That's surprising. I knew the blast doors were tough, but you'd think they could get in after a day. They must have brought explosives with them."

"They did, sir. Here let me show you. Here's the camera showing the outer blast doors."

"The screen is black. There's nothing there," Smith observed.

"That's real time. I can rewind from these controls." Vinson rewound the image, and the outer blast doors appeared. Figures in green khaki scrambled around the door, which had several small holes blasted into it. The fast motion made them look comical.

Vinson slowed the playback to normal speed. "Okay, these guys are engineers. They wear plain green uniforms, where the airborne guys have the mottled pattern."

"Airborne? Not army?" That surprised Smith.

"Yes, sir. I was able to zoom in on an arm patch and identify it. They are members of the PLA 44th airborne division. See here, this older guy who looks pissed and is yelling at everyone? He's a lieutenant general, according to his collar insignia. Probably the commanding officer of 15th Airborne Corp. I don't have audio, but it's obvious he's not happy with the delay. Here, watch. General Hissypants screams at the engineers to use more explosives, which they put around the door to cut the locking pins. See the packets they're handling? Those look like regular plastic explosive bricks, but that door is made of hardened steel and designed to stand up to a nuclear blast wave. Why they're not using shaped charges, I'll never know. Here, let me fast-forward to the explosion... Okay, here. I memorized the time code. Three... Two... One... boom."

The area around the door erupted in an orange and black fireball. The camera went black a split second later. "Now let's shift to the interior entrance camera."

The camera changed, and he could see the interior of the blast door was unharmed.

"That's the back side of the second blast door, sir. They still have to get through that once they punch a hole in the outer door. Might take them another day, assuming they brought enough C-4. Might be easier for them to blast through the wall."

"Good. Glad to see something going our way, finally. Those must be the explosions the others are hearing. They'll get in eventually, but not quickly. When they do, let me know.

Don't swivel any of the cameras. We don't want them seeing camera movement. It's a small advantage, but one we might be able to use later." Smith took his coffee and got up to leave. The smell of bacon beckoned him.

"One more thing, sir. With your permission, I can try to access the cameras at the other sites."

Smith didn't hesitate. "Do it. Just keep a low profile."

"Yes, sir."

On his return to the kitchen, he found that Tyler had a toasted bacon sandwich waiting on a small plate.

She handed it to him. "There you are, sir." Much more quietly, she added, "I'm sorry about the way I acted last night." She walked off before he could respond.

Noel made space for him at the kitchen table and indicated he should sit. The bacon sandwich was the finest he'd ever had.

* * *

With Chief Duggan behind him, Reid conducted his daily submarine inspection, walking down a deck to the torpedo room. The scene before Reid looked typical. Several men were working around the area nicknamed the "dance floor." A large area that could have its layout changed to accommodate any mission the *John Warner* found herself on. The officer responsible for the space, a young lieutenant junior grade named Aceveds, came up to him with an eager smile. "Morning, Captain."

Reid nodded. "Morning. Anything to report?"

"No, sir. All's well. We're just doing routine maintenance on an ADCAP."

An enlisted man with his back to the three of them roughly tossed a pair of pliers aside, grabbed a vertical support with both hands, and muttered something.

Chief Duggan moved to the man's side. "Is there a problem, Petty Officer Wyatt?"

A pause followed where Wyatt didn't move, then he pushed himself off the support and whirled to face the chief. His voice rose as he talked. "Yeah, Chief, there's a problem. We're stuck in this tin can bobbing in the Pacific while my wife and infant daughter are blind and helpless at home. The Chinese are invading and probably on the mainland by now. We need to get back to port and make sure they are taken care of!"

Duggan had none of it. "Wyatt, you need to focus on the task in front of you and get that ADCAP functional. While we're on patrol, anything in the outside world is not your concern—"

Wyatt prodded Duggan's chest. "My family's health is not my concern? You can shove that torpedo up your ass, Chief! You selfish—"

Duggan floored him with a single quick punch.

One moment, Wyatt was ranting, and the next moment he was down, holding his cheek in one hand. Wyatt looked murderous.

Duggan turned to the other enlisted men in the compartment. "P.O. Wyatt is relieved from his duty and is to be confined to his bunk for the rest of the watch. Get him off the deck." He turned back to the captain. "Sir, may I have a word?"

Reid nodded, and the two men went up the stairs to the command center. "Let's step into the wardroom, Chief."

As soon as the door had been closed, Duggan said, while looking at the floor, "Sir, I'm sorry."

"Why? Everything that happened down there was Wyatt's fault. He shouldn't have touched you. That was assault, and you were within your rights to stop him. He's on the hook for insubordination and refusal to follow orders. You stopped him from facing more serious charges. He'll have to face a captain's mast for that."

"Yes, sir. It's just…" Duggan looked hesitant to speak further.

"Speak your mind. You're chief of the boat. I need to know your thoughts."

"Captain, Wyatt's a decent P.O. That's not typical of his behavior."

"That'll be taken into consideration, of course. However, he assaulted you and disobeyed orders in what could be considered wartime operations. The penalty for that is a lot more serious than normal."

"I'll go talk to him when he calms down and explain things, sir."

"No, you won't. You need to keep clear of him, otherwise it may complicate things. Talk to the senior chief in the torpedo room and have him do the talking. I don't want you interacting directly with him until captain's mast. The next one's scheduled for the day after tomorrow at zero eight hundred hours."

Duggan looked dubious but nodded. "Yes, sir."

"Dismissed, Chief."

* * *

General Secretary Gao leaned back into his chair at the head of the table, waiting for everyone to take their places. He brought the politburo meeting to order as the doors closed. "Gentlemen, I'm very proud of our men in uniform this day. All major goals—save one—have been achieved by the PLA airborne forces, and our plan is solidly on track. Casualties have been minimal, less than four percent, where we forecasted twenty to thirty. All major American government bunkers have been neutralized. Strategic command and control aircraft and facilities are under our control, including both Air Force One aircraft. We have their vice president, joint chiefs, and the vast majority of their Congress in custody. Only President Calvin eludes us, having run for his life. I'm assured his location is known, and troops are on route. His capture is imminent. In any event, he's been separated from any communications, and there's no hope remaining for him.

"Fighting on the ground has been brief and sporadic. The sheer mass of troops we deployed ensured short battles. In summation, the United States of America is no longer in existence. Today, we form the new eastern provinces of China."

Gouliang Jang said, "Positive results indeed. Were there any complications?"

Gao's smile faded. "Some, yes. Before the blindness took effect, many of their major power generation stations were turned off or significantly lowered in output. Their military units sabotaged fuel facilities and pipelines in Hawaii and Alaska, rendering them useless as midpoint refueling stations. We hoped to capture those facilities intact. Estimates run into weeks to correct this, if not months.

"Only ten aircraft have returned to China as a result. The rest are stranded in place until those repairs can be made. They are not needed in any event, as additional troops are seen as unnecessary, given our success to date."

Jang placed his elbows on the table while leaning forward. "Can the power plants be brought back up to produce electricity?"

Gao shook his head. "In the short term, no. There are so many plants, many with dissimilar designs. Oil, gas, hydro, nuclear, etc. We can't spare the engineers from our own infrastructure to work on them without crippling our own industries. This is an inconvenience only. The occupying forces arriving by ship will not require power. We can address those issues once they arrive."

Bohai Quishan said, "If I may, I would like to congratulate our general secretary and all at this table on the flawless execution of a fine and noble plan." There were several nods around the table. Quishan continued, "I do have concerns regarding President Calvin being free. Even though he is blind, he could be seen as a rallying point for a resistance."

Gao nodded slowly. "Yes. I share your concerns, of course. However, we are vigorously interrogating their senior government politicians and advisers. His location was easily determined, and the airborne are on the way to collect him. Besides, any resistance is doomed to fail. Few people are still capable of seeing, and when spotted, they'll be liquidated. The vast majority of the U.S. population will die of hunger before our ships even get there. The few remaining alive when our liberation forces arrive will be put down quickly."

Guoliang Jang leaned back in his chair. "As we now have vast new provinces at our disposal, we should discuss the establishment of provincial committees and potential names of candidates to run them."

Gao took a breath to respond, but Wei Sun spoke before he did, referencing a series of notes before him. "While I applaud the progress to date, the 'provinces' you refer to are still weakly controlled. Provinces need people to run the system and many workers to implement the directives of the party. At the moment, we have none.

"We discussed sending civilians once the ships carrying the troops returned, which is at least a month away. We still have the remaining foreign territories nearby to consider, as well. I suggest the appointment of a military governor to take care of the U.S. cleanup. Once the PLA troops arrive by ship and the situation has stabilized, we can then transport workers east and incorporate them under the existing provincial system at a more leisurely pace.

"New arrivals will need shelter, food, and fuel to achieve success. The military can establish stockpiles for those newly arrived workers. Naturally, we should only send stalwart members of the party east to minimize any political adventurism."

Shen tapped the table with his palm. "Yes! Well spoken, and a brilliant approach. As workers arrive, they can establish infrastructure and rebuild to our needs. Then, when enough progress has been made, we can designate official provinces and leadership, as we did in Tibet. The existing military campaign will transition naturally into the party taking responsibility over those areas."

The overall mood around the table was positive toward the idea, Gao saw. He had no objections, himself. "Very well. We shall consider that suggestion at our next meeting. I think that will be all for now, gentlemen. We shall stand adjourned."

Gao stayed seated as the meeting broke up.

Wei Sun looked pleased with himself. On the way out, Shen gave Sun a familiar pat on the shoulder. *Sun has intellect and a desire for power. He could decide to try to sit in my chair one day, unless I preempt him. Shen looks to be on good terms with Sun, so he must also be watched, to ensure they do not oppose me.*

* * *

Doctor Krause ran into Oscar Blake as he delivered another armload of food to the people in the waiting room. He didn't see her, and she watched him handing out the small cookie packets. *Taking the time to talk to each person in turn and even making them laugh where he can. What a lovely man.*

Blake turned suddenly. "Hey, Doc. You need me for something?" He strode up to her.

"No. I'm just going downstairs to see if Doctor Wiater has made any progress."

"Who's that? Oh, would you like some cookies?" He offered a single packet. It looked to be his last.

She was hungry and happily took the packet. "Thanks. He's a geneticist working in the lab downstairs. He may have an idea about the cause of all this."

"Mind if I tag along? Need to stretch my legs a bit."

"Of course." They turned and made for the stairwell. "I'll probably be able to take the bandage off your eye tomorrow. It should have healed enough by then," she said.

"Great news. Thanks." He gallantly held the door open for her, and she smiled at him as she went by.

She nibbled on a cookie as they walked to the lab. She found Doctor Wiater sitting with his eyes pressed against a stereomicroscope. She waited until he pulled back before asking, "Any progress, Doctor?"

Wiater turned. "Yes, I think so— Oh, good morning."

Krause indicated Blake with an open hand. "Doctor Wiater, this is Oscar Blake. He's the man I was operating on when the fireworks went off. Oscar, this is Doctor Wiater."

Blake and Wiater shook hands. Blake reached into a shirt pocket, "I have a packet of crackers and cheese if you're hungry, Doc."

Wiater grinned slightly and took the offered snack. "Good timing. I was about to look for something, thank you. Doctor Krause, I suspect I know what the cause is."

"Excellent. What have you learned?" she asked.

Wiater peeled the plastic cover open and began spreading cheese on a cracker. "I did an analysis of the eye tissue. Are you familiar with protein RB?"

She nodded. "Yes, it's a tumor suppressor protein in a gene that regulates cell division. When absent, it's a direct cause of retinoblastoma." For Blake's benefit, she added, "RB actually stands for retinoblastoma."

"Correct. The gene is called *RB1* and is found on chromosome thirteen. The incidence of normal retinoblastoma cancer is roughly one in fifteen thousand people and primarily affects children. In all of the tissue samples I checked, the RB protein is there, but dormant." He bit off a piece of cracker.

She nodded. "So to stop this, we just need to reanimate the RB protein?"

"That would stop further growth but not reverse the damage. People would still be blind. I need to find a mechanism that both kills the cancerous cells and reanimates the gene, and quickly." He took a bite of cracker.

Krause felt a little confusion. "Why the rush?"

"Unchecked, the cancer will continue to grow and spread along the optic nerve to the brain at a rapid rate. Normally, that process would take years, but given the accelerated rate of growth I'm seeing, if we don't solve this within three months, then everyone affected will probably die."

Blake took a half-step forward. "We have even less time than that, Doc."

"What do you mean, Mister Blake?" Wiater asked with a frown.

"Simple practicality. The people upstairs need food, and we're running out. There may be a day, maybe two days' food left in the hospital kitchen. We can raid supermarkets in the area, but even that won't be enough to support a thousand people for months. And that's just the people in the hospital. Seattle has millions of people in their homes, then there's the rest of the country. Hell, this is all over the world. Starvation and disease are inevitable."

Wiater looked at the floor, nodding slightly. "Yes. I never considered that. I've been focusing on the problem in front of me. You're right. Time is against us for multiple reasons."

"So what do we do?" Krause asked.

"If you can keep people alive in the short term, I can work on a cure. We have to keep going. All we can do is our best."

Blake smiled. "Works for me. I'll round up a couple of people who can see, take a trip to a local store, and look for food. I'll look for some diesel, as well."

Krause frowned. "Diesel?"

Blake nodded and pointed at the lights above. "Yes, the hospital's emergency generators run on diesel. I checked the tanks earlier, and they're below a third full. We'll need more to keep the power on."

Wiater said, "Everything in this lab needs power to function. The generators are essential."

"I'll get going, then." Blake left the room.

Wiater tossed the remnants of the cheese packet into a nearby garbage container. "We're very lucky to have Oscar with us. He's a practical man and thinks ahead, identifying issues before they arise."

She smiled. "He's been helping the nurses as well wherever he can. I wish we had a dozen more like him. I need to go and do my rounds. We'll talk later."

As Krause left the lab, she felt conflicted. The scale of the problem was staggering, but there was hope of a cure. Doctor

Wiater had made progress in understanding the cause of the blindness pandemic. They could pull this off.

However, Blake was right. Even if they had a cure right now, a lot of people would still die, because they wouldn't be able to get it to them in time.

July 7th

Chapter Thirteen
Observations

Colonel Smith walked into the living room to find Vinson sitting on the couch, staring at the laptop screen and looking furious. "What's wrong?"

Vinson's eyes never left the screen. He simply pointed at the laptop. "Look what they're doing."

Smith sat beside Vinson to see what he was talking about. In what looked like a meeting room, two Chinese soldiers held a silver-haired man stripped to his boxers. A third, larger soldier wearing black gloves pounded the gray-haired man with blow after blow to his body and face. Blood flowed freely from multiple cuts on the victim covering his front in an almost unbroken sheet of red.

"Where is this?" Smith asked.

"Site R. I got onto their surveillance system about twenty minutes ago."

"Poor bastard," he said quietly.

"That's the vice president." Anger dripped from Vinson's voice.

"No... They caught him?" Smith looked again and recognized President Calvin's running mate. "Why in God's name are they doing that to him?"

"We don't have audio, but I'm assuming they're interrogating him. Here's another camera." Vinson brought up another internal video feed from Site R. A man in his mid-fifties, wearing nothing but his underwear, rolled on the floor while being kicked repeatedly by four soldiers. A second man lay still against the wall, his face and upper torso a bloody mess.

"Who are they?" Smith asked quietly.

Vinson tapped the edge of the screen. "I'm not sure, but given the location, I think they're two of the joint chiefs. A marine dress tunic is in the corner. I can't see the rank, but it has a lot of ribbons."

Smith shook his head in bewilderment; he, too, was starting to get angry. "Beating defenseless and blind men senseless... It's... It's..."

"It's war," Vinson said simply.

Smith bridled. "I don't care if it's war. This can't be tolerated."

"As long as the Chinese are in a position of power, we can't stop it, Colonel. The only way to end this is to beat them."

He couldn't disagree with that. He pointed at the laptop. "Are you recording this?"

"Yes, everything is going onto a backup server. The Internet has dropped out twice since I've been connected, but I can reconnect in a few seconds. I've got copies of everything I've seen so far."

"What about Site MW? Can you get onto their cameras?"

"I've been trying, but their firewall's a little trickier. I'll get Noel to help me. He thinks more outside the box than I do and might have some insights."

"All right. Whatever you need to do, do it." Smith rose and went into the kitchen. "Noel, go help Vinson!"

Noel eyed him oddly, and Smith realized his tone had been a lot sharper than it should have been.

"I'm sorry, that was uncalled for. Can you please help Vinson in the living room?"

Noel nodded as he rose. "Certainly, Colonel."

Smith stomped into the master bedroom and sat down on the edge of the bed. He needed to get off the turf farm and go for a long jog to work off some of this stress, but he couldn't because of the nearby Chinese.

Tyler knocked politely on the doorjamb and came into the bedroom. "Is everything okay, sir?"

"No, Captain, it isn't. The Chinese are mercilessly beating the vice president and at least two of the Joint Chiefs of Staff, and we can do nothing to stop it."

She went down on one knee and placed her hand on top of his. "Not yet, but we will in time, Colonel. Don't lose faith in yourself."

Her hand felt soft and soothing, and he calmed slightly. "It isn't a lack of faith. It's my inability to change things. We need to rally whatever military forces we can and hit back, even if it's guerilla-style tactics to begin. Those troop ships from Qingdao will be here by the sixteenth or seventeenth of the month. After they get here, our options drop dramatically."

"Sir, with respect, we need information first. We have to know where they're strong and where they're weak so we can hit them effectively."

Smith raised his head. "That sounds like something from Sun Tzu's *Art of War.*"

She nodded. "It is. The advice of one of their most famous generals should be valid if we're fighting the Chinese."

He snorted with amusement. "I can't argue that." Her hand was still on his; he took his free hand and sandwiched hers between his. "Thank you."

She smiled at him, and he felt all the better for it. He released her and she stood to leave.

"Thank you, Captain."

* * *

Lieutenant General Lam stood well back from the Cheyenne Mountain bunker tunnel and waited for the next explosion. Teams of engineers scrambled out of the tunnel entrance to get clear. The last two men out pulled a roll of wire between them. They ran past him and hunched down, connecting wires to a detonator.

Lam looked over at the pair of Chinese bodies a dozen feet away, lying beneath a concrete wall that was pitted with bullet holes. Two engineer majors had failed and paid the price. Now the senior captain of the engineers was in charge and had six minutes left before he joined his superiors.

"Clear!" came from one of the engineers.

Lam put his fingers in his ears. The other engineer twisted the stubby handle on the detonator.

A sharp explosion sounded and echoed around Lam. The blast vibrated deep in his chest. Smoke and minor debris flew out of the entrance. Lam waited several seconds to make sure the larger pieces of debris had settled and entered the tunnel. The engineer captain hurried past him with a lit flashlight and got to the bunker doors first. He disappeared through a hole in the outer doors.

Lam got to the hole and waited for an update.

The captain coughed repeatedly inside the hole and emerged, looking desperate for air. He kept coughing even as he spoke. "Sir, the inner... door is... breached. The hole is... large enough to gain entry."

Lam turned up the tunnel and faced the entrance. He was relieved that they had gotten into the bunker. The chances of his being shot had just declined, but he could not celebrate yet. "Assault element! Forward!" He screamed.

Close to a hundred armed men ran up the tunnel, led by an airborne major. They unceremoniously pushed the engineer out of the way. Soldiers scrambled into the small hole.

Lam stood aside, forcing himself to be patient. The troops would suppress any resistance inside. He paced in front of the door, ignoring the captain who still lay on the rubble pile.

Lam's aide marched up with a half-dozen soldiers, carrying the gear he would need to set up his headquarters inside.

Without warning, hydraulic motors sounded, and the outer door of the bunker slowly swung open. Lam entered as soon as he could walk in. The inner door was also opening, and Lam went through them without stopping.

Inside, a pair of airborne troops stood near what appeared to be the door controls. They came to attention as Lam passed.

Lam heard no gunshots or screams and took that as a good sign. The best place to mount a defense was at the front door.

Entering the main chamber, Lam could see several white pre-fabricated buildings before him. A soldier, chosen for his English skills, indicated the arrow on the wall and pointed the way to the main operations room. He entered operations and stopped just past the threshold. The desks were abandoned, but displays showing North America were still active.

The large desk at the rear of the room had obviously belonged to a high-ranking officer. A U.S. Air Force uniform jacket, adorned with many colorful ribbons, was draped over the high-backed chair.

Lam sat down in that chair with a smile. He slowly swiveled in the chair, savoring the moment.

His aide entered the room, followed by several soldiers, ending the general's muted celebration. Lam pointed to the other desks in front of him. "Set up headquarters staff on those desks there. I want communications circuits operational in five minutes."

"Comrade Lieutenant General," the aide responded, and the men set to work.

They produced laptop computers and radio gear from the backpacks. One soldier opened a laptop, placed it on a desk, and plugged the network cable into a free port on the desk.

* * *

Colonel Smith sat at the kitchen table, watching the airfield through binoculars. He had seen little movement today. New rows of sandbags had been put in place by the Chinese soldiers near the hangars and perimeter, but beyond that, he saw little else. A clink of dishes distracted him. He glanced over to see Tyler stacking dishes. *She shouldn't feel obliged to do that. We need to take it in turns to cook and do dishes.* He opened his mouth to say just that when a shout stopped him.

"Sir! Colonel!" came from the living room.

Smith rose from the kitchen table and hurried out of the master bedroom, unlatching the top of the holster and placing his hand on the pistol, ready to draw.

Smith entered the living room to find Vinson waving him over. "What is it?"

"I'm able to access the Chinese military network directly." Vinson pointed at the screen.

Smith saw a series of Chinese characters on Vinson's laptop. "How is this possible?"

"They've occupied Cheyenne Mountain. They plugged their own computers into our network, and they used a VPN package through the Internet to tunnel back to their servers in China. Whoever set up their laptops screwed the pooch, and I'm able to access their entire network through that PC. Sir, we have access to pretty much anything the Chinese military has."

Smith didn't read Chinese, but he didn't need to. This was big. "First, I want you to go slow and not jeopardize this resource. This is our first break, and I don't want to lose it."

"Yes, sir," Vinson said happily.

"I need you to find three things. Tell me what's on board those ships coming from Qingdao, what forces are already in North America, and whatever you can tell me about the blinding warheads they used. Clear?"

"Yes, Colonel. Leave it with me."

Smith left him and returned to the kitchen. Folsom had the binoculars to his eyes, and Tyler sat beside him, eating a sandwich.

"Captain, can I talk to you out front?"

"Yes, sir," she responded.

The pair exited through the living room, out onto the front landing made of concrete. Smith closed the door and sat down on the steps, his elbows on his knees. Tyler sat beside him.

"Vinson found a backdoor into the Chinese military. He's tracking down intel on the forces already in the States and those coming by ship. It'll give us an idea of what we're up against, if nothing else."

"That sounds great!" She smiled at the news.

"Also, I asked him for information on the blindness weapon. Hopefully, they developed a cure in addition to their warhead. Assuming he can deliver both, we'll be back to a level playing field."

"I told you to have faith, Colonel."

"Faith aside, it's going to be a long haul. How are you holding up?"

Tyler's smile faded. "I'm worried about my parents. They live in Severance, New York. It's in the Adirondacks out in a fairly remote area."

"Did you try calling them?"

"Dad has a cell phone, but he always forgets to charge it. I left a voicemail, but they didn't respond before the trouble started. Normally, I wouldn't be concerned. Dad's an outdoorsman and built the two-bedroom cabin they live in by Lake Paradox. Mom's a baker. She makes cakes, cookies, and muffins every day. It's just that if they can't see... Well, you know."

Smith rubbed his temples with a thumb and forefinger. "Yeah, I know. At the end of the day, we're fighting for everyone in that same situation. All we can do is stay positive and perform to the best of our ability."

A few moments of silence passed. He was unsure if he should say more.

"Did you enjoy your breakfast?" she asked out of the blue.

Smith faced her. "Yes, thank you. I live alone, so a home-cooked meal is a rarity unless it comes off the barbecue."

"We'll have to work on that," she said, smiling again, and she checked her watch. "I need to relieve Folsom."

Tyler got up and went in the front door, leaving Smith sitting on the stoop. Neither of them had used ranks or honorifics since sitting down, and he didn't mind that one bit.

He began casting his eye toward the mountains in the distance. On the drive there, he'd seen very few people outside. Passing them without stopping to help caused him a lot of discomfort, but ultimately he was trying to save everyone in the country. Helping individuals would only distract him, and his people from getting rid of the Chinese as fast as possible. *We need a cure. Everything hinges on that.* He hoped Vinson found something soon.

* * *

Keith Hurst lay on his sleeping bag. "With Carter and Ogden out at the store, it's quiet, isn't it?"

Calvin laughed. "It's so quiet, you can hear my thoughts. That's exactly what I was thinking. Mount Weather had air conditioning and generators making lots of white noise. There were always people talking, phones ringing... Here, it's so still."

Calvin almost never laughed in the Oval Office. Hurst wondered if being blind and the break from being president was actually helping his friend. "When we get things back to normal, you can come here on weekends instead of going to Camp David."

"Funny," Calvin said flatly. "Get back to normal. I wonder if 'normal' will ever return. I've been thinking, Keith. If we do find a cure, if we're successful in getting rid of the Chinese, it's not going to stop there. This sneak attack is a thousand times worse than Pearl Harbor or 9/11. A lot of people have died, and more *will* die over this. Surviving relatives are going to be screaming for revenge and Chinese blood. Congress will jump on the bandwagon so they don't get lynched, and only the most drastic act will satisfy them. They'll push for an OPLAN 8044 option, and frankly, they'd be fully justified."

Hurst's job placed him in the position where a discussion of exchanging nuclear warheads was commonplace. "Nuking the Chinese will result in us getting hit right back. They only have a pair of ballistic boats, but that's twenty-four ICBMs with four warheads each. Each one targeted at a major U.S. city."

"I know the stakes, Keith. It's keeping me up at night. If we lose, the country is theirs. If we win, there will be nuclear war. Asking everyone in the world to forgive and forget is unrealistic."

A long silence followed. Hurst could think of no other options than what Calvin had outlined. The future looked dark indeed.

An idea struck him. "We could build an international coalition and blockade them, like Kennedy did with Cuba."

Calvin sighed. "Potentially, but that assumes we find a cure and can spread it worldwide quickly enough. The Chinese aren't going to sit around as we do that. They have a formidable military and could occupy a lot of countries in a few days, if they haven't already."

After more silence, Hurst finally said, "None of those choices are acceptable."

"The only way to develop more options is to get updated information. As long as we're cut off from the world, that isn't going to change," Calvin said.

Hurst couldn't disagree. "Then we wait for a miracle. Nothing else will do."

* * *

The sound of a tooting horn at the emergency room entrance got Doctor Krause's attention. She placed her stethoscope over her shoulders and went out to find a beaming Oscar Blake and a pair of her surgical nurses standing beside a pickup truck, crammed full of canned goods, sacks of rice, flour, and other bulk items.

Blake slapped a pile of cans. "We got lucky. On the way to the store, I spotted a warehouse. It's a distribution center for a grocery chain, so we'll have a decent amount of food for some time. We could make twenty more trips and not dent the supplies we found there. Where do you want it?"

The kitchen was the obvious place, but that was on the opposite side of the building and not very convenient without staff to run it. There were a stove and large fridge in the staff break room, however. She pointed. "The break room is down that hall, second door on the left."

Blake grabbed two flats of plastic-wrapped cans and began to carry them past her.

She couldn't help notice his well-developed biceps and shoulders. She motioned for him to stop but realized she was on his blind side. She touched his shoulder. "Mister Blake? Thank you."

He stopped near her and turned to see her with his undamaged eye. "Call me Oscar, Doc. I think we're past formalities, at this point."

He smiled again and carried on past her. As she watched him walk away, a certain warmth began to spread through her. It had been a long time since she'd felt that way. Her smile couldn't be stopped, and her cheeks felt warm.

Dorothy, one of her surgical nurses, came up to her with an armload of food. Krause turned to face her. She nodded toward Blake, who turned the corner and disappeared. "He's single."

Her face heated further. "What? I don't... I mean I..."

Dorothy tilted her head slightly and raised an eyebrow in amusement. "Unlike many people around here, I'm not blind. I just thought you'd like to know." She went inside, leaving Krause behind.

To cover her embarrassment, Krause took a flat of cans into the ER and made her way down the hall to the break room. Blake had already tipped a couch up onto its end to clear a space and begun setting up a stack of cans in the far corner. Dorothy handed her items to him and left, winking at Krause on her way past. Dorothy closed the door behind her.

Krause handed over her cans. He added them to the pile.

"I can bring the rest in, Doc. I know you're busy," he said.

"I'm going to take that bandage off tomorrow." She'd already told him that, but it tumbled out on its own. She wanted an excuse to talk to him.

"Yes, I know. I'm going to miss my royal status," he said with a slight grin.

She frowned from confusion. "Sorry?"

Blake pointed at his face. "'In the land of the blind, the one-eyed man is king.'"

Krause groaned, rolled her eyes, shook her head, and smiled at the same time. "That was bad."

"I'll be here all week. Don't forget to tip your waitress, and try the veal cutlet," he joked.

"I'm going to get back to my rounds. If you need any help, just ask."

"Sure, Doc."

She walked to the door and stopped. Krause felt conflicted. She was his doctor, and the Hippocratic Oath she had sworn to uphold was clear. There were to be no sexual relationships between doctors and their patients. Under normal circumstances, the American Medical Association could take her license away.

Yet, these were hardly normal circumstances. There was no government, at any level, no police or fire department, and certainly no AMA. She had no idea if they would find a cure, and even if one magically appeared right this second, the world would still take a long time to recover. Krause didn't want to face that alone.

"Linda," she said quietly with her hand on the doorknob.

"Excuse me?" he asked.

"My name. It's Linda." She flipped her hair back as she turned back to face him. "I think we're past formalities, as you said."

"Okay, Linda. I'm here if you need me."

Krause left without saying anything else. She went back to her rounds. The reduced food intake was causing a few minor issues with some of the people. That would grow over time, but at least they wouldn't be starving to death, thanks to Oscar.

They were lucky. The hospital had power, and the people who could see were mostly trained medical professionals who could take care of the rest. Krause wondered how the rest of the country was coping. Blind people stuck in their homes, or out in the country at remote farms.

Then she remembered the entire world had been affected, and thoughts of millions, if not billions, in the same circumstances made her melancholy indeed.

* * *

As Colonel Smith scanned the air force base with the binoculars, he wondered if he should check in with the president. He decided that until they knew something of substance, contacting him would be premature. While he wanted to hear how things were going, the cell phone was a tenuous link, only to be used in an emergency. *I wonder if he's still alive…*

Smith dismissed the thought immediately. The president's safety was in the hands of others. *His* responsibility was to protect the nation.

The level of activity on the airfield had remained the same. Chinese patrols were inside the fence line, but Smith hadn't seen any out on the civilian roads. *So their focus is securing the Peterson AFB facilities. Probably to ensure no resistance when the main body of troops arrived by ship. They're staying in one place to concentrate their military defenses. With fifteen hundred troops, there's nothing we can do to harm them in any significant way.*

So if they're focusing on facilities tied to command and control, it's possible other bases aren't being occupied. While the Chinese had a lot of troops, they can't be everywhere. I just need to figure out where they are weakest.

The sound of a bowl being placed before him on the table made him pull his eyes away from the binoculars. Tyler placed a second dish containing freshly sliced bread and butter beside the soup, which looked like minestrone. It smelled delicious.

"There you are, sir. Dinner is served. That's the last of the fresh bread, so enjoy."

"Thank you, Captain." He handed the binoculars over to Folsom and picked up a spoon.

The soup was canned. He'd seen her open it earlier, but she'd added some pepper and spices. He felt an enjoyable little bite on his tongue, reminding him of a Cajun meal.

Tyler moved through the kitchen, handing out bowls to the others. He was glad for the distraction. While eating, he didn't worry about the Chinese or contacting the president. His troubles took a backseat.

As Smith ate, he realized he knew very little about Folsom. "Where are you from, Tech Sergeant?"

"Small town outside of El Paso, sir. So small that I joined the service right after high school just to get the hell away from it."

"Ever been back?" Smith asked between mouthfuls of soup.

Noel kept the binoculars to his eyes. "Just for my father's funeral. I'd been gone almost ten years, and nothing had changed. Same people doing the same jobs, hanging out in the same bar. It was depressing."

Smith picked up a piece of bread and dipped it into the soup.

Folsom asked, "Do you play golf, Colonel?"

"No, never. How about you?"

"I love the game. I play every chance I get. I started out as a bogie golfer, but I finally got my handicap to a decent level. You know, I'd spend the rest of my days on a golf course if I could."

Smith paused, the spoon just under his lip. "I played football in college, but I never had the desire to do it full time. Today, I'd be happy with a canoe and a calm unoccupied lake with bass... Maybe when we retire, we'll get what we want."

After he finished eating, Smith carried the dishes over to the kitchen sink.

Tyler took the bowl out of his hands as he approached. "I'll do them, sir."

"Captain, you don't have to be only chief cook and bottle washer. We can take it in turns."

She smiled at him again. "I grew up with four brothers, Colonel, and helped my mother with every meal growing up. I enjoy cooking and don't mind a bit. When I'm not keeping watch on the airfield, I'm going stir-crazy."

"All right. Just don't feel it's mandatory. If you feel like a break, let me know."

"Certainly, sir. If you want to help, you can dry while I wash," she suggested.

Smith hated drying dishes. He didn't mind washing them, but at home he had a dish rack, and he would just let them drip dry. Still, she'd asked for his assistance, and it would give him an excuse to stay with her a little longer. He grabbed a dish towel off a hook. "Four brothers? You were the only girl?"

Tyler plunged the dishes into the sink full of hot foamy water. "Yes. They liked to tease me a lot, but once I knew where to hit them and grew my nails out, they backed off. Dad always backed me up, so that helped, too. What about you?"

"I had no family. I was left on the doorstep of a fire station when I was four months old."

She paused washing and turned to him with a look of wide-eyed concern. "Seriously? Oh my…"

"I went through a lot of foster parents, some good, some not so much. Worked my way through college, then joined the Air Force. I wanted to see the world."

Tyler went back to scrubbing plates. "Did you ever find your parents?" She handed him the dish.

"I never looked. They gave me up, so I left it up to them." He dried the plate as best he could, then he added it to the stack in the cupboard.

She didn't say anything for a long time. While silent, she handed him dishes, plates, and pots to dry.

He decided to try a different topic. "Are you intending to make the Air Force a career?"

"That's a good question. I've been asking myself that for a year or so. I considered going back to school and getting my master's, but I can do that in the service. I still have two years left before I need to make a decision. I'm not really comfortable in uniform. I know women today are supposed to be in business and climbing the corporate ladder, but I'd be happy staying at home. I'm like my mother in that respect. She bakes, does needlepoint, and volunteers at the local nursing home to keep busy. There's pros and cons both ways. I suppose now it depends how this situation plays out. I may find myself somewhere I never imagined."

"Like hiding out from Chinese paratroops on a turf farm." He put the latest dry plate back into the cupboard.

"Ha! Something like that." She went quiet again but continued to work on the sink's contents.

Smith continued drying until everything was done.

Tyler pulled the stopper from the drain and turned, smiling at him. She dried her hands on the dish towel in his hands, then touched him lightly on the arm as she left. "Thanks for the help."

July 8th

Chapter Fourteen
Trials and Tribulations

Doctor Krause went down the stairwell into the hospital basement. She found Oscar Blake already in Doctor Wiater's lab, in the middle of handing Wiater a shiny metal tube. She hadn't expected to see Blake there. "Good morning."

Blake turned and smiled at her. "Morning, Doc."

I told him he could call me Linda. Why isn't he?

"Doctor Krause," Wiater said. "I believe I've made some progress."

Krause joined Wiater and watched him put the metal tube down on the lab table. The metal was hollow, about eight inches long, and just over two inches in diameter.

"As I said earlier, we need to find a mechanism that not only reactivates the RB protein to stop future growth, but also kills the cancer cells already in place."

"Yes. I can imagine that won't be easy." She stood beside Blake. She could feel the heat of his bare forearm near her. She sidestepped slightly, to get away from that distraction.

Wiater handed her a series of printed pages. "This is what I found concerning cancer radiation therapies. The one on top is from the Institute of Biotechnology, University of Texas Health Science Center at San Antonio. The authors claim to have used beta radiation from the rhenium-188 isotope to successfully curtail retinoblastoma in tissue samples from affected children. It not only stopped further growth, but it also killed the existing cancer cells. I consider this worth pursuing."

Krause read the science paper carefully. The text was detailed and technical, but Wiater's summation had been accurate. Then she noticed an issue. "It's promising, but it says here—they haven't done human trials."

Wiater sat down on a stool while nodding slowly. "Yes. They applied for phase one human testing. As you may or may not know, the FDA has been dragging its heels on approving new radiotherapy processes since several radiation-related deaths were highlighted by the *New York Times* a few years ago."

Krause placed the paper back on the pile. "How do you want to proceed?"

Wiater reached over and picked up the metal tube and handed it to her. "I asked Oscar to look around, and he found some stainless steel storage vessels that can safely contain the rhenium-188 radiation. We have a small supply of the isotope here. If I can calculate the precise amount of material to use, along with the exposure time, we should be able to test it on a few blind people in the hospital."

Krause regarded the cool metal in her hand. His theories made sense, but she had doubts. "If we get this wrong, a lot of people will suffer."

Wiater nodded slowly, grim faced. "I know. They say desperate times require desperate measures. As M.D.s, we swear to 'Do no harm,' but lengthy testing will mean millions will die of disease and starvation. I can't tell you how knotted my stomach is over this, but we need to do something and soon. This is the best solution I've found so far."

"So are there alternatives?" With millions of lives at stake, they had to be right the first time.

"Yes, the most promising avenue is with proton therapy. It should be more effective and the technology has been thoroughly vetted, but the equipment is massive, requires a lot of electricity, and there are very few units across the country. Many of the people who know how to run them are blind, as well. The smaller tubes could be hand carried and taken to the most isolated of areas. They would not require any external power, and they could be put together quickly."

Krause still had reservations. "How do we control the exposure time?"

Blake leaned forward. "I can help there. I took a few years of metal shop in high school. Before you came in, we were talking about using shutters on the end of the tube. Rigging something up should only take couple of hours. I just need to find a workshop with the right gear."

Krause handed back the tube. Time was against them, there was no perfect solution, and Wiater was right. They needed to do something. "We should start small. Four to six volunteers, no more. Whatever we do, we can't make things worse."

Wiater stood, holding the tube against his chest. "Agreed, I'll start on the calculations for the amount of rhenium-188 isotope to use and determine a specific exposure time. Oscar, you get to work on the shutters, and Doctor Krause can assemble the volunteers. Let's meet back here in—" He looked at his watch. "Will four hours be enough time?"

"Should be, I still need to go out and locate some diesel. I've drawn blanks searching so far, but I'll wait until I'm done here before I leave," Blake said.

Krause suspected she would have no issue finding volunteers in the desperate group upstairs. "All right. I'll see you then."

* * *

The compact wardroom of the USS *John Warner* had multiple functions out of necessity. The space was normally used as the mess and recreation area for the commissioned officers on board. This morning, the television was off, the board games were stowed, and the mood was anything but relaxed.

Captain Reid, Executive Officer Maddox, and Chief of the Boat Duggan were present wearing dress blue uniforms. Only Captain Reid sat at the large table. The rest stood off to his left with their backs against the wall in the limited area that remained.

Reid adjusted the files and paperwork in front of him. He had to move his glass of water over a few inches to make room. Over the last twelve hours, tensions had risen significantly throughout the sub. Smiles had disappeared, the crew avoided eye contact with him, and the little conversation there was ended when Reid walked into the compartment. Secrets were almost impossible to keep on a submarine. Word of Wyatt being put on captain's mast had spread through the boat.

Masts were a necessity. It would not be a trial, although the accused could opt to have a general court-martial. Few chose that path, as punishments in a mast were typically lighter than those given in a court-martial. Reid had already reviewed Petty Officer Wyatt's official record and found no blemishes. Indeed, Wyatt had several exceptional performance reviews, as well as a letter of appreciation for charity work he had done onshore during his leave.

Reid caught Chief Duggan's eye. "Bring him in, Chief." He took a drink from his glass of water.

"Yes, sir." Duggan marched to the wardroom door and opened it, revealing Petty Officer Wyatt standing there with Chief Petty Officer Marquez, who was senior NCO in the torpedo room.

Marquez marched Wyatt in, halting him just before the wardroom table as Duggan closed the door behind them. Wyatt saluted, removed his cap, and tucked it under his arm while remaining at attention.

Wyatt's dress blue uniform was clean and pressed properly. *He's obviously a good sailor who made a stupid error. If he plays this right, his career will not be adversely affected.*

Reid picked up the piece of paper with the formal charges and read selected parts. "Petty Officer Second Class Wyatt, you are charged with three violations of the Unified Code of Military Justice. Specifically, refusal to follow a direct order, assault of a superior, and insubordination. You have the right to stay silent, the right to request a lawyer to assist you, and the right to appeal to a higher authority for a court-martial. Do you wish to exercise any of these rights at this time?"

"No, sir," Wyatt replied immediately, his gaze was focused at a spot on the wall above Reid's head.

"Very well, Petty Officer Wyatt, were you ordered to perform routine maintenance on an ADCAP torpedo yesterday?"

"Yes, sir."

Reid laid the paper in his hand on the paperwork pile before him. "Who ordered you to do that?"

"Petty Officer Marquez, sir."

Reid looked at Marquez, who was sweating. "Is that correct, P.O.?"

"Yes, sir. I directed Petty Officer Wyatt and Seaman Archer to replace a defective sensor in the torpedo propulsion unit on that weapon."

Reid turned back to face Wyatt. "Later in the day, you exchanged harsh words with Chief Duggan. You stopped working on the TPU, and after Chief Duggan ordered you to return to the ADCAP, you struck him several times in the chest. He—"

"I just poked him, sir." Wyatt interrupted, looking Reid in the eye as he said it.

He disliked being cut off. "Petty Officer Wyatt, assault is defined as the threat of harm combined with the ability to carry out the threat. Your comments made at the time were threatening, therefore your 'poking' is considered assault."

Wyatt's gaze refocused over Reid's head.

Reid again referenced the paper listing the charges. "The insubordination charge stems from your use of the phrase, 'shove that torpedo up your ass,' to Chief Duggan. Did you say that to him?"

"Yes, sir."

"Do you have anything to say in your own defense?" Reid placed his hands on the table in front of him, intertwining his fingers.

"No, sir. No excuses, sir."

Just as I expected, he's being smart. No arguments or whining. Reid turned his attention to Petty Officer Marquez. "Petty Officer Marquez, what's your assessment of Petty Officer Wyatt's abilities?"

"Sir, P.O. Wyatt is one of my better people. He's the lead trainer on all gear in the compartment, and until this incident, I've never seen any negative behavior from him. I feel he has a strong future in the navy, Captain."

Reid took another sip of water and regarded Wyatt, who still stood at attention, his expression blank. He placed the glass back on the table before speaking. "Petty Officer Second Class Wyatt, as long as I'm in command of this vessel, I'll not tolerate any NCO behaving as you did. I find you guilty on all three counts. I've taken into account your record to date. Both Chief Duggan and Petty Officer Marquez have spoken positively about you. I therefore award[19] you thirty days extra duty. You will forfeit half your base pay for thirty days and be reduced one pay grade. You shall also be restricted to the boat for thirty days."

Reid thought that punishment appropriate. Restriction to the boat meant no shore leave, but the sub had just started a four-month deployment, so Wyatt would not be inconvenienced by that. The thirty-day pay reduction and extra duty were roughly half the sixty-day maximum that Reid could levy. Wyatt's decent performance record had counted to reduce the sentence. It was a slap on the wrist, nothing more.

Reid began to gather the paperwork off the table in front of him. He was about to dismiss the accused when two gunshots rang through the submarine, followed by three more in rapid succession. "What the hell?"

Reid began standing as several people moved for the wardroom door.

"Freeze!" Wyatt screamed.

---

[19] In the U.S. Navy, the term "award" is used for positive things like medals and for negatives like punishments, as they are both earned by the individual.

Reid turned.

Wyatt had a pistol in his hand. The muzzle pointed directly at Reid's face.

Wyatt looked him in the eyes. He was smiling. "Looks like you're not in command anymore, Captain."

* * *

Colonel Smith made himself some coffee in the kitchen before striding into the living room. He found Vinson in his usual spot on the couch, tapping on his laptop keyboard. His feet were up on the coffee table, and he stared intently at the screen, scowling. Vinson's undone bow tie hung around his collar. Smith had always thought the ties were clip-ons.

Smith sat on the couch beside him. On the laptop screen, he saw indecipherable Chinese characters filling web and terminal windows. He put his mug down on the table. "How are you doing?"

Vinson finished typing a long series of commands and never looked up from the screen. "Hit and miss. I'm into the core switches for their military network, but they've been configured to restrict traffic along the routes I need to get to. Much of the equipment is dated, and standard commands are not working. I'm having to frequently stop and figure out the correct syntax to proceed to the next stage. Having to translate everything is also slowing me down."

"Did you sleep last night?"

Vinson gave him a puzzled look. "Sleep? No. I've been working on this since we talked last. I'm fine."

"Turn the laptop off. I want you to get some food and rest. I can't have my only resource into their network burning himself out."

"Colonel, I—"

Smith grabbed the Ethernet cable leading to the laptop. "You either take a break, or I pull the plug."

Vinson looked as if he would argue, but seconds later his shoulders slumped. "All right, but we have to keep the laptop connected, or I'll have to redo a couple hours' work."

Smith released the cable. "I don't want to see you on it for eight hours. Get some food then lay down. This is going to be a long haul for all of us."

Vinson closed the lid of the laptop and headed to the kitchen, sidestepping Captain Erica Tyler on the threshold as she came through the opposite way.

She smiled as she saw Smith and sat down beside him. She clasped her hands together, resting them on top of her knees. "Colonel, can I ask how long we're staying here?"

Smith picked up his coffee. "Eager to go somewhere?"

"No, sir. It's comfortable and we have lots of food, but shouldn't we be trying to gather forces for a counteroffensive or something like that?"

Smith took a sip of coffee as he considered the question. The liquid was hot, so he put the cup down to cool a while. "Ideally, yes. My goal in coming here originally was to observe what the Chinese were up to—to try to gain some insight into why they were here and how they were operating. That changed slightly when Vinson got into their network. We may be able to learn a great deal about their forces and intentions now. If we can understand what they want, then we can move to oppose them."

Tyler pursed her lips. "I sense a huge 'but' coming."

"Yeah." Smith put the mug back on the table and leaned closer to her, lowering his voice so only she could hear. What he had to say could undermine morale if the others heard. "When we were at NORAD, the Chinese offensive looked to be focused on our strategic assets. From what I can see, they've succeeded at neutralizing our nukes and everyone who could order their launch, except for the president. Since then, they've done nothing except hold position, at least here. Logically, we can consider nullifying our command and control as their phase one. We know they have a surface fleet on the way with additional troops. That's their phase two.

Until they arrive, we have a window of opportunity, but we have little to no offensive capability with everyone in the military blind."

"We should be organizing some form of resistance," she said defiantly.

Smith jerked his thumb in the general direction of the airbase. "We need a cure first. That's the key. If we can get even a single division of troops mobilized, we can roll them back. The problem is, where do we look for one? If one of the big government labs had a lead on this, the president would have known about it. We have nothing right now. That's why we're sitting here. I'm hoping Vinson can find a clue on the Chinese network about how they caused this. It's logical to assume they have a cure for themselves. If we can find that, then we can oppose them."

Tyler pulled a leg under herself, twisting on the couch to face him. "Assuming we find a cure, then what? Where do we go?"

"It would have to be a base that had no strategic ties. The closest I can think of is Hill Air Force Base near Salt Lake City. They're an AFMC base that has a fighter wing of F-16s."

"Surely, the bases in Colorado are closer?" Tyler protested.

"Yes, but the issue is their proximity to Peterson. Buckley AFB, Schriever AFB, and even the army base at Fort Carson are only a short drive away. The Chinese would have no problem taking those establishments out in the first day. Indeed, they'd be stupid not to. No, Hill in Utah is the best bet."

Tyler seemed to be mulling over the issue. "Why the delay?" she asked quietly.

Smith reached for his coffee mug. "What do you mean?"

"Why the delay between phase one and two? Why are they just sitting on the strategic assets, waiting for the ship-borne troops to arrive? Why not spread out and eliminate the other bases?"

"Ahhh. Two reasons." He took a long sip while maintaining eye contact with Tyler, deliberately taking his time.

He needed to phrase his response delicately. "First, they want to safeguard the sites they took. If anyone did try to take them back, they have more than enough troops to stop them. Second, why waste the bullets and risk casualties, when you can just wait for everyone opposing you to die?"

"That's… That's just—" she stammered.

"Efficient. From their perspective, anyway."

* * *

Captain Reid wanted to tear the pistol out of Wyatt's hand and beat him senseless with it. *How dare he risk the lives of everyone on board by trying something this asinine! God knows who or what has just been shot.*

Petty Officer Wyatt kept the barrel of the pistol pointed directly at Reid's head. All movement had stopped in the wardroom. "Get up and don't try anything, Captain. We're going to the command center. The rest of you stay here."

Reid stood slowly. Being ordered around on his ship at gunpoint did not sit well with him. "Do you know what the penalty for mutiny is in times of war, Petty Officer?"

"You had your chance, Captain, sir." Wyatt jerked the tip of the pistol toward the door. "Move."

Reid opened the wardroom door. Chief Duggan looked as if he would jump Wyatt as he passed, but Wyatt sidestepped to keep Reid between them. *I don't need more people hurt, and there are others involved other than Wyatt. I need to find out more before we act.* Once the two men were in the corridor, Wyatt closed the wardroom door. He stayed a few paces from Reid, making it impossible for him to try to grab the weapon. He pointed toward the command center and Reid moved in that direction.

On entering the command center, Reid saw several stations unmanned. Two seamen he recognized from the Torpedo Room held pistols on the duty crew, and a pair of bodies lay motionless on the floor. He recognized Petty Officer First Class Blevins lying on his back. He had been on duty at the fire control station. The other man was face down and had two bloody bullet holes visible in his back. Reid didn't know who that was; his uniform was that of an enlisted man.

"Petty Officer Wyatt, those men need medical attention," Reid said.

"I keep saying you're not in command anymore, Cap'n." Wyatt turned to the Ship Control Station. "Pilot, set course for Naval Base Point Loma. We're going home."

Reid looked over to the Ship Control Station[20]. Both the pilot and copilot positions were occupied by junior officers.

The man in the left-hand pilot seat looked over his shoulder. Reid recognized him as Lieutenant Junior Grade Pennington, the youngest man on board, only twenty. This was his first tour on a submarine. He didn't even have his dolphin submarine qualification badge yet.

"Captain?" Pennington, his hands on the maneuvering controls, sounded confused and nervous.

Wyatt didn't let Reid respond. "I said set a heading for Point Loma, Mister Pennington."

Pennington ignored Wyatt and locked gazes with Reid. "Sir?"

Reid had to say something, or he'd lose control of the boat. He ached for revenge, but he forced himself to keep his comments civil and calm to let the crew know he was still captain. Reid spoke to Pennington, but his words were for every man in earshot. "Lieutenant Pennington, Petty Officer Wyatt and the others have taken up arms against lawful authority in a time of war and must be considered mutineers. You need to decide where your loyalties lie: with him, or with the United States Navy."

Pennington took a few seconds to consider that, then simply nodded. "Yes, sir." He faced his instruments, took his hands off the steering joystick, and folded his arms. The officer seated in the copilot position to Pennington's right did the same.

---

[20] *Virginia*-class submarines have a pilot, copilot, and relief pilot, which replace the traditional Diving Officer, Chief of the Watch, Helmsman, Planesman, and Messenger positions from older submarine designs.

Good man! If Pennington had buckled and followed Wyatt's orders, half the crew would probably have followed suit. Now we have a chance to fight this.

Wyatt strode over to Pennington and ground the tip of the pistol barrel against the back of his head, forcing it to an uncomfortable angle. "Turn this boat toward home, sir, or I'll shoot you as an example."

Pennington stayed still.

Reid didn't wait for Wyatt to decide whether to make good on his threat. "How many bullets do you have, Wyatt? It's three of you against a hundred others. Are you going to shoot everyone? Can you operate and navigate this boat alone? I don't think so. One bullet hitting the wrong piece of equipment, and we all die. You said you want to see your wife and daughter again? How will that be possible, when you're in the brig waiting to be hanged?"

"Shut up, damn you! I'm in charge here. We're going home. They'll do what I tell them to do!" Wyatt turned the gun back on Reid.

Reid had no doubt Wyatt wouldn't succeed, but he needed to end things before Wyatt got desperate and started firing. "Pilot, all ahead full, twenty degrees down bubble," Reid ordered.

"All ahead full. Twenty degrees down bubble, pilot aye," Pennington replied immediately while pressing the joystick forward. His counterpart beside him advanced the engine throttles to full. The nose of the sub sharply began to tilt down.

"What are you doing?" Wyatt asked incredulously.

"I'm taking my boat to crush depth, Petty Officer."

* * *

Doctor Wiater asked Oscar Blake to go and get Doctor Krause early. As soon as Blake left, Wiater ran through his calculations twice more to check the numbers. He then set up a series of microscopes with sample slides.

When Doctor Krause came into the room alone, he had everything ready.

"Oscar said you wanted to see me?"

"Doctor, yes, I did. I have good news and bad news. I came up with a baseline calculation for the rhenium-188 exposure and subjected some fresh autopsy samples to timed exposure. If you care to look, the first microscope shows the unexposed tissue I used as a control."

Doctor Krause checked through the microscope. "That looks like the original tissue with out-of-control cancerous growth."

Wiater said, "The second microscope shows similar tissue after a timed radiation exposure. Two hours have passed since initial dosage."

Krause looked through the eyepiece to view the second sample. "That's an impressive reduction. The cancerous cells look severely disrupted, and I can see the tips of a few rods and cones have been uncovered."

Wiater nodded as Krause pulled away from the microscope. "Yes, given these results I calculate most, if not all vision, will return within four to five hours. That's good news, but I'm afraid it ends there."

Krause sat down at a workbench. "What's the catch?"

Wiater pointed to a nearby whiteboard, filled with formulas and charts he'd drawn while working. "My calculations have defined the amount of rhenium-188 isotope needed to the gram. The initial time of beta radiation exposure must be exactly thirty-four seconds. That time will increase due to the short sixteen-day rhenium-188 half-life. Any less exposure, and the cancer cells may survive. Any more, and the rods and cones themselves will be damaged. It's a fine line, and we can only give one treatment per person at these levels of exposure."

Krause looked surprised and pointed to the second microscope. "If it kills the cancerous cells and returns vision, then I fail to see the issue. Isn't that what we wanted to achieve?"

Wiater nodded before sitting down on a lab stool. "Yes, and that's the good news. We can return vision, but the effects of radiation exposure are cumulative. If the blindness weapon is ever used again, anyone treated with the therapy can't be treated again. They'll be permanently blind, and there's no hope of a cure after that. This is literally a one-time treatment."

Krause stood, protesting, "We can't hold back the cure for fear of another attack, Doctor."

"I'm not suggesting we do, but those are the risks. Whoever is behind this can easily do it again and undo everything we've accomplished here."

Krause crossed her arms. "With that aside for the moment, are you ready for human trials?"

Wiater picked up a metal tube from the lab workbench. "Yes, your friend Oscar helped me a great deal. This is our prototype. He figured out how to use a motorized camera iris instead of shutters. Plus, we rigged up a timer for an exact dosage. You place the eye here, press this button, the iris opens, and a timer starts. Once it counts down to zero, the iris closes and you repeat on the second eye. Theoretically, each tube should be able to treat fifty people an hour. With the amount of isotope I have on hand, we can make ten tubes."

Krause's eyebrow jumped up for a half second. "Impressive. Five hundred people an hour is a good rate. I have four volunteers ready to go, and another two dozen waiting behind them. Is there any reason not to proceed with human trials?"

The whole process had gone far too quickly for Wiater to be comfortable. Normally, years of closely monitored clinical trials needed to be done before something of this type was attempted. He'd come up with a new radiation therapy treatment and a delivery mechanism in the space of a few days. He wanted to play it safe, redo all the calculations, double- and triple-check everything. He desperately wanted half a dozen colleagues to go over his work, looking for flaws.

But delays would cost lives as people died of dehydration, disease, hunger, and any one of a hundred other causes. There was no other viable alternative, and they were running out of time. "We can proceed."

Chapter Fifteen
The Depths of Despair

President Calvin dreamed of strolling in a vast rolling green field of spring flowers. He held the hand of his wife, who smiled at him in that special way she reserved for him alone. Carrie squeezed his hand gently. Her blond hair sparkled in the sunlight, and her light laugh seemed to come at him from every direction. The sun was so bright and warm. Birdsong came from all around. A perfect day.

Someone shook his shoulder. The dream dissipated, and darkness returned. Calvin jerked up, reaching for her. A hand grabbed his wrist.

"Mister President, you asked me to wake you. Your breakfast is ready, sir," Agent Nance said quietly, releasing his hand.

The dread feeling of losing his wife returned. He sat up slowly and rubbed his face. "Yes... Yes, thank you." The stubble on his chin had grown. Calvin was usually quite particular about his appearance. He never knew when a photo would be taken of him, and as president, he could not afford to be seen in a negative light. *God forbid I ever be seen in a creased shirt in the Oval Office. Society would crumble at the very sight.*

"We have oatmeal with a little brown sugar this morning, sir."

"Give me a moment, please." The dream lingered. The vivid colors and sounds had made him feel almost joyous, but now everything was black once more. *Is my mind compensating for the lack of vision?* He didn't know. All he knew was that he'd held his wife's hand for a moment and that had been glorious while it lasted.

Time to come back to reality. He got up out of the sleeping bag. Nance guided him to the small table, and he sat down.

He realized Keith had not said good morning. "Keith, are you there?"

"No, sir," Nance said. "Agent Carter escorted him and Mister Ogden to ground level for some fresh air. He said he'd be back down in a bit. Coffee?"

"Thank you." Calvin listened while Nance placed a bowl of oatmeal and a coffee cup in front of him.

"The bowl is in front of you, and the coffee is the left of the bowl. They're both hot, sir."

He carefully located the mentioned items and a spoon with his hands. The oatmeal, he had to admit, tasted pretty good.

"It was raining earlier and looked like it would last a while." It sounded like Nance was doing something with the dishes.

"As we're not going anywhere for a while, I don't think that's a problem." He heard what he thought was a laugh from Nance, but he felt melancholy. If no one could find a cure, then he wouldn't be moving from that dank hole in the ground. The thought of hiding there for the rest of his life depressed him.

The Chinese troop ships would be ashore in just a week. The most powerful military on the planet had been rendered helpless. Without a cure, the United States would fall under the heel of barbarian invaders, just like the Roman Empire.

He had not heard from Colonel Smith for some time. There might be a handful of others he didn't know about, but not in the numbers required to stop a massive invasion from the Chinese. The aging bunker would protect him for a while, but they would find him eventually.

Will I be the last President of the United States?

He ate his oatmeal, mentally pleading to the god he didn't believe in to throw everyone a break.

* * *

"Captain, depth is four hundred and eighty feet, with twenty degree down bubble indicated, engines answering full ahead," Pennington called out.

"Thank you." Reid said and did nothing further, except for looking at Petty Officer Wyatt.

Wyatt hurried to Reid and shoved the pistol in his face. "Order the boat to surface, or I'll kill you!"

Reid ignored him. "Report our depth."

"Passing five hundred forty feet, sir," Pennington replied.

"You're going to kill everyone on board!" Wyatt screamed.

"Yes," Reid said, letting his anger show. "This is a warship of the United States Navy, and I will not surrender my command to a thug with a pistol! Order your men to put their weapons down, or I keep this boat on course past crush depth. That's somewhere around eight hundred feet. No one really knows what this hull will take, so it looks like we'll find out together."

"You're mad!" Wyatt looked around at the other men with pistols.

"Pilot, call out depth every fifty feet," Reid ordered.

"Pilot aye. Now passing six hundred feet."

The hull groaned under the massive external pressure, sounding like a wounded animal in a lot of pain.

Wyatt frantically waved the gun in Reid's face. "Stop this! You won't kill yourself. You're bluffing."

"Passing six hundred fifty feet," Pennington stated.

Reid said nothing. He leaned back against the plotting table and crossed his arms, giving Wyatt a hard stare. Wyatt needed to decide if he wanted to live or not.

"Seven hundred feet," Pennington's voice had risen a half-octave.

One of Wyatt's armed mutineers could take it no longer and threw his pistol onto the rubber floor mat in front of him, held his hands up, and stepped back from it. No one made a move for the weapon.

There were still two men with guns in the command center. "Seven hundred and fifty feet."

With a last desperate look at Reid, Wyatt threw his gun down and raised his hands. He turned to the last holdout. "Roberts, drop the gun!"

Roberts did so. Crewmembers moved without orders to take the three men prisoner. Others rushed to give first aid to the two shot men prone on the deck.

Reid picked up the 1MC handset. "Corpsmen, XO, Chief Duggan, report to the command center on the double." He replaced the handset and waited.

"Depth eight hundred feet. Captain, your orders?" Pennington twisted in his chair to make eye contact.

"Steady as she goes, Mister Pennington," Reid said as the XO and Chief Duggan entered the command center. "Chief, grab those weapons and bag them as evidence. Find out how they got access to them. XO, secure those prisoners. Make sure they're isolated from the crew and not able to cause trouble again."

"Eight hundred and fifty feet," Pennington stated, looking over his shoulder with wide eyes.

The hull emitted a second louder groan as the surrounding water pressure pressed in. Wyatt screamed, struggling against the grip of the pair of men holding him. "We're past crush depth and still going down! Bring the boat up, or we'll all die!"

A pair of corpsman appeared from the rear hatch, carrying trauma bags.

Reid ignored Wyatt. "Corpsmen, take care of those men. Move it, XO, get the prisoners out of my sight."

The XO complied and took charge of the three mutineers, taking them to the rear of the sub. The corpsmen began tending to the fallen men.

"Nine hundred feet, Captain."

Reid saw many concerned faces around him, but no one said or did anything untoward. He calmly ordered, "Pilot, level off at nine-five-zero feet."

Pennington immediately pulled back on the joystick before replying rapidly, "Level off at nine-five-zero feet, pilot aye."

The nose of the sub rose up sharply. Reid kept an eye on the instrument readouts. Pennington didn't exceed nine hundred and fifty feet, and he brought the boat to an even keel.

"Sir, my depth is nine hundred and fifty feet."

Reid strode over to stand behind Pennington's padded seat. "Are you nervous about being at this depth, Mister Pennington?"

He looked over his shoulder. "First time this deep, sir, so yes, I am."

"No need to be. Your faith in your boat should equal your belief in your captain." He patted Pennington on the shoulder to reassure him.

"Yes, sir."

"Pilot, ahead one third. Five degrees up bubble. Bring her up to three-zero-zero feet."

"Five degrees up bubble. Ascend to three-zero-zero feet, pilot aye."

Reid walked back to the plotting table. He leaned over the large display, placing his hands on the console to stop the shakes of relief. His bluff had worked, and no one else had been hurt. Publicly, the crush depth of the sub was eight hundred feet. Reid and his XO were the only ones briefed on the actual classified figure, which was several hundred feet deeper. The boat had never been in any real danger. He had wanted Wyatt to suffer waiting for the hull to implode.

The two men being treated on the floor looked dead, and as captain, the fault rested on his shoulders. Reid had failed them.

* * *

Doctor Linda Krause looked over the square hospital room she had chosen for the tube trials. She'd chosen four names from the patient list, trying to get an assortment of ages and genders for the trial. The four beds were neatly made and ready to accept patients. Two visitor chairs and four adjustable-height rolling tables were the only other furnishings. The door to a compact bathroom was ajar. Krause peeked in, and everything looked clean and sanitary. Normally part of pediatrics, this room had heavy curtains to limit the light in the room.

The scent of the recently mopped floor irritated her nose. Blake had volunteered to clean the floor, and he apparently hadn't diluted the disinfectant with enough water. She cracked open a window. A gust of fresh air brushed against her face, and the smell dissipated quickly.

If she had done that during a normal day, the fumes and noise of street traffic would've forced her to close it immediately.

Krause prayed the tubes worked. While the lab tests looked promising, no one could predict what the real world trials would accomplish, if anything. Nervousness and optimism both fluttered in her, and she couldn't bring herself to celebrate quite yet.

Oscar Blake appeared at the room threshold with a middle-aged woman who held onto his forearm for guidance. "We're going through a doorway now. Careful. There, you're in. Doctor Krause, this is Mrs. Antonio. She's from Kirkland originally."

Krause smiled before remembering Mrs. Antonio couldn't see it. "Good morning, Mrs. Antonio. Thank you for volunteering."

Blake escorted Mrs. Antonio to the bed farthest from the door on the left and helped her sit down. He faced Krause as the volunteer lay back. "Mrs. Antonio wondered if her sister could come up to be with her. She's downstairs."

That was a good idea. Any results would take hours, so the patients might as well be comfortable. "Of course. I'm heading downstairs in a few minutes and will bring her up with me."

Mrs. Antonio asked, "When are we starting the tests?"

Krause walked over to stand near her bed. Oscar motioned that he was going back out. Krause nodded at Oscar and, as he left the room, spoke to Mrs. Antonio. "We'll begin once we get all four volunteers up here. For now, just relax. I'll be taking your blood pressure and keeping an eye on you throughout the trial."

Mrs. Antonio reached out for her but missed. Krause gently caught her hand, held it, and lowered it to the bed. "Do you really think this will work, Doctor?"

"The lab tests we did look promising, so we have an excellent chance to succeed." Krause released her hand and patted it. "Let me go get your sister while the others are being brought up."

"Thank you. Her name is Lydia, and she was wearing a green skirt. We were sharing a mattress together in the waiting room. It was in a corner, but I can't tell you which one, I'm afraid."

"I'll find her. You just take it easy, and the others will be here soon." Krause strode out of the room, to the stairwell.

She descended past the first floor and into the basement and went to the lab Doctor Wiater occupied. She found him hunched over a microscope. "We're assembling the volunteers now. Any further developments?"

Wiater sat up and turned toward her while rubbing his eyes. "No. I've been observing the cadaver tissue since treatment with the tube. The level of beta radiation, while high, does not seem to have any effect on the rods and cones. The cancerous cells have been disrupted and don't seem to be regenerating, but until we do trials on living humans, I can't be sure of anything, including potential relapse." Wiater reached for a tube beside him on the bench. "Here, this is my mark II design. I applied a thin sheet of lead foil inside the tube and iris for better radiation containment and added a countdown LED timer. The timer automatically adjusts to the half-life degradation. As time goes by, the treatment times will get longer. Once it reaches the theoretical minimum for radioactivity, the LED will display three X's and the iris will not open. The batteries are new, so they should last for a couple of thousand treatments." He handed her the tube.

Krause bounced it in her hand for a moment. "It's heavier than the prototype. How long until the rest are finished?"

He shook his head. "I'm not going to do any more until we're sure these work. I have all the materials to make them ready to go, but until we see promising results…"

"Okay. That makes sense. I'll be upstairs with the volunteers in room two-oh-seven. You should come by and meet them at some point. Spending all your time in this lab isn't healthy. Come and see the people you're helping."

"Maybe later. I'm still going through the research material and reviewing my notes. Without thorough peer review, I need to be absolutely sure of every single aspect of this treatment."

Krause could tell from the sound of his voice that arguing with him would be fruitless. "I'll be upstairs, if you change your mind."

Krause left the lab with the tube in hand. Halfway up the stairs to the ground floor, she began examining the tube. The increased weight over the prototype made her consider it much more seriously. *The fate of the entire world is resting in the palm of my hand… No pressure.*

* * *

Captain Reid hadn't moved from the plotting table when he saw his XO, Commander Harry Maddox, return to the command center. Reid made eye contact and nodded toward an unoccupied corner. They met up and spoke in low tones. "Where did you put them, XO? They give you any trouble?"

"Escape trunk. They moaned and complained about it, but we stuffed them in along with a pair of mattresses and a bucket to crap in. It's crude, but with no SEALs onboard, the space shouldn't be used for anything else. If they try to get out, only one will fit through the entry hatch at a time. I left a pair of engineers on guard with some large wrenches to discourage anyone from leaving. I told them if they made any problems we'd just flood the space with seawater. That shut them up."

Reid looked across the compartment to see a seaman mopping up the blood from the dark rubber tiles. He tried to keep his voice low, but his rage at their mutiny was barely contained. "They killed a good man. My first inclination was to fire them out of a torpedo tube."

"You mean 'men,' don't you, sir?" Maddox asked with a frown.

Reid shook his head, calming a little. "No. P.O. Blevins is dead. The other man, Evans, lost a lot of blood, but he's still breathing. The corpsman says he's got a fifty-fifty chance."

Maddox made the sign of the cross. "Thank God. I thought we'd lost them both."

He had never seen any form of religious expression in the XO before. He decided to ignore it. "We still might. Until we get back to port, the prisoners are not to communicate with anyone. Make sure no one from the Torpedo Room is assigned guard duty. All three prisoners are from that compartment, and I don't want this spreading."

"Aye, sir." Maddox paused a moment. "Captain, what's the plan?"

Reid frowned. "Sorry. I don't follow."

Maddox glanced around the room before continuing, voice very low. "The airwaves have been silent since the message from Pearl arrived. The blindness affliction looks to be widespread, and it's obviously affected command and control. What are we going to do?"

Reid crossed his arms, not liking where the conversation was leading. "We're a warship of the United States Navy, Commander. We're going to continue our patrol as ordered and stand by for further instructions from the NCA."

"And if no further orders arrive? Then what?"

Reid shifted his weight, uncomfortable. He simply didn't know the answer to that question. "We'll handle that situation when the time arrives, XO. We don't have the luxury of independent action here. Otherwise we'll end up in a brig ourselves. I know it looks bleak. The lack of communication has me deeply concerned, as well. Until comms are reestablished, we shall stand to our duties as long as our supplies last."

Maddox nodded toward the men in the Control Center. "A lot of the men have families, sir. What happened with Wyatt could happen again as time goes by."

Reid uncrossed his arms. "Are you siding with mutineers, XO?"

"No, sir, I am not!" Maddox took a breath and glanced down. "I am trying to do *my* duty and follow your orders."

"My orders?" Reid frowned. *What's he talking about?*

"The first order you gave me when I came on board as XO. You told me that when we were in private, you wanted my honest opinion, good or bad. That's all I'm doing. We need to stay on patrol and do our jobs, but the men are nervous. Unless we can reassure them and give them something to focus on, then what happened with Wyatt will happen again. Only next time, it'll be half the boat rising up."

Reid *had* given him that order. However, Maddox was a natural conversationalist and had a similar personality to Reid, so they communicated freely regardless. Reid held out his hand. "You're right, Harry. I shouldn't have questioned your integrity."

Maddox shook his hand firmly. "No apologies needed. We're all in this together. May I make a suggestion?"

"Of course." Reid leaned against a chair.

"Military channels are blacked out. If we move to the edge of our patrol area, we'll be closer to the U.S. coast. We may be able to pick up civilian radio stations to get some sort of update as to what the hell is going on with the world."

That made perfect sense. Reid began moving toward the plotting table. "All right, I'll order a course correction."

Maddox held up his hand to stop him. "Captain, I'll do that. You go get some rack time, and I'll call you when we get close to the coast. From here, it'll be four hours."

Reid opened his mouth to argue, but he did feel weary, and four hours' rack time sounded good to him. "Very well. XO has the conn. Call me in four hours."

He strode out of the Control Center and entered his compact cabin. He stripped off his dress whites and sat on the edge of the bed in his underwear. He considered his door, then stood up, and threw the bolt, locking it. It was the first time he'd ever done that.

* * *

Colonel Smith had just finished his shift watching the airfield from the kitchen when Vinson called for him from the living room, sounding excited.

Smith turned the corner of the threshold to see Vinson waving him over with a huge smile. "What's up?"

"I was able to get into the Wenchang Satellite Launch Center. They're the ones who launched the rockets for the orbital fireworks."

Smith sat down on the couch beside Vinson and looked at the screen, which was filled with indecipherable Chinese characters. To Smith, they looked like squiggles made by a three-year-old, and he had no idea what they meant. "What did you find?"

"I located a manifest of the total load carried by each rocket. It's a spreadsheet listing specific contents, purpose, and exact weights. Fuel, electronic packages, communications, the chassis of the rocket itself—It's all in there.

"One line item stood out. It's listed as 'activity six-eight-nine' and has a weight of two hundred and seventy-four kilos. That's it. No description, documentation, purpose, or responsible agency is listed. See here in the spreadsheet. This line is for six-eight-nine…"

That line item had many empty fields. No other entry had any empty fields. "Okay, I see the empty fields, but why is that important?"

Vinson used his hands for emphasis. "Before coming to NORAD, I did a two-year tour in Kyrgyzstan. We have an intercept station on the top floor of our embas... Ummm, you might want to forget I said that, sir. Anyway, all sorts of documentation from several Chinese agencies came across my screen daily. The China National Space Administration is a huge bureaucracy and has a lot of oversight. They go into painstaking detail about everything in their documentation. For them to list payload information without that detail indicates that it's classified. It would take someone in a position of great power to authorize withholding that level of information. I'm sure that's the warhead they used. I feel it in my bones."

Smith failed to see how it could help them and tapped the entry on the screen. "I still don't understand how this benefits us."

Vinson smiled broadly. "Sir, up until now we've been searching in the dark. I've spent hours going through information almost randomly looking for clues. Now we have something specific to search for."

"Won't searching for a specific name, especially a classified one, be dangerous? Is there any chance they'll see you looking for it?" The possibility of losing their only intelligence source worried Smith greatly.

"It's doubtful, the way I'm doing it. At worse, any trace will end up on the military laptop plugged into the network at Cheyenne Mountain. I'm confident I can do this without compromising our access."

Smith stood and met Vinson's gaze. He nodded once. "Go ahead. We're desperate for information, and we'll have to risk it. Take every precaution as you work, and call me if you need anything."

* * *

As a precaution in case the recovering patients would be hypersensitive to light, Doctor Krause made sure the curtains were completely drawn to keep light in the hospital room to a minimum. Her eyes adjusted to the dimness. The four volunteers lay on their respective beds, waiting to see again. Mrs. Antonio and her sister held hands and pushed the beads of a rosary through their free hands as they finished each prayer.

The three other volunteers were less active. Two were fast asleep, and the last, a Mister Darwin, tapped his fingers on his chest. She assumed he was remembering a favorite song.

Krause checked her watch. She didn't need to check vital signs for another ten minutes.

She was beginning to get concerned. Doctor Wiater had seen results after two hours in the lab with the eye tissue taken from cadavers. The volunteers were coming up on the four-hour mark after receiving beta radiation treatment, and no progress had been noted. Krause had taken their vitals every half hour and noted nothing out of the ordinary, but the amount of time that had passed without positive results could mean the treatment was a bust.

She began to feel the first effects of despondency—not for the four volunteers, but for the rest of humanity who were struggling in the dark.

Oscar Blake entered the room with his usual confident smile. He carried a tray of juice boxes, along with small cellophane bags of snacks. Krause smiled back immediately. He'd been a rock throughout the crisis, dependable and strong. She knew she could rely on him.

Blake kept his volume low. "Hey, Doc. The generator tanks are full. I found a truck with four thousand gallons of diesel. Want a snack?"

"No, not right now, thanks. I'm sure the rest would, though."

Over Blake's shoulder, she noticed one of the previously sleeping patients sit up. She walked around Blake to reach him. "Good afternoon, Mister Vernon. Would you like a juice box?"

He rubbed his eyes and yawned. "Yeah, thanks."

Blake went over by the bed. Vernon took a juice box off the tray.

Krause looked at Blake in disbelief. "He can see?" She turned back to Vernon, feeling elation. "You can see?"

Vernon stopped fiddling with the straw glued to the side of the box and looked up at her. Surprise and wonder crossed his face. "I can. I can! I was so groggy, I didn't even realize it."

Krause turned around. Mrs. Antonio had sat up and was looking around the room with her mouth and eyes wide open. "Thank God. Thank God. Thank God…" she repeated.

The other two volunteers were smiling, as well.

Krause turned back to Blake, who had put the tray down on an empty chair. She ran up to him and wrapped her arms around his neck, hugging him. "They can see, it worked!"

Blake spun her around in a full circle and gently put her down. Relief surged through her, and for a moment, she experienced nothing but pure happiness. *There's hope. Finally, there's a cure.*

Relief flowed over her, and Krause began to cry. She pressed her face into Blake's hard chest. The smell of a freshly showered man surrounded her. She could feel his strong, wide muscular shoulders beneath his soft flannel shirt.

She pulled away slightly to look up into his eyes. Blake wiped a tear from her cheek with the side of his left thumb. He smiled down at her, and in that instant, Doctor Linda Krause didn't want to be anywhere else.

* * *

Captain Eric Reid lay in his bunk, dreaming of better days. Every year, he would take his family to a large lake and rent a two-bedroom cabin for a week. There, they could run, swim, and relax. No radio, television, or Internet intruded on the idyllic scene. There were other cottages spread sporadically around the lakeshore, but everyone kept to themselves, only occasionally exchanging waves from a distance. At night, weather permitting, each cabin built a bonfire. The kids would roast marshmallows and hot dogs. After the children went to bed, he would sit out by the crackling embers beside his wife and look up at the brilliant stars above.

In his dream, he sat there, holding his wife's hand. The other cabins were illuminated by their fires. He breathed a deep sigh of satisfaction.

Across the lake, he noticed a distant fire on the opposite shore growing dimmer. It eventually died out completely. A second fire went out soon after. The fires about the lake faded, one by one.

He looked up at the stars. One after the other, they winked out, too.

Under the dark sky, he returned his attention to his own bonfire, the only remaining source of illumination, which was also dying. He grabbed some firewood at his side and fed the fire, but tossing pieces of dry wood into the pit did nothing.

Blackness descended, leaving him in pitch darkness.

Reid tossed and turned on his bunk as he flailed in the night to find his family.

* * *

After examining the four recovered patients and making notes on their conditions, Linda Krause led Blake to an examination room in the ER. There were a few people in adjoining beds, but they appeared asleep. "Sit on the gurney, and we'll see how your eye turned out."

Blake sat, and Krause pulled a rolling tray of instruments over to her side. She realized with annoyance that a few things were missing, but she had what she needed to remove Blake's bandage.

Stepping in toward him, she looked down on his face. She selected a pair of surgical scissors. "Hold still."

She placed her palm against his cheek and placed her thumb over the gauze. She peeled back the white adhesive tape from his forehead and cheek. The last piece went over his temple. She used the scissors to cut that tape while holding the bandage in place with her thumb. She placed the scissors back on the tray, saying, "Close both your eyes for a moment."

She pulled the bandage away from his eye. The lid over the eye she had operated on had minor bruising but looked better than she expected. She discarded the gauze in a nearby trash container. "Your eye may be sensitive to light, so open it slowly."

His lids fluttered as he opened his eyes. He blinked a few times.

Krause held up an index finger and began moving it. "Follow my finger."

He seemed to have no issues following her motion.

"How does it feel?"

Blake smiled. "It's a bit itchy, but I can see fine."

"Excellent. Let me take a look at the stitches. Lean your head back a little, please." She picked up an ophthalmoscope, turned on the internal light, and examined the minute stitches in his eye at fifteen times magnification. She saw no issues or post-surgical tears. His eye was healing nicely and the suture she had used would be naturally absorbed by his body over time. She placed the ophthalmoscope back on the tray and her hands in the lab coat pockets. "Everything looks good, Oscar. You're healing well, and I see no problems at all. Let me know if you experience any itchiness or swelling, but I suspect you'll be fine."

He smiled up at her. "Great. Thanks, Linda."

She smiled with closed lips, stepped back from him, and nodded toward the rolling tray. "That's all for now. If you'll excuse me, I need to restock this tray."

"Of course. I'll go see if Doctor Wiater needs anything." Blake left.

Krause went to the nearby supply cabinets and pulled out the missing items to replenish the tray. The duty nurse was supposed to do that, but everyone was so busy, it had been overlooked.

Just as she was finishing, Blake came back in the room with his hand behind his back.

"Back so soon?" she asked with a raised eyebrow.

Blake handed her a bouquet of long-stem pink roses. "You said you wanted pink roses, so here you are."

She gasped in surprise. "Oh, they're beautiful. Where did you get them?" She sniffed them, smelt nothing, then realized they were made of silk.

"When we went to the food warehouse, I spotted a flower shop. The real flowers were all wilted when I went in, so I hope those will do. You kept your end of the deal, so there's mine."

"They're perfect, and I'll be able to keep them forever. Thank you." She clutched the roses to her chest. She felt like she was sixteen again, on her first date. She looked up into his green eyes. *Kiss me; kiss me; kiss me.*

"Glad you like them. I'll see you later." Blake stepped in closer, gently touched her upper arm, and then left the room.

What the... Why didn't he... Couldn't he tell I wanted him to...? As his footsteps faded, Krause looked at the silk flowers and heaved a sigh. "Men."

July 9th

Chapter Sixteen
Optimism

Doctor Krause entered the lab where Doctor Wiater was conducting his research to find him on a stool, hunched over a laboratory counter, with his head on his folded arms. His breathing was shallow, his eyes were closed, and he looked to be soundly asleep.

The poor man must be exhausted. But he had been so worried about the trials—he'd surely want to know the results as soon as possible. Besides, sleeping on a hard bench couldn't be comfortable. She glanced back at the door. Blake stood on the threshold, holding up his hand to those waiting in the hallway.

Krause gently shook him by the shoulder. "Doctor Wiater? I have excellent news."

Wiater sat bolt upright with a sharp intake of breath, his hands placed on the counter before him. "What…"

"All four of the volunteers got their sight back. You did it, Doctor. The cure works."

Wiater placed his face in his hands. "It worked? My God, it worked. I don't believe it."

Due to her hand on his shoulder, she felt him shudder. *He's crying.* She looked around then pulled a large absorbent wipe from a dispenser on a shelf above the counter. "Here, take this."

Wiater took it in both hands and held it to his face. After a brief pause, he wiped it downwards and then crumpled it up into one hand and wiped his nose with it. "…Sorry," he said eventually. "I'm sorry."

Krause put her arms around him and gave him a brief but reassuring hug. "You've done the work of twenty people over the last three days, Doctor, and achieved the impossible. I'm so very grateful."

Wiater nodded, sniffed, and looked as if he were beginning to get a grip on himself. "We need to observe the volunteers and make sure there's no regression. We still have a lot of work ahead of us."

"Agreed, but first the volunteers want to meet and thank you."

Wiater tossed the wipe onto the counter. "Yes, yes, I'll get upstairs at some point. For now, I need to—"

Krause interrupted. "No, Doctor. I mean turn around and meet the people you've helped."

"Huh?" Wiater turned.

Krause waved Blake in from the corridor. He escorted the four volunteers through the doorway.

As they came in, Krause said, "Doctor Wiater, this is Mrs. Antonio, Miss Lee, Mister Vernon, and Mister Darwin. They all insisted on coming down to meet you."

Mrs. Antonio was the first to get to Wiater. She grabbed him in a tight hug. "You wonderful, wonderful man. Thank you."

Miss Lee held Wiater tightly from the opposite side. "Thank you so much, Doctor."

That left the two male volunteers. Vernon moved in and gripped Wiater in a bear hug, lifting his feet off the ground for a few seconds before releasing him and holding his biceps. "You tell me what you want as a reward for this, and I'll make it happen, Doc. Anything at all."

Wiater said nothing. He simply nodded as Vernon took a step back.

Darwin simply shook hands with Wiater.

Seeing Wiater's face, Krause reached for a fresh wipe. If he didn't need it, she suspected she would.

* * *

Colonel Smith stared at the kitchen calendar taped to the side of the refrigerator. He ignored the bright image of sunflowers on the upper half and focused on the grid of dates below. The Chinese ships were due to arrive on the west coast of the U.S. in a week, and he had nothing to stop them—absolutely nothing. No navy, no coast guard, no army.

He realized that wasn't entirely true. There were still submarines in the ocean, both SSBN[21] missile boats carrying nuclear missiles and SSN[22] hunter-killer submarines. They had been underwater during the fireworks and therefore should've been immune to the effects of whatever blinded the world.

But he had no way to warn them there was an invading force on the way. If a sub chanced upon the convoy, it wouldn't be regarded as hostile—the boats were civilian merchantmen.

He sighed heavily through his nose. *Without a cure, we are well and truly—*

"Colonel, may I see you outside on the front step?" Captain Erica Tyler asked, interrupting his thoughts.

"Of course." He indicated she should go first. Smith followed her through the living room. He couldn't help but look at her shapely backside, but he kept his glance brief so no one would notice. He passed Vinson, who was still on the couch, huddled over the laptop. Tyler had already opened the door for him before he'd reached it.

He closed the door behind them and sat down on the stoop with Tyler to his right.

"Sir, I need to speak frankly."

"Go ahead." He twisted on the concrete to face her directly.

---

[21] Submersible Self-propelled Ballistic Nuclear. *Ohio*-class submarines that carry ballistic nuclear missiles.

[22] Submersible Self-propelled Nuclear. Current SSNs in service include *Los Angeles*-, *Seawolf*- and *Virginia*-class submarines.

"I'm getting concerned about you, Colonel. Over the last few days, you've stopped talking to everyone except Vinson, and that's only irregularly. You're drinking so much coffee that you're not sleeping. I can see the stress on your face. Just now, you were staring so hard at the calendar that I thought your ears would start bleeding."

"What's your point, Captain? We do have Chinese troops occupying our country, in case you haven't noticed."

Tyler clasped her hands together. "Yes, sir, I have. My point is we need you—healthy and thinking clearly. If something happens to you, I can't take over. I'd have no idea what to do. I work in the NORAD headquarters administration unit. My days are spent working with forms, memos, files, and records. I only became your aide because I didn't lose my sight. I'm not the natural leader you are, and I don't have the knowledge or experience to deal with this. You said you wanted me to be your conscience. My advice is to lay off the caffeine, get a solid eight hours sleep a night, and talk to me."

The last part of her sentence took him by surprise. He raised an eyebrow. "Talk to you?"

Tyler nodded. "Yes, sir. It's obvious you're under a lot of pressure. Tell me what's on your mind and get it off your chest. I don't have to understand the issues, but I'll listen to you as you describe them. It'll help."

Smith held his breath. His gut reaction was to rebuff her, but he stopped to consider what she had said first. The hardest thing he had learned to do as a leader was objectively assess the opinions of his staff. In this case, objectivity was much more difficult, for he was the topic of discussion. But she was right that he wasn't sleeping well. "Look—"

High-pitched squealing brakes interrupted him as a khaki green Humvee came to a halt on the road at the end of the turf farm driveway, three hundred feet away. The two Chinese soldiers in front were arguing loudly. Tyler started to jump up, but Smith pressed down on her thigh, keeping her in place.

"Don't move!"

* * *

The phone mounted to the bulkhead above Captain Reid's head rang. He felt as if he'd just closed his eyes. Instantly awake, he twisted around and grabbed the handset. "Captain."

"Sir, you asked me to call you after four hours. We're approaching the coast." The voice was Commander Maddox.

"Thank you, XO." He hung up and fell back into his pillow, rubbing his face with both hands. He sighed, sat up, and rolled out of bed. Looking at himself in the small wall-mounted mirror above the sink, he decided he should shave to look presentable.

While scraping the stubble from his cheeks with a disposable razor and shaving cream, he considered his reflection. The obvious circles under his eyes normally didn't appear on his naturally dark black skin until the last month of a tour at sea, but there they were after only a week. He shook his head slightly in disgust as he rinsed the plastic razor in the sink.

Once done, he dressed in a short-sleeve service uniform and a dark blue baseball cap with "USS John Warner, SSN-785" embroidered in gold thread.

Reid grabbed his door handle and pulled. The door remained where it was, and his fingers slipped from the small handle. Cursing himself for forgetting he had locked it earlier, he threw the bolt and opened the door. The narrow corridor was dark with red lighting to simulate night. It helped keep the crews' circadian rhythms normal on long undersea deployments.

Half a dozen steps brought him into the command center. Reid instinctively looked to see the boat's current course, position, depth, and speed presented on a navigation screen. His XO greeted him by handing him a cup of coffee. Reid nodded in appreciation.

"Morning, Captain. We're directly between Santa Catalina and San Clemente islands heading north. I was about to go up to photonics depth for our first scan."

"Proceed." Reid went to take a sip of the extremely hot coffee, but it was too hot to drink. He pulled the mug away from his lips before tasting it and placed it on the plotting table to cool.

Maddox called down to the sonar operator. "Sonar, conn. Report all contacts."

"Conn, sonar. I show no contacts at this time."

"Very well, pilot, take us to photonics depth," the XO ordered.

"Ascend to photonics depth, pilot aye."

The sub's nose came up slightly. The coffee in Reid's mug inclined toward the back of the boat. The ascent was slow and uneventful, and by the time they made it to photonics depth, Reid was able to sip his coffee.

"Raise ESM[23] mast," the XO commanded.

"Sir, I'm raising the ESM mast," came the reply from the radar console operator. The dim sound of hydraulic actuators sounded for about five seconds. "Sir, ESM mast is raised. There are no contacts."

The XO nodded. "Thank you, Captain, your orders?"

Reid didn't hesitate. "Raise the communication mast. Let's see if anyone's talking." A minute later, he asked, "Do we have anything coming over the CSRR[24]?"

Chief Holgrim at the CSRR station replied, "No data, sir, but I do have carrier signals on all bands. Terrestrial and satellite comms are up, but no one is talking."

Reid stepped closer to the CSRR station. "What about civilian bands?"

"Scanning those now, sir. Will take a while. I have to dial those frequencies in manually," the chief replied.

---

[23] ESM (Electronic Support Measures) is a passive system, used to identify and track active electromagnetic transmissions like radar from distant sources.
[24] CSRR (Common Submarine Radio Room) is standardized technology that combines radios, cryptography, and messaging systems to unify tactical and strategic communications on all *Virginia-*, *Los Angeles-*, *Sea Wolf-*, and *Ohio-*class submarines.

Reid turned back to the XO. "Keep moving north at photonics depth and let Chief Holgrim see if he can hear anything. Do you need a break?"

"No, sir. I'm fine for now," Maddox replied.

Reid picked up his coffee mug from the plotting table. "I'll grab some breakfast and be back to relieve you."

* * *

Colonel Smith kept his eyes on the two Chinese soldiers, his hand stayed on Captain Tyler's thigh so she couldn't stand up from the stoop. He whispered, quietly but firmly, "The human eye is drawn to movement. They won't see us if we stay perfectly still. The morning sun's on the opposite side of the house, so we're in the shadows."

The Chinese soldier driving the Humvee got out of the vehicle while gesturing wildly and yelling back at his passenger. Both men wore sky gray camouflage fatigues. The driver walked to a fence post, unzipped his fly, and began urinating while looking back over his shoulder at the Humvee and continuing his animated discussion with the passenger through the open driver's door.

Smith watched the Humvee passenger. He was looking in their general direction, and if anyone saw them, it would be he. The passenger had a long-barreled weapon between his knees, and a second—probably the driver's—beside him, leaning on the seat. Smith was armed, but the two men were three hundred feet away, and at that distance, his pistol would lose against their rifles. The gunfire would likely carry to the airfield as well, which would bring reinforcements. *Stay still. Be patient. He's just taking a leak and will be gone soon.*

What sort of rifles are those? I should recognize them, but I don't.

Smith became conscious of the heat from Captain Tyler's thigh against his palm. He wanted to move it, but he needed to stay still.

The driver zipped his fly, turned, and climbed back into the Humvee. He yelled something to the passenger, slammed his door, and drove down the road to the south.

The second the Humvee was out of sight, Smith yanked his hand from Tyler's leg and began to stand. "That's it. We're leaving."

Smith quickly got up and ran inside. "Everyone, pack up! Chinese patrols are starting on the roads. We need to bug out."

Vinson stood up from the couch, pointing at the laptop. "Sir, I just got into the secure database at the launch site. We can't leave now."

The rest of the small group appeared from the kitchen. "We have no choice. Download what you can and then pack up." To the rest, Smith said, "We're moving in five minutes."

Vinson came around the coffee table. "Colonel, I need more time! Give me a half hour at least! If I kill the connection now, I may not be able to re-establish it. It's taken me days to get into their secure database, and we may never have this opportunity again."

Smith considered the risk. Their position was still secure for the moment, and if they waited, the Humvee they had seen would be farther away. "All right, a half hour. The rest of you, we need food, water, and supplies for the road. Let's move!"

* * *

Doctor Linda Krause felt elated as she finished up entering her notes on the tube trials in the break room. She used a stack of canned food as a makeshift standing desk. A second test group of eight volunteers had just regained their sight and were up and about. Even better news—the original four volunteers had remained stable with no changes in their vision. The possibility of a relapse seemed distant to her.

Oscar Blake came up beside her. "Linda, Doctor Wiater has finished building all the tubes he could. We have a dozen ready to go. The only question is, what do we do now?"

Linda put her pen down on the notes. "What do we do? We cure everyone."

Blake raised his palms up for a moment. "That's the issue. We can get to everyone in Seattle fairly quickly, but no aircraft are flying. What about the South, the East Coast, Canada, Europe, Asia?"

"Oh, I see what you mean..." Time was against them. They needed to get this cure out to all affected areas. "We should try and let the president know about this. I'm sure he has some resources he can use to help us spread this. Washington DC—"

"DC is too far." Blake paced off to the corner. "It's a four- or five-day trip by road when the highways are clear. It'll be a week and probably more in these conditions."

"We don't have that amount of time. People are suffering out there," Krause objected.

He returned to her. "I know... I saw a TV documentary on a huge bunker in Colorado a few weeks ago. The one they built under a mountain in the fifties, what was it called?"

Krause had heard of it. "Cheyenne Mountain! They designed it to withstand a nuclear attack, so it would make sense that they wouldn't be affected by this. They would still have power, radios, and the means to spread the cure. It's a long way away, though, near the center of the country."

Blake nodded, his hand under his chin. "It is, but I drove down through Colorado last year on my way to Dallas. I was helping friends move furniture. Once you get away from Seattle, there are very few towns along the way. The route goes through the least populated states in the U.S.—Washington state, Oregon, Idaho... Few people, so there should be limited road obstructions. Plus, as you pointed out, Colorado is in the center of the country. Distribution from there should be easy for the military."

"How long would it take me to get there?" she asked.

"We did it straight through without stopping, save for gas and food, and it took us less than a day to get to Denver.

Assuming there's some sort of problem on the way, it would be two days at most, if we push it."

"We? You're planning on coming with me?" She smiled at him.

"Well, I'm not going to let you go alone. I've been that way, I know the roads, and I owe you for this." He tapped below his damaged eye while moving closer to her.

"I… I mean, I'd like the company, I think." She beamed at him.

He smiled back. "We should go and talk to Doctor Wiater first. Make sure we're all on the same page."

She pointed at the file on the stack of cans. "I'm done here. Let's go see him now."

Blake led the way to the stairwell. He opened the doors for her along the way, which she appreciated. They descended down the staircase and found their way to Wiater's lab.

Krause turned the corner to find Wiater hunched over a microscope. "Doctor?"

Wiater sat up and turned to face her. "Ahh, I'm glad you're here. The tubes are finished. Including the prototype I gave you earlier, we now have thirteen." He went over to a cardboard box further down the counter.

Krause joined him and could see the tubes within. "Oscar and I were just talking about that. We think taking them to a command bunker in Colorado would be best. The military should be able to spread it to the rest of the country from there."

Wiater looked away slightly and nodded slowly. "I hadn't considered that, but did have an idea myself. A dozen tubes won't cure the entire country in a timely manner. We need more, many more. The rhenium-188 I used was manufactured at the Oak Ridge National Laboratory in Tennessee. If we can get their staff and feeder reactors working, we should be able to manufacture more rhenium isotope and subsequent tubes.

"By the way, here's a schematic of the tube design. On the back, I included all my calculations. That's everything anyone needs to make more tubes."

"Thanks. Oak Ridge is even further than Colorado. I suppose we could carry on once we talk to the people in the bunker." Blake came up beside her.

Wiater shook his head, folding his arms. "No. You should go to Colorado. I'll find other volunteers to go to Oak Ridge. No need to put all our eggs in a single basket, as it were."

Krause couldn't argue with that logic.

Blake chimed in, "How do we split up the tubes? We need some here to bring Seattle back to life."

Wiater touched the cardboard box of tubes. "You have the prototype. We can keep four here. Give two to the Oak Ridge team, and that leaves six for Colorado. As people are cured, they can bring in more of the blind, and over time, we should be able to get the city back up and running."

Krause had a thought. "If we focus on the airport, we can take planes and get to both places in a few hours."

Wiater shook his head. "The rest of the city is largely without power. We'd need to locate qualified pilots, maintenance crews, and get power online for fuelling. Just finding the right people's houses will take days, and there's no guarantee they're still there, or even alive. Driving there is the simplest solution for the moment."

Krause looked over at Blake, who simply shrugged.

"What he says makes sense, Doc. Give me an hour to collect some supplies and a vehicle, and then we can hit the road."

"All right. Go ahead."

Blake left the room.

"The second group of volunteers successfully regained their sight," she told Wiater.

His eyebrows momentarily lifted. "Any side effects noted?"

"Nothing so far. Why, were you expecting some?" she asked, concerned.

"No, not really. I chose rhenium-188 specifically for minimal side effects, so that's good to see. After you leave, I'll set up a system to get people in here for treatment. There's a police station just down the road. Getting them and the firefighters back on the road before the others is probably a good idea."

"You don't expect anyone to cause trouble, do you?"

"Frankly, I do. Human beings have an annoying habit of being selfish and taking advantage of situations for personal gain. The last thing we need is organized crime or some skinheads taking control of the cure. Can you imagine? Splitting up the tubes will give us a much greater chance of success for curing everyone."

Krause began taking the tubes she would be transporting out of the cardboard box. "That's a fairly cynical attitude, Doctor. I'd like to think people are better than that."

Wiater pointed to the wound on his bicep that she had stitched up earlier. "I tried to help someone and got stabbed for my trouble. Cynicism is hard to ignore when you face such things. Do me a favor. When you're on the road, be careful. You're going to meet a lot of desperate and ignorant people. If you treat someone, get clear before they regain their sight. That tube in your hand will make you a target if you don't."

"I'll be fine, Doctor." *People always pull together in a crisis, don't they?*

Chapter Seventeen
On the Road

Captain Reid stood near the plotting table and looked over at Chief Holgrim, who was manning the CSRR station. Holgrim had insulated headphones clamped over his ears. He delicately adjusted a radio receiver-tuning dial with the tips of his fingers, looking like a safecracker from a 1930s film. He had the same position and level of concentration.

"Here's the coastal chart from our current position up to San Francisco, sir." Maddox interrupted Reid's train of thought as he came up beside him. He unrolled the chart he carried on the plotting table.

The *Virginia*-class submarines had a fully integrated state-of-the-art electronic navigation system, but all course plots were still done by hand, on paper charts. If the computers ever failed, the paper charts would tell them exactly where they were. Reid took the chart and unrolled it, placing various items from the plotting table at the corners to keep the paper flat. Picking up a fine-tip marker from a cup full of similar pens, he then checked a digital display suspended from the overhead, showing the boat's current position. He located those coordinates on the chart and marked it with a press of the marker. "We're here, and our baseline course takes us to... Here. If there's anything transmitting on shore, we should have a good chance of picking it up."

Maddox indicated the CSRR station. "Chief Holgrim hasn't taken a break all day, sir. He's refused relief twice now."

Reid capped the marker and checked his watch. "His watch ends in an hour. We'll give him a break then. I'm not going to come down on him too hard. He comes from California— Berkeley, I believe."

Chief Holgrim pulled the right side of his headphones off to one side. "Captain, I have something on the FM band."

"Put it on the overhead speakers, chief."

Holgrim flipped a switch, and a female singer was heard. Everyone listened for a few moments.

"That's Beyoncé," said the seaman at weapons control.

"No, it isn't, Berman. That's Katy Perry. It's from her new album," said the chief beside him.

"Quiet on deck," Maddox ordered.

The song ended, and a man's deep bass came over the speaker. "KHOP-FM at ninety-five point one FM. All the hits."

Then a series of male and female voices came over the speaker, accompanied by background music. "Modesto... Ninety-five point one... All the hits... We love K-HOP...! The best music... Stockton... Fifty thousand watts... The best giveaways... Fresno... K-H-O-P!"

Silence followed.

Reid turned to the CSRR station. "Chief, did we lose the signal?"

"No, sir. I still have the—"

A Black Eyed Peas hit started playing.

"Captain, it's an automated station," Maddox said. "The silent part is where the DJs would talk. Everything else is pre-recorded."

"Makes sense. Chief Holgrim, feed that signal through the boat. Keep the volume reasonable."

"Aye sir," Holgrim responded.

Reid turned to Maddox and pointed to the chart. "Modesto is about here on the mainland. Looks like they still have power at least."

Maddox grimaced. "Probably a backup generator. Most of the larger stations would have them for earthquakes, that sort of thing. No one is talking, so we're listening to a hard drive with queued recordings. Good idea to pipe it through the boat. Will do the men a world of good to hear something normal."

"Doesn't give us any actionable information though." Reid tapped the end of his capped marker on the plotting table.

"Right now, sir, all we can do is wait for someone in command to pull their thumb out and establish contact with orders that make sense."

"Yeah. You know how much I love sitting around and waiting." Reid placed his fists on the plot table. "But you're right. Without an operational reason, I can't leave our patrol area. Leave the music on for a while. Even the insurance commercials will build morale, at this point."

"Yes, sir."

* * *

Smith ordered Tech Sergeant Folsom to back their van up to the front stoop of the house to facilitate loading. As a human chain, the group loaded food and water into the back of the van. Sleeping bags, blankets, and pillows taken from the home went in next.

Satisfied they had everything needed to survive on the road, Smith returned inside to find Vinson, who still sat on the couch.

"Thirty seconds, Colonel, and I'll be done. Downloading the last of the exported database now."

"Right." Smith walked deeper into the home and checked they were not leaving anything of consequence behind. He picked up the briefcase containing communication authentication codes from the master bedroom and checked the lock. Smith didn't expect anyone would try to get into his case, but seeing the locks were secure made him feel better. He carried it in his left hand, cast one last look around the bedroom, and couldn't see anything else to take. He went back into the living room to see Vinson packing up his laptop.

"All done, sir. I found some really good intel and downloaded copies." Vinson's smile beamed. "Oh, and here's your cell phone back. I charged the battery off my USB port."

"Thanks. We'll talk about it on the road. Get moving." Smith pocketed the cell phone in his breast shirt pocket, checked the living room, found nothing of import left behind, and strode out the front door.

Everyone else save Vinson was already seated and ready to go. Vinson placed his laptop case under a rear seat with care, then hopped in, closing the side door behind him. Smith got in the passenger door, placing the briefcase in the passenger footwell.

Smith nodded to Tech Sergeant Folsom.

He pressed the brake, started the engine, put the truck in gear, and turned to face Smith. "Where to?"

Smith realized he had neglected to tell anyone but Tyler where they should go. "Hill Air Force Base in Utah. They're the closest non-strategic military location. Let's stick to the back roads until we clear the area. I don't want the Chinese to see us."

Folsom nodded. "Yes, sir." He began driving down the long dirt driveway to the road.

Smith pulled his seat belt on, twisted around as best as he could, and faced Vinson…who had taken the time to do up his bow tie. "What did you learn?"

"The Chinese don't have a cure for the blindness. I found a top-secret memorandum dated three weeks ago from the director of the Wenchang Satellite Launch Center to the officer in charge of warhead development. They used unspecific language, but it's clear they were talking about the blindness warheads. He asked about a cure in case of 'accidental exposure' for his workforce. The response clearly states there is no cure, and there was no chance of an accidental warhead detonation."

Smith felt the disappointment to his core. "Then there's no hope?"

"There's something else. I found a manifest showing the contents of the special satellites they launched. There are still three blindness warheads in orbit. They substituted different pyrotechnics for the shows over China so their own people were not affected."

"How does that help us?" Smith asked bitterly.

"If we can figure out how to drop them, we could send them into the Pacific Ocean and get them out of Chinese hands." Vinson raised his hands, palm up, for emphasis.

"That doesn't help stop the invasion convoy or do anything to improve our situation," Smith observed.

"What about dropping the warheads on the invading troops instead? It wouldn't tip things in our favor, but would even the playing field somewhat."

Smith turned back to face the road to examine that question. *The only advantage we could gain using them here, assuming we could figure out how to launch them, is blinding the invading troops. Everyone in China would still be able to see, and they could ship over more soldiers. It would be a delay, rather than a solution. Plus, the few U.S. citizens who can see would be blinded.*

We could use the warheads on mainland China. The Chinese troops in the U.S. would still be able to see, and their numbers combined with the convoy soldiers could be a quarter million. They wouldn't be able to resupply, but America has a lot of resources to plunder. If we blinded their country, they would be pretty pissed off as well. Of course, they've been bayoneting helpless people already, so could things get any worse?

He also didn't have the authority to attack another country. NORAD was a defensive organization.

Neither solution presented a satisfactory outcome, in his opinion.

* * *

Doctor Linda Krause walked out through the emergency room doors, carrying the tubes wrapped carefully in surgical towels.

Blake had told her to meet her outside so they could start their road trip to Colorado.

She saw him and stopped dead. He wore black leather pants and jacket, but that wasn't the reason she stopped.

She gaped at the, the... *thing* he was close to. "What the hell is that?" she asked, both frowning and half amused at the same time. She'd never seen a vehicle like it before.

"It's a Spyder Can-Am Roadster. I thought it would be a good choice for a long-distance trip."

She looked it over. There was a vague similarity to a motorcycle, in that it had seating for two and handlebars, but there were two wheels up front and one in the rear. The seats were burgundy and the body a burnished silver. The wheel rims and body highlights were chrome. A matching trailer was connected to the rear on a pair of smaller wheels.

Krause moved closer to look it over.

"She has a stable ride and a high seating position so you have a good view around you. Cruise control, power steering, traction control, heated seats, GPS, and tons of storage. Has everything most cars have today," Blake informed her.

She nodded and turned to him. "Exactly, so why not take a car?"

"There's bound to be places where there's limited space to get through. Plus, the weather should be reasonably warm for a bike ride, and she gets forty miles to the gallon. I've got spare gas in the trailer, but we won't need a lot to run her."

What he said made sense. It wasn't as if there would be gas stations open every thirty miles, so economy would be a necessity. Besides, their main cargo was the tubes, and they were relatively compact. She ran her fingertips across the body. It did look quite sleek to her. "Where did you get it?"

"Right off the lot. I spotted it earlier while I was out scavenging for food." Blake walked around the bike.

"You stole it?" she asked, her hands on her hips.

"Borrowed. I had to improvise." Blake smiled, displaying that he was joking, and pulled a key ring out of his pocket.

"I don't know." Krause didn't like stealing.

"Linda, the food we gave to the people inside was technically stolen. The fuel truck filled with diesel I pulled around back to keep the generators going was stolen, too. It isn't like I'm going around all the jewelry stores grabbing as many diamonds as I can. I'm trying to get the world back on its feet. The bike is necessary to get us to Colorado, so yes, I'm borrowing it. If they want to arrest me after we get everyone's sight back, then I'll face the charges with a light heart."

Embarrassed, Krause dropped her gaze for a moment. She had judged him based on the world being normal. He was correct. They had all stolen things, but for a noble cause. "You're right. I'm sorry."

She'd ridden on motorcycles before, and they scared her. She looked at the strange vehicle with trepidation.

"I've already loaded some food and supplies, but you'll need to pack a few things for the trip. We can drive over to your place so you can grab some clothes," he offered calmly.

"Okay. We can try it out. I'll need a helmet."

Blake pulled two black helmets from behind the bike. "I got two in different sizes for you. Try them on."

She did after putting the wrapped tubes on the seat of the roadster. The first helmet was far too tight—she couldn't even get it over her head. The second fit perfectly. Her hand touched something by the left side of her face. "What's this?"

Blake reached up and pulled it down. "It's a microphone. The helmet has a built in walkie-talkie so we can talk. It turns on with this switch, here." He guided her hand to the rubber-covered button on the left side of the helmet. She pressed it, and a burst of static sounded in both ears.

He reached for his helmet, put it on, and turned his microphone on. "Testing. Testing."

"I hear you fine. I need to pack the tubes away." She went to open the mounted side bag closest to her.

"No, wait!" Blake said, reaching to stop her. "Not in there. That's where I put the diamonds."

She turned toward him with wide eyes and an open mouth. Her momentary shock ended when she saw the grin forming on his face. She backhanded him lightly across the shoulder. "Argh, I almost believed you for a second."

She opened the side bag and found nothing within. She carefully placed the tubes within and secured it. "All right, let's get on the road. Hop on."

They climbed onto the seat. The padded backrest and handles to hold onto made her feel secure. She wiggled into place. "This seat is really comfy, and I love the backrest. It feels like a normal chair."

Blake inserted the key and fired the bike up. "This is a long-distance cruiser. They designed it for comfort. Which way do I need to go?"

"I have an apartment on 14th Avenue South. Turn left, and I'll show you where to go."

"Okay, here we go."

Krause gripped the handles on either side of her seat. A former boyfriend in college had once taken her on the back of a Kawasaki racing motorcycle. It had been horrifically loud, a high-pitched wail that irritated her senses, and she'd had to hold onto him for dear life as he sped around the tightest of corners.

She clenched her teeth in anticipation of the same sort of ride, but Blake accelerated with care. They turned the corner out of the hospital without leaning. The ride was surprisingly smooth, and the engine purred along.

She relaxed her hold on the handles and began to enjoy herself.

She directed him which way to go, and they arrived at her apartment in under five minutes. He pulled up in front of the building, turned off the bike, and hopped off before offering her his hand. Krause took it, even though she could have easily made it off the bike on her own. She smiled at his gesture and pulled her helmet off.

"One sec." Blake went to the front of the bike and opened a compartment. He withdrew a compact roller bag and handed it to her. "There you go. That suitcase is designed to fit in the front compartment, so you can use that."

She looked it over. "It's perfect. Thanks. I'll only be a few minutes."

* * *

Colonel Smith looked through the van's windscreen at the city of Denver coming up in the distance. Highway 25 was remarkably uncluttered, with only a few abandoned vehicles, so their progress had been steady.

No one spoke. They either dozed or engaged with their own thoughts.

Smith kept running through scenarios, but no matter which way he approached the issues, everything pivoted on a cure; nothing else made a realistic difference. Without that, they would never have enough forces to oppose the enemy troops.

Tech Sergeant Folsom interrupted his thoughts. "Colonel, we're coming up on the intersection for the 430 highway, if you want to avoid going through the city."

"No, stay on this main road. The 430 would take us close to Site D, and the Chinese probably have troops there."

"Site D?" Folsom asked, frowning.

Smith realized he'd spoken without thinking. The tech sergeant obviously wasn't cleared for that location or he'd know where he was talking about. "Never mind. Stay on the highway. We're making good progress. How's the fuel holding up?"

Folsom checked the dash. "Just over a quarter tank. We should be able to get through Denver and can look for gas on the other side."

Smith nodded and looked toward the horizon. "Good. We'll need to find a place to hold up for the night. I don't want to drive with lights on if we can avoid it. We would be easily seen."

Folsom rubbed his chin. "Cheyenne is around the halfway mark. We should be able to find a place to overnight there."

"I was thinking Laramie. If we turn off at Fort Collins, we can take Highway 287 and cut the trip by at least thirty miles."

Folsom glanced at him. "True, but I've never taken that road before. Is it any good?"

"I've used it before. I used to go camping in Rocky Mountain National Park. It's half decent. I wouldn't take it in the winter, but this time of year, it should be a breeze."

"All right, sir. We'll go that way. I'll keep an eye on the gas and try to get us to Fort Collins. May as well fill up there, if we have to turn off the highway anyway."

Smith began thinking again of the issues before him. He pulled out his cell phone and saw there was still service here. That was encouraging. At least parts of the infrastructure were still working. He put the phone away, and they passed through the city of Denver. He had never seen the streets so empty and lifeless. There must have been people there, but he assumed they had heeded the president's warning and stayed home.

He wondered how many were still alive. He had been so busy dealing with the Chinese that he hadn't thought about the impact on the population. They would be groping in eternal darkness, unable to go beyond their homes without assistance. The thought depressed him, and it combined with the knowledge that there was no cure, producing despondency. His chin touched his chest, and he breathed deeply to fight off the tears forming in his eyes. The feeling of powerlessness almost overwhelmed him. Every aspect of society had been affected by the Chinese weapon. Even if the invaders could be thrown out, would the country be able to survive?

A soft hand touched his shoulder. He wiped his eyes on his shirtsleeve and turned to see Captain Tyler leaning forward to comfort him. He patted her hand before turning back to face the road. Her hand left his shoulder, and Smith forced himself to begin thinking over the next steps for the group.

* * *

Doctor Linda Krause was enjoying herself. The raised rear seat of the Spyder let her see the surrounding countryside as Blake drove them down Highway 90. The only noise came from the vehicle's engine and the dull roar of wind noise. The ride was so stable and smooth, she didn't bother to hold the seat handles. She wore a tan leather jacket that she had pulled from the back of her closet. It kept her warm enough, as Blake's torso blocked most of the wind.

Apart from the highway itself, there was nothing save endless rolling green forest around them. As a doctor, she seldom got outside. She worked all day in the hospital, then worked out at the gym, and finally went home to her apartment. The ride was the longest she'd been outside in years, and she realized what she'd been missing.

She'd chosen to come to Seattle partly because of the natural beauty of the area and almost immediately turned her back on it…and she knew why. She'd come to Seattle to get away from Donovan, her ex. He'd been such an emotional and financial drain that a clean break into a new city was the only thing that had kept her sane. She had thrown herself into her work to forget him, and she'd succeeded for a time. Then those flowers had arrived and the memories returned.

She realized something and spoke into her microphone. "Oscar?"

"Yes."

"You called me both 'Linda' and 'doctor' earlier. Why?"

"I only used Linda when we were alone. When others were in the room, I called you doctor. It seemed to me to be the respectful thing."

"Okay, thanks." Since he couldn't see her, she let herself smile broadly at his chivalry.

"Why are you smiling?" he asked.

She looked around rapidly. *Oh my God, he can see me in the side mirror.* Her smile vanished as she felt herself blushing. "I'm just happy to be outside. It's a beautiful day."

"Sure is. The sun feels great… Linda, I've been thinking. I'd like to make Boise our overnight spot, but that will mean driving in the dark for an hour or so."

"I don't mind. The more progress we make today, the less we have to do later."

Blake nodded. "I agree. Are you comfortable back there?"

"Yes, everything is great. I shouldn't have doubted you."

Looking at Blake in the side mirror, she saw him smile. She realized he was the exact opposite of Donovan in almost every way. If Blake saw a problem, he didn't whine or complain and blame others; he simply fixed it. He gave selflessly, and he did so with good humor and a smile. Donovan was a loser, and Blake was a winner in every way.

She regretted that the Spyder drove with such stability, because she badly wanted an excuse to wrap her arms around him.

July 10th

Chapter Eighteen
Convergence

Linda Krause awoke in her hotel suite, relaxed and happy. She stretched, moaning contentedly as she sat up and the luxuriously soft sheets fell away from her. The mattress of the king-sized bed felt like a cloud, and she had slept blissfully. It felt as though she was on vacation.

She got up to look out the window, straightening the long pink T-shirt she'd used as a nightshirt for years. The sun was just rising over the horizon, and the abandoned streets of Boise stretched out before her.

She turned to look at the room, which she had only briefly seen by flashlight the previous evening. It looked much better in the daylight. The king bed had a teak headboard with matching nightstands, and brass lamps were secured to the wall above. An unpowered alarm clock sat on the right-hand nightstand, beside her watch and the glass of water she had poured herself the night before. The building power was out, but the water pressure seemed unaffected for some reason. The flush toilet was appreciated, but she was not looking forward to a cold shower.

Beside the bathroom, the door to the adjoining room was wide open. The matching door leading into the other room was closed but unlocked.

Knowing Blake was in the other room made her feel safe and that, at least in part, had contributed to her sound sleep.

He had been a perfect gentleman. Remembering his broad shoulders, his strong arms, the way his green eyes would focus on only her… she started to feel warm inside. She took a deep breath, closed her eyes, and sighed lightly.

The heavy knock at her hotel room door sounded like someone kicking the door, which struck her as strange. Blake would use the adjoining door between the rooms, wouldn't he?

The Berber carpet had a thick underlay, and her bare feet sunk into it. "Yes?"

"Linda, it's Oscar. Open up, please."

She undid the lock and chain on her door then opened it to reveal Oscar, holding a huge steaming pot with oven mitts.

"Back up. This is scalding hot."

She retreated to let him enter.

He carried the pot into the bathroom and placed it on the sink. He took a bath towel, folded it, laid it on the counter, and moved the pot onto it. "Don't want to burn the surface. There you go. I can't provide a hot shower, but that should help."

"How did you get hot water with no power?" Krause moved to close the door.

He took off the oven mitts. "There's a barbecue outside. Didn't take long at all. Oh, wait! I forgot." Blake went out into the hall and retrieved a paper bag and Styrofoam cup. He handed them to her. "It's just instant coffee, yogurt, and a couple of ripe bananas, but breakfast is served."

Krause was floored. She had expected nothing, and he delivered both breakfast and hot water to wash. "Thank you. That was sweet." She gave him a hug, which he returned. Her thoughts began to wander to things she hadn't thought of in months. She began to blush and became self-conscious about holding him while wearing only a T-shirt. She released him. "Now, you'd better go. I need to get dressed."

"Sure. I'll see you down at the bike in thirty minutes. We're making good progress so far. If we push, we can be in Colorado tonight." He smiled and went out into the hallway. She glimpsed at his backside and muscular legs as he left.

The door closed, and she placed her back against it before blowing out slowly. *Whew, maybe that cold shower is a good idea after all.*

* * *

Colonel Smith woke to a knocking on his motel room door. He got up and went to the door in his underclothes. He opened the door to find Captain Tyler standing there in civilian clothes holding a coffee mug. "Good morning, Colonel. You wanted me to wake you at eight. Here's some coffee, compliments of Mister Noel. He raided the restaurant down the road. What it lacks in taste, it more than makes up for in strength.

"I hope you don't mind me out of uniform, Colonel. I just couldn't wear it in the condition it's in."

Smith rubbed his eyes then took the coffee. "No problem. Laundry facilities are few and far between. Sleep well?"

"Not bad. Tech Sergeant Folsom and I had the last watch, so we've been up since four. He's waking up the rest now. We had a quiet night. No traffic on the road, and we haven't seen anyone moving. Noel said he found around a dozen bodies scattered between here and the restaurant. Looked to him like they died of exposure; the bodies were badly sunburned. He wanted to go search through the local neighborhoods, but I told him not to."

Bodies? There'll be more if we fail. "Good call with Noel. No one should wander off alone. I want to get on the road as soon as possible." He felt his chin with his free hand. He needed a shave. "Let's say twenty minutes." He took a sip of the coffee. It wasn't bad at all.

"Yes, sir." She nodded and left.

He closed the door and went into the compact bathroom. The window over the tub let in the morning light. He washed himself with a washcloth then shaved with one of the disposable razors he had brought from the turf farm. The water dribbled out of the tap at an annoyingly slow pace, far too slow to rinse the stubble out from between the blades. Frustrated, he ended up pulling the top off the toilet tank and rinsing the razor in the water there. When finished, he began to feel human again.

Back in the bedroom, he pulled on his uniform. He had worn it since escaping from the Cheyenne Mountain bunker. He could have changed into clean civilian clothes, but he was still the head of NORAD, and to him, that just didn't feel right. It might have been soiled and stinky, but the uniform represented his duty.

He left the motel room and walked down to where they had parked the van. Everyone was standing around, chatting in low tones. Tech Sergeant Folsom had the hood up, apparently checking the oil.

"Morning, everyone. We ready to hit the road?"

Folsom slammed the hood closed and joined the rest of the group while wiping his hands on a rag. He also wore his uniform. "The van's good to go, sir. Full tank of gas, and the fluids check out."

"Thank you, Tech Sergeant. Let's go. We should be able to make it to Hill by the afternoon."

Everyone climbed into the van. Smith took the front passenger seat, and Folsom drove. They were heading west down Highway 80 only minutes later.

* * *

James Calvin made his way to the small dining table without effort. He was getting used to being blind. Occupying the same room almost continuously for several days meant he knew where most things were. Outside the room, he was as helpless as a newborn kitten, but within, he could at least get around without assistance. Calvin sat down.

"Mister President, your oatmeal is in front of you, sir. There's a glass of orange juice on the right side of the bowl," Agent Nance said from the corner.

"Thank you." Something occurred to Calvin as he reached carefully in search of the orange juice. "Agent Nance?"

"Yes, sir?"

"I've never asked. What's your first name?" The back of his hand brushed against the cool exterior of the glass. He picked it up, being careful not to spill it.

"Karl. Nance comes from the German last name, Nantz. My grandfather changed it when he came to America in the 1920s, but all of the boys in the family still got German first names."

Calvin could hear Nance was washing something metallic in the plastic washtub. He took a sip of the orange juice. "Do you mind if I call you Karl?"

"I'm not sure if you should, sir. We were trained not to be on a first-name basis with our protectees. I know several agents who were reassigned duties because of that."

"I can respect that, but I do have a question for you. If you were running things, what would you do different?" Calvin put the glass down and felt for a spoon.

The sound of dishwashing stopped. "Mister President, I'm not sure I should say anything. I'm not qualified to give any form of intelligent opinion at your level. Maybe Mister Hurst could assist you better? He's your national security advisor, after all. I don't mind going up to get him."

Calvin picked up his spoon and mixed his oatmeal. "Humor me. I have no aides to talk to. All of my staff are out of contact, and I already know Keith's thoughts. If you were president, what would you be doing?"

"Well, sir... I'm not sure if I could do anything different. The majority of the country is blind, we have no viable military forces remaining, and without a cure... I'd say we were screwed."

Calvin raised a spoon of oatmeal to his lips, but it was too hot to eat. He gently blew on it. "We have identical opinions, Agent Nance. Without a cure, we have few options. Now, assume we have a cure. What do we do?"

There was a moment of silence. "We learned in college about how important communications were in times of strife. Revolutionaries always try to control the newspapers and radios, as an example. If you wanted to take the country back, you need to deliver orders, coordinate forces, and gather intelligence. To do that, some sort of communications network is needed."

Calvin ate some oatmeal. While he swallowed, he considered what Nance had said. Parts of the cell network were still up, but that wasn't viable for military orders. There was little to no security on cell phone calls. With the Chinese in control of the bunkers and other strategic assets, access to military radios would be difficult. He'd have to think about that more. "That's a good point, then what?"

"There sir, we enter the realm of speculation. It all depends on a cure. If it's something that will only cure a couple of people a day, then guerilla tactics are the only option. We resist with hit-and-run raids until the numbers of people who can see increases, then hit them full force. Same tactics we used against the British in the War of Independence, really. However, that said, without a cure, none of that's going to happen."

Nance didn't know about the Chinese ships inbound to the West Coast. Calvin didn't mention it, for he didn't want to depress him. The thought of those reinforcements certainly made Calvin feel more than a little dismay. There was still no word from Colonel Smith, either, and that did nothing to raise his spirits. Calvin recalled the cell phone they had taken with them. "How is the battery on our cell phone holding out?"

"Oh sorry, sir—I thought Agent Carter had told you. We picked up an identical spare phone and battery when we went into town. We swap batteries out every day and charge the spare down here. We never have less than sixty percent charge on the phone upstairs."

"Good thinking. Thanks." Calvin returned to eating his breakfast in silence. *A cure. It all comes down to a cure.*

* * *

Doctor Linda Krause looked up at the blue sky as they traveled along Highway 84. The strange three-wheeled motorcycle ate up the miles, and she looked out at the horizon they were driving toward. *There are more clouds today, and the ones on the southern horizon look positively ominous.* The highway was clear of obstructions, and Blake maintained a steady pace. The mountainous terrain of Washington State had slowly changed into the rolling hills of Idaho.

Blake's voice came over her earpieces. "Linda, my morning coffee has come back to haunt me. I'll need to pull over."

"I could use a bathroom too," she said.

"All right, I'll pull into Mountain Home. That's only a few miles away."

They took the interstate exit and slowed down significantly. Krause saw a Burger King sign, but as they got closer, she saw the roof had collapsed. Charred red brick showed evidence of a bad fire that had gutted the restaurant.

Blake took them deeper into Mountain Home. They passed several homes and light industrial buildings on their left. There was little to their right save open fields. He turned left onto a residential street and stopped in front of a large house.

He stepped off the bike and removed his helmet. "Looks like a decent place. I'll go check it out. Mind staying here for a bit?"

"Okay." She also removed her helmet but stayed seated.

Blake walked up the driveway and knocked on the front door.

Krause looked around. There was no sound at all. In the hospital, even at night, there was some sort of noise—footsteps, conversation, air conditioning, *something*. Here she heard nothing. She realized no birds sang. *Are animals affected by the blindness, as well?*

She looked back toward the house and saw Blake step through the open door. She stepped off the bike, placing her helmet on the seat.

"Are you real?" a voice asked quietly from behind her. She spun around in surprise to find a black-haired man in his mid-thirties—wearing black gym shorts, white running shoes without socks, and a tan polo shirt—standing ten feet away from her. He hadn't been there before, and she had not heard him approach. He simply stood there.

"Sorry. I didn't see you," she said.

"You *are* real. I heard the bike and thought I was hallucinating. I'm Tony. Do you know what's going on? Why is everyone blind?"

"Hi, Tony, I'm Doctor Linda Krause. We're not sure what caused the blindness, but we think the July 4th fireworks had something to do with it."

"Yeah, that's what we thought, too. I was asleep and missed them. You're a doctor? Can you look at my sister? She's been ill for a few days now, with cramps and nausea." He pointed over to a nearby house.

Krause nodded. "Of course. I'll go once my friend gets back. Is it just you and your sister or...?"

Tony waved his finger around to indicate the houses around them. "I gathered up all the people on the neighboring streets and brought them to my house. I've been taking care of them as best as I can, but there's a lot more out in the town. People were told to stay home, but no help came."

Blake came up beside her. "Hello."

"Oscar, this is Tony. His sister is ill, and he's taking care of several afflicted people. I'm going to go check her out."

Blake moved toward the side pouch on the bike. "Sure, I'll follow with your equipment."

Krause knew he was referring to a tube so she turned to go with Tony, and they walked across the street toward his house.

Before entering Tony's home, Krause looked over her shoulder to see Blake carrying a wrapped tube in his hands.

"This way. They're all in the living room," Tony said while holding the screen door open, and she stepped into his hallway. She turned the corner into the living room and counted fourteen people. Some sat on the couch and chairs;

others lay on the floor in blankets. They all stirred when she entered. From the smell, she doubted they had washed in some time.

Tony spoke to the room. "Everyone, this is Doctor Krause. She's here to help Maggie."

Everyone spoke at once, asking questions; some rose up. They were all blind.

Tony raised his voice over all the others. "Everyone, calm down! There'll be lots of time for questions. Maggie, I brought a doctor."

Maggie was a twenty-something blonde with deep black roots. She was clutching her abdomen, face contorted with pain. "Doctor, my guts are cramping badly, and I have to run to the bathroom all the time."

"Okay Maggie, I'm Doctor Krause. Let me feel your head… Okay, no fever. That's good. How long have you had the symptoms?"

"Two days ago. I was fine until then. Ahhhhhhhh! Ow, that hurts."

Krause examined her quickly. She had no medical equipment with her, save a basic first aid kit on the bike. However, given the conditions they were living in and the symptoms, she had an idea what was probably bothering her. "Maggie, it looks like amebic dysentery. Are you pregnant?"

"No."

"All right, you just need some antibiotics. I'll tell your brother what to pick up. You just relax and make sure you drink lots of water to keep your fluids up."

Krause stood and turned to Tony who was hovering nearby. "You'll need to go to a pharmacy and get some metronidazole or paromomycin. I'll write down the amounts for you along with the schedule."

Tony smiled. "Thank you, Doctor."

"Oscar, can you hand me the tube?" Krause asked.

Blake unrolled the tube from the surgical towel and handed it to her.

"What's that?" Tony asked.

"It's a cure for the blindness. We can give everyone their sight back."

"Oh my God, really?" Tony asked.

Everyone in the room began moving and talking excitedly.

"It takes about four hours to work, but we've seen some really promising results." Krause moved to the first person to begin administering treatment.

* * *

Reid stood in his usual place near the plotting table. He made sure to check all stations periodically in the command center, but he was glad to see no issues.

Commander Maddox approached him with a clipboard in his hand. "Captain, I compiled the list of supplies you wanted. Given current food supplies, we can last a hundred and thirty-five days if we cut back from standard rations."

Reid took the clipboard and looked over the figures. "What about cartridges for the scrubbers[25]?"

"We've got enough lithium hydroxide absorbent on board for six months of normal operations, not including the emergency supplies. The newer model of scrubber canisters on board is fifty-five percent more efficient than the older one. It isn't a concern at this time."

Reid flipped through the several pages of inventoried items. He saw nothing that needed his attention. Maddox was a good XO, and little escaped him. Reid handed the clipboard back to him. "What's our current weapon status?"

Maddox held the clipboard against his chest and recounted from memory. "All ADCAPS are operational, as are the mark 50s. We have a Harpoon down for maintenance; it isn't linking to the targeting computer. Repair time is roughly three hours."

---

[25] Nuclear submarines recycle the same air repeatedly. Special air filtration equipment called scrubbers removes the CO (carbon monoxide) and CO2 (carbon dioxide) exhaled by the crew and supplies oxygen back into the sub.

"If any weapon goes down for any reason, I want to know and have them working on it immediately," Reid ordered while adjusting his baseball cap.

Maddox moved closer and lowered his voice. "You expecting trouble, Captain?"

Reid answered just as quietly, "We have to keep the men occupied—idle hands and all that. Let's set up a fire drill for this afternoon. It'll give them something to focus on. To answer your question, with no news coming from command, I'm expecting all sorts of trouble. I just have no idea what shape it'll take. If the Chinese are attacking by air, there isn't a lot we can do with torpedoes." He sighed. "We've heard nothing, and there's that saying about the quiet before the storm. So XO, in the grand tradition of the navy, I'm preparing for the worst, while hoping for the best. That'll be all for now."

"Yes, sir."

* * *

Colonel Smith checked his watch and saw they were making good time. He looked into the back of the van. Many of his people were dozing. Noel's red head rested on the shoulder of his neighbor, Vinson, who also appeared to be asleep. Smith smiled at the sight before making eye contact with Captain Tyler, who returned his expression with a full-toothed grin. He turned back to face the road, hoping she knew he was not smiling at her.

"I'd say we're about an hour away," he said to Folsom.

"Yes, sir. I agree. We're just passing Morgan now. We should be getting to the airbase—"

The relatively quiet interior of the van was broken by a sudden *WHOMF* from the back, followed by Tyler screaming and the sound of air rushing into the cabin. His first thought was a tire blowout, but the van maintained a straight and smooth course.

Folsom began slowing. Smith looked back to see the entire left rear window pane had shattered into thousands of glass nuggets that had spread over the people and supplies piled in the rear. Tyler was brushing pieces of glass out of her hair.

Smith then heard *TAK-TAK* as a bullet hole appeared in the left side of the van. "Floor it—someone's shooting at us!"

The van's engine revved up.

"Everyone get down!" Smith looked out the windows but could not see anyone. The surrounding terrain sped up. After driving for a minute, Smith decided they were past the ambush.

"Sound off—is everyone okay?" Smith screamed over the wind noise.

"I'm fine, Colonel," said Vinson, who was also looking back in the direction of the assailants.

Noel poked his head up. "I'm good, sir."

Tyler brushed glass shards off her jacket. "Were they Chinese?"

Smith felt relieved no one had been hit. "Folsom, you can ease off the gas. We're clear... Folsom."

The tech sergeant lifted his left hand from his side. His palm was full of dark red blood.

"Pull over. Noel, we need the first aid kit! Folsom's hit."

The van slowed and came to a stop on the gravel edge of the highway. Smith reached over and threw the van's transmission into park. He undid his seat belt, got out of the van, and ran around to the driver's side door, which had a bullet hole in the doorframe. Folsom had already opened the door slightly. Smith yanked it open to see a large area of blood on Folsom's side.

He undid Folsom's seat belt and brought him outside. "I've got you. I've got you. Just sit down."

Folsom's eyes were half closed. "I don't want to die. I don't want to die. I don't want to die..."

Noel came around the back of the van, carrying the first aid kit. In his haste to open it, many of the contents spilled on the gravel. Smith grabbed the thickest bandage he could see, tore it open with his teeth, and pressed it against Folsom's side. The bullet had entered just under his armpit. The white bandage quickly turned red. "Noel, here. Take my pistol. You and Vinson keep an eye on the highway. They may try coming after us."

"I'm sorry, Colonel." Folsom's voice rasped. "I didn't see—" He closed his eyes and went limp, collapsing onto the ground.

Captain Tyler came around the front of the van, getting a clear view of Folsom for the first time. She gasped and then stood there with her hand over her mouth.

"Help me, Captain. Apply pressure on the bandage," Smith ordered.

She knelt down and did as she was told.

Smith checked for a pulse and felt none. He began chest compressions. "Come on. Come on, Tech Sergeant... I didn't bring you this far to have you quit on me now, damn it."

He continued giving chest compressions for several minutes.

Tyler checked Folsom's pulse. "Sir. Sir! He's gone."

Smith kept going.

"Alvin, he's dead," she said quietly while placing her hand on top of his.

He stopped, looking down on the motionless body. Tears fell freely, and he clenched his fists, mentally cursing the ones who had done this.

"We need to go, Colonel." Tyler said, placing her hand on his shoulder.

Moments passed.

"Get a blanket. We're not leaving him in a ditch," Smith ordered.

Tyler got up and went to the rear of the van. She returned, shaking glass pieces off a large red blanket. Together, they wrapped Folsom up in it.

Noel, Vinson, Tyler, and Smith all lifted him up and placed him in the rear of the van. No one spoke. Smith closed the doors, retrieved his pistol, and walked to the driver's side door.

Smith got in, adjusted the seat, and put on the seat belt. Tyler slipped into the front passenger seat. When everyone was inside, Smith put the van in gear and pulled back onto the asphalt.

* * *

While Doctor Krause waited for the timer on the tube in her hand to reach zero, she looked around Tony's living room. Everyone appeared relaxed, and even Maggie had stopped moaning; she rested with her eyes closed. *Hope is soothing their suffering. They're no longer expecting death in the dark. They know that in a little while, they'll see again.*

The LED display on her tube changed from "01" to "00." As it did so, she heard the iris snap closed. She took the device away from the eye of Dora, who was the last person to receive treatment.

Krause rubbed her forearm. The tube weighed several pounds, and holding that weight motionless for multiple treatments was a strain. "That's it. We're done."

Dora jerked up slightly in surprise. "I didn't feel a thing. Are you sure this will work?"

"We tested it in Seattle. You should recover your sight in about four hours," Krause stated.

"Thank you, Doctor."

Krause stood and walked over to Blake, who stood near the foyer. She handed the tube to him, and he carefully wrapped it back up in the light green surgical towel.

"Ready to go?" he asked.

She nodded. "Yes, there's not a lot else we can do, and—"

Tony appeared in the kitchen doorway, drying a stainless steel soup ladle with a dish towel. "You can't leave—there's hundreds of people in town who need that cure."

Their goal was to heal the country, not just Mountain View. They needed to get to Colorado. "They will be cured, once we get the tubes distributed. We need to get this—"

Dora called out, "My sister is in Bruneau. It's just down the road. You have to help her."

A young man named Greg said, "My parents are across town. It'll only take five minutes to get there."

The others began pleading with her as well for others. Krause raised her voice to be heard over them. "They'll all be helped once the cure gets mass produced. We can't stay. I'm sorry."

"You're not leaving," Tony said in a dead calm voice. "We need that cure."

Blake stepped forward, but Tony swung the soup ladle, catching him on the temple. Blake fell back against the wall. Krause tried to intervene, but Tony pushed her deeper into the living room. "Get her! Hold her down! Grab the cure!" he yelled to the others.

Everyone in the living room flailed, trying to locate her. She twisted to avoid them. When one man got too close, she shoved him back with both hands, sending him backpedaling back onto the couch. That created a temporary hole she took advantage of, and she broke for the hallway.

Blake had recovered from the hit. He stood with the wrapped tube cradled in his left arm, while he protected himself from Tony with his right. As she made it out of the living room, Tony turned to look at her, and Blake lunged forward and landed a jab to his chin. Tony hit the wall by the stairs, slipped, and went down hard onto the wood floor.

"Come on, Linda!" Blake pushed the front door open, and she ran through it, heading for the bike as fast as she could run. Once at the roadster, she put on her helmet while seating herself on the rear passenger seat.

Blake came up to her a second later and handed her both the tube and his helmet. "Hold onto those," he said, digging into his pocket.

Keys in hand, he jumped onto the driver's seat and started the engine. As soon as she heard the motor start, he twisted the accelerator and put the steering hard over to the left. The savage acceleration forced her to grab a hold of him to stay on the back seat.

As the roadster turned around, Tony appeared on the porch of his house, shaking the soup ladle and screaming something that was drowned out by the noise of the accelerating engine.

Blake drove rapidly, turned back toward the highway, and stopped on the on-ramp. He turned around to look at her. "Are you all right?"

"I'm fine. My heart is racing, though." His temple looked red and slightly swollen. She reached up to feel it, but he pulled away.

"No time for that now, Linda. I want to get away from here as quickly as possible in case they come after us. Hand me my helmet."

She did so, and he slipped it on. He faced the road and accelerated the bike up the on-ramp.

Several miles passed without either of them saying anything.

She looked over her shoulder but saw no signs of pursuit. "I don't think anyone is following," she said into her microphone.

"Doesn't look like it. We were lucky they didn't have knives or guns. That would've played out a lot worse for us if they had. The next town I see, I'm going to pull over and find a pistol. I'm not going to lose you without a fight."

"Edmund warned me about this," she said to herself.

"Sorry? I didn't catch that."

"Doctor Wiater said people would react that way, and I didn't believe him. How can people be like that?"

"They're afraid. They're regular people, driven into hectic circumstances. They want to help and protect their own families and friends. If you or I were in the same situation, we might act the same way."

Krause shook her head. She refused to believe she would hold someone against his or her will, but also recognized she hadn't lost her sight for the better part of a week, either. All she did know was Blake had gotten her out of that situation.

She inched forward so her thighs touched him. She placed the tube between her legs, pressed forward, wrapped her arms around him, and held him close. She rested her cheek against his back.

Chapter Nineteen
Hellos and Good-byes

Colonel Smith drove toward Hill Air Force Base in silence. Folsom's death weighed heavily on him. He'd seen death before—the massacre of the air force personnel at the Cheyenne bunker entrance came immediately to mind. But Smith hadn't known those people, or at least he'd been far enough away that he didn't know their identities. Folsom had a face, name, and personality that he knew well. Now he was dead, and as far as Smith could tell, for nothing.

He doubted the attack had been by the Chinese, as they had no reason to be there. The town of Morgan was in the backcountry of Utah, with no military bases nearby. The bullet holes indicated a large caliber rifle, like a .308 hunting rifle. Chinese paratroops carried 5.8mm rounds, and they would have riddled the van with hundreds of bullets in seconds.

The idiocy of the attack angered him. Folsom, a good man, had died because a couple of yahoos with guns had shot at them, for no reason whatsoever.

He realized he was clenching the steering wheel far too tightly and relaxed his grip somewhat.

Smith saw a sign indicating a turn, labeled "Hill Air Force Base – 3 Miles," and turned onto Highway 193. On his left, he saw a sign advertising the Hobbs reservoir; to his right, the Mountain View School. He pulled into the school parking lot and threw the van into park.

Tyler asked, "Why are we stopping, Colonel?"

Smith undid his seat belt and turned sideways to face the small group. "I want you three to stay here until I check out Hill. I want to make sure there's no Chinese. If I don't come back within three hours, assume the worst and get away from here."

Tyler objected, "Sir, we should stick together and scout—"

Smith held up his hand. "No, I'm going alone. That's an order. There's no need to risk everyone, and if the Chinese are there, I'll get back here as fast as possible. I should be back in an hour at most. Wait for me for three. Here, take my cell phone." He handed it to Tyler.

Vinson was the first to reach for the door handle. "Good luck, Colonel."

Tyler and Noel left at the same time. As soon as they closed their doors, Smith turned back to the dashboard, put the van in gear, and drove for Hill Air Force Base.

The few miles passed uneventfully. Smith purposely drove slowly while scanning the area. A large Chinese presence would be obvious. The gate of the airbase appeared ahead, and Smith finally saw movement. A single sentry in air force uniform stood with an M-16 rifle in his hand, the barrel pointing to the sky. Thinking it might be a Chinese soldier wearing the uniform, Smith approached cautiously, but when he got closer, the dirty blond hair of the airman became obvious. The guard saw him and placed the rifle butt to his shoulder, but he didn't point it at him, which Smith took as encouraging.

Smith parked the van fifty feet from the gate and turned off the engine. He got out slowly and approached the gate.

"Halt! Identify yourself," the airman shouted.

He stopped walking. "Colonel Smith from NORAD. I need to see your CO."

"Advance slowly. Keep your hands where I can see them, sir."

Smith moved closer, keeping his palms outward and away from his body.

"Halt," the airman called out when he was ten feet away. His nametag read "Fabian". "Slowly take out your ID and place it on the ground."

Smith did as he was told and carefully took his laminated air force identity card out from his wallet. The bar code, visible gold-embedded smart chip, and Air Force seal told him at a glance that he had grabbed the right one. He laid it on the asphalt.

"Back up please, sir."

Smith walked backwards about ten feet until Fabian said, "That's good there, sir."

Fabian walked up and picked up the ID card without taking his eyes off Smith. He checked the front and back of the card. He walked back to the gatehouse and picked up a walkie-talkie. "Control, gate two. I have a Colonel Smith from NORAD here wanting to see the CO."

The radio was turned down too low for Smith to hear the reply.

Fabian said, "Roger." He put the walkie-talkie down. "Colonel, someone will be along in a few minutes."

Smith nodded then waited. Fabian was too far away for casual conversation, so he scanned the area but saw no troops. The airfield itself was quiet, but he could see many parked aircraft, including at least three tail fins of Hercules transports. Smith had counted twenty-two F-16 fighter jets when an approaching engine interrupted him. A khaki green Humvee with white "MP" markings came up to the gate and stopped.

A second lieutenant, who Smith thought looked to be barely over twenty, stepped out of the cab and marched up to him. He saluted smartly, saying, "Good afternoon, Colonel Smith. I'm Second Lieutenant Greer. If you'll come with me, sir, I'll take you to the CO. This way, please."

Smith returned the salute and walked to the Humvee. Fabian handed him his ID card as he passed the gatehouse. Smith put it back in his wallet and got into the passenger seat of the Humvee.

Greer didn't waste any time. He reversed the Humvee into a three-point turn, and drove into the base proper.

Smith waited, but Greer said nothing. "How many pilots do you have who can see?"

"Sir, I've been ordered not to say anything about operational matters. You can talk to the C.O. about that."

Greer's comeback effectively killed any further conversation. After a few minutes, they pulled up in front of the base gymnasium with a sign reading "Warrior Fitness Center". Greer parked directly beside the front doors. "Here we are, Colonel. Just head inside and you'll be escorted the rest of the way."

Smith got out, and Greer drove off. He walked through the metal and glass doors to find cots in neat rows in the entry hall. The air had a strange, subtle smell. It was hauntingly familiar, but he couldn't place it.

Two pairs of steel double doors were wedged open to the right, and Smith could see many more cots inside the main gymnasium. Men and women of all ages and ranks were sitting or lying on the cots. All were obviously blind. The men had several days of stubble. No one came forward, so Smith began walking toward the gym, careful not to disturb anyone resting on the cots.

Just as he got to the door, a technical sergeant, clean shaven and in an immaculate uniform, came through the opening. He had a clipboard under his left arm. He saw Smith, stopped, came to attention, and saluted. "Good afternoon, sir. Please come this way."

Smith returned the salute. The tech sergeant turned smartly and marched deeper into the gym. The tech sergeant went straight down the wide corridor that had been established between the cots. Smith followed, consciously matching his pace to that of the NCO. He observed pilots in flight suits, ground crew in coveralls, and many other trades in parts of various uniforms.

Halfway through the gym, he realized the scent niggling him was chlorine. *There must be a pool in the building.*

Smith looked ahead and saw some offices with glass windows built into the far wall of the gymnasium. He assumed they had been offices for the physical education staff. The tech sergeant went up to one of the office doors and indicated he should go in.

Smith stopped on the threshold. Just inside the door, a large hip-high metal mesh box of basketballs waited. He stepped in and found another cot inside the door, but the sheets and pillow looked as if they had been ironed into place, and the blanket had been tucked in with precision. Past the cot was a large wooden desk that looked as if it came from the 1950s and had the usual office items on top. The only thing that stood out as unusual was a glass jug of ice water and a couple of glasses.

Behind the desk, a short black-haired woman sat with her forearms on the desktop. She wore the dress tunic of a colonel and had the same distant look as the rest of the blind people in the gym.

Smith said, "Good afternoon, Colonel...?"

"Barton. You're from NORAD?" she responded.

"Yes."

"Good. Have a seat. Maybe you can tell me what the hell's happening to my people."

* * *

Krause hated to slow down the excellent progress they were making on the roadster, but nature called. She spoke into her microphone. "Oscar, I need a pit stop."

"GPS says we'll be in Blackfoot in fifteen minutes. Is that okay?" He replied.

"That's fine, thanks." She looked around at the farmland passing them by. It looked so idyllic and peaceful... normal. She wished the rest of the world could return to the way it had been.

But then, the "normal" world prior to July Fourth hadn't been that great. Political partisanship resulted in constant government gridlock, tensions between various religious bodies were at an all-time high, wars and conflicts continued unabated…

Would any of those things wane in the face of global blindness, or would this experience exacerbate the issues? *If everyone got their sight back today, would the world be a better place?* Probably not, she decided. People would angrily point fingers and blame others. Decades-old grudges would work their way to the fore, and personal agendas would be thrown in front of any progress. The rhetoric would build, and eventually, almost inevitably, blood would be spilled.

Does humanity deserve a cure?

The thought shocked her. *Why would I ask that question?* As a physician, she was trained to heal, but sometimes diseased tissue had to be removed for the greater good. As a teen, Krause's neighbor had put down a rabid dog. She could remember the late night gunshot as she lay in bed, followed by a hideous scream of pain from the animal. She'd cried for that dog but known that ending its life was merciful in the long run. *Is this the same situation?*

She mulled that over and decided the question shouldn't be, "Does humanity deserve a cure?" *It should be, "Has humanity earned a cure?"*—and that question stumped her.

"Uh-oh," Blake said.

Krause snapped out of her pensiveness. "What's wrong?"

"Look ahead. That's the town of Blackfoot."

She peered over his shoulder to see a decimated city before them. Columns of dense black smoke rose up from many destroyed buildings. Most if not all buildings were either smoking or aflame. "Oh my God, how can something like that happen?"

Blake replied, "I don't know. The GPS is telling me to go through there, but I don't want to risk going through downtown. The map shows a secondary highway on the other side of the Snake River. It'll let us avoid that mess. I'm afraid your pit stop is going to be delayed a little longer."

She regarded the smoking ruins ahead. "That's fine. I don't want to stop here."

Crossing the Snake River brought the stench of charred wood and burning buildings to her nose. Blake drove slowly past wrecked and fire-gutted buildings. To her left, the red brick wall of a three-story building collapsed inwards with a rumble.

As they went past the fallen wall, a thin teenager in a black baseball cap, jeans, and gray hoodie appeared from behind a parked car to her left. The teen started blowing a loud whistle and pulled out a handgun from the small of his back. Blake apparently saw the same thing and gunned the accelerator to get away. She heard two bullets whiz past her head.

Blake randomly steered left and right, causing her to clutch at him to stay on the bike.

Looking over her shoulder, she could no longer see the shooter. She blew out her breath. *We're clear.*

Returning her attention to the street ahead, Krause caught sight of a flaming bottle flying toward them from the left. Blake jammed on the brakes, swerving madly to avoid the Molotov. The bottle barely missed the handlebars and impacted on an abandoned sedan off to the side of the road. She felt the explosive heat from the fireball on her side and instinctively recoiled from it. Another teen ran into view from between two buildings on her right. This one had shocking red hair to his shoulders and a blue bandana. He also pulled out a pistol and began taking aim at them with a two-hand stance.

Again, Blake accelerated and weaved randomly to try to get away. She saw a third teen—this one with short black hair— emerge from the right side of the street and turn toward them with an unlit Molotov in his hands. The teen tried to light the rag dangling from the mouth of the bottle with a silver lighter. The handle of a pistol tucked into his jeans was unmistakable against his white T-shirt.

Blake turned directly toward him. The teen had to dive to get out of the way. As he did, the bottle broke on the ground, and the gasoline ignited. The bike passed him as he rolled on the ground, engulfed in flames and screaming.

She clutched Blake's torso tightly. Blake kept the accelerator wide open until they were clear of the city and surrounded by farmland. They pulled up an overpass, and she saw the sign for Salt Lake City whiz by. He eased off the gas, returning to a normal driving speed. "You okay, Linda?"

She said nothing, too shocked for words. Her entire body shivered.

Blake began to slow the bike. "Linda! Are you hurt?"

"No... No, I'm fine," she said finally.

* * *

In Colonel Barton's gymnasium office, Colonel Smith gave her a rundown on the overall picture—the global pandemic, the invasion by Chinese airborne, the follow-on forces coming by ship, and the neutralization of all U.S. military command and control. He finished describing the vice president being beaten by Chinese soldiers.

When he was done, she sat in wide-eyed silence. Smith was wondering if he should say something more, when she took a deep breath in.

"The Chinese blinded the world, kidnapped the entire House of Representatives, the cabinet, and joint chiefs. They've captured our command bunkers and, to top it all off, are invading the United States with upwards of a quarter million troops," she said flatly.

"That's an estimate," Smith replied. He'd spoken so much his throat was dry. He poured himself a glass of ice water.

She shook her head. "You know just how implausible that sounds."

"Colonel Barton, it is what it is. The sooner you wrap your head around it, the better." Smith had no time for doubters with the country at stake.

There was a long pause.

"You said the vice president was being beaten. What about the president?" Barton asked.

"He got away. As far as I know, he's still safe." He took a sip from his glass.

"Do you have any way of contacting him?" Barton leaned forward.

"Yes, but I won't, not until we have some sort of plan we can put in action. How many of your people can see?"

Barton pressed her palms to the desk. "Things may have changed, Colonel. We need to talk to him and get an update. Besides, I have a few ideas I want to put to him concerning—"

"Colonel, the president can contact me if needed. Communicating with him prematurely may disclose his location to the enemy, and I'm *not* going to do that," Smith said with an edge in his voice.

Colonel Barton stood, keeping her hands against the desk. "What's your date of rank, Colonel?"

If her promotion date to colonel is earlier than mine, she would be the senior officer, which would usually make her outrank me, but... "General Wachowsky placed me in the position as commander of NORAD, Colonel. As I hold the positional authority of a four-star general and am acting on direct presidential orders, I'm the senior officer here."

A long silence passed. Even though Colonel Barton was blind, she seemed to stare directly through him.

She sat down slowly. "Yes, sir."

"How many of your people can see?" Smith sipped his water. It made his throat feel better.

"We started off with nine, various ranks. Three have been AWOL since then. The six that remain are running around almost without rest standing guard, gathering food, or keeping the lights on. They've been doing an outstanding job so far."

"I have fou— Sorry, three people with me who have their sight. A captain and two analysts. Do you have any pilots that can see?"

"No, sir. We had a huge celebration for base personnel and their families for July Fourth. Even the on-duty pilots watched the fireworks from the flight line."

"I see." Smith slumped back in his chair. A pilot would have given him some mobility. Not that he had anywhere to go at the moment, but it would have been nice to have that option.

"What are your intentions?" Barton asked.

"As of now, there's not a lot we can do without a cure. All we can do is survive and pray for relief. You've done an exceptional job keeping your people alive. I just hope we can get them back in the fight somehow."

"Sit and wait? Not a very proactive plan." Barton said flatly.

"I'm listening, if you have a suggestion." He placed the half-empty water glass on her desk.

She remained silent.

"I need to go pick up the rest of my group, but before that, I have something to ask of you, Colonel Barton."

* * *

They had traveled a dozen miles past the smoking ruins of Blackfoot, and Krause couldn't wait for the bathroom any longer. She tapped Blake on his shoulder. "We really need to stop for the bathroom."

"Sure. There's a trading post on the Indian reservation just ahead. I used their toilet on my last trip. We'll be there in a minute."

Blake pulled up directly in front of the trading post doors. She slid off the back seat of the roadster and pulled off her helmet. Walking up onto the covered porch, she saw two bloody hatchets embedded in a column. Blood from the blades had run down the pillar and dried. She shivered and moved closer to the doorway.

Her foot kicked an empty water container. A second one lay farther down the porch. She looked inside the building to see a path had been made through the stuff on the floor. Then, through an open door, she saw the toilet. It had been smashed completely.

She turned to Blake, who was still on the bike. "The toilet's not usable. It's broken."

Blake looked around then pointed down the road. "That's the closest house over there. I'll pull up to it on the bike."

She jogged over to the house, which was only fifty feet away. The wind had picked up, and a stiff breeze blew through the area. A junked car and wire mesh fence blocked her way to the front door, so she went to the rear. In her haste, she barely noticed deck chairs and a barbecue, but she didn't stop. The back door was open, and she rushed inside.

"Hello!" she called through the kitchen. There was no answer.

Krause located a half bathroom just past the kitchen. She went in, locked the door out of habit, and used the toilet. As she sat there, she saw the bare toilet paper roll and cursed. When done, she stood and flushed. The handle moved easily, but nothing happened. *No power or water...* She spotted a container of baby wipes on a shelf and used those to clean her hands.

She left the bathroom and went out the way she came in. The backyard looked as if some high winds had gone through. A couple of chairs were on their backs, and the area was riddled with trash and beer cans. A motorcycle without a front wheel lay on the dirt, looking as though it had fallen off its blocks. Tools lay nearby, along with the loose wheel. A blue tarp lay over a low mound. She spotted a cooler beside a chair and opened the lid, revealing three cans of beer in two inches of water. The water felt cool, so she took two beers—one for herself and the other for Blake. It had been a hot and trying day, so they could relax for five minutes before continuing their journey.

"Linda, are you okay?" Blake called from around the house.

"Fine! Be right there," she called back.

Looking over, the barbecue lid looked slightly open, and she could smell something burnt. *Maybe there's some food on there.* She walked over and saw the gas burners were turned on, but could hear nothing. She placed her hand over, then carefully on, the metal lid. It felt cool. *They left it on, and it ran out of propane.* She opened the barbecue.

Three charred human heads faced her. Their eyes were hollow sockets, and the black skin around their mouths formed grotesque smiles.

She backpedaled in horrified shock.

Krause's heel caught on the loose motorcycle wheel, and she fell backwards, landing beside the tarp. As she tried to get up, a gust of wind blew back the tarp, revealing three headless corpses lying together beside her.

Doctor Linda Krause screamed and screamed and screamed.

July 11th

Chapter Twenty
Dum Spiro, Spero

Doctor Krause awoke in her hotel room. The mattress felt just as comfortable as the one she had stayed in the night before. The sheets were even softer. However, her night had not been an easy one.

She was in the town of Pocatello, only five miles south of where she'd discovered the headless bodies. Blake had brought her here the previous evening. She had been completely distraught and couldn't see for tears. He had picked her up off the bike and carried her to this bed. After hugging her and stroking her hair, he left her alone.

Krause had been awake more than she slept. The horror of the previous day haunted her thoughts and her brain refused to let go. As a result, she felt like a porcelain doll—completely hollow and terribly fragile.

Does humanity deserve a cure? Yesterday, that question had weighed on her, and she'd had no answer. This morning, her disgust toward the people who tried to steal the cure for themselves, the teens who burned Blackfoot to the ground, and whoever had killed those three decapitated men was pushing her toward the answer no.

A knock at her door got her attention. She threw back the top sheet and went to the door in her pink T-shirt nightdress. The peephole revealed Oscar Blake holding a tray. She opened the door, and the smell of cooked eggs, coffee, and bacon teased her nose.

"Morning, Linda. I made some breakfast sandwiches for us. Feeling better?"

"Yes," she lied reflexively. "Come in."

He walked over to the compact round table with four chairs in the far corner of her room and laid out the breakfast. She sat opposite him and looked at the paper plate he placed before her. She'd had fancier breakfasts in the past, and the simple plate of scrambled eggs, bacon and fried tomato he had made for her looked clumsily thrown together. The plastic knife and fork looked remarkable cheap and flimsy, but she appreciated the meal more than any other she ever had.

"The winds picked up today, and it's cloudier. Might get some rain, but the good news is we'll be getting to our destination this afternoon at the latest," he said, placing a medium-sized paper cup of strong-smelling coffee in front of her.

"Good," she said quietly. She wanted this trip to be over.

"We'll get going as soon as you're ready. No rush." Blake tucked into his breakfast, and she did the same.

Blake had mixed light salt and pepper in the eggs. It gave them a little bite, which she appreciated. She ate while stealing glances at Blake—at his muscular hands, broad shoulders and green eyes. He was a handsome man, and she was so glad he was there for her to lean on. He was her rock, and she knew he would never fail to support her.

"Sorry there's no toast," he said. "I couldn't find any decent bread."

"That's fine, Oscar. Thank you."

He smiled briefly and chewed on a piece of crisp bacon.

When they were done eating, he collected the paper plates and stacked them on the tray he had brought in. They were left with only coffee.

After a few minutes, he asked, "Is something wrong?"

"No," she replied.

"I can make more eggs if you like." He glanced toward the tray.

She rose and took his hand, leading him up and out of his seat. She led him to her bed. "That's not what I'm hungry for."

* * *

Colonel Smith stood off to the side of the fourth hole fairway of the Hubbard Memorial golf course. They were just inside the tree line, deep into the rough. Hill Air Force Base stood off to the west, barely visible through the thin line of trees on either side of the neighboring twelfth hole fairway.

The morning was chilly, but he tried to ignore that. He had worked with Noel and Vinson in turns for over an hour to dig a deep enough grave for Technical Sergeant Folsom. His labors had kept him warm enough. The earth taken from the ground was shoveled onto a tarp to keep it off the green turf below. Captain Tyler sat huddled on a groundskeeper's golf cart bench, wrapped in a wool blanket. The trailer, towed behind the cart, bore Folsom's body, wrapped in canvas.

A shovel was tossed up out of the hole, and Vinson helped Noel out of the grave.

Noel turned to Smith. "That should do it, Colonel."

"Let's get him," Smith replied.

The three men went to the trailer and retrieved Folsom's canvas-wrapped body along with several coils of rope. They carried the canvas between them and laid him down gently at the side of the opening in the ground.

Captain Tyler came to the graveside. They eased Folsom up and lowered him into the hole. When he rested at the bottom, they dropped the rope ends into the grave.

"Would anyone like to say something?" Smith asked.

No one spoke, so Smith felt obligated. Though not a religious man, he forced himself to say, "Lord, we ask you take care of the soul of Technical Sergeant Folsom, a good NCO who was taken from us prematurely." *And for no good reason,* he didn't say out loud. "May he find peace, surrounded by the game he loved."

He hadn't known the man well, but at least he knew Folsom had loved golf. There was nothing else he could think of.

After a silence of several seconds, Noel said, "Amen," followed immediately by Tyler and Vinson repeating the word.

Smith picked up the shovel, took a load of earth, and dropped it into the hole. He filled it halfway, and then the others took turns to help. When done, the tarp was folded away, and they stood looking at the dirt mound.

"What are we doing for a headstone, sir?" Tyler asked.

"Colonel Barton will arrange that once things get back to normal. *If things don't get back to normal, he won't need a grave marker. No one will be left to see it.* "Until then, we need to pitch in and help keep the base going. Mister Vinson, I arranged for an office for you with several high-speed computers and Internet access. I want you to update your information from the Chinese network. Mister Noel, you'll be working with the base staff, filling in where needed. Myself and Captain Tyler will be looking for food in the local area. Supplies on base are running low, and we have a lot of mouths to feed."

Smith stole one last glance at the grave. A feeling of loss pushed his head down. He forced it back up again and trudged to the golf cart.

* * *

Keith Hurst decided his friend needed to do something to break the monotony. "Come on, Mister President. You've been underground for days. It's time to get out of the bunker and get some fresh air. It's rejuvenating."

"All right, I'll do it just to stop your nagging," Calvin replied.

"Agent Nance, could you escort us up the stairs, please?" Hurst asked.

"Of course, sir. If you gentlemen can hold onto my shoulders, I can lead you both to the stairs."

Nance took Hurst's hand and placed it on a shoulder. Hurst felt the material of the Secret Service agent's suit jacket.

Nance led them out of the heated room they lived in, and the temperature dropped noticeably. The sounds of their footsteps on the gritty concrete floor sounded unnaturally loud.

"I need to go to the left a little to avoid a pillar," Nance warned before turning slightly.

They made it to the doorway leading to the metal stairs.

Nance took Hurst by the hand. "Mister Hurst, here's the railing. There are nine steps per section, then the stairway turns to the right. You can start up, and I'll follow with the president."

Hurst counted the steps as he ascended. He'd been up and down them twice a day since they'd been here. Nance was needlessly over-explaining things.

Then Hurst realized that Nance was talking to him for Calvin's benefit. He didn't want to be seen telling the president directly and treating him like a blind man. Hurst smiled. The secret service agent protected not only Calvin's life, but also his pride.

Hurst was halfway up the first set of stairs when he heard Calvin coming up behind him. Hurst didn't slow down.

"Good morning, Mister Hurst," Agent Carter said as Hurst reached the top.

Hurst felt a chill and a wetness in the air. "Morning. How's the weather today."

"Overall, a dreary day, but it looks like it's clearing up. Regardless, the entrance here shelters us from any bad weather," Carter replied.

"The president is on his way up. I thought he could use some fresh air." Hurst felt the edge of the doorway and sat down on the folded blanket that was his usual spot.

"That's a good idea, sir. The bunker can get a little stuffy, with no airflow."

Hurst heard approaching footsteps on the metal staircase behind him.

"Two more steps, sir," Agent Nance said. "There, you're up. We have a folding deck chair you can use, Mister President. Just turn a little to the right. There you are. Just sit."

Hurst heard light metal squeaking as Calvin sat.

"Thank you. Smells like rain."

Carter said, "It's cloudy, but looks like it's clearing up."

"Agents Carter and Nance, could I have a few minutes with Keith?"

"Of course, Mister President. We'll scout the perimeter and be right back," Carter said before walking off.

Several moments of silence passed.

"Keith..." Calvin said.

"Yes, Jim?"

"Today's the eleventh?"

"Yes." Hurst wondered what the date had to do with anything.

"The Chinese fleet is due on the West Coast on the sixteenth?"

"That's the earliest estimation. It could be the sixteenth or seventeenth depending on their speed."

"Only five days..." Calvin sounded on the edge of being distraught.

"You sound a little down, Jim," Hurst said, understating what he heard.

"Discouraged, certainly; we've had no positive news since this began. If only we had something to hold onto. Some hope..."

"*Dum spiro, spero.*" Hurst replied.

"I know you enjoy being cryptic, Keith, but just this once can you say it in simple English?" Calvin asked impatiently.

"It's Latin for 'While I breathe, I hope.' As long as we draw breath, there's the possibility of something positive happening. Yes, we're facing long odds, but Churchill probably felt the same way in 1940 during the darkest part of the Blitz. The Germans were bombing RAF airfields into oblivion, and they came closer to going under than most people know. They persevered in the face of overwhelming odds, and when the *Luftwaffe* switched over to bombing cities, they rebuilt their airfields and pulled off one of the biggest victories ever."

A moment of silence followed.

Calvin said, "I know that, Jim, and I've not lost hope completely, but I'm discouraged. I don't see a way out of this."

"You have to stop thinking about Carrie." Hurst knew the real reason for his despondency, and it was time to address the metaphorical eight-hundred-pound gorilla in the room.

"I'm not—" Calvin began.

"Damn it, stop denying it. I've heard you call her name out when you're sleeping downstairs. Every. Single. Night. You feel down because you were unable to save her, and now you think the country is in the same position. You see the U.S. circling the drain, and it's pulling you back to when she died while you were holding her hand at her bedside."

"I don't want to hear this!" Calvin objected.

"I know you don't, but I'm the only one here who can bring you out of this stupor." *Talk to me, Jim. Vent; get it all out.* "Your wife died from cancer, and there was nothing you could do to save her. You've obsessed on that for years, and it's time to let her go."

"Agent Nance!" Calvin yelled out.

Hurst restrained himself from saying more. He'd made his point. The rest was up to Calvin.

He heard Nance run up. "Yes, Mister President?"

"Take me downstairs, please. I've had enough fresh air."

"Yes, sir."

* * *

Colonel Smith pulled up in front of the Hill Air Force Base gymnasium in his van. His burying of Folsom only hours ago still weighed on him.

Captain Tyler waited for him outside of the front doors. He was surprised to see she had changed out of civilian clothes and was wearing ABUs[26] with subtle rank insignia on the collar. She also wore calf-high combat boots and a green web belt with thigh-strapped pistol holster. She hopped into the passenger seat.

"You changed?" he observed.

She looked down on the camouflaged uniform while placing her hand over her chest. "Since we got on base, I felt self-conscious about wearing civvies. I got one of the supply people to issue me with these. They're more comfortable than what I was wearing, and best of all, clean."

"Well, you look…" He was going to say "great", but realized that would be inappropriate. He finished with, "…Ready to get to work."

"Yes, sir. Where are we heading?"

Smith pulled a road map of Salt Lake City from above the visor and unfolded it against the steering wheel. He pointed. "Colonel Barton tells me they've scavenged everything locally, and she has teams to the south. She asked we go north and look in and around the Ogden area."

Tyler looked over her shoulder into the rear of the van. "Not a lot of room back there if we find anything, and there's a lot of mouths to feed inside."

"We're just scouting. If we find any sizable food supply, we mark it on the map and Colonel Barton will send out a work party with a deuce and a half to bring it in. They're limiting the use of the heavy trucks to maintain fuel supplies. That reminds me, if we see a gas truck, we report that, as well. Clear?"

"Yes, sir. Let's go."

Smith handed her the map, put the van in gear, and drove off. As they passed the front gate, he saluted the sole armed guard and turned onto the civilian road. "We'll take Highway 15 north. I'm told it's been cleared."

The drive passed in silence. Further north, Highway 15 merged with Highway 84.

---

[26] Airman Battle Uniforms are camouflaged light green shaded clothing worn in the field by Air Force personnel.

Tyler reviewed the map. "The Ogden turnoff should be in a couple of miles… Looks like a decent day. The heavy cloud is well off to the east and shouldn't be coming this way."

Smith nodded. "Yes, decent weather is the only good break we've had so far. When this is over, I plan on taking as much leave as I can, head to some resort with nothing but a beach, sunshine, and a waiter bringing me drinks regularly."

"Mmmmm, sounds divine. Throw in a hammock with a fruity drink, and I am so there." Smith glanced over at her, and she smiled back at him. *Is she saying she likes the idea of a vacation or a vacation with me?*

Smith decided not to open Pandora's box by asking, so he focused on the road and driving.

"There's an airport off to the left. Want to check it out? The secure side should have bulk food for their outlets," Tyler asked, pointing at the obvious civilian airfield.

"We'll drop in there on our way back. I'm hoping to find large grocery stores or a food distribution warehouse, if possible. Hill has thousands of staff, so the bigger, the better."

"Understood."

When they reached the Ogden turnoff, Smith turned down the off-ramp. He rolled through the stop sign and turned right onto West 21st Street. He kept a slow twenty mile-per-hour pace and began scanning for possible locations where food could be.

"Congratulations, Colonel. We're making history," Tyler said suddenly.

"For what?" He had no idea what she was referring to.

"We're the first black people to drive a van full of bullet holes through Utah and *not* be pulled over by the cops."

He moaned, chuckled, then laughed, as what she said sank in. In seconds, both he and Tyler were laughing hilariously.

A loud bang stopped their merriment. The back end of the van jerked to the right, accompanied by numerous thuds, and the vehicle shuddered. Smith slowed rapidly, safely bringing the van to a halt.

"Is someone else shooting at us?" Tyler wondered out loud, looking all around her with her hand on her pistol butt.

"Don't think so. I think we blew a tire. I'll check." He jumped out and immediately saw the driver's side rear tire was deflated. He looked around, ready to jump back in the van at the slightest provocation. There was no other noise and nothing moved. No sign of any threat.

I hope we have a spare in the back.

* * *

Linda Krause sat on the backseat of the roadster as they sped along. She leaned into him, with her arms wrapped solidly around Blake's torso. She didn't need to find an excuse anymore. They were lovers now, and she could hold him all she wanted.

Krause hadn't wanted to leave the hotel. She'd had everything she wanted within arm's reach. With the world falling apart around her, staying in bed with her man sounded wonderful to her. Blake had encouraged her to finish the trip so they could return to Seattle and be together. That motivated her to get up. All she had to do was deliver the tubes to Colorado and give the cure to the government. Then the military would take over, and they would be free.

"Linda."

"Yes, Oscar?"

"We're just over empty on the gauge and need gas. I'm going to pull down the next off-ramp. One more fill-up should see us all the way to Cheyenne Mountain."

"Great. It'll be nice to stretch my legs. Where are we?" Krause released her grip slightly and rotated her shoulders to stretch out her back muscles.

"Just north of Salt Lake City." Blake began to slow and turn off the highway.

"Wow, time flies. We've traveled a lot further than I thought."

"Yeah, we should get there just after dark, at this pace."

The roadster turned onto the city street, and she began scanning the area for a gas station. It didn't look as if there was power in this neighborhood, but Blake had a siphon hose and didn't mind the taste of gas. At least, that was what he said. The look on his face when the fuel entered his mouth was priceless, she thought. *I need to get him some breath mints if he's going to be kissing me tonight with gasoline mouth.*

"Heads up," Blake said flatly without any discernible emotion.

"What's wrong?" She looked over his shoulder to see what he did.

"There's a van pulled over with two people. Looks like they're changing a tire. Hold on tight. I may need to take off quickly."

She saw them, then—two black people, a man and a woman. The rear wheel was off, and the rear of their van was suspended up on a scissors jack. The man was tall, over six feet, and wore what looked like a uniform: light blue shirt, darker blue pants, and black shoes. The woman wore military camouflage clothing and boots. As they drew closer, Krause could see both people had pistol belts. She gripped Blake's torso in case he decided to run. Blake had picked up a pistol and belt holster, but that was under his jacket. He wouldn't be able to get to it in a hurry.

The people at the van noticed them approach and stood to face them. Blake stopped twenty feet away. His helmet radio was still on, so she heard him say, "Afternoon. Are you with the air force?"

She had to lift the side of her helmet up to hear the man answer "Yes, where you heading?" with a single nod.

Sunlight reflected from some sort of silver insignia on his collar. *He's an officer of some sort.*

"Cheyenne Mountain. We're making a delivery," Blake answered.

"You don't want to go anywhere near there. The Chinese took it over days ago and control that whole area," the black man said.

"The Chinese?" Blake asked, saying exactly what she was thinking. "What are you talking about?"

Holding his hands out from his sides to show he was no threat, the uniformed man approached slowly. "I'm Colonel Smith from NORAD. I was in the Cheyenne Mountain operations bunker when the Chinese airborne attacked. They're the ones who orchestrated the blindness worldwide so they could invade us." Smith got close enough to Blake to hold out his hand. "It's nice to meet people who can see. There's not many of us around."

Blake shook hands with him. When done, he surprised Krause by turning off the ignition. "Oscar Blake, and this is Linda Krause."

Smith held out his hand to shake with Krause. She took his hand to be polite. His grip was firm but not overpowering.

Blake turned slightly and indicated the camouflage-wearing woman. "This is Captain Tyler." Tyler approached the group as her name was mentioned.

Blake slipped off his helmet, so Krause did the same. More handshakes introduced Tyler to the group.

Blake asked, "Was it the fireworks on the Fourth?"

Smith nodded. "Yes. I can't say how we know, but we have direct evidence the Chinese were responsible for what happened."

Blake shook his head. "My God, how could they do something that... heinous?"

"For the same reason all invaders have. To take what we have by force," Smith said matter-of-factly.

Blake twisted on his seat slightly. "If you're in the military, you must have a plan to kick them out?"

Smith folded his arms, looked down, and shook his head. "Until we get a cure in place, there's nothing of consequence we *can* do. The vast majority of the military is blind, and we have zero chance of opposing them right now."

Blake twisted around toward Krause and raised an eyebrow. "Do you want to tell him?"

Smith frowned. "Tell me what?"

Krause looked at Smith. "I'm a doctor of ophthalmology from Seattle. A small team at my hospital found the cause of the blindness, and we've developed a cure to reverse it."

Smith stepped back a half step as his jaw dropped. He looked as if someone had just slapped him hard.

Tyler stepped forward. "You're serious! How long does it take to reverse the blindness?"

Krause replied, "Four hours. It varies slightly by individual, but only by a few minutes."

Smith recovered himself. "Doctor, I need to get the spare tire on the van. When I'm done, can you come back with us to Hill Air Force Base? We have several thousand military staff who need that cure."

Krause looked at Blake. The two air force officers looked genuine to her and what they said rang true, but she was still uncertain. Was following them back to their base a good idea? With the news that Cheyenne Mountain was in enemy hands, their original plans were in tatters. She looked at Blake, who simply nodded once. She turned back to face Smith. "Of course."

Blake placed his helmet on the handlebars and slid off the roadster seat. "I'll help you with the tire, Colonel."

* * *

Captain Eric Reid had finished his daily inspection walkthrough of the USS *John Warner* and sat down alone in the wardroom for coffee when the 1MC squawked. "Captain, contact the command center. Captain, contact the command center."

Reid looked up at the handset on the wall. He could use that to talk to the command center, but he decided to go there instead. He left the coffee on the table and strode rapidly up the narrow corridor. He habitually checked the boat's course, speed and depth on a nearby monitor upon entering the command center. The XO came up to him from the CSRR station.

"What's up?" Reid asked.

"Sir, we're coming to the edge of our patrol area and have had no additional civilian traffic save the Modesto station. We need to change course to stay in the designated patrol area, unless you want to keep going north."

As captain of the boat he did have the discretion to exit his patrol area if he felt it both advantageous and necessary. However, he had no reason to do so. The radio watch on civilian stations had not produced any news, and they were just in the dark as before. Heading farther north would serve no purpose, and if he did leave his patrol area without a damned good reason his command could be revoked.

He raised his voice slightly, "Pilot, come to course one-niner-five."

"Come to course one-niner-five, pilot aye," the officer manning the dive controls repeated back.

Reid turned to the radar operator. "Retract all masts."

The female singer warbling on the ship's speakers faded out. "Sir, all masts are retracted."

"Pilot, take us down to three hundred feet, ten degrees down bubble. Report when we get to depth," Reid ordered.

"Descend to three hundred feet, ten degrees down bubble, and report when at depth, pilot aye."

The submarine's deck tipped slightly downward.

Reid motioned for Maddox to join him at the navigation table. He pointed to a chart. "XO, let's head back to the center of our patrol area here. It's deep water, and we should get decent convergence zone[27] coverage. We'll stay there unless we get a contact to investigate. Any ship out here needs to be looked over."

Maddox rubbed his chin. "You expecting—"

---

[27] Convergence zones (CZ) occur in deep water. Some frequencies of sound do not reach the bottom, as deep isothermal layers bend sound back upwards. This can result in passive sonar detection of ships from a considerable distance. You can have multiple CZs. If the first is at thirty nautical miles, the second would be at sixty, and so on. Each CZ is only a mile or two wide.

"Captain, my depth is three hundred feet," the pilot called out.

"Thank you, pilot. All ahead one-third."

"All ahead one-third, pilot aye."

Reid faced Maddox. "You were saying?"

"Are you expecting the Chinese navy to come through our area?" Maddox tapped the paper chart.

"It makes sense. If there was an air invasion, there should be some sort of resupply by sea. Troops in the field need lots of ammo, food, and supplies to be effective. Only ships can carry those loads. Our patrol area includes the area off Los Angeles, Long Beach, and San Francisco. The first two are among the largest commercial ports in the world. Logically, they need to go through us."

Maddox slid his finger up the coast to Seattle. "You're forgetting the Sea-Tac[28] container ports. They could off-load there."

Reid shrugged. "Potentially, but my money's on L.A.— Long Beach. There's better road connections to go cross-country from there. Besides, if they do head to Sea-Tac, we'll hear them on sonar. We can do a speed run if we hear any significant traffic heading up there. Without any intel or orders, it's the best I can come up with."

Maddox studied the navigation chart. "I concur. All we can do is wait for them to come to us."

* * *

Colonel Smith parked his van in front of the gymnasium. Both he and Captain Tyler got out. Blake and Krause arrived soon afterwards, pulling their three-wheeled motorbike up directly behind the van. Smith led the group into the base gymnasium and escorted them to Colonel Barton's small office. Everyone had to squeeze in.

---

[28] Refers to the Seattle-Tacoma area of Washington State.

Smith began, "Colonel, we may have found a cure for the blindness. We need to get some volunteers to prove it works."

After a long silence, Barton responded, "I send you out to look for food, and you come back with what? Magic beans?"

Doctor Krause stepped forward, addressing Smith. "We've already tested the cure on many people. It's worked on everyone who has been treated."

Barton asked, "Do you have any evidence of that?"

"No, we left all our clinical notes behind," Krause admitted. "It wasn't practical to—"

Barton interrupted, "Can you even prove you're a doctor?"

Krause's mouth opened slightly. She looked dumbfounded, and while her lips moved, no words came out.

Smith leaned forward. "That's unfair, Colonel. This may be exactly what we need."

Barton stood and tried to face Smith, but her blind eyes focused at a point just over his shoulder. "This sounds like snake oil to me, Colonel Smith."

"Yes, it could be. That's why we need volunteers to prove it works or doesn't."

Barton objected, "I just don't see why you need my people to be guinea pigs. Can't you go out and get some civilians to test your theories on?"

Getting tired of Barton's intransigence, Smith raised his voice. "Civilians can't stop the Chinese invasion force! If we're to have a prayer of doing that, we have to get your base back up and operational ASAP. We need your jets in the air."

Barton closed her eyes and placed her hands on her desk. "I just don't see why I should trust people who could very well be taking advantage of this situation for personal gain!"

Smith began to object, but a red-faced Doctor Krause stepped forward. "Colonel Barton, people are dying by the thousands out there from starvation, dehydration, and disease every minute. Others are giving up, committing suicide, or burning entire cities to the ground. I'm not in this to sell you anything. I'm not here for money or fame. All I want is to get the country back on its feet before it is destroyed.

"This cure works, Colonel. We've seen it work on everyone we've treated. If you don't want us here, then say the word, and we'll go back to Seattle. The cancer in your eyes will continue to grow, creeping along your optic nerve. When it reaches your brain in three months, you'll die. You have a choice. You can either let us cure you or keep your officious attitude and live out the remainder of your short life in the dark."

Blake put his hand on Krause's shoulder. It had been quite the tirade, and Colonel Barton obviously didn't like it. Smith hadn't interrupted, though. He agreed with Doctor Krause. That the blind had only three months to live was new to him, though, and it underlined how important it was to fix this.

"Get out! All of you—get out of my office!" Barton screamed.

Tyler hurried out while shaking her head. Blake escorted Krause out. Smith took a deep breath. He had larger problems to deal with than Barton's insubordination. It wasn't worth responding to. When he was alone with Barton, Smith said, "I'm sorry you feel that way, Colonel. I asked for this meeting as a courtesy only. Thank you for your time."

Smith walked outside, where he found the small group waiting for him. Behind them were row on row of blind men and women on their cots. Smith came to attention and in his loudest voice ordered. "*Aten-hut!*"

All conversation in the gymnasium ended. The military personnel got to their feet as best as they could, but it took time and a few stumbled against their cots while doing so.

Once the noise subsided, Smith projected his voice. "Good evening, ladies and gentlemen. I'm Colonel Smith. I have a doctor with me who claims to have a cure for the blindness, and we require some volunteers to test it. If you wish to volunteer, please raise your—"

He didn't see a single blind person in the gymnasium who didn't have their hand up.

July 12th

Chapter Twenty-One
By The Dawn's Early Light

Linda Krause dozed on a gymnasium cot in the upstairs weight room, provided by Colonel Smith. Most of the overhead lights had been turned off. She wore her clothes and lay on top of the blanket. This habit came from her time as an intern. A gentle shake of her shoulder brought her out of her light sleep.

"Linda?"

She stirred and sat up, a little confused as to where she was. "Yes… What?"

"You wanted me to wake you."

She focused and saw Blake standing there. He had a paper cup in his hand. Steam rose from the top.

"They don't have any coffee at this time of the morning, so I made you some green tea. I hope that's all right."

She swung her feet onto the floor and straightened her shirt collar. "Yes, that's fine. Thanks." She took the tea, holding it in her palms. The intense heat that came through the paper told her it would be too hot to sip.

Blake sat down beside her. "Can I ask you something?"

Krause turned to face him. "Of course you can. Ask me anything."

"You tore into Colonel Barton pretty badly last night. I've known you for a while, and that didn't seem characteristic for you. Why did you say that?"

"Yeah… I regretted it after, but she reminded me of an administrator at the hospital I deal with all the time. She's a bureaucrat, and they irritate me. They never make decisions or take responsibility; they just follow policy. They point blindly to paperwork, memos, and binders and don't care about suffering or the impact on people's lives. Barton's that type; she's as arrogant as she is ignorant. She'd rather be blind than wrong—you could see it on her face. She gets away with it because she's a colonel, and those beneath her can't speak up without retribution. Well. I'm not in the air force, so I can tell the truth. I'd say I was sorry, but I meant every word. People *are* dying—the entire country is dying—and those deaths will only increase unless people like her shut up and either help or get out of the way."

Blake smiled. "If it's any consolation, I spoke to Colonel Smith, and he agrees with you. He's waiting impatiently downstairs for an update."

Krause looked across the room. The four volunteers who had taken the radiation therapy hours earlier rested on their own cots, wedged between the exercise equipment across the room. She checked her watch. Oscar had woken her exactly on time. *They should be regaining their sight soon.* "Oscar, have you had any sleep?"

"I've been so busy helping around the building, I haven't had a chance."

She looked at him with a doctor's eye. His eyes were bloodshot, and he looked tired. She stood up. He tried to do the same, but she held the tea in her left hand and placed her right hand on his shoulder. "This cot is now yours. I'll wake you in six hours. You need the rest. Your eye injury won't heal properly if you don't."

"I'm fine, Lind—"

"No, you're not. No arguments. Doctor's orders… You need to rest." She pressed him back onto the pillow. He didn't resist. She kissed him on the forehead and stroked his temple with her fingertips.

She walked over to the four volunteers. Smith had randomly chosen three men and a woman. They had been introduced before the treatment, but having just woken up, she couldn't remember their names. She walked up to the woman. She was the only one of the four to have her eyes open. *What was her name? Betsy? Betty? Betty.*

"Betty, it's Doctor Krause. How are you feeling?"

"Kinda weird, Doc. I thought I was imagining things, but I'm definitely seeing little flashes of light. They're there for a split second then gone. I only see white flashes. No colors. Does that mean it's working?"

Blake sat beside her on the cot. "Yes. The cancer that's covering your rods and cones is slowly dying off. You should see in black and white to begin with. Colors won't be visible until later."

"Would you mind telling me what rods and cones do? I've heard of them, of course, but don't know how they work." Betty waved her fingers a few inches in front of her own face.

"Of course. Rods are what you use to see in the dark. They work best in low-light conditions and only see in black and white. Cones let you see in bright light and in color." As an eye doctor, Krause had answered that question many times.

Betty turned her head. "I'm seeing a little more now. It's like I'm in a really dark room. I can just see the outline of your head."

"Rods greatly outnumber cones; the ratio is around twelve to one, so that's why everything will be dark for a bit. Once the cones become exposed, you should regain all your sight."

"I didn't think this was going to work so quickly. I can almost see again. I hoped…" Tears formed in Betty's eyes. "I prayed for this day."

Krause held Betty's hand.

Betty squeezed it tightly. "Thank you, Doctor. Thank you so much."

Krause smiled. This was why she had become a doctor—to heal and help people make their lives better. "Just lay back and rest. I need to go check on the others."

* * *

Colonel Smith had to leave the base gymnasium to go and see Vinson, who had been placed in a neighboring building. One reason for that was that the gym had no computers or available space, but more importantly, Smith didn't want anyone to know they had a back door into the Chinese networks.

Smith walked up the corridor. Vinson was easy to find. His office was the only one with the lights on. He encountered the smell of brewed coffee as he got closer. Smith entered the office to find Vinson sitting behind a desk with three wide-format monitors. The windows behind the desk had closed venetian blinds. A coffee maker had been set up on one of the window ledges.

Vinson looked up as Smith entered; he had his hand wrapped around a coffee mug. "The vice president is dead, Colonel. They beat him to death."

"When?" Smith was shocked at the news. He walked around the side of the desk to see what Vinson was looking at.

"Two days ago, when we were on the road. I just finished reviewing all the video footage I missed when we were traveling. They were questioning him, showing him papers, but he kept shaking his head. When he did, two guys moved in and pounded on him. I didn't see him speaking, so he must have resisted right to the end." Vinson's voice sounded brittle.

"Wait, you said earlier there was no audio? Couldn't he just be unconscious?" Smith looked at the screens, which were full of Chinese.

"No, sir. They put him in a body bag. I followed the soldiers who carried him on internal cameras all the way to the morgue. They threw him on a stack of bodies waist-high. He's gone, Colonel." Vinson drank the last of his coffee.

Smith sat back on a window ledge. He felt weak, as if the oxygen had been removed from the room. "Any good news?"

"No, sir, but no real bad news either. I'm still able to get into the Wenchang launch facility servers. Plus, I've got access to the authorization codes for launching the last three blindness warheads." Vinson rubbed his eyes.

"Can we change the codes to something they don't know?" Smith asked while standing back up.

Vinson shook his head. "I don't recommend that. We could do it, but alarms would go off, and they could easily reset them. We'd be throwing away our only access for a token result."

"What about the ships from Qingdao?"

Vinson tapped a yellow legal notepad on his desk. "Noel gave me his access credentials for NRO resources. I was able to link to an IKON satellite and get this…" He handed Smith a piece of paper with several lines of notes. "Course, speed, and numbers for the Qingdao fleet as of forty minutes ago. They are traveling in a two-column convoy on a direct course to L.A. If they keep their current speed, they'll be entering port midday on July the sixteenth."

Smith audibly blew out his breath. "That means we have four days to come up with a plan to stop them."

Vinson reached for the coffee pot to refill his mug. "Without a cure, that's going to be impossible."

"We may have one," Smith said.

Vinson almost dropped his mug. Coffee pouring from the pot hit the back of his hand. He hissed and hastily put the mug down, then shook his hand to get rid of the searing liquid. "What? Really? When did this happen?"

"We found a doctor who claims to have a radiation treatment that reverses vision loss. We're running a trial now with some volunteers." Smith checked his watch. "I need to get back and see if it works."

Vinson seemed to forget about the spilled coffee. "Can you get Noel in here to help me? If you do have a cure, I'll need him to keep tabs on the ships, generate some overhead imagery, and identify the PLAN escort ships. I can then focus on getting intel from the Chinese network."

"Of course, but let's make sure there is a cure first. It may not work." Smith began moving to the door.

"Colonel," Vinson said. Smith stopped and turned. "If the cure works, what's your plan?"

Smith crossed his arms. "That's what I need to figure out. Getting a cure will help, but it isn't the only obstacle. We still have quite a few in front of us."

"Anything I can help with?"

Smith usually wouldn't discuss such things with an analyst, but Vinson had proven himself, and there were few people he could talk freely to. *Maybe talking it out will help.* "The biggest issue is coordination. The Chinese have control of our strategic assets and bases. The only combat-ready force we have are submarines. We don't have access to any military radios capable of warning the sub forces. Nor do we have the troops required to take back our bases—not in four days, anyway."

"What about Navy SEALs? If we could get someone down to Coronado and get them operational, they could—"

Smith cut him off with a raised hand. He appreciated the input, but Vinson's background in analyzing *foreign* armed troops wasn't helping. "The SEALs are effective troops, but they have very small numbers. A SEAL team only has a hundred and twenty men. There were fifteen hundred airborne troops protecting Peterson alone. We'd need a division to assault it effectively. That'll happen in time, but for now, we don't have that option.

"No, the key is stopping the ships. Do that, and the airborne troops will be isolated and without supplies." Smith began pacing the office. "To reach a submarine at depth requires an ELF[29] radio. All ELF land bases are probably occupied, and the only other resource that has ELF are E-6 Mercury aircraft. They fly out of Tinker, Travis, and Patuxent River; all of which are occupied by the—"

Tyler had mentioned something about an E-6 earlier. What the hell did she say? Something about maintenance? He couldn't remember.

---

[29] Extremely Low Frequency

A lot had happened since then. He needed to talk to her. "Sorry, I need to go. If the cure works, I'll get Noel in here."

"Thank you, sir."

* * *

Doctor Krause was more than satisfied with the results from the first group of volunteers. All of them had recovered their sight and could see normally again. Word had spread quickly, and there was a long line of air force personnel waiting at the door of the weight room, pleading to be next.

Krause glanced over at Blake, who slept on her cot. She'd let him sleep as long as possible. He'd earned it. She smiled at him.

Colonel Smith came through the people milling around the door. He strode up to her. "Doctor, how are the volunteers?"

"Why not ask them yourself, Colonel?" She turned to the others in the room. "Betty, gentlemen, come say hello to Colonel Smith."

The four volunteers came over to them, some having to avoid weight exercise stations, which they did easily.

"You can all see?" Smith said, his mouth hanging open.

They said, "Yes, sir."

Betty added, "It's amazing, Colonel. I can see as well as before."

Smith asked Betty, "Any pain or side effects? Anything negative at all?"

"No, sir. I'm feeling perfectly normal and ready to get back to work."

"Me too, sir," said one male volunteer.

"And me, sir," said another.

"I'm good to go, Colonel," the last man stated.

There was a period of silence. Krause thought Smith looked subdued, as if he didn't know what to say.

Krause jumped in. "With your permission, Colonel, I can show these four how to do the treatments, and they can start on the rest."

Smith turned to her. "No objections at all, Doctor. I'm just amazed it works that well. Ha! You could tell me the sky was purple with polka dots right now, and I'd believe you. We'll need to start with the Herc pilots and ground crews, then F-16 pilots and support staff. I'll get others to help you organize that."

She didn't understand. "Sorry? You said 'Herc'?"

"Yes, Hercules aircraft. They're four-engine transports designed to carry cargo over a long distance. We're going to need them to spread the—what did you call them, tubes?"

"Yes, I see, thanks. I'll get started right away." Krause turned back to the volunteers. She needed to explain how the tubes worked and how to use them, to treat people safely.

"Doctor?" Colonel Smith asked. "Thank you. You don't know what this means."

She turned back to face him. He looked to be on the verge of tears.

* * *

President Calvin dreamed of days past. He sat on the edge of his wife's hospital bed, holding her hand gently. Her fingers suddenly clasped his, and she took a sharp intake of breath. The cancer caused her considerable pain, and he stroked her fingers until they relaxed again. He looked down on her, unable to do anything. The I.V. needle in her arm supplied the strongest possible pain medication they had, but even that was failing her. She was dying, and he was powerless to stop it.

"It's time for you to leave, Jim," she said with closed eyes. "You can't stay here anymore."

"I'm staying, Cassie. I want to be with you," Calvin said softly.

"Mister President, you're needed in the Oval Office," a female voice said from behind him. He ignored it.

Another voice, this one a man: "Secretary of Defense Blackburn is here for his appointment."

Calvin yelled, "Not now!"

Another woman's voice. "The Malaysian ambassador wishes to speak with you, Mister President."

Calvin whipped around in a fury. "Leave me alone, all of you!"

He saw no one. The room was unoccupied.

He felt his wife's fingers slip out of his hand. He turned back, reaching for her, but found only an empty unmade bed.

Cassie's soft voice came from all around. "It's time to let me go, Jim. You need to live your life without me. Don't worry. I'll always be with you."

Calvin stood, looking around for her. "No, Cassie. Don't leave me alone... Cassie? Cassie!"

She was gone.

Someone began shaking his shoulder. "Mister President... Mister President... Colonel Smith just called on the cell phone for you."

He awoke, half sitting up as he did. "Huh? What? Who?"

"Colonel Smith, sir, from NORAD. He just called the cell phone. He'll try calling again in five minutes."

Calvin recognized Agent Carter and remembered where he was. "Colonel Smith... Of course. Help me up. Let's get upstairs. Where's Keith?"

"He's sleeping, sir." Carter said.

"No, I'm not. What's up?" Hurst replied, before coughing a few times.

"Smith wants to speak to us. Let's get up top." Calvin was wide awake now.

Carter assisted Calvin up. "Wait one moment, Mister President, and I'll help Mister Hurst."

"What time is it?" Hurst asked.

"Just after three in the morning, sir," Carter replied. "Okay, Mister President, just place your hand on my shoulder. Mister Hurst, same thing... All right, ready? I'll walk slowly."

They made their way upstairs. Calvin was given the folding chair to sit on. An uncomfortable silence followed. He needed to say something, but he had no idea what.

Carter said, "I have the phone, sir. I'll accept the call then hand it over."

"Can you put it on speaker as well, Agent Carter? I'll want Keith's opinion on this."

"Yes, sir."

"Don't forget to mention a baseball team when he rings back, Mister President. It will tell him you are not held under duress. He should mention a star constellation in return," Hurst said.

"Right," was all Calvin could muster in response.

At least another minute of silence passed.

The cell trilled. Carter answered it quickly and handed it to Calvin. "Speakerphone is on, sir. May I suggest you don't use titles or real names, sir? This is an unsecure line."

"Hello. Have you caught a Colorado Rockies game lately?" Calvin said.

"No, sir. I've been too busy looking up at Orion." It certainly sounded like Smith, and he used the code. "We found a cure."

Calvin sat bolt upright. "You're positive? A lot's riding on this."

"Four volunteers were treated, and all four recovered one hundred percent of their sight. I've ordered base personnel to receive the cure. We should be combat capable in twenty-four hours."

"Which base?" Calvin wanted to know.

"Sir, I'd rather not say. This is an open line. My intention is to send someone to brief you and also establish more secure communications. We have access to Hercules aircraft. I just need to know where to send it to meet up with you."

"Stand by. Can the phone be muted?" Calvin felt the phone being taken from his hand.

"Phone's muted, sir," Carter replied.

"Well, Keith?" Calvin asked. "What do you think?"

Hurst sighed. "He used the proper code, so he's not under duress, and talking in unspecified ways isn't helpful. We have no choice, really. We need to be briefed and get secure communications in place. Agent Carter, what's the nearest airfield that can take a Hercules?"

Carter paused before answering, "Pottstown Heritage Field Airport is quite close, so we'll hear any airplane on approach. Short runway for a Herc, but should be doable. If he lands there, I can go in a car and check them over before bringing them back. Just don't tell them where we are. If there's an issue, Agent Nance can get you away in the spare vehicle."

Hurst said, "I agree with Agent Carter. It's a safe play."

Calvin also agreed, but said nothing. "Unmute the phone, please."

"Done, sir. Here you are."

Calvin felt the phone return to his hand. "You can land at Pottsdown Heritage Field Airport in Pennsylvania. We'll meet the aircraft on arrival."

Smith replied, "Understood. I hope to get them up in the air within twelve hours, but the condition of the aircraft is unknown at this time, so there may be delays."

Calvin thought he heard some tension in Smith's voice and decided to explore it. "Anything else?"

"Yes, sir. I'm getting flak from a local commanding officer. She's not in the NORAD chain of command, and while I technically outrank her, she's, well, resisting my orders." Smith stated.

"Will the Hercules be returning to you after coming here?" Calvin asked quickly.

"Yes, sir."

"I'll send back written orders to make things easier for you. The stakes for this are too high for obstinate personalities to get in the way." Calvin said forcefully.

"Thank you, sir. That's all from me for now."

"Godspeed and good luck."

"Good-bye, sir." Smith hung up.

Calvin held the phone out, and Carter took it from him.

"A cure?" Calvin said. "Keith, I wouldn't have thought it possible."

Hurst sighed audibly. "It's a weight off my mind, too. We have a fighting chance now. Let's hope Colonel Smith can get a decent-sized military force pooled up in time."

"Agent Carter, could you leave us for a moment?" Calvin asked.

"Yes, sir. I'll be close by. If you need me, shout out."

Calvin heard Carter's footsteps fade away. "Keith, I'm sorry for the last time we spoke. I was out of line."

"Don't worry about it. I had it coming. I pushed you a little too hard," Hurst replied.

Calvin moved on. He didn't want to dwell on the negative. "We'll need some sort of printer to produce Smith's orders. A laptop as well, unless Mister Ogden doesn't mind sharing his."

"I'm sure one of the agents can go into town and get those for us. In the meantime, what's our overall plan? Smith has the military side of things covered, but the political aspects need to be planned out for the long term."

"We'll wait on that until we get briefed, but I agree, we'll need options. The Chinese can't get away with this barbaric act. Blinding the world? They need to pay."

"Agreed, Mister President."

* * *

Colonel Smith awoke to the high-pitched beep of his watch alarm. He had forced himself to take four hours' sleep knowing he needed to be mentally alert over the coming day. The four hours also coincided with the second batch of people getting the radiation therapy. He hoped the Hercules pilots and ground crew would be up and ready for duty when he got to the gym.

Smith shut off the alarm and swung his feet to the ground. He had set up a cot in an office down the hall from where Vinson worked. He had pulled aside the desk to make room for the cot. The building was otherwise unoccupied, and Smith wanted the privacy. He had always hated dormitories, and the base gym had been turned into a huge one, with noises sounding at all hours.

He walked down to the small bathroom in his boxers and, seeing the shower stall, decided to shower and shave. He got away with looking grungy when people were blind, but as a command officer, he needed to look his best when people regained their sight.

Standing in the shower, he wondered where he could get a new uniform. The one he'd been wearing had not been laundered since leaving the Cheyenne Mountain bunker, and frankly, it reeked. He resolved to find a new one that morning.

He dried himself and wrapped the towel around his waist before walking back to his room with boxers in hand.

Smith turned the corner to find Captain Tyler, wearing freshly pressed dress blues and hanging up a man's uniform shirt and trousers on the free-standing coat rack.

"What's this, Captain?" Smith asked, feeling somewhat perplexed.

"Morning, sir. It occurred to me that as people recover their sight, you'd need a clean uniform. I talked to my supply contact and arranged for this."

Did she just check me out? Smith moved into the room, holding where the towel tucked into itself. *I don't need a wardrobe malfunction with a junior female officer in the room.* "While I appreciate the thought, this isn't your job."

Tyler's eyebrows rose. "Sir, you made me your aide back in Colorado, when the first Chinese planes were inbound. So, with respect, this is exactly my job."

Smith remembered that. "I did, didn't I? All right, thank you." He realized he held his boxers in his other hand. "It's too bad you couldn't get some underwear, as well."

"The bag on the door handle behind you has three pairs of black socks and three pairs of black boxer briefs. I hope I got the sizes right."

Smith turned and saw the white plastic bag. He'd missed it, as the door was wide open and back against the wall. He laughed and turned back to face her.

"Something funny, sir?"

"It isn't often that someone exceeds my expectations. You seem to do it consistently."

She just smiled at him and said nothing for several seconds.

"Thank you for the clothes," he said.

"You're welcome, sir," she replied, not moving.

He indicated the door with a flat hand. "Captain, I need to get dressed."

She jumped slightly. "Oh! Of course. Sorry, Colonel." She left the room.

Smith closed the door, removing the bag from the handle. When it was closed all the way, he allowed himself a chuckle.

* * *

Linda Krause walked up to her cot in the gym's weight room with a plastic tray in her hands. Blake slept blissfully on his right side. On the tray she had placed a glass of orange juice, a banana muffin, and cup of coffee. She tapped the leg of the cot with her foot. "Oscar... Oscar! Wake up."

It took more kicking, but he finally stirred. "What's up, Linda? What time is it?"

"Time for breakfast," she said with a faint smile.

He sat up, bringing his feet to the floor. She placed the tray on his thighs.

"No eggs or bacon?" he said, looking at the meal.

"Not this time. Too much fat and sodium. From the limited menu they do have, this is better for you, and doctor approved." She sat down beside him.

Blake drained the orange juice in four swallows. "Mmm, freshly squeezed."

"One of the food scouts found a refrigerated warehouse with a backup generator still running. It was full of fresh fruit and veggies. We'll have fresh OJ for some time. Luckily, one of the few who kept their vision is a base cook. They didn't have to worry about starving. I had a word with her and got you this special breakfast." She bumped shoulders with him.

"I appreciate it, especially the coffee." He held up the mug.

"The four volunteers I cured are treating the rest of the blind downstairs, but they have no plan to go out and help the surrounding civilians. I'm more than a little concerned about that."

"Given the threat from the Chinese, I think they have to do it that way." Blake peeled the paper liner from the bottom of his muffin.

"I know, and I'm not suggesting we take anything away from that effort." She looked around to make sure no one would overhear. "I still have the prototype tube that Doctor Wiater made. We can go out and try to help as many civilians as possible. At least, until some sort of mass production is worked out for the tubes. That's still a week or two away, though. Even healing a hundred people should help. What do you think?"

Blake took a bite of the muffin. After chewing and swallowing, he said, "You know I've got your back. Besides, these military types will probably kick us off base soon, anyway."

She smiled and kissed him on the cheek. "Thanks. You're so supportive."

He bumped her shoulder with his. "I go where you go, or haven't you figured that out?"

She kissed him, but this time it wasn't on the forehead.

* * *

Colonel Smith felt normal again. The shower, shave, and clean uniform helped buoy up his spirits. With a working cure, his confidence was at the highest point it had been since the fireworks had started. Captain Tyler had done a decent job getting him a uniform in the right size. Even the socks and underwear fit. He'd never worn boxer briefs before, but he didn't mind them at all.

Smith strode down the hallway to Vinson's office. He found him behind the desk. *Does he ever sleep?* "Morning."

"Morning, Colonel. I'm just updating the position of the ships. They're still on the same course."

Smith walked around Vinson's desk and sat on the window ledge. "Is Noel helping out?"

"Yes, sir. He's been working up background information on the ships. A pair of Chinese PLAN destroyers has joined the convoy, and he's generating a threat assessment."

"Good. I have a job for you."

"What's up?" Vinson turned to look at him.

"I need you to go brief the president in Pennsylvania. We should have a Herc spooled up within a few hours, if we're lucky. You'll be taking two of the tubes with you, as well."

"Okay," Vinson said flatly.

"I know it's a surprise, but there are several good reasons." Smith counted on his fingers as he said, "First, you have the best intel on the Chinese. The president and Keith Hurst need that info more than we do. Besides, you'll be setting up secure communications back to us and can pass on any relevant info we need to know.

"Second, once he can see again, you need to show the president the video of the V.P. and joint chiefs. That's something we can't hold back.

"Last, you have the launch codes for the remaining orbiting warheads. The president should control those as well. Do you have any questions?"

Vinson felt his bow tie and straightened it. "Yes, secure communications. What capabilities do you want? Voice, data, fax?"

Smith wanted to keep things as simple as possible. "For now we just need voice, but data and fax would help, if possible."

"Okay, we're on an air force base, so that should be doable. I'll see if I can track down some satellite gear."

Smith stood up. "Make sure you bring Noel up to speed. He'll run this end of the link. You'd better get a move on. I'm hoping to get the Herc in the air as soon as we can."

"Yes, sir," Vinson replied, turning back to his screens.

Smith walked out of the office and to the gym. He walked through the doors to find several people walking around. They were obviously able to see, and that made him feel more positive about things in general. A major in a khaki green-zippered flight suit walked up and saluted. He had several patches on his chest. The first showed a Hercules aircraft taking off and "C-130J-30 - Super Hercules" written on it. Another round patch showed his unit, 514th Flight Test Squadron. "Colonel Smith, I'm Major Kerouac. I've been tasked with flying my Herc out east for you."

Smith braced to attention and returned the salute. "Come over here, Major. I don't want anyone to overhear... I have a man I need to get to the Pottstown Heritage Field Airport in Pennsylvania. Once there, you'll be given orders for me to bring back."

Kerouac frowned. "That will be right at the edge of my range unless there's fuel available."

Smith shook his head. "Assume there isn't."

"I don't know that airfield, but as long as it's within my airframe's capabilities, I'll get him there."

"It may be a short runway, Major. I know the Hercs can land on those, but taking off is another matter."

Kerouac smiled broadly. "Sir, the 514th is a test squadron. We have access to all sorts of toys. Don't worry. We'll get him there and get back safely."

Smith nodded, appreciating the pilot's confidence. "Good. He'll have some equipment with him. I suspect less than five hundred pounds. This mission is deeply classified, Major. No flight plan, radio silence throughout, and that destination is *not* to be given to anyone else—including your copilot, until you're airborne. Even then, you're not to repeat where you went or why."

"Understood, sir. The light load will certainly help improve my range."

"Report to me when you're ready to go," Smith ordered.

"Yes, sir," Kerouac said, but he remained where he was.

"Something else, Major?"

"Colonel, I saw the sunrise this morning. That wouldn't have been possible without you bringing the cure here. I wanted to thank you for that, sir. Everyone here owes you their lives."

Smith felt embarrassed. He'd simply been doing his duty and following the president's orders. He was certainly no hero. "Thank me later when the Chinese are completely gone. Until then, we all have jobs to do. Dismissed, Major."

Kerouac saluted. "Yes, sir."

Smith returned the salute, and Kerouac marched off toward the front entrance.

Captain Tyler came down the stairs, saw him, and came over. She carried a yellow notepad on a clipboard. She stopped, and saluted precisely.

Smith's brow furrowed for a moment, but he returned the salute. "You're quite formal all of a sudden, Captain."

She remained at attention. "Before, sir, we were refugees in a storm. Now that people are getting their sight back, I don't think we can act like scruffy vagabonds anymore."

Smith couldn't deny the truth in her statement. The time had come to return to the military lifestyle. "Perhaps not. At ease, Captain. Walk with me. I want to see how people are getting on in the gym. Report." He marched toward the gymnasium entrance.

"In the last four hours, we've treated close to eight hundred people. All of the Hercules pilots and ground crew were first as you ordered. The F-16 squadrons should be up within eight hours. After that, I've scheduled the A-10 pilots, and then—"

Smith stopped in the doorway to the gym and faced her. "A-10s? Here?"

"Yes, sir. The maintenance wing on base is a depot for all air force A-10 squadrons. They replace the wings on the Thunderbolt IIs to extend service life of the airframe. There are eight on base at the moment. Two are hard down—they have no wings—but six can be made operational within twenty-four to thirty-six hours."

Smith felt his heartbeat speed up. He'd seen A-10s in action on the range. To say they were formidable in battle was a dramatic understatement. "I'll want those aircraft given high priority. As a ground attack airframe, there's none better. Even six will dramatically affect the odds. We need 'em." Smith turned back to the gym entrance and entered the huge space.

Many of the cots were empty, he was glad to see. A few people were still blind, but an hour should see the rest taken care of. The base had roughly twenty-five hundred people. He quickly calculated that everyone on base should be seeing by day's end.

Smith recalled what he wanted to ask her. "Captain, when we were in Cheyenne Mountain, you mentioned something about an E-6 being in maintenance."

"Yes, sir. One E-6 was getting its systems upgraded by Raytheon at their facility in Centennial, Colorado. They were due to be back on duty last week, but obviously because of the fireworks—"

"Yes. It may also be our saving grace. Centennial is a civilian airfield. It's well away from Peterson and Site D, so it's highly unlikely the Chinese are there, and that means we may have a platform capable of communicating with the subs."

Tyler made a note on her notepad. "It's certainly likely, sir."

"Anything else for me?" Smith asked her.

"Sir, Colonel Barton has refused to take the treatment," Tyler said while making notes on her clipboard.

"Really?" He shook his head. Doctor Krause had called that one. "We'll have to go directly to the squadron COs. Also, find the deputy base commanding officer for Hill and have him report to me. We need to get an offensive planned, and I can't wait for any one person."

Tyler tucked her clipboard under her arm. "Sir, Hill is an Air Force Material Command base and not technically under NORAD command. Shouldn't we try to get some front line units involved that are?"

Smith shook his head. "There's no time. Material Command or not, they have F-16s and A-10s we can throw at the Chinese. Besides, the front line bases have probably been occupied. Hill is still an air force base, and they shall be expected to defend the United States."

"Yes, sir."

"Let's go take a look at the flight line. I want to see if there's any issue we don't know about."

"I have a golf cart waiting outside, Colonel." She pointed a thumb over her shoulder.

"Golf cart?" That didn't seem like typical transport for an air force base to him.

"Yes, sir. There's quite a few. One of the support staff told me about them. A half-dozen were plugged in and fully charged, so I had a lot of choice."

"Fine. Let's go."

Chapter Twenty-Two
Change of Scenery

Colonel Smith ordered Captain Tyler to drive the golf cart to the flight line. The sound of a high-pitched turbine engine came to his ears as they passed a hangar.

"Turn that way," he commanded, and she complied.

As they pulled onto the concrete apron, Smith spotted a Hercules transport aircraft with several people working in and around it. "Take me over there, please."

As they got closer, Smith saw a technician working on the portside brakes. A pair of men in dirty coveralls stood on a set of maintenance stands by the inner starboard engine, which had its access panels open. They looked to be adjusting something on the engine. Smith had never seen a Hercules with six bladed propellers. He assumed the aircraft was a newer model.

Tyler pulled up beside the aircraft, just behind the cockpit. The noise of the aircraft APU[30] coming from the other side of the aircraft was barely tolerable. Major Kerouac emerged from the side access door just forward of the port propellers and saluted as he approached. Smith stood up and returned it. He noticed Kerouac had small orange earplugs in his ears.

---

[30] Auxiliary Power Unit. A power generator built into the airframe that supplies electricity to an aircraft in places where external power is either unavailable or impractical. The APU typically allows aircraft to start their engines without assistance, allowing them to operate at remote locations.

"Colonel, give us twenty minutes, and we'll be up in all respects. Just fixing a fuel line leak and bleeding the brake lines, then we're good to go. Mister Vinson is already here with his gear. The loadmaster is getting him settled in the back. I checked the target airfield, and we can land with no problems. Do you have any further instructions?"

Smith shook his head. "No, Major. Take off as soon as you can. You should buzz the town at least once to let people know you have arrived. I don't know who'll meet you, but I'm sure you'll know them when you see them."

"Yes, sir. We'll be back before dark," Kerouac said confidently.

"Come back safe. I'll have another job for you tomorrow. Carry on, Major."

"Yes, sir." Kerouac saluted.

Smith returned the salute and watched Kerouac return to the aircraft. Smith followed, entered the access hatch, and turned toward the cargo area. In the rear of the aircraft, the noise of the APU diminished significantly. He found Vinson with the aircraft loadmaster.

Vinson was speaking loudly while pointing animatedly at a pair of large duffel bags on the deck. "Make sure you treat those bags with respect! Don't tie them down too tightly." Vinson turned toward Smith as he approached. "I've got everything I need, Colonel. We'll be taking off soon."

"Yes, I know. Did you make sure you had everything before you packed it up?" Smith indicated the bags.

"Three times. I'm taking two complete satellite communication units, plus spares to play it safe. Noel and I set up the unit he'll be using here. He moved into the office I was using and has all the crypto codes he'll need. The link works beautifully."

"Excellent. Make sure you brief the president on everything you told me. Lead off with what happened to the V.P. and joint chiefs. He needs to know that ASAP."

"I will, sir," Vinson answered.

"Do you have the tubes?" Smith asked, looking around.

"Yes, I packed those in my laptop bag over there." Vinson pointed at a bag sitting on a red webbing seat by the side of the aircraft. "I'll keep them safe."

Smith hesitated, unsure if he should say the next thing on his mind. "If you get a chance—and this is completely unofficial—see if you can track down Captain Tyler's parents. They live in Severance, New York, near Lake Paradox in the Adirondacks. She hasn't heard from them since this all started. Again, that's unofficial. She didn't ask for this, but I think it would be good for her to know one way or the other."

Vinson smiled. "No problem, Colonel. She's good people. I'll see what I can do."

Smith nodded once and patted him on the shoulder. "Thanks. Safe trip."

He left the aircraft the way he had come. He marched to the golf cart and sat on the passenger side of the cart bench. He turned to Tyler and said, over the noise of the APU, "Let's go see Noel."

Tyler accelerated the golf cart as Smith fell into deep thought about what still needed to be done.

* * *

Linda Krause was just finishing packing her few belongings into a side bag on the three-wheeled roadster when Oscar Blake came out of the doors of the base gymnasium and headed her way. He carried a full plastic grocery bag in his hand.

"Any luck?" she asked when he was close enough.

Blake held his hands palm up and shrugged. "No one's seen Colonel Smith in several hours. They said he's out getting the base back on its feet."

She checked her watch. "He's probably busy. He'll figure out we left eventually. It would have been nice to say good-bye, though. Ready to get on the road?"

"Speaking of that, I have a lead." Blake reached into his jean pocket and produced a piece of notepaper. "I wrote it down to make sure I got it right. One of the airmen said there was a FEMA shelter set up at the T.H. Bell Junior High School. She gave me directions."

"That sounds good. We can head there first. What's in the bag?" Krause asked.

"Ahh, something I suspect we'll need." He dug into the bag and produced a battery-powered megaphone. "This should get people's attention."

She gasped in surprise. "It's perfect! Where did you get that?"

"One of the supply people. I told him we were going to look for survivors, and five minutes later, he gave me this. He told me it never existed and just winked at me." He put it back in the bag and stowed it in the trailer. He retrieved both of their helmets before locking the lid.

"That's fantastic, Oscar. That'll save us knocking from house to house. Ready to go?"

"Yes." Blake handed over her helmet before putting his own on.

Krause slipped on the helmet and got onto the rear seat. Blake jumped on seconds after. She wrapped her arms around his torso without hesitation. Blake started the engine, and within a few minutes, they were waving at the four armed gate guards on duty as they passed.

Blake spoke over the helmet radio. "If we ever want a free night of drinks, we just need to come back here. Lots of people are grateful you came along, Linda."

"People are grateful to you, as well," she countered. "I wouldn't have gotten here without you."

The trip went swiftly. Paths had already been cleared through the numerous cars and obstructions. Blake turned off the main highway, and Krause spotted the large sign for the high school on the front lawn. Beside it was a piece of fabric nailed to a pair of wooden posts. A corner nail had let go, and the loose fabric moved in the gentle breeze, but she could see it said "FEMA Shelter".

Blake pulled into the drive and had to slow because of all the cars. He parked outside the front doors then turned off the engine.

Krause slid off the seat, pulling her helmet from her head. She took the prototype tube Doctor Wiater had given her from the side bag where she'd stored it. Blake took her helmet from her, and she waited until he locked it up in the trailer with his.

They walked inside together. Blake held the door open as she passed. In the main corridor, the distant sound of many voices singing came to her ears. "This way, I think," Krause said, pointing.

Krause came to a large pair of steel double doors under a sign saying "Gymnasium". As she opened the door, Krause recognized the melody of the song and also heard a guitar. "That's 'Sweet Caroline.'"

She went inside the gym, where perhaps three hundred people were singing to the tune. A man in a priest cassock played guitar at the opposite end of the room. Many people were lying on gym mats spread on the floor, but at least two-thirds had folding cots, pillows, and blankets.

Krause saw two people standing. One of them, a black-haired woman, turned and did a double-take. She walked over, smiling at them.

"Good morning. This is a surprise; we haven't seen anyone new in several days. I'm Lisa." She held out her hand.

Krause shook hands with her, followed by Blake. "Morning. We were told there was a shelter here. I'm Doctor Krause, and we have a cure for the blindness."

Lisa's eyes almost doubled in size. "What, really?" She turned and energetically waved over the other person on his feet, a man who was tall—almost seven feet.

"Michael, this is Doctor Krause. She says she has a cure!" Lisa said it so loudly that surrounding people turned toward them, and the priest stopped playing in mid-sentence.

Michael frowned, turning toward her. "Seriously, you have a cure?" The tone of his voice indicated disbelief.

Others around them began talking and shouting out questions.

Krause nodded to Michael. "Yes, we just came from Hill Air Force Base. When we left this morning, almost everyone on base could see again."

Lisa jumped up and down, clapped her hands, and smiled broadly. "That's fantastic."

Michael was much calmer. "Hold on a sec, Lisa. Let's see what sort of *cure* they are offering and what they want in return."

Krause objected. "There's no charge. We're simply trying to give people their sight back. It's caused by a form of cancer that covers the rods and cones in the eye. We have a radiation treatment that kills the cancerous cells. Everyone treated recovers their sight in about four hours."

The guitar-playing priest hobbled up to them. He walked strangely and used a pair of forearm crutches. Lisa took him by the arm and guided him the last few steps to the group. "This is Father Peters. He's blind like the rest, but he's been amazing. Keeping up our spirits, tending to the elderly, and he can play any song you can name on the guitar."

"Good morning, Father," Krause said.

"I heard what you said," Father Peters said. "What's the isotope you're using for the radiation treatment?"

Krause moved closer. "Rhenium-188. It's a beta—"

Peters raised his hand slightly, stopping her. "Yes, I know what it is. What area do you specialize in, Doctor?"

"I'm an ophthalmologist," Krause replied.

Peter nodded slightly. "Then please describe Eale's Disease to me, and don't be afraid to use the big words."

His request surprised her. Few people had even heard of that disease. "Eale's Disease, or idiopathic retinal periphlebitis, is quite rare in North America. It's mostly seen in young men in India and South Asia. The veins of the eye become inflamed, and the patient's vision becomes blurry. Patients report seeing floating particles or specks—"

"Doctor, I said not to be afraid of using the big words."

Krause decided to talk to him like an intern. "It's diagnosed by exclusion, as many other retinal disorders can have the same symptomatology. Dilatation of capillary channels, spontaneous chorioretinal scarring, and tortuosity of nearby vessels are primary indicators. Posterior microaneurysms will typically be present."

Father Peters nodded and grinned. "Thank you, Doctor. Michael, let's make our guests comfortable. Doctor Krause, please sit down. Let's talk further about this cure of yours."

* * *

Larry Vinson rode a Jet Ski at maximum throttle. The *thump-thump-thump* of the fiberglass hull pounding against the waves caused him to bounce up and down. The odd burst of salt spray hit him in the face, but that added to the excitement, and he didn't slow. The firm breasts of his curvy, redheaded, bikini-wearing companion pressed into his back. The bouncing made that feel all the better. He glanced over his shoulder. The pursuing seventeenth-century pirate ship was under full sail and was rapidly closing the distance between them. Buccaneers were visible at the bow of the ship, waving cutlasses and screaming at him. The noise of the jet ski engine drowned out their shouted threats.

"Oh no, Larry, they're gaining on us!" she said, squeezing him.

"Hold on!" He threw the jet ski hard to port. The small watercraft turned around almost a hundred and eighty degrees. He steered the jet ski to run parallel to the pirate ship. He gave the crew the finger as he passed.

"We're safe! You're so brave. How can I thank you?" she asked, slipping her hand inside the waistband of his damp board shorts. Her soft fingers moved down, wrapping around his—

Someone roughly shook his shoulder. His eyes popped open. "Mister Vinson, sorry to wake you," the loadmaster yelled, to be heard through Vinson's ear defenders. "The pilot wants you up in the cockpit right away, sir."

Vinson took in the area around him. The two green duffel bags tied to the floor, the red fabric jump seats, and continuous drone of aircraft engines. *I'm in the Hercules cargo bay.*

"Mister Vinson, did you hear—"

He held up his hand and closed his eyes for a moment. "Yes, yes... Give me a second." Vinson tried to stand but had to undo his seat belt before he could get up. He rubbed his eyes.

The vibrations he felt through his feet told him they were still airborne. He made his way through the cargo area, up the steps, and past the bunk beds into the cockpit. Major Kerouac was in the left-hand seat, and his copilot, an officer called Hennessy, sat in the right.

Kerouac turned, saw him, and pointed at the wired headset hung up on a peg behind the copilot.

Vinson removed his ear defenders and put the headset on. The padded earpieces made most of the external noise disappear.

Kerouac pointed out the window, saying over the headset, "That's Pottstown Heritage field down there to the left. Do you see the problem?"

They were a thousand feet in the air. The white runway was easy to spot... as was the medium-sized two-engine aircraft that had burned and broken in two, almost exactly halfway down the only runway. That ruined airplane blocked their landing from either direction.

"Damn it," he said, before realizing his voice could not be heard. He picked up the control box on the headset wire, pressed and held the button. A brief click sounded in his headset. "Does that mean we go somewhere else?" He released the button.

Kerouac shook his head and pointed again. "No, look beside the runway. There's a taxiway. I'm going to aim for that. It's not very wide, and it's certainly not designed to land on. If we drift off onto the grass, it's going to get real bumpy, real fast. So buckle up tight. If we do crash, the loadmaster will help you get out. I'm descending in three minutes."

Vinson keyed his microphone. "Will you be able to take off again?"

Kerouac flashed him a grin. "We have JATOs loaded on board. That's one of the benefits of working in a test and evaluation squadron. It'll be one hell of a show when we leave. Better get below and in your seat."

"Right." Vinson had no idea what Kerouac was referring to, but he was eager to get strapped in before landing. He replaced the headset with his ear defenders and went down the steps, back into the cargo hold, then over to his seat.

The loadmaster was waiting for him. He made sure Vinson was securely strapped in before he sat down on the opposite side of the aircraft. The loadmaster was tightening his seat belt as much as he could, which worried Vinson. *He's obviously preparing for something bad to happen.*

The engine noise and vibration reduced in volume and violence. The nose of the aircraft tilted slightly downwards. The loadmaster pointed down. *Here we go.*

A loud thump sounded from behind him, which made him jump. The scream of hydraulics came after. The next noise was probably the landing gear, Vinson thought.

The loadmaster waved at him and mimed holding onto the front edge of the jump seat they were both sitting on. Vinson mirrored his grab.

A moment later, there was a gentle bump, accompanied by the familiar *CHIRP* noise from the tires hitting the ground. *We're down.* He relaxed his grip. *That wasn't so—*

The airframe shuddered violently, bouncing him around. He clasped the aluminum tubing of his seat and held on for dear life. The engines roared, and he was thrown forward as the aircraft slowed. Several Gs of force pulled his body sideways, then gradually stopped.

The loadmaster undid his seat belt and rose up, indicating Vinson should remain where he was. The loadmaster went to a porthole in a rear access door and looked out. The engine noise returned to a reasonable level, and the aircraft stopped. The propellers immediately wound down. The APU was already running.

The loadmaster gave him a thumbs-up as he headed to the front entry hatch, behind the cockpit access stairs. Vinson took that to mean he could stand, so he undid his seat belt. By the time he got to the hatch, it had already been lowered. Using the steps built into the door, he went outside. A black SUV pulled up just off the wing tip, so he walked over to it.

The driver got out. His suit was badly in need of dry cleaning. The dark material had white powder and dirt on it. His white shirt looked faded and had a few visible stains. He had shaggy growth on his chin and a gold circular pin on his lapel.

The transparent radio earpiece and coil of wire leading under his suit jacket identified him. *I've come to brief the president, so he must be secret service.* Vinson couldn't see anyone else around, and he wondered where the president was. Vinson smiled, approached, and held out his hand. "Hi, I'm—"

The driver's right hand whipped aside his suit jacket, where he had a pistol in a hip holster. He placed his hand on the pistol but did not draw it. "Freeze! Keep your hands in sight. What's your name?"

That wasn't the friendly reception Vinson had imagined. Were they expecting another Hercules to land here today? "Larry Vinson. I'm with the NSA."

"Are you armed?" the secret service agent demanded.

"No."

"Do you have I.D.?" the agent asked loudly.

"In my wallet." Vinson didn't like this third-degree questioning.

"Bring it out, slowly, and place it on the hood," the agent instructed.

Vinson did as he was told. He glanced at the card he pulled out to make sure it was his NSA identity card. The laminated card itself was plain. A head and shoulders photo on the left, with his name and employee number to the right. The lower part of the card had a bar code and an embedded gold security chip. It said nothing about whom he worked for. Vinson placed it on the hood and backed away without being asked.

The agent closed in, scooped up the card, and examined it. He looked up at Vinson, then back at the card. His hand came off his weapon, and he handed the card back. "I'm Agent Carter. Grab your bags and load them in the back. I need to see the pilot."

Agent Carter walked up the access door steps into the Hercules, and Vinson followed. The agent kept going to the cockpit, while Vinson turned right into the cargo bay. The loadmaster had his bags unstrapped and ready to go.

Vinson shook his hand. "Thanks for the lift."

"Anytime," the loadmaster replied. "You need a hand?"

"Nah, I'm good." Vinson took his luggage and returned out the way he'd come. The rear of the SUV was unlocked, and he lifted the bags inside. He took off his ear defenders and placed them through the handle of one of the duffel bags.

Carter came out through the access door of the Hercules. The loadmaster appeared in the doorway, and seconds later, a propeller began to turn.

Carter climbed into the driver's seat, so Vinson got in the passenger's side. Carter started the engine and began driving off the tarmac.

Vinson asked, "If you don't mind, I want to see it take off. The landing was pretty rough, and with the runway blocked, the pilot said he had something special planned."

"Sure. If we wait until he's gone, we can drive straight across the runway," Carter replied. He parked the SUV nearby with the windscreen facing the Herc.

The Hercules moved into position on the taxiway. It stopped. A minute passed, then the revs on the engines picked up considerably. The aircraft began rolling forward. Eight jets of yellow flame appeared around the rear cargo bay, billowing thick black smoke out behind the aircraft. Vinson wished he hadn't taken off his ear defenders.

The aircraft accelerated quickly. Vinson counted fifteen more seconds before the flame cut out. The aircraft was a hundred feet in the air and climbing rapidly.

"Wow, I've never seen that before. He only used half the taxiway before he got airborne," he said out loud.

"It's called jet-assisted takeoff. I started in the Marines and saw that a few times. You ready to go?" Carter put the vehicle transmission in drive.

"Yeah, where we heading?" Vinson looked around. He'd never been in Pennsylvania before.

"You'll see when we get there."

* * *

Colonel Smith continued his base inspection on the golf cart driven by Captain Tyler.

Tyler spoke to him as they passed the base exchange. A few men and women were going in or out of the main doors. "It's starting to look like a regular base again, Colonel."

Smith couldn't disagree. He had been thinking the same thing a few minutes earlier. However, his thoughts had moved onto other more important things. "Once we get everyone on base treated, we should get the tubes to other bases. We'll need one with us tomorrow, but the others need to be flown to California."

"Why California, Colonel?" Tyler asked.

Smith turned to face her. "If we can get the E-6, I'm fairly confident we can alert the navy, and with the F-16s here, we should be able to stop the convoy. However, if any ships leak through, we need to oppose any landings and bottle up any Chinese troops that do get ashore. We need to get bases like Camp Pendleton, Twentynine Palms, Fort Irwin, and Coronado operational to do that. Even a couple of companies of soldiers will make a difference. We should make the Marines our priority, though. Their bases are closer, and they're a hard nut to crack."

"We'll have several Hercs serviceable by day's end. We can start airlifting people to those bases anytime afterwards," she said.

"Agreed, but I want one of the tubes kept with us. We'll need it in the morning. I intend to use Major Kerouac for that mission, but if he doesn't make it back, then we'll need another Hercules."

"Are you hungry, sir?" she asked. "We can head to the mess for lunch."

Smith was. "Yes, lunch sounds good to me. We can't do anything until Vinson sets up secure communications to the president."

Tyler turned the golf cart toward the mess.

* * *

Larry Vinson looked with trepidation at the metal staircase leading down into pitch darkness. Rust stains and peeling green paint on the interior concrete walls told him the place had not been maintained properly in decades. He tested the top tread on the metal staircase before placing his full weight on it. He swapped his laptop bag to the opposite hand to take a hold of the rounded hand railing.

"Go ahead. It's solid. We use this staircase daily," Agent Carter said from behind him.

Vinson took the next step, then the next, slowly gaining confidence. The stairs did feel solid underfoot, but he slowed nonetheless. Each step down sank him further into darkness. With no illumination, he had issues seeing, and he hadn't brought a flashlight.

Light appeared above him as Agent Carter turned on a bright wide-beamed light. He aimed the beam at Vinson's feet, letting him see where to step.

Carter said, "Sorry about that. I know this staircase so well, I don't use the light."

Vinson didn't respond, but he was glad the light was on. He made it down to a landing. The stairs carried on descending, so he headed for the next set of stairs, but Carter stopped him.

"We're going through there." Carter indicated a metal door with his light.

The door was at least four inches thick, with a panic bar on the inside. He went through. Ten or so feet along, there was another identical door, also open. Vinson went through that and found himself in a large open area. The walls were mostly a beige color, with supporting pillars painted orange. The floors were messy. Old newspapers and trash littered the floor. The air smelled dank and felt cool, bordering on cold. He shivered once.

Fluorescent light fixtures, suspended from the ceiling on wires, were dark. The only source of illumination was Carter's light.

"This way," Carter said stepping out ahead of Vinson. He strode to the far wall. The color of the pillars changed from orange to blue as he walked to a normal door. He entered without knocking, and light from the inside flooded out. He turned off his light on the threshold.

Vinson came to the doorway as Carter said, "Mister President, Larry Vinson from the NSA is here to brief you."

Warmth came from the room. After entering the room and turning the corner, Vinson took a sharp intake of breath. He recognized the president sitting at a rickety-looking card table, but Calvin didn't look anything like his photos. He looked like a street bum. His clothes were disheveled and dusty. He had several days of beard growth, but the most striking thing about him was his eyes. They were bloodshot, sunken, and tired. He didn't look the least bit presidential.

There were two other men in the room. One lay on a sleeping bag beside the president. His clothing looked as if he had been in it for some time. He was trying to get up. *That must be the national security advisor, Keith Hurst.*

The third man could see and had stood when Vinson entered, looking him in the eye. Vinson simply nodded to him then returned his attention to the president. "Mister President, I'm Larry Vinson. I'm glad to see you alive and well."

The president stood and extended his hand. "Good day, Mister Vinson. I hope you had a pleasant journey."

Vinson realized the president couldn't see him and took a step forward to shake his hand. "Yes, sir. I brought a cure for the blindness with me. If you have no objection, I'd like to get the healing process underway before I brief you." He released the president's hand, unzipped his bag, and reached inside.

He had the stainless steel tube halfway out of the bag when Carter's hand gripped his wrist.

"I'll need to see that first," Carter said sternly.

Vinson handed it over and watched Carter examine the tube carefully. He tested its weight and pressed the red plastic button. The end of the iris opened, and the LED counter began counting down. Carter started to look into the tube.

"No!" Vinson yelled, as he pushed the open end of the tube away from Carter's face. Carter took a half-step back, putting his hand on his pistol grip. Vinson held up his hands in front of him to indicate he had no intention to do anything else and explained, "They warned me. If you have your sight, the radiation in the tube can damage your eye over time, and you'll go blind. Don't look in there."

Carter held the open end toward the wall. "I can't let an untested and unexamined piece of gear get near the president."

Vinson didn't know what to say to that. *Then why in God's name did I fly over half the country to get here?*

The man on the sleeping bag had stood up. "Then use it on me first. I'm Keith Hurst."

The iris on the tube snapped closed.

"Sir, I'm not sure I should allow that, either," Carter objected.

Hurst sighed. "Agent Carter, this young man came halfway across the country. He brought us the cure we so desperately need. Time is against us. I say we let him use it on me as a test. Mister Vinson, please proceed."

There was a pause, and Carter handed over the tube. The agent kept his hand on his pistol, however.

Vinson stepped over to Hurst. "Just stand still, sir. Keep your eyes open. You don't need to do anything." He held the tube in front of and perpendicular to Hurst's left eye and pressed the button. He heard the iris snap open, and the LED counter counted down. "It's important you only receive one treatment per eye. Repeated exposures can burn out your retina and blind you permanently."

"You've had good success so far then?" Hurst asked.

"Yes, sir. We treated the entire base at Hill Air Force Base in Utah. Over two thousand people could see when I left."

The LED counter counted down to zero, and the iris snapped closed. Vinson moved the tube to Hurst's right eye and pressed the activation stud again.

The president said from behind Vinson, "Is that where Smith is now? Utah?"

"Yes, sir. As soon as I get the satellite communications up and running, you'll be able to talk to him directly. I should brief you on what's going on before you speak with him. Colonel Smith told me to make that a priority. There's been, well, let's call them dramatic developments over the last week."

The iris snapped closed.

Hurst asked, "Is that it? Are you done? I didn't feel a thing."

"Yes, sir. You should recover your eyesight in four hours or so." Vinson began to return the tube to his laptop bag.

The president said, "All right, treat me next. I've been blind long enough."

Chapter Twenty-Three
X Y Z

Doctor Krause set up a small area at the front of the junior high school gymnasium to treat people. Michael and Lisa brought her people who would be treated, then they took them back to their cots.

Father Peters hobbled up beside her as she worked. He had been one of the first treated and now waited for his sight to return. Even though he couldn't see, his ability to move within the gym amazed her. He felt the back of a nearby chair and tried to sit. The forearm crutches, combined with his lack of sight, made that an effort.

Krause took hold of his elbow to assist him. "Let me help."

He pulled away. "I've been dealing with my condition for many years, young lady. I can take care of myself," he said calmly before sitting. He laid the forearm crutches on the floor beside him.

"Muscular dystrophy?" she asked.

He nodded. "Yes, I thought God didn't like me much when I was diagnosed." He touched the crucifix around his neck. "However, we've worked through our differences successfully... I pray this cure works."

"It will. Our trials in Seattle went very well, and we cured several thousand people at Hill Air Force Base." She began treating the next person, a young teenager. "Do you have medical training?"

Peters came close to laughing. "Me? No."

"You seem remarkably well informed on rare diseases of the eye, so it's a natural assumption," she countered.

"It isn't anything remarkable. I have an eidetic memory. I can recall most things I've ever read or seen," Peters said.

Krause was impressed nonetheless. Eidetic or photographic memories were rare. "That explains your guitar skills and ability to find your way around the gym, too."

"I know this gym as I was in it two years ago. The real challenge was learning the location of the cots and mats. Once I knew where they were, navigation was relatively easy. I stepped on quite a few people the first day."

She swapped the tube over to the teen's other eye. "I'm surprised to find a Catholic priest in Salt Lake City. You only hear of Mormons coming from here."

Peters chuckled. "I have a small but energetic parish. The area is quite diverse religiously. My weekly bridge partner is a rabbi."

Krause finished with the teen and marked the back of his left hand with a marker pen, a practice that would ensure only one treatment per person. She waved Lisa over who then took the teen away.

Peters lowered his voice. "I'm very glad you came along when you did, Doctor. Lisa and Michael have been amazing keeping us supplied with food and water, but rations lately have been running low. We couldn't have kept this up for much longer. There must be thousands of similar groups in FEMA shelters all over the country in the same circumstances."

Krause nodded before realizing he couldn't see. "Yes, I know. The cure isn't widespread, and my fear is many will suffer before we can get it to them. When I left Seattle, we were trying to get mass production underway for these tubes, but I've no idea how successful they've been. When we're done here, Oscar and I will try to get to as many as we possibly can. Speaking of Oscar, I wonder where he is."

"He just went out with Michael. They're making a grocery run to stock up on supplies. He should be back in an hour or so."

She smiled. *Of course he is. He's pitching in where he can.* "Glad we can contribute something."

"God will bless you both for your efforts, Doctor."

* * *

Colonel Smith was glad they were driving on base in the golf cart. If they had been in a regular vehicle, he wouldn't have heard the Hercules landing. Captain Tyler pulled out onto the tarmac in time to see the ground crew placing chocks under the wheels of the aircraft. The six bladed propellers spun down, and the left side access door opened.

"Get me over there, Captain," he ordered.

Tyler drove rapidly, bringing the cart within a dozen feet of the access door. The loadmaster stepped out, stifling a yawn with the back of his hand. Major Kerouac appeared behind him and pressed past to go down the steps. He carried a white envelope in his left hand. He walked up to Smith just as he stood up off the bench seat on the golf cart.

Kerouac saluted. "Successful mission, sir."

Smith returned it. "Vinson's on the ground?"

"Yes, sir. Here's a letter for you. A secret service agent gave it to me. He said I had to hand-deliver it to you." Kerouac handed it over.

"Thank you. I'll need you and your crew at first light tomorrow for something special. Make sure your aircraft is ready. Briefing will be at the flight operations building at oh-five hundred."

"We'll be ready, Colonel."

"Dismissed."

Kerouac and Smith exchanged salutes. Smith got back on the bench seat of the cart and opened the letter in his hand. He pulled out two pieces of white letter paper.

Smith scanned the page. The first letter was short. There was no logo or seal on the header, and the paper was common in quality. He read the date, which was the same day's, and his eyes widened at the rest:

From the Office of the President of the United States
Ref: Colonel Alvin Smith, USAF

The President of the United States, acting as lawful Commander-in-Chief of the United States Armed Forces, hereby bestows Colonel Alvin Smith with the rank of Brigadier General, USAF, effective this date.

The letter was signed: *James Calvin.*

Smith reread it three times before saying, "Damn."
"What, sir?" Tyler asked.
He simply handed the letter over to her and began reading the second, which was not only longer, but even more surprising.

From the Office of the President of the United States
Ref: Defense of the United States of America

The President of the United States, acting as lawful Commander-in-Chief of the United States Armed Forces, hereby grants Brigadier General Alvin Smith the acting rank of Lieutenant General, USAF as of this date.

Acting Lieutenant General, Alvin Smith shall, as of this date, be responsible for the defense of the United States of America and is formally appointed Commanding Officer of NORAD.

Acting Lieutenant General Alvin Smith may, at his discretion, bring any unit under his command, from any service of the United States military, to aid in his mission.

Acting Lieutenant General Alvin Smith is acting under direct authority of the President of the United States. All officers and men, regardless of their branch of service, and all citizens of the United States, shall cooperate with Acting Lieutenant General Alvin Smith to the best of their abilities.

The letter was signed: *James Calvin.*

He looked at Tyler, who was beaming at him. "Congratulations, General Smith."

"It gets better," he replied, handing over the second letter. He waited while she read it.

"Three jumps in rank in one day. That's amazing!" she said finally.

He looked off into the distance. "It's temporary, and it shows just how desperate the situation is. That's a powerful piece of paper and exactly what I need though. Now I have the authority to order navy, marine, and army units into position. Damn, we might just win this. Can you photocopy the second letter? We can send copies with teams going to other bases. It should make things easier."

"Yes, sir. And General?"

He looked over at her. It sounded so strange to be called general. "Yes."

"I'm proud of you, sir."

* * *

President Calvin listened as Vinson briefed him on everything he had experienced since leaving the Cheyenne Mountain bunker. It took some time, but Calvin didn't interrupt. The brutal death of the vice president and abuse of the joint chiefs hit him particularly hard. With all members of the House of Representatives and his cabinet captured or dead, he was effectively the entire executive branch of government of the United States. If he was killed or captured, there was no one left in the constitutional chain of succession to lead the country.

Vinson concluded his brief, informing him of the remaining warheads in orbit and his ability to release them on command and of the detail that the Chinese didn't have a cure for the blindness they had created.

"Thank you, Mister Vinson. You've gone through a lot to bring me this information, and I appreciate it. Could you excuse us? I need to discuss this with Keith."

"Of course, Mister President. I'll go up and get the satellite link active. You should be able to talk to Colonel Smith within the hour," Vinson replied.

"Smith has been promoted to general," Calvin corrected. "Without his efforts in getting a cure organized, we'd still be helpless. Yes, please get the link up as quickly as you can."

"Yes, sir." He heard Vinson leave.

"I'll help you unload your bags," Carter said, before closing the door.

"Congratulations, Keith," Calvin said.

"Huh? For what?" Hurst asked.

"You're now the vice president."

"Vice president? What are you talking about?"

Calvin shifted himself on his chair to get comfortable. "Continuity of government. With Hamilton Kendall dead and everyone else in detention, I need a new V.P. in case something happens to me. You're the best choice."

The reaction was silence.

"Problem?" Calvin asked finally.

Hurst answered in a much quieter voice than normal. "I'm trying to wrap my head around this. What about the confirmation hearing?"

Calvin answered as he placed his arm on the table. "Legally, as Congress is not in session, we'll have to get you confirmed later, but I suspect that'll be a while. Until then, you'll be the V.P. with full powers of the office. We've got a couple of years until the next election, and if we can't stop the Chinese, it's moot anyway. What do you say?"

After another pause, Hurst said, "I serve at the pleasure of the president."

* * *

Linda Krause sat beside Father Peters and watched him play guitar for the crowd to pass the time after their treatments. She thought he had talent. He turned to her after finishing a Bob Dylan song, "Knockin' on Heaven's Door." "I can see again, Doctor. Things were fuzzy when I began to play, but now I can see as clearly as ever. Thank you."

Krause touched his arm. "That's wonderful news, Father. You were one of the first treated, so the rest will be able to see soon."

"What's your favorite band?" Father Peters asked.

"I listen to a lot of different music, but when operating, I always listen to Pink Floyd," she responded.

He looked down for a moment, and then began strumming one of her favorite tunes, "Wish You Were Here."

Everyone in the gymnasium began to sing. It was a melancholy song. Krause looked out over the people. Several were cuffing away tears. *They're remembering the loved ones they've lost.* Krause herself felt moist eyes beginning when Oscar walked in the far side of the space. She walked over to him, wrapped her arms around his neck, and held him close.

He returned the gesture. "What's wrong?" he asked quietly.

She thought about that and answered from the heart. "When I'm in your arms, nothing."

* * *

General Smith strode out of the mess with Captain Tyler. His lunch had been smaller than usual. Mulling about the best ways to oppose the Chinese invasion had stolen his appetite. The pair had made it back to their golf cart when an airman ran up to them. "Colonel, Mister Noel asked me to find you. You have a call, sir."

Smith still wore colonel insignia, so he didn't correct the young man's use of his former rank. "Thank you, airman."

Only one person would be calling him through Noel: the president. He turned to Captain Tyler. "Drive me over to Noel's office, please."

"Yes, sir," Tyler responded.

The drive itself passed in silence. Smith used the time to solidify his strategizing for how he'd counteract the Chinese.

The golf cart halted outside the office block Noel occupied. Smith got off the bench.

"Sir, I need to grab a few things," Tyler said. "I'll be back in ten or fifteen minutes."

Preoccupied, Smith just nodded and walked into the building as she drove off.

He marched down the hall to the office Vinson had handed over to Noel. Several offices were now occupied by air force personnel, and the sounds of typing and office equipment came to him. *Things are slowly getting back to normal.*

At the end of the corridor, Dennis Noel sat where Vinson used to. A few things had changed since his last visit. Several thick black cables came in through an open window and were plugged into a khaki green telephone handset, which sat on the desktop.

Noel looked up as he entered the space. "Morning, General. Congratulations on your promotion. I was rather surprised when they asked for 'General Smith.'"

Smith appreciated Noel's good wishes, but they had more pressing matters to deal with. "Thanks. The president called?"

Noel stood. "No, sir, Keith Hurst. He said to find you and have you call them back. I sent out three air force people to find you."

"Okay. How does this work?" Smith indicated the handset.

"Just like a regular phone. Pick up the handset and dial 898427. The link is running through an AEHF 3 satellite in geosynchronous orbit. There's a quarter-second delay, but otherwise, you talk normally. Everything is fully encrypted. Want me to step out?"

Noel knew everything they were going to discuss, and it would be nice to have him there in case of issues. "No, but close the door, please. Eight nine eight four two seven?"

Noel closed the office door. "Correct."

Smith raised the handset and dialed. He listened and heard a regular phone ring sound in the earpiece. It didn't ring long.

Someone answered, "Vinson."

"It's General Smith, calling for Keith Hurst," Smith said formally.

"One moment please," Vinson responded.

Moments later, Smith heard, "General, this is James Calvin. What do you think of the Cardinals chances this year?"

Smith recognized the code phrase and responded with his own. "Mister President, I give them the same chances as us getting to Tau Ceti. It's good to hear your voice, sir." He sat down behind the desk, resting his elbows on the surface.

"Yours as well, General. Where do we stand on the readiness of our military forces?"

"Hill Air Force Base is operational. All personnel have their sight back, and we have two squadrons of F-16s at our disposal. After a week of sitting idle, the maintenance crews are working around the clock to get them serviceable. Tomorrow, I'll be sending teams out to marine, navy, and army bases to get as many troops pooled up as possible. If any Chinese troops do get ashore, I want them contained. Mister Vinson took tubes with him. You can use those to get East Coast units in the fight." Smith saw an open ream of photocopier paper just out of reach. He waved at Noel and pointed at the paper. Noel retrieved several pages and handed them over.

"Good thinking. What about stopping the Chinese invasion ships?" the president asked.

"I'll be heading to Colorado tomorrow, sir. I have a lead on an E-6 Mercury aircraft I can use to alert navy submarines to the threat. That's only half the problem though, sir." Smith pulled a pen out of his pocket to make notes.

"The other half is the airborne troops already occupying key bases and command bunkers," Calvin stated flatly.

"That's correct, sir. We won't have the firepower to oppose them directly for some time. I'm suggesting we use whatever land forces we have to contain them. It's a large force and will need a lot of food and water to keep going. If we blockade them, we can weaken their positions and starve them out. It's easier to lay siege when we have such limited forces."

"I concur," Calvin said immediately. "It's a sensible approach. The vice president will be traveling to New Jersey and setting up an eastern command post at Joint Base McGuire-Dix later today. He'll be taking the tubes with him. I'll follow after he confirms the area is secure."

Smith sat up. He'd watched the vice president die on a video recording. "Sorry sir, did you say the vice president?"

"Yes, Keith Hurst is my new V.P.," Calvin stated.

Smith made a note. "Oh, I see. I can send a couple of Hercules aircraft to McQuire for him to use. Will make it easier for him to get around."

"Thank you, General. I'm sure that would be appreciated. He'll be arriving there later this evening. Anything else we need to discuss?"

Smith put his pen down. "I'd like to thank you for the letters and promotion, Mister President."

"General, you earned the promotion by keeping your head and finding the blindness cure. If we can't stop the Chinese, it won't amount to anything in the long term. However, with recent developments, I suspect we now have a fighting chance."

"Yes, sir, I agree. That's all for now, Mister President."

"Right. Good-bye, and good luck."

Smith hung up and addressed Noel. "Tomorrow, prior to my oh-five hundred briefing, I'll need an updated ship count for the Chinese fleet with their position, course, and speed."

"No problem, Colon— Sorry, General."

* * *

Linda Krause sat on the rear seat of the Can-Am roadster and pulled on her helmet. Around her, a dozen well-wishers, including Father Peters, stood around the bike to see her off.

"Were my directions clear enough?" Father Peters asked.

Krause patted her jacket pocket, where she had placed his map. "Yes, we should be able to find those two other FEMA shelters easily. Hopefully, they'll lead to others. The more people we can cure, the better."

"I'll miss you, but I know you have to leave. Where's Oscar?" Peters asked.

"He's taking a last-minute bathroom bre— Oh, wait, there he is." Oscar emerged through the main doors and came down the few stairs.

As she watched him coming, she noticed something else, and her eyes opened wide for a moment. She couldn't say anything as he made his way through the crowd. Several people were near him, slapping him on the shoulder. He slipped onto the front seat of the roadster and took his helmet off the handlebars.

"Thanks for everything, Father," Blake said as he shook Father Peter's hand.

"Go with God's blessing, my son," Peters replied.

Blake strapped on his helmet, started the bike, and with a final series of waves, pulled away from the building. "All right," he said over the helmet radio. "I'll get onto the highway and we can make our way to the next shelter. It feels good helping people."

"Feeling like a hero, are we?" she teased.

He answered, "I help people daily in my job as a park ranger, but it's always giving people directions or answering basic wildlife questions. I don't get to help them in a significant way except for the few who injure themselves. So yes, I guess I am feeling like a hero today. Why?"

She had to struggle not to laugh. "Oh, nothing, but before we get to the next shelter, you might want to do up your fly to maintain that heroic image."

* * *

The President of the United States blinked repeatedly and stared at something forming from the darkness. He turned his head slightly, trying to gain perspective to decide what he was looking at. He had no idea what it was.

Staying patient was not easy. After a week of being blind, he wanted this affliction gone.

His sight brightened somewhat, and he realized he was looking at a shelf with several paperback books. The titles were too fuzzy to read, but it didn't matter. He was starting to see again, albeit crudely. Movement from the corner of his eye drew his attention. Colors still eluded him, but a man he didn't recognize sat in a corner chair with a notebook computer on his lap. "Mister Ogden?"

"Yes, sir?" asked the man in the corner, looking up.

"I believe I can see you." Calvin sighed in relief. "I can't tell you just how good you look."

Ogden smiled and folded his laptop closed. "Shall I go get one of the agents?"

Calvin shook his head. "No need. At the rate I'm getting my vision back, I'll be able to walk upstairs in a few minutes. I see you have your computer. Is the Internet still up?"

"Surprisingly, it is. Many websites are off-line, but a few of the major news sites are still up. There's been nothing new posted for over a week, though."

Calvin felt confident enough with his vision to stand. "There will be soon. General Smith's cure is working. Now we just have to get it to everyone and boot out the Chinese, and life can get back to normal."

Calvin looked around the space he had lived in for a week. He was glad he'd been blind. The entire space was crudely furnished, dirty and unkempt. The surface of the table he'd eaten his meals from was stained, cracked, and slightly warped. The "kitchen" comprised a two-burner electric stove on cinder blocks and a pyramid stack of canned food nearby. He looked over at his sleeping bag near the wall. The dirty concrete floor under his mattress pad had peeling paint flakes on it, and the roof over the sleeping bag was buckled and distorted.

Ogden had lived here for some time out of necessity.

A small mirror hung on the wall. He looked into it and saw an almost unrecognizable haggard, bearded man staring back at him. Calvin rubbed his chin, and the derelict in the mirror did the same. The sight surprised him, but he realized it shouldn't have. He had not washed properly for days and felt grungy, plus he smelled.

Still, he'd never seen himself in such rough shape before. Looking away from the mirror, he looked down to see his clothes were in dire need of a wash.

"Mister Ogden, could you show me how to boil some water, please? I think I'm well overdue for a shave."

* * *

General Smith marched out of the office building. He saluted a lieutenant in a flight suit coming into the building and spotted Captain Tyler waiting for him in the golf cart.

He jumped onto the bench seat. "Let's go to flight ops. I want to see how they're set up for briefings."

The cart didn't move.

Tyler was shaking her head. "I'm sorry, sir, but I can't take you anywhere as long as you're out of uniform."

He glanced down at himself. *What the hell is she talking about? I'm wearing the correct air force uniform.*

Before he could voice a counterargument, she pulled a small paper bag from a cubbyhole in the dash of the cart. "Here, sir. You'll need these."

He took the bag. Inside he found two pair of epaulettes with lieutenant general rank stitched onto the surface.

"I got you an extra pair for a coat, as well," she said with a smile.

He pulled a pair from the bag and undid the buttons on his shoulder epaulettes. He removed the colonel rank from his shirt and slipped on the ones she had given him. He had an issue getting the buttons done up, and she helped get them secured.

"Now you are dressed correctly, sir," she said.

He was moved that she had thought of this. "Thanks. That was good of you."

She swiveled back into driving position, and the golf cart accelerated toward flight ops.

* * *

James Calvin walked up the stairs toward the surface entrance to the bunker. He used a small LED flashlight Ogden had given him to illuminate his path. As he got closer to the top, the air got a lot less stuffy, and he found himself breathing in a lot more deeply than normal.

Coming up the last few steps, he spotted Keith Hurst and Agent Carter talking together. Hurst had the same heavy beard stubble and dusty clothes that Calvin had possessed minutes before. Hurst stopped talking and glanced over at him. *He can see, as well.*

"It looks like it's going to be a decent evening, Mister President," Hurst said.

Calvin walked over to his closest friend and embraced him briefly, while slapping his back. "It's the best one in a long time. You never know how much you rely on something until you lose it." He looked out at the surrounding trees and hospital just past them. The last rays of the sun were fading. "Damn, I missed the sunset. It's been so long, I was hoping to see it."

"There'll be many more. Agent Nance is loading up one of the SUVs. We're taking one of Mister Vinson's satellite systems with us so we can communicate securely. We'll be leaving as soon as everything is loaded. I suspect we'll be a day or two setting up a secure command post," Hurst said.

Calvin felt his smooth chin. "Are you going to clean up first? I can't describe what my first shave in a week felt like."

Hurst shook his head. "I'll wait until I get there. I'll have several hours waiting for base personnel to regain their sight, so there's no rush. If I'm truly lucky, I'll be able to nab a hot shower as well."

Agent Nance came from the parking lot. "All set, Mister Vice President. We can leave whenever you're ready."

"Thank you." He turned back to face Calvin. "I think it's best I leave right away. The sooner I get there, the better. Once we get everything secure, I'll send an airplane to pick you up."

The two friends shook hands. Calvin added, "I'll look forward to hearing from you. Good luck."

Hurst walked off with Nance. They hopped into their SUV, slammed the doors, and drove off into the evening. Carter said nothing and stood off to the side, watching the area.

Calvin spied the folding deck chair he had used previously. He sat down in it and stared up at the sky. The sky was slowly transitioning to black. He'd seen nicer evening skies, but at the moment, he couldn't remember when. The realization that he was one of the few people who could see this night sky made him shiver. *So many are still in the dark. We need to do something about that, and quickly.*

July 13th

Chapter Twenty-Four
A Message from Mercury

General Smith stood behind the lectern in front of the small group he had assembled over the last twelve hours. The flight operations briefing room could hold up to seventy people, but it was only a quarter full at the moment. He sipped the hot coffee in his hand to let the caffeine drive away the last vestiges of sleep from his body. He hadn't slept well, not with so much weighing on his mind.

Major Kerouac sat in the front row beside his copilot. Behind him were the half-dozen military police who had been asked to provide security. Their leader, a senior master sergeant, stood behind those men with a notepad in his hand. His last name was Ortega, and he looked like one tough S.O.B. He'd been in Delta Force at one point, according to Tyler. He certainly looked formidable in his camouflage fatigues and webbing.

On the opposite side of the room were a dozen technicians, mostly airmen and women who looked nervous. Their officer, Lieutenant First Class Unger, was pale, and he constantly looked around the room.

Captain Tyler stood near the rear of the room by the light switch.

Smith turned to double-check the screen behind him. The solid blue background with "Hill Air Force Base - Flight

Operations" logo was unchanged. Smith checked his watch. Oh five hundred. *Time to begin.*

He caught Captain Tyler's eye and nodded. She dimmed the overhead lights, and conversation in the room stopped.

Smith pressed his handheld control, and numbers appeared on the screen. "Good morning. I won't keep you long. These are the tactical frequencies we'll be using to communicate between the aircraft and the ground assault element."

Everyone in the room began making notes. Smith waited until the writing stopped, and advanced the slide. A large-scale satellite image appeared. "This is the latest overhead imagery for Centennial, Colorado." Smith pressed the top of the handheld control and used the red laser dot as he spoke. "Our destination is the airfield located here. It's a civilian field used primarily by private charter outfits. We have no firm info on the site, nor do we know if the Chinese have a presence there."

Smith advanced to the next slide, an overhead image of the airfield. Overlaid arrows pointed to points of interest and a specific aircraft hangar. "Our mission is to secure the Raytheon maintenance hangar located here.

"We'll take a single C-130 piloted by Major Kerouac. We'll approach from the south to avoid Denver Airport, land on the main runway three-five right, and taxi to this spot. Major Kerouac, I want to arrive there as close to 0900 hours as possible."

"Yes, sir," Kerouac acknowledged, making further notes.

Smith returned his laser dot to the screen. "From here, Senior Master Sergeant Ortega and his people will spread out and secure the Raytheon hangar as quickly as possible. The objective is an E-6 aircraft held inside. It's the only one we know of that's not in enemy hands. We need the strategic communications gear on board that aircraft to coordinate our defense.

"The Hercules call sign will be Larry. The ground assault team is Curly, and the maintenance team is Moe. Once that's done, Lieutenant Unger will move his maintenance people in, to get the aircraft flight ready. We're hoping to find Raytheon support staff and hopefully a navy flight crew for the E-6, but can't count on it. Major Kerouac tells me he has time on the Boeing 707 airframe and can fly it if needed, but locating a crew with specific E-6 qualifications would be preferable. We simply don't know if there's any crew at the location, so keep your eyes open and do not fire unless fired upon. We will have a tube with us to cure people's blindness.

"As soon as the E-6 is serviceable, we fly it out of there and use it to coordinate any available naval assets. On this mission, there is no backup or reinforcements. Questions?"

Ortega spoke up. "I only have six MPs, General. If we encounter severe opposition, what's the evac plan?"

Smith leaned on the lectern. "If you meet a force you feel you can't handle, make a fighting withdrawal back to the Hercules, and we get out of dodge as fast as possible. We're only taking a limited force to minimize complications. We don't have enough troops for a large-scale ground offensive, so I'm scaling this mission back as much as possible."

"Yes, sir," Ortega said, with a single nod.

No one else said anything.

"If there are no more questions, be on the flight line in fifteen minutes to load up. Dismissed."

* * *

Linda Krause awoke to find Blake's muscular arms wrapped around her naked body, his front pressed against her back. She snuggled back against him with a blissful grin.

They were in the bedroom of an abandoned home, just west of Weber State University in Ogden. The bedroom was bright with daylight. After spending the previous afternoon and evening treating close to seven hundred people in the FEMA shelter on campus, they'd gone to bed late, feeling exhausted. They hadn't waited to see everyone regain their sight. At this point, Krause knew their treatment worked, and weariness had forced her to look for a place to lie down.

She lay there, eyes closed, feeling the warmth of his body against her. She was sleeping a lot more than normal. Krause checked her watch. Typically, when on duty at the hospital, she got no more than six hours a night with a few catnaps during the day. The constant travel, irregular diet, and long hours had combined to keep her in bed for almost nine hours. She knew she should get up to get ready to move to the next FEMA shelter, but a selfish part of her wanted to stay where she was, comfortable, relaxed, and happy.

Blake slid out of bed on his side. She groaned with disappointment and twisted around to see his naked body disappear around the corner.

He must have heard her, for he said, "Sorry, I need to use the toilet." She heard the door close.

She lay back and stared at the ceiling. There was so much to do! They could only cover a very small area and treat roughly one person a minute. The seven hundred people yesterday had taken over eleven hours to treat.

She had no idea how Doctor Wiater was doing in getting Seattle back up and running, nor did she know if Oak Ridge had been successfully reached. Oak Ridge was the key to this disaster. With their reactors, they could produce enough isotopes to create hundreds of tubes. With no way to contact either location, she was left in a state of ignorance regarding the fate of the majority. She took solace in the fact that she had cured roughly five thousand people, but there were at least five billion still blind worldwide, and the difference between those two numbers made her melancholy.

The toilet flushed, and she heard Blake remove the porcelain toilet tank lid. She sat up, wondering what he was doing until she heard water being poured. The previous night, he had carried two buckets of water into the house from the backyard pool to fill the tank. Lying back, she entwined her fingers on her belly and returned her thoughts to the many who were still blind.

The bathroom door opened, and Blake emerged. She ran her eyes over his naked torso and legs, and she watched as he picked up a clean pair of underwear from his open bag and began to pull them on.

"Why don't you come back to bed? We're in no rush," she said quietly, patting the mattress where he had been.

He dropped the underpants and slid back into bed.

She didn't think of anything negative for the next half hour.

* * *

General Smith stepped up onto the lowered access ramp on the back of the Hercules. He could see everyone else was already on board. Every man and woman on board sat on the red webbing jump seats with an M-16 rifle between their knees. Two pallets of gear, lubricants, and various spare parts were secured to the cargo deck.

He turned back to speak to Captain Tyler, who stood on the tarmac. Smith had to speak loudly to be heard over the noise of the APU. "I'll be gone for a day, at least. I'll have Kerouac send updates to flight ops over the HF link. While waiting, have Noel get overhead shots of LAX and any other airports in the surrounding area. I want to know which airfields are usable as forward operating bases. With the numbers of aircraft we have, we'll need several.

"Have the squadron commanders organize advance parties to any viable airstrips later today, to assess their usability, check fuel supplies, etc. We don't have a lot of time to organize."

"No problem, sir." Tyler replied.

Smith turned to walk up the ramp when Tyler called, "General!"

He turned to look at her. "Yes?"

"Please be careful, sir. Some of us would miss you if you didn't come back."

Smith gave her a closed-lipped smile. "I'll be back in a day or so, Captain."

He walked up the ramp. Senior Master Sergeant Ortega had a space available on the seat beside him. Smith buckled himself into that jump seat. Once done, he asked Ortega, "I understand you were in Delta at some point?"

Ortega looked down and tapped his right knee. "Yes, sir. I was, for three years. Blew out my knee on a HAHO[31] insertion onto rocky terrain in Yemen one dark and miserable night. We were supposed to meet tribal leaders who never showed, and I had to walk out of the desert on it. It healed eventually, but I still have issues, and it killed my career in SpecOps."

That made Smith feel better about the mission. Ortega's training and experience would make all the difference if they did get into a fight.

The loadmaster came up to Smith. "Pardon me, General. Major Kerouac's compliments. He has a place for you up on the flight deck."

"Thank you, but I'll stay here for takeoff," Smith replied.

"Yes, sir." The loadmaster moved to the rear of the cargo area and began raising the rear ramp.

* * *

Less than an hour later, General Smith watched the loadmaster enter the cargo bay from the forward access hatch. The loadmaster moved along the line of men, repeating, "Two minutes, buckle up! Two minutes, buckle up for landing."

Those few who had undone their seat belts quickly did them up again.

Heading into an unknown situation made Smith feel anxious. The Hercules was rugged and reliable, but it was just as susceptible to an anti-air missile as any other aircraft. *That's all it would take. One Chinese private getting a lucky shot with their version of a Stinger missile, and America falls.*

The butterflies in his stomach multiplied.

---

[31] High Altitude High Opening. The parachutist jumps from an aircraft at high altitude (30,000–40,000 feet) opens the chute almost immediately and glides onto a drop zone several miles away. HAHO typically involves specialized gear, including oxygen masks, and they can be in the air for one to two hours.

Beside him, Senior Master Sergeant Ortega used the charging handle on his M-16 and chambered a round. The MPs nearby did the same.

The Hercules banked sharply. There were groans of displeasure from all around Smith. The aircraft leveled out, and Smith heard a sharp *eeerrrpppp!* as the tires touched the ground. The pitch of the engine noise immediately increased, and Smith felt himself being pulled toward the front of the aircraft. That eased over time, and as soon as he felt normal, Ortega undid his seat belt and moved to the back of the aircraft. His men followed.

The loadmaster lowered the rear ramp as a light box above their heads turned red. Ortega said something to his men that Smith couldn't hear over the engine noise. The light box above the ramp door turned from red to green, and Ortega ran off the end of the ramp, waving for his men to follow.

Smith undid his seat belt and jogged forward. He went up the stairs into the flight deck and tapped Kerouac on the shoulder.

Kerouac pulled his headset away from over his ear. "So far so good, sir. No opposition on landing."

"Good. Let me know when you hear from Ortega on the radio."

Kerouac nodded and pulled his padded earpiece back into place.

Minutes passed, feeling like hours. The engines of the aircraft were still running, in case they needed to make a rapid escape. The noise grated on his nerves.

Kerouac turned. "General, Ortega has called all clear. The hangar's secure. He's ready for Moe."

Smith left the cockpit and descended down the stairs and through the cargo area to Lieutenant Unger. "Deploy your people, Lieutenant."

"Yes, sir!" Unger eagerly replied.

Smith didn't wait. He kept walking out the rear door and down the ramp. He had to place his hand to jump off the end, as it was a good three feet above the concrete, but he landed without issue and half-jogged toward the Raytheon hangar while scanning the surrounding area.

One of Ortega's men stood at an open access door recessed into a monstrously large hangar door. He pointed the way to go. Smith entered to find himself looking up at an E-6, built on a Boeing 707 airframe. It was a large aircraft. The outer skin was painted pure white—"anti-flash" white, which would reflect heat energy from nuclear detonations away from the aircraft. The smooth skin of the airframe had many antennas and bulges along its length.

"Back here, sir!" one of the MPs called while waving him toward the rear of the hangar where there looked to be a series of offices.

Smith nodded at the MP and passed through a pair of double doors. The smell of unwashed bodies came to his nose as he crossed the threshold. He discovered a small canteen lit by a single portable battery lantern. There were around fifty men, women, and children huddled against the walls, or in chairs. Most of the men wore white coveralls, but a few were in navy uniforms.

Smith spotted Ortega in the back corner, talking to some of the men. He went to join them.

Ortega stopped talking and turned to face him. "General, this is Dale Marvin. He's senior man here. This is Bill Darber—he's the lead maintenance manager."

Smith took a knee to get closer to them. "Gentlemen, I'm General Smith of NORAD. Can you tell me if the E-6 outside is serviceable?"

Marvin responded. "It needs a couple of minor checks, but otherwise it's ready to go back to Tinker. The navy crew was supposed to take it back when this blindness thing hit. What the hell is up with that anyway? The only reason we survived this long is because two of our guys can see. They were able to gather our families together and take care of us."

Smith looked up at Ortega. "Get the tube." He then addressed Marvin. "That's great news. We have a cure for the blindness, and it'll take about four hours to take effect. I can explain what's going on in the meantime."

Marvin frowned. "Wait a sec. You said you're from NORAD? They have nothing to do with the TACAMO[32] program!"

Smith pulled over a chair to sit on. "Let me fill you in on what's been happening for the last week."

* * *

Linda Krause finished her second canned fruit cup, sitting at the kitchen table of the abandoned house. The small cans of fruit hardly constituted a breakfast, but that was all Blake could find that hadn't spoiled. There was no coffee in the house, but the sugar-laced syrup in the cans certainly woke her up. Blake sat across from her.

"Oscar, as we make our way to the next FEMA shelter, we should use your bullhorn on the way. It's possible there are people in their homes. We can call out and try to help as many people as we can."

"Wouldn't it be more efficient to treat the people in the shelter?" he asked. "There'll be a lot more people there, and we can treat them quickly."

"That may be so, but who knows when a mass-produced cure will be ready? It could be another week until someone else comes through here. We should at least try and see how it goes," she countered.

"You're the boss." He patted her hand. His palm was rough but warm, and it brought back pleasurable thoughts from the night before. "We have no dishes to do, so we can get on the road right away."

---

[32] "Take Charge And Move Out," abbreviated to TACAMO, was first used by Director of Naval Communications, Rear Admiral Roeder, USN in 1962. TACAMO is a strategic communications platform that allows presidential orders to be sent to land- and sea-based nuclear missiles. The naval TACAMO program replaced the better-known U.S. Air Force "Looking Glass" program in 1998.

"Sounds good," she said while standing.

Blake stood, as well. "We should keep an eye out for a local road map. If we're going to cover the streets between here and the next shelter properly, we'll need a decent reference map."

She remembered seeing filler pumps and a small adjoining convenience store the day before. "Good idea. We passed a garage yesterday, by that mini-mall. They should have them."

"That'll be our first stop. We may be able to find something for lunch there, too," Blake said.

* * *

James Calvin walked up the stairs from the bunker. The cables on the satellite communication gear were not long enough to get down the stairs, so to take a call, he had to go up to the surface. The walk up the stairs felt good. The past week had not allowed him to be as active as he would have liked.

Ascending up the final steps, he saw Vinson waiting for him. He held out the handset to the president as he approached. "The vice president, sir."

Calvin nodded in thanks and took the handset, placing it to his ear. He sat down in his folding deck chair and said, "Keith? I'm here."

"Morning, Jim. I wanted to let you know that things are going well here. We have a couple of National Guard army units taking the cure now, and Smith sent two Hercs to use as transport. Let me know when you're ready, and I'll send one up to get you."

"Thanks." Calvin checked his watch. "Have them here by three p.m. our time."

"No problem. I also have some good news. I finally got a call through to Oak Ridge to see where we stand. A team from Seattle got to them and gave them the cure. Their staff is spooling up reactors for mass production of rhenium isotope now. They'll be able to start tube production beginning tomorrow."

Calvin raised a triumphant fist. "That's fantastic. We'll give priority to military units and get them operational. After, they can go into their local communities and set up clinics for civilians. We can't forget our neighbors and allies, either. We need to get some over the border to Canada, Mexico, and over to the U.K. as quick as we can. Think on how we can spread the tubes worldwide."

There was a pause over the connection, and Calvin wondered if the call had dropped.

Then Hurst said, "Have you thought that through, Jim? Spreading a cure will alert the Chinese. We're still weak, and if they decide to nuke us, we'll have zero warning and a lot of dead people."

Calvin thought about that briefly, but didn't change his mind. "We can't deal with 'what if' scenarios and live in fear of retaliation. Nor can we let the rest of the world suffer in darkness for some sort of tactical advantage. Once Smith hits the incoming ships, they'll know something is up. Anyone who does not get the cure has a death sentence hanging over them from the cancerous growth along their optic nerve. If we don't start healing the world now, we'll lose millions of lives.

"Even looking at it from a purely humanitarian point of view, we have to spread the cure, Keith."

"All right. I'll get that organized and will send the Herc to pick you up at three. I'll see you soon," Hurst responded.

"Bye." Calvin hung up the handset and turned to Vinson, who was standing nearby, monitoring the communications gear. "We're leaving here this afternoon at three from the local airfield. Can you let Agent Carter know?"

"Of course, Mister President."

"I'll be downstairs."

* * *

General Smith stepped through the E-6 hangar to find a hive of activity. After regaining their sight, the Raytheon staff and navy crew had launched themselves into action to get the aircraft serviceable. Smith had informed them about the cause of the global blindness, Chinese airborne invasion, and the inbound convoy.

Lieutenant Unger's maintenance technicians looked like ants against the huge airframe. They brought in spare parts, hydraulic fluid, and oil. They moved stands and equipment where needed. The pace was frantic, and Smith stayed out of the way. There was nothing he could do to improve either their motivation or performance.

Dale Marvin stepped up to him. He still had several days of shaggy beard growth. "General, we'll have her ready for flight in an hour."

"So quickly?" Smith asked, surprised. "That's amazing!"

"Not really. We were in the process of acceptance checks to turn the bird back over to the navy when the blackout hit. Everything was ready at that point. We just need to check for fluid levels and leaky seals. We'll haul her outside for some gas in a half hour, and you'll be good to go. Part of the EW[33] suite is the only thing that's not working in the back end. We were expecting parts, but they never arrived. However, all comms, ESM, and radar systems are operational. The navy crew has loaded the daily crypto settings you provided. With the updated gear we installed, as long as they have a radio turned on, you can communicate securely with any military unit."

Smith felt exhilarated. That report was much better than he had expected. They'd finally caught a lucky break.

"Thank you, Mister Marvin. That's excellent news." Smith looked back at the airframe. This was turning out to be a good day.

"Are you planning on landing back here when your mission is done?" Marvin asked in a low voice.

Smith turned back to face him. "Probably not. Why do you ask?"

---

[33] Electronic warfare. A series of electromagnetic receivers and jammers designed to confuse enemy forces and weapons.

"Once you fly out, I plan on heading home with my family. I suspect the rest of the staff will, as well. This airport will be a ghost town a half hour after you have wheels up."

"That's understandable. I can't imagine what you've been through over the last week. Just make sure you and your people stay clear of the Chinese airborne troops. They're centered around Denver airport, Peterson Air Force Base, and Cheyenne Mountain as far as we know, but could be elsewhere."

"I'll let my people know. We live near here and most of us belong to the local gun club, so we're not exactly defenseless," Marvin said confidently then added, "I have to go make sure we have a fuel tanker lined up."

Smith shook Marvin's hand. "Next time I come through this way, I'll buy you and your people a round of drinks."

"That sounds like a plan." Marvin smiled before shaking his hand. "Good hunting."

* * *

Krause sat behind Blake on the roadster as he drove slowly down a residential street in Ogden. Off in the distance, the green and brown broken hills surrounded the town. She had the bullhorn in her hand and called out to the mostly redbrick, single-story bungalows. "My name is Doctor Krause. We have a cure for the blindness. Come to your front door, and we can treat you." She swapped the bullhorn to her other hand, pointed the cone to the opposite side of the street and repeated herself.

No one had appeared on the block since they had started making announcements. Was this really the best course of action? Many would have gone to the FEMA shelters. Others would have gone to assist family members in other parts of the city. She had a nagging feeling that many people were in their homes but couldn't come to the door, and she didn't want to think about that.

Movement caught her attention. An older woman in a sundress stood on her doorstep waving a white dishtowel in one hand and holding the white screen door open with the other. Krause tapped Blake on the shoulder and pointed at her. He slowed the bike, and Krause alit. She pulled the helmet from her head and retrieved her tube from a side bag.

She walked toward the older woman. "Hello. I'm Doctor Krause."

"Lord, oh Lord! Finally, someone answered my prayers," the woman said.

Krause came up onto the stoop. "What's your name?"

"Alice Bonner. I was hoping my sister would come over, but it's been so long. What's happening to me? Why can't I see? I called 911, but kept getting a busy signal, and now my phone doesn't work at all. There's no power, and I'm out of food."

"Well Alice, it's a long story, but the fireworks caused everyone to lose their sight. I can give you a treatment, and you'll get your sight back in four hours."

"Four hours? That's wonderful, but will it hurt?"

"Not at all. You won't feel a thing. Just stand still." Krause raised the tube, aimed it at Alice's eye, and pressed the button to open the iris. The LED counted down to zero, the shutter closed, and Krause repeated the process on the opposite eye to repeat the process. When done, Krause said, "That's it. You're all done. Just go rest, and in four hours, you'll see normally."

Alice hugged her. "Thank you, Doctor. I'll go check on my sister when I can see again."

Krause's earlier misgivings disappeared in the warm embrace. She had helped Alice, and that made her day. "You're welcome. I have to go. There are lots of people who need the cure. Good-bye and good luck."

"Good-bye and thank you, Doctor," Alice replied.

Krause returned back to the three-wheeled roadster.

* * *

The acceleration of the E-6 pressed General Smith back into his high-backed chair as it hurtled down the runway. Smith didn't hear much engine noise, as his noise-cancelling headphones were the best money could buy. He did feel the heavy vibration of the four CFM56-2A engines at military power for takeoff.

The nose of the aircraft came up suddenly, a lot faster than a civilian flight, and the airframe leapt into the air. Smith was glad to see the navy pilot not wasting time, as they had little left. The E-6 banked hard to the west.

Surrounding him at various workstations were ten men and women. Four naval officers and six enlisted personnel manned the various stations throughout the cabin of the aircraft.

Smith waited until the climb rate eased slightly before reaching for his keyboard. The centrifugal forces of the climb made his arms twice as heavy as usual, and that made it tough to type anything.

But he began typing quickly anyway, and he reviewed the output on his monitor. Smith had been building the message in his mind for several days and had a good idea what he wanted to say.

A female voice came over his headset. "General, navigator. We'll be feet wet in one hour, fifty minutes."

Smith keyed his microphone. "Roger." He returned to composing his message.

* * *

President James Calvin found David Ogden in his heated room in the bunker. "We'll be leaving soon. I just wanted to thank you for sharing your home with us. If you can use them, you're welcome to the sleeping bags and any other supplies we brought. We won't need them anymore."

Ogden rose from the dining table and went over. The two men shook hands. "Thank you, Mister President. I hope you have a safe trip."

Agent Carter stood on the threshold. "Sir, our aircraft just went overhead. We can leave whenever you're ready."

Calvin turned. "Let's go."

Carter moved toward the stairs. Calvin paused a moment, took one last look at the derelict bunker, and strode to follow Carter toward the exit.

* * *

Since finishing his message, Smith had spent his time learning the onboard command and control systems. He had assistance from the navy crew who were eager to show him the capabilities of the aircraft.

"General, navigator. We are now feet wet," announced First Lieutenant Jennifer Warden.

"Roger. Thank you. Activate the ELF." Smith replied.

A low-frequency radio signal began transmitting along a twenty-eight thousand-foot long wire trailing behind the aircraft. The transmission rate was slow. Only six characters were sent out over five minutes.

* * *

"Captain, to the command center! Captain, to the command center!"

Relaxing in his bunk and reading a novel, Captain Eric Reid started at the loud excitement in his XO's voice. *What's caused that?* As he raised himself up off the bunk, dropping the novel on the blanket behind him, he wondered if the three prisoners were causing issues.

He made it to the command center in a few steps. As Reid stepped through the door, he noted the course, position, and depth of the sub on a nearby monitor. He saw the depth was a hundred and fifty feet and slowly decreasing. One of Reid's standing orders was the boat could not go shallower than one hundred feet without his direct order. The XO stood near the tactical plotting table. Their eyes met.

The XO moved immediately to him. "Sir, we've received an ELF transmission alerting us we have orders waiting. The message code group covers all submarine units in the Pacific Ocean. I've ordered the boat to a hundred feet. Awaiting your orders."

Reid didn't hesitate. This was the moment he'd been waiting for. "I have the conn."

"Captain has the conn," XO Maddox repeated.

Reid called over to the sonar station. "Sonar, report all contacts."

"Conn, sonar, I detect no contacts," Tolly replied.

"Pilot, ten degrees up bubble. Take us to photonics depth. Make your speed four knots," Reid ordered.

An officer seated at the dive control station gave his acknowledgement. The nose of the boat began to rise.

Maddox came closer. "Could it be a trick, sir?"

"You think the Chinese got into our codes?" Reid asked quietly. The same thought had crossed his mind as well, but after a week of hearing nothing, he simply had to check. Receiving a radio message wouldn't betray their position.

Maddox inclined his head to the left, raised an eyebrow, and shrugged simultaneously.

Reid nodded. "It's possible. We'll have to make contact to see."

"Captain, we're at photonics depth," the pilot stated.

"Thank you. Raise the ESM mast and report all contacts," Reid replied.

"Raise ESM mast, report contacts, aye," repeated the radar console operator.

There was a pause and hiss of hydraulics as the ESM was raised.

"Sir, I have one contact, airborne radar on the edge of our detection range. He's well away to the north, northeast, sir. It'll take a moment to firm the contact up... There, the triangulated range is four hundred nautical miles. Signal has a staggered PRF and the frequency is— Captain, that's one of our E-6 Mercurys."

Reid walked over to look at the radar operator's monitor. The screen had a single line indicating the direction to the aircraft. The line changed slowly as the aircraft flew along. On the right of the screen, the signal characteristics of the radar were listed.

The P.O. manning the station, Farber, was one of the more experienced submariners aboard.

"Are you sure, P.O.?" Reid asked.

"I saw the same signal last year during RIMPAC[34] when on the *Connecticut*. I'd bet my sea pay on it, Captain," Farber said confidently.

Reid clapped Farber on the shoulder. "That's good enough for me. Raise the communications mast."

A moment later, Chief Holgrim at the CSRR station replied, "Comm mast is raised, sir." "I have an incoming message over AEHF relay... It's a big one, sir."

"Decode it as soon as it finishes." Even though Reid was impatient to read the message, he walked away to the plot table to give Holgrim space to work.

Reid placed his fists on the table, staring unseeingly at the chart below him. His mind impatiently ran wild trying to think of what was coming. No one in the command center spoke.

Chief Holgrim came over carrying a clipboard, which he handed over. "Here you are, sir. All attached data has been transferred to the tactical plot table. Sign this, please."

Reid signed the message receipt, took the printed pages, and returned the clipboard. Holgrim retreated back to his station.

Reid took a deep breath, exhaled, and read the long message.

<MSG START>

---

[34] RIMPAC or Rim of the Pacific Exercise. RIMPAC is held during June and July of even-numbered years and is the world's largest international maritime warfare exercise, involving ships from many countries bordering on the Pacific Ocean.

MSID:
96b2fca2e8baba8a9d20d6a67b430d3a69e9c168f9239a30
71bf87d5bd55136a
TO: 24G
PRI: FLASH
FROM: NCA VIA NORAD
SUBJ: PRC INVASION FLEET

Current situation - Three PRC airborne divisions occupy all major U.S. strategic bases, facilities, and communication stations. Congress, cabinet, and joint chiefs in enemy hands. Many POWs bayoneted by PRC troops. Vice president tortured / killed in captivity. POTUS safe at undisclosed location. Blindness cure developed and being circulated globally as fast as possible.

PRC surface fleet departed Qingdao, PRC, July 5. Currently on course for commercial berths, Los Angeles - Long Beach, speed twenty knots. ETA late morning, 16 July. Fleet comprises sixteen civilian container and RoRo vessels, two PLAN Luyang-II Class destroyers as escort. Estimate of PLA troop numbers in convoy are 150,000 to 250,000 enemy combatants.

USN command and control not currently viable.

Per NCA directive, all PACFLEET forces fall under NORAD command, effective immediately.
Air Force units will strike when PRC fleet comes into range, morning of July 16.
All available SUBPAC units to engage escorts, then remainder of fleet, starting no earlier than 0600, July 16— repeat, 0600, July 16.

Command is to make all efforts to stop ships landing troops. Marine and army units defending shore, but numbers limited. Most recent intel and communication schema attached.

All units shall adopt DEFCON TWO. No nuclear option at this time.

—Smith, A.L. - Lt. General, Commander NORAD
<MSG ENDS>

Heat washed over Reid as he read about the extent of the Chinese occupation. The bayoneting of prisoners and brutal death of the vice president made his teeth clench. That the navy was now under NORAD made him raise an eyebrow slowly, but if the regular navy command and control was unusable, then that made some sense. He handed the message over to XO Maddox. "Sounds like real orders to me. This Smith guy doesn't sugarcoat things."

While Maddox read the message, Reid used the electronic plot table to open the data package sent along with the message. There were overhead images of the Chinese fleet, a course plot showing their locations over the last week, and up-to-date specifications on the Luyang-II destroyers. Another file gave call signs, communication satellite frequencies, and other needed information.

Maddox placed the message on the plot table and whistled in a descending tone. "Damn, a quarter million troops of the People's Liberation Army! If they get ashore, they'll run rampant. We have to stop them."

"We will," Reid said with finality. "When is sunrise on the sixteenth?"

Maddox looked up the number in the navigation charts. "It's at five fifty-six. Is that why they chose zero six hundred?"

"The sun rises in the east, so it'll be directly in their eyes. Aircraft can come straight at them unseen," Reid explained.

Whoever General Smith was, he'd planned his assault using common sense. Giving yourself every advantage saved lives in battle, and Reid fully approved of that.

Maddox picked up the message. "What do we tell the crew?"

Reid pointed emphatically at the message. "Post it, exactly as it is. Make sure everyone understands 'POTUS'[35] means the president. They need to know what they're fighting for."

"Yes, sir," Maddox responded.

Reid turned to the CRRS station. "Chief Holgrim, let's get the satellite comms warmed up. We need to send a response."

Holgrim walked over with a clipboard and pen ready. "What do you want to send, Captain?"

Reid thought for a moment. "Take this down... Exactly."

---

[35] POTUS stands for President of the United States. It was created in 1879 by Walter P Phillips, Washington bureau chief for the Associated Press, and is one of the earliest known acronyms.

July 14th

Chapter Twenty-Five
En Prise

General Smith sat at a spare desk in flight ops. There were a few officers on duty, but they worked on the opposite side of the building and left him alone. He leaned way back, stretched, then rubbed his eyes. He decided he needed another coffee to stay awake. His flight the day before had lasted nine hours. He'd tried to cover as wide of an area as possible and returned back to Hill Air Force Base well after dark. Since landing, he had stayed in flight ops to plan his air assault against the Chinese fleet.

Several Pacific-based submarines had checked in, but only one SSN was in a position to do anything about the incoming fleet. The USS *John Warner* had responded to his message. Smith unfolded the printed message form and read the text again:

> *On station off Los Angeles. Have full mission capability. Can execute requested attack on schedule.*
>
> *"The Eyes of all our Countrymen are now upon us, and we shall have their blessings, and praises, if happily we are the instruments of saving them from the Tyranny mediated against them."*
> —*Captain Eric Reid*

Reid hadn't recognized the source of the quote, but one of the navy communication staff on the E-6 had penciled "George Washington" on the printed message.

The next closest submarine was an SSBN in the Bering Sea. However, it would take eighty hours at maximum speed for them to get there. Smith had ordered that captain to remain on station.

Smith rose and shuffled over to the small kitchenette. His dismay upon seeing the empty coffee pot was short-lived when he realized he'd been the last to take a cup. He took a coffee can from under the open cabinet and prepared the basket with a fresh paper filter. After adding water to the machine and ground coffee to the basket, he flipped the switch, and eventually gurgling hot water began to flow.

He placed his hands on the worn counter to wait. Impatient, he glanced out the small window.

It was daylight outside.

He checked his watch and saw it was just after seven in the morning. Time had gotten away from him. *I have a meeting with the squadron COs in a half hour, so sleep is out of the question.*

Steam began to rise from the edge of the lid, and the smell of the coffee wafted to his nose. He closed his eyes and ran his mind over the preparations he still needed to make. The list was almost endless. Only half of the advance parties sent out the day before had checked in. Time was quickly running out, and he needed their information. They needed airfields to stage attacks, but to attack, the squadrons needed to have fuel and weapons. If an airport didn't have those things already, then he'd need to supply them from elsewhere. The number of serviceable transport aircraft he had was limited, and his attack was less than forty-eight hours away.

The progress of the people he had sent out to cure marine and army units was also unknown. *Will I have defenders in place on the shore if any ships get through?* He had no idea.

He sighed and opened his eyes to find a full pot of coffee waiting for him. Smith frowned, wondering how long he'd been thinking. He shook his head to clear it, took a mug, and prepared coffee for himself.

He returned to his desk and stood holding his mug, regarding the mass amount of stacked paper waiting for him. Maps, supply reports, flight schedules, and other needed paperwork waited his attention.

A door closed behind him. Smith turned to see Captain Tyler march up to him in dress blues. She carried a pressed man's shirt on a hanger over her shoulder, and a file folder and a paper bag in the other hand. "Good morning, sir. The duty officer told me you had been here all night, so I brought you a clean shirt and breakfast." She placed the bag on the desk. "Croissant sandwich with ham, cheese, and egg with a slice of sausage. Better to eat it while it's hot." She hung the shirt up on a wall-mounted hanger near some flight helmets.

"Thank you," he said, genuinely meaning it.

She opened the file folder and withdrew several stapled pages, which she handed to him. "This is the latest information we have on the advance parties, marine, and army units, along with updated estimates of enemy troop locations already in the country. The president and vice president have relocated and have established a link over satellite with our comm center."

Smith flipped through the pages. He'd been waiting for that information. Scanning the message headers, he realized they had arrived several hours earlier.

Tyler continued, "The last page is your itinerary for the day. You have a meeting in twenty-five minutes with the squadron commanding officers to discuss the establishment of forward operating bases. Immediately after that, you have a meeting with Major Kelly from base supply. He has some concerns about logistics and scheduling the available transport flights needed. Then you have a fifteen-minute break followed by—"

"Captain! Why wasn't this information brought to me immediately? I've been waiting for this."

"Sir, the staff compiled it overnight. Once they established—"

"I need to see this information as soon as it comes in. Why wasn't it given to me?"

Tyler paused, came to attention, and took a deep breath. "Permission to speak freely, sir?"

Subordinates only used that phrase when they had something unpalatable or objectionable to say, but Tyler hadn't yet acted without good reason. "Proceed," he said formally.

She took a deep breath. "Sir, with respect, you're a lieutenant general now. That means you let your staff handle the nuts and bolts. They're all experts in their fields, and you need to let them do their jobs so you can focus on the overall effort. People can't run to you with every single message and update, nor can they bring every small issue to your attention. That would be micro-managing and would tell everyone that you didn't trust them. If they did come to you with everything, you'd be burned out by the time of the attack and useless to everyone. Last night, you had no sleep. You can't do everything by yourself, General. That's all I have to say, sir." She remained at attention when done.

Smith was tired and irritable, and his first instinct was to lash out at her, but he recognized more than a kernel of truth in what she said. When he had been a colonel on NORAD watch duty, he needed to know everything, but he only communicated up the chain of command when necessary. If the photocopier broke, he didn't pick up the red phone. He handled it without anyone above him even knowing, most of the time. He deeply resented people who tried to micro-manage him for the same reason Captain Tyler had voiced.

He'd jumped up three rank levels and was still acting like a watch officer. She was right. He'd had no sleep the night before and felt like a dog's breakfast. After another caffeine-fueled day of stress and no rest, he'd be useless.

Smith had initially named her his aide simply because of expediency. Now, he was glad he had. "At ease, and sit down, Captain. Let's discuss my itinerary."

* * *

Captain Eric Reid tapped Petty Officer Second Class "Tolly" Toledo on the shoulder. "Got anything, Tolly?"

Tolly pulled back his headphones and twisted in his chair to face Reid. "No, sir—at least, nothing concrete. I've lowered the input filters to absolute minimum on the Q-10[36], and I'm hearing whale farts twenty miles away. We're getting the odd blip of noise, but it's distant, and we can't track it."

"Keep me posted," Reid ordered.

"Aye, skipper." Tolly pulled his headphones over his ears and returned to monitoring his screens.

Reid returned to the tactical plot table. He looked at his XO standing nearby and shook his head, saying nothing. Maddox simply nodded once in acknowledgement. "Could this be a ruse, Captain? Something designed to draw us out?"

Reid placed his hands on the plot table. "I thought about that, but it doesn't make sense. If they did have access to our crypto, they'd order us to the nearest occupied port or tell us to surface at a specific location and time for an ambush. Then there's what Smith said about the navy command and control being shot to hell. We know it is from that message we got from COMSUBPAC himself. If they developed a cure, they'd only have limited numbers of people. NORAD has deep bunkers, so it's logical they'd avoid seeing the fireworks. Smith was probably one of the few commanders to keep his sight. The overhead images they provided show a large eastbound convoy with Chinese military escorts. No other scenario I can come up with fits those facts."

Maddox crossed his arms. "The cure is good news. Too bad we didn't hear about it sooner. It might have stopped Wyatt and the others."

---

[36] AN/BQQ-10 (V) or Acoustic-Rapid COTS (Commercial Off-The-Shelf) Insertion, designed to replace different pre-existing submarine sonars with one standardized suite across all classes. A single central processor for the BQQ-10 has more processing power than the entire *Los Angeles* class of subs combined.

"Good news for us, but not him or the two others. A cure means the country will recover and they'll eventually face court-martial for what they did. Anyway, we have more pressing matters. Weapons are all operational?" Reid asked while picking up a navigation compass.

"Yes, sir. All Torpedo Room ordinance is up at this time," Maddox confirmed. "It's a shame our Tomahawk missiles are the land attack version. We could cause some serious grief with anti-ship models on board."

With the compass, Reid drew a circle around their current position on a chart. He replaced the compass with a ruler and pointed at the circle. "This is our theoretical sonar detection range, given current conditions. Assuming no change in course, they should come through here."

He laid the ruler down to show the enemy course, then picked up a thin-tipped marker to draw a line. The line passed within ten nautical miles of the sub's current position. He pulled aside the ruler and tapped the paper chart with the end of the marker. "We can tighten things up once sonar gets updated tracks, but we shouldn't have to maneuver much to line up for an attack.

"Starting tomorrow at the end of the morning watch, let's get the crew rested. Set up a barebones rotation to get as many people in their racks as possible. We'll go back to full crew watches at 2200 Zulu[37], then battle stations soon after."

"Aye, sir," Maddox agreed.

* * *

General Smith not only had time to change his shirt before the commanding officer briefing, but he'd also taken a shower and

---

[37] Zulu used to be a reference to GMT or "Greenwich Mean Time." It began as a standard time reference by the military to coordinate military actions globally. Each time zone has a different letter. Eastern is "R" or "Romeo," Central is "S" or "Sierra," Mountain uses "T" or "Tango," and Pacific uses "U" or "Uniform." The more accurate Coordinated Universal Time (UTC) replaced GMT in 1972, but the term "Zulu" remains in use.

shaved in the pilot changing room. Even though he hadn't slept the night before, he felt somewhat rejuvenated and ready to face his meeting with the squadron commanders.

There were two F-16 squadrons represented at the meeting, the 4th and the 421st. They made up the 388th Fighter Wing based at Hill and had forty-four aircraft total. A black-haired woman in a flight suit, Captain Sarah "Ducks" Margolis, sat quietly across the table from Smith. She was senior pilot of the small A-10[38] contingent. Her flight had been pieced together from numerous aircraft in for maintenance at Hill. They sat around a table in flight ops with various airport runway maps and charts showing all of Los Angeles and southern California.

The squadron COs had reviewed his attack plan and slowly worked through the difficulties. They were currently discussing where to stage their fighters from in Los Angeles, based on reports made by the advance parties.

The senior squadron commanding officer, Colonel "Advil" Harnell, commanded the 4th Fighter Squadron, the "Fightin' Fuujins. " He was only five foot four and built like a fire hydrant. "Of the six choices I see here, my squadron will have to base out of LAX. With twenty-nine aircraft, we'll need the room." He pointed at the map of southern California. "It's the closest to the sea, has four good length runways, plus their facilities look to be in good shape."

Colonel "Stretch" McConvey of 421st Fighter Squadron bobbed his head and tapped the map further inland. "That works for me. With my fifteen falcons and Ducks' half-dozen warthogs, Los Alamitos is my choice. Two runways and decent facilities. The 'hogs can use the shorter runway, and the falcons can take the longer one." McConvey looked over at Margolis.

She nodded, saying, "That works for me, sir. You want us to begin deployment tonight, General?"

---

[38] The A-10 Thunderbolt II, colloquially nicknamed "The Warthog," is a Close Air Support (CAS) aircraft designed to deliver ordinance in direct support of troops in combat. The A-10 is heavily armored and has redundant flight controls to offset battle damage.

"Affirmative. If you can get a couple of Herc loads of techs in place to prepare for arrival, the aircraft can leave at first light tomorrow. Then you'll have all day to prepare and load up. I'll authorize supply flights to both locations as soon as we conclude this meeting. We should have enough weapons available for the op. However, we're light on transports, so a second strike may not be possible. Make sure you have an armed security detachment going out on the first flight to secure the perimeter. Any other issues?"

McConvey stood. "No, sir. We'll do you proud. Oh, do we have a name for the op?"

Before Smith could answer, Harnell, also getting to his feet, chimed in, "When I played football at college, we'd call this a 'Hail Mary' play."

Margolis collected her notepad and stood. "Seems appropriate."

Smith got up last. "'Operation Hail Mary'? All right, we'll use that. At least until a bureaucrat comes along and spins it to something more politically correct."

That got the laughter Smith was after. "Dismissed. We'll go over the plan again at zero four hundred tomorrow before you leave."

"Yes, sir," the three officers said simultaneously.

As they left the room, a major marched in. He carried an accordion file folder in his left hand. The major stopped near the table, came to attention, and saluted. "Morning, General. Major Kelly reporting."

Smith returned the salute, then indicated a nearby chair. "At ease, Major. Please sit. I'm told you want to discuss supply issues..."

* * *

President James Calvin walked into the large conference room located in the base headquarters of Fort Dix with Agent Carter immediately behind him. Vice President Hurst, already seated at the table, stood and walked over to shake his hand.

Someone in the room called "Ten-hut!" and the other military officers, eight in all, stood quickly.

Calvin shook hands with his friend. "Morning, Keith. At ease, everyone. Please sit down."

Hurst came closer and asked in a low voice, "Sleep well?"

"Yes, thanks. After having spent a week in a hole in the ground, it's nice to be able to wake up on a decent mattress with a breeze and sunshine coming through the window," Calvin said, meaning every word. He had slept very well, had a long hot shower, and shaved. Agent Carter had tracked down a decent suit for him to wear. He didn't wear the jacket—the July temperatures made it unnecessary. Still, he felt part of the human race again.

Calvin sat with Hurst beside him.

Hurst began. "To bring you up to speed, Mister President, seventy percent of the personnel at Joint Base McGuire-Dix-Lakehurst have received the cure so far. I had the 174th Infantry Brigade put at the head of the line so they could provide security. They are fully restored and have secured the base perimeter. The rest of the personnel will have their sight back by midnight. Once that's complete, a unit from here will be sent to Fort Drum in New York State to heal the 10th Mountain Division. After that, Fort Detrick and NAS Patuxent River will be next. At that point, it becomes problematic. The other bases near here like Andrews are probably occupied by PLA."

Calvin thought Fort Drum was prudent. At some point, they would have to start fighting back. "Approved. Does anyone have suggestions for other units to mobilize?"

"Mister President, if I may." An army colonel from across the table leaned forward and said, "I'm Colonel Hollister, commander of the 174th. The 101st Air Assault Division is at Fort Campbell, Kentucky, and the 82nd Airborne is based at Fort Bragg, North Carolina. Both of those units would shore up our offensive capabilities. Hercs can land at both their locations, but we have a limited number of tubes. Is there any way we can get more?"

Calvin looked at Hurst. "Keith, how is Oak Ridge coming along?"

Hurst checked his wristwatch. "Last update we had, they should be producing tubes now. We shouldn't forget the Army Rangers or marines."

Calvin turned back to Hollister. "Colonel, I want you to detach a company, get it on a Herc, and fly down to Oak Ridge. You'll provide security for the staff and production lines, and set up a delivery system to get tubes to all commands as quickly as possible. Place the emphasis on combat units, then logistics. The vice president is heading up the effort to heal the civilian population, and you'll report to him."

"Understood, sir," Hollister said while scribbling notes.

Calvin looked around the room. "Let's get tubes out to the 101st and 82nd, as well. Where is the base commander?"

An air force officer raised his hand at the far end of the table. "Sir, I'm Colonel Monk."

"Colonel, until we're able to re-form the joint chiefs, I'm going to need your services as my military advisor. Having run a joint base of air force and army personnel, you are uniquely qualified." Then, to the rest of the room, he said, "If there's no further business, I'd like Colonel Monk and the vice president to remain behind. Everyone else may return to your duties."

Everyone who was not named stood and left. Once the room emptied, Agent Carter closed the door.

Calvin turned to Colonel Monk. "Can we get a large-scale map of the United States in here? The three of us are going to decide how to take back the country."

* * *

Linda Krause repeated her amplified message from the back of the roadster to either side of the street as they drove along. She spotted a man and boy standing in a house doorway and stopped using the megaphone. The man held his screen door open with one arm and waved with the other. He shouted something, but she didn't hear what over the motorcycle engine noise. She tapped Blake on the shoulder and pointed at them. He pulled over and parked the bike in front of their house.

"I'm going to take a bathroom break while you treat them, Linda. Make sure you stay in sight," Blake said. He withdrew a roll of toilet paper from under his seat before heading for the opposite side of the street.

She headed for the pair in the doorway. When a dozen feet from them, she said, "Hello, I'm Doctor Krause."

The man said, "I'm Doug Landau. You said you had a cure?"

She began to ascend the steps. "Yes, it will cure you in about four hours."

"It's about time. We've been blind for days now," Landau griped.

Krause decided not to tell him it had been a week. She raised the tube level with his eye. "All you have to do is stay still and look ahead." She began the treatment.

"Are you with the government?" Landau asked.

"No, I'm a doctor from Seattle. We developed the cure after everyone went blind. We're just starting to get the cure out to everyone." She swapped the tube over to the other eye.

When Landau was treated, she used the tube on the young boy.

A sudden loud *boom* echoed throughout the neighborhood, vibrating the glass in the aluminum screen door. Linda Krause jumped involuntarily, as did the man and child she was treating.

"What was that? Billy, are you all right?" asked the man.

"I'm fine, Dad."

"I don't know what that was, but it was close. Sounded like thunder." Krause looked around, but saw nothing. The LED counter on the tube in her hand reached zero and the iris closed. "Well, that's it. You're both done. You should both get your eyesight back in four hours."

She heard movement coming from the street. Blake was running toward her, his pistol in one hand and the waistband of his open jeans in the other. She would have normally found that funny, if not for his concerned expression. "What was that? It sounded like a shotgun."

"I don't know," Krause replied, still searching for the source of the noise.

"If you're done, we should get out of here," Blake said, scanning the nearby houses.

Something in his voice motivated her to move. *He sounds afraid.* "Yes, I'm done."

The pair returned to their bike. Blake did up his pants and holstered his pistol on the way. They put on their helmets, jumped on, and Blake started the bike. He pulled away using every bit of the throttle, forcing Krause to cling to him.

After a few seconds, Blake spoke. "I'm heading back to Hill. We'll go talk to Colonel Smith. He should be able to provide some security."

"It was just a gunshot. It wasn't even aimed at us."

"Maybe, but this isn't the first time we've been exposed to danger. There's a lot of desperate people out there, and my one pistol isn't much of a deterrent. Besides, shooting someone isn't something I really want to do."

She hadn't realized that he might have to shoot someone. She knew she wouldn't want to live with that and could understand his trepidation. Besides, a small group would work more efficiently. "Okay, Oscar. I see your point. Let's go back to Hill. Can you slow down, please? No one's after us, and you're going too fast."

After a brief pause, Blake eased off the throttle.

* * *

General Smith sat down at the desk in Noel's office to take the president's call, making sure to have a notepad and pens to make notes. A few air force technicians had rearranged the original wiring Vinson had used to tie into the satellite transceiver so the wires came through the wall rather than the window. The installation looked a lot neater, more professional.

He waited alone, with the door closed. He wished he'd gotten coffee, as his eyes were closing with nothing to do. He stood and paced the office to get his blood moving again. He promised himself to get a solid eight hours of sleep later.

The satellite phone chirped, indicating an incoming call. Smith sat and picked up the handset. He pulled the yellow notepad closer and tapped the end of a pen with his thumb. "General Smith."

"James Calvin. Been to any decent games lately?"

"No, Mister President. I'm hoping NASA goes to Rigel, though."

"I've relocated, General. I'm now at Fort Dix and surrounded by an infantry brigade. As we're now on a secure link, I think we can do without the baseball and star references from here on."

"Understood, sir. May I proceed with your briefing?" Smith asked.

"Go ahead. I have you on speakerphone. Vice President Hurst and Colonel Monk are also on the phone."

"Eddy Monk?" Smith asked, startled.

"Yes, sir," his old friend answered. "Congratulations on your promotion."

Smith wanted to catch up with his old friend, but there were more pressing matters, and the president and vice president were waiting. "Colonel Monk and I were roommates at OCS, Mister President. Anyway..."

Smith went through what had happened since they had last spoken. The retrieval of the E-6 Mercury, contacting the USS *John Warner*, selection of forward operating bases in California, and a quick outline of his strike plan. As he spoke, he doodled a crude turtle on the blank page in front of him.

When he was done, Calvin asked, "Colonel Monk, what's your opinion of the attack plan?"

"Sir, overall it sounds solid, given the resources available. It's unfortunate we only have one sub in range, but a *Virginia*-class SSN is the best we have. General Smith, will there be enough weapons for a second strike if the first isn't enough?"

Monk wasn't dumb. He'd hit the nail right on the head. "No, with the limited numbers of transport aircraft we have, we can only support one major attack. We may have enough extra for a dozen aircraft to conduct a secondary strike, but with the time bombs take to transport... We simply don't have a lot of time left."

Calvin said, "Then General Smith will need to impress the pilots with just how important the first attack is."

Smith made a brief note and underlined it. "Yes, Mister President. The limited supply of tubes is slowing us down. If we could get more, I could detail people to round up the transport aircraft we need, plus additional ground forces in case any PLA forces get ashore."

Keith Hurst said, "We're getting Oak Ridge spooled up as fast as we can and have tubes being produced now. I'm looking into setting up a distribution system now. That would normally be a FEMA job, but with their leadership afflicted with blindness or in enemy hands, that process will take time. We'll need to use military resources, and that takes away from the overall effort to get rid of the Chinese."

Smith wrote "FEMA?" on his notepad. The sound of a motorcycle engine came to Smith's ears. He turned to see Doctor Krause and Oscar Blake go past on the road outside. An idea formed, and he turned back to the phone.

Chapter Twenty-Six
The Beginning of the End

Linda Krause slipped off the back of the bike and removed her helmet. Blake parked in the lot by the gymnasium rather than in front as they had done previously. She looked around and saw why. Everyone she saw had their sight. People were driving, walking, and there were a few people jogging. It looked so normal, she almost cried.

Captain Tyler came up to her. "Good afternoon, Doctor. Would you have a moment to speak with General Smith? He'd like a word with you."

General Smith? Who is...? Wait. "He got promoted?"

Tyler beamed and nodded eagerly. "Yes, by presidential order. Do you have a minute? It won't take long."

"Sure," Krause replied, puzzled. She turned back to Blake.

"Go ahead," he said while turning on the engine. "I'll see if I can find some gas for the bike. We're running low."

Krause followed Tyler into the office building. She'd never been through it before. The single-floor building had many small offices with glass windows facing the hallway. Venetian blinds were lowered and closed on most, but she could see through enough of them to see regular-looking desks with people in uniform working at them.

Tyler walked all the way to the end office. She knocked politely on the open door, and General Smith rose with a warm smile and came around the desk. "Doctor Krause, please come in and sit down. Would you like coffee or tea?"

She shook his hand. "No, thank you." Apart from the multiple computer monitors on the desk, the office looked quite normal. File cabinets, a portable shredder, etc. There were two phones on the desk. One looked normal, while the second had a thick cable running into the side of it.

Smith moved back around the desk and sat in the office chair. He looked over Krause's shoulder. "That'll be all, Captain. Close the door on your way out, please."

He returned his attention to Krause, and she heard the door close behind her.

"Oscar and I have been going into the residential neighborhoods to try and get the cure to as many people as possible. He thinks it's prudent to have security as things get more desperate out there. Is there any way you can provide us with an armed escort?"

"I think I can do a lot more than that," Smith said before leaning forward and pressing a button on the bulky phone on the desk. "Are you still there?"

A man's voice came over the speaker. "Yes, General. Doctor Krause, it's nice to speak with you."

The voice sounded familiar, but she couldn't place it. "Thank you. Who am I speaking to?"

"President James Calvin. I've also got Vice President Hurst with me."

Krause blinked once, holding her eyes closed for a long moment while she tried to process what she had just heard. She then looked at Smith. "Good day, Mister President, Mister Vice President. I'm sorry; I wasn't expecting to speak with you."

"We were on the phone with General Smith discussing other matters when you pulled in. I understand you're one of the people responsible for the blindness cure."

Krause sat up a little straighter and leaned forward toward the telephone, to be heard better. "Doctor Edmund Wiater in

Seattle did the lion's share of the work. I simply collaborated with him, ran the clinical trials and follow-up examinations."

"That's a notable contribution, Doctor, and I thank you for it. That brings me to the reason I wanted to speak with you. How would you like to oversee the distribution of the cure nationwide?"

"I'm sorry?" She couldn't comprehend what he was offering.

Calvin clarified, "We're attempting to get the military back in operation to take on the Chinese, but as you know, the civilian population is in dire need, as well. We need to get the cure that's currently being produced by the Oak Ridge reactors to the people. General Smith thinks you have what it takes to lead the effort to do that. What do you think?"

Krause felt relieved that the process to cure the public had begun, but... "That's going to be a huge undertaking. There's no infrastructure to either ship or distribute the cure," she said finally.

"True," Calvin replied. "However, we have national guard units in every state. They could be easily utilized. They can also provide a communications network, support, and security."

"Yes, that would work." She fell silent, considering the many obstacles still in the way.

"Do I take your silence as hesitation, Doctor?" Calvin asked.

She placed her hand on the desk. "No, no, not at all. I'm just thinking it through. There's a lot that needs to be done."

"Doctor, you'll have access to an operating budget of thirteen and a half billion dollars."

"Thirteen and a..." The sum staggered her. Her hands fell into her lap.

"That's the annual budget for FEMA. As their administrator, you'd have the authority, the money, and my backing. What do you say?"

"I'll do my best, Mister President." She felt there was nothing more to say.

Smith nodded once and smiled at her across the desk.

"Excellent. You'll report directly to Keith Hurst until we can get the cabinet reformed. If you have any issues or concerns, contact him. General Smith will give you details on how to contact us and can arrange to take you anywhere you need to go."

Krause's first destination was obvious. "I need to go to Oak Ridge to see their production lines and find out how many tubes we can produce. We can't plan anything until we know how many tubes we have to work with."

"Agreed. We're currently sending a Hercules with troops to secure Oak Ridge. Once it drops them off, I'll have it fly to Hill Air Force Base and pick you up."

"Yes, sir. I'll do my best," she responded.

"General Smith, we'll talk later as we discussed. Thank you, and good-bye."

"Good-bye, Mister President," Smith said before hanging up.

Krause collapsed against the back of her chair, feeling as if the air had been sucked from the room. She was light-headed and blinked rapidly several times. "Wow, I was just a simple eye doctor until a few minutes ago. Now this…"

Smith laughed and stood. "A week ago, I was just a colonel; today, I'm a lieutenant general. Just shows how desperate they are for people, if they're scraping the bottom of the barrel for people like me."

His joke brought a grin to Krause's face.

July 15th

Chapter Twenty-Seven
Reactions

Linda Krause had never been on a Hercules transport aircraft before. The bare metal struts of the walls and the visible cabling running through the ceiling supports looked strange to her. Unlike a regular airline flight, there were no stewardesses, no pre-flight safety briefing pointing out the exits, and no offer of a beverage. The engine vibration and noise were a lot stronger than she was used to, as well.

She didn't have to wear hearing protection on civilian jets. Her feet buzzed against the cold metal floor of the aircraft. Even the seats gave her pause at first—made of inch-wide strips of red fabric stitched into a lattice over a thin steel frame, they looked like wide deck chairs. Their slender supports gave an impression of fragility, but were a lot tougher than they looked. The loadmaster for the Hercules had told her they were called jump seats and would carry men with parachutes and full equipment weighing up to three hundred pounds each. Even so, she found them to be quite comfortable.

Blake was beside her, and she was thankful for that. For a portion of the flight, she had leaned against him and dozed. The need to wear ear protection and the strong engine noise discouraged even simple conversations. They were the only passengers.

A man in an air force flight suit appeared from the front of the aircraft. He caught her eye and pointed down a few times then mimed an aircraft landing on a runway.

She nodded in return and looked over at Blake. The rough conditions hadn't fazed him one bit, and he snoozed with his arms folded. She elbowed him in the side, and he jerked awake then looked at her with a mild look of confusion. She made the same aircraft landing gesture the air force man used. Blake just nodded and closed his eyes again. She checked his seat belt—it was secure. Hers was also tight, so she went back to looking around the cargo area.

Several pallets of supplies had been taken aboard at Hill destined for Oak Ridge. They were for the soldiers sent to Oak Ridge. She scanned the boxes, and only one stood out. According to the outside label, it held sixteen thousand 5.56 caliber bullets. She wondered why they needed so much ammunition.

A high-pitched mechanical scream sounded, interrupting her thoughts. *What was that?*

A minute later, the aircraft bumped onto the tarmac. She felt herself pulled toward the front of the aircraft for twenty seconds as the aircraft slowed. After a short taxi, the aircraft stopped, and the air force man dropped the rear ramp open.

The airport was pitch black. She checked her watch and saw it was 4:42 in the morning.

Four soldiers in camouflage uniform jumped up onto the ramp. Blake stood up, and Krause undid her seat belt and did the same.

One of the soldiers approached her. "Doctor Krause?"

She realized she still wore her hearing protection; she edged an insulated cup away from one ear, decided it could come off, and removed the protection altogether. "Yes."

"The lieutenant's outside, waiting with your transport."

"Thanks."

Blake grabbed their small bags, and they walked toward the ramp together. As she passed the end of the pallets, she heard a soldier say, "Palmer, grab the grenades. Kenny and I will..."

Damn it, they only sent sixteen thousand rounds. We asked for sixty!"

Her eyes widened at that number, but she kept on walking. Blake hopped down the three-foot drop at the end of the ramp and helped her descend.

The only vehicle nearby was a green Humvee. A heavily tanned man stood at the passenger door with a black radio handset to his ear. He saw her and waved them over.

As she approached, she heard him say, "Get those roadblocks up by oh five thirty. Seven delta four niner, out." He tossed the handset inside the vehicle and turned to her. He shook her hand, then Blake's. "Doctor Krause, I'm Lieutenant Ashford of the one-seven-four. If you jump in, I'll take you to the facility. Sorry for the delay. I'm trying to get additional reinforcements. Oak Ridge is a lot larger than we thought and surrounded by forest. With only thirty men, it's impossible to secure completely. There were several members of the Tennessee National Guard on site, but almost all were blind as well."

Krause and Blake slid into the rear seat of the Humvee. She smiled at the driver, also dressed in camouflage, but he turned back to the road, remaining detached.

Ashford got into the vehicle, slammed the door, and told the driver, "Administration building."

The Humvee accelerated into the night.

Ashford twisted toward them, saying, "It's a twenty-mile drive. We're having quarters set up for you, and there'll be a staff briefing at oh six hundred for you in the main conference hall to bring you up to speed. Did you need anything in the meantime?"

They'd eaten late, and Krause wasn't hungry. "No, I think we're good. I did have a question, though."

"Yes, Doctor?"

"Why do you need so much ammunition?" she asked. "One of the men inside the plane said you requested sixty thousand rounds. That seems excessive."

He nodded. "I have a thirty-one man company. Each rifleman carries two hundred rounds, plus frags... Sorry, grenades. So I need six thousand rounds just to give them a basic loadout. If we do get in a fight with the Chinese, we'll burn through that very quickly. Combat eats up supplies. We have no resupply scheduled, and reinforcements are unlikely, so I asked for extra. No officer ever got court-martialed for having ammo left over after a battle."

"I see, thanks," Krause replied.

Ashford turned back and faced the road. She glanced out the window. There was no external lighting, and everything was pitch black. She looked at Blake then took his hand in hers. She was so glad he had insisted on coming with her. She returned her view out the side window.

* * *

General Smith marched out of the front entrance of the Mountain View Inn, also known as Hill Air Force Base Building 146. It acted as temporary housing for base staff. He walked out under the large red exterior canopy over the front doors feeling rested and relaxed. With almost nine hours of sleep, he felt normal again. Captain Tyler waited for him on a golf cart parked just outside the main doors.

He slid onto the seat. "Good morning, Captain."

"Morning, sir. Sleep well?" she asked while slipping the cart in gear and driving away.

"Yes, the apartment you arranged for me is excellent, thank you. Let's head to flight ops. I want to see how the deployment is going."

"Yes, sir. In the cubbyhole in front of you, I have your messages, briefing papers, and itinerary ready for your review."

Smith grabbed the paperwork and read the contents. The overnight messages were arranged in order that they arrived. He flipped through them. The advance parties reported Los Alamitos Army Airfield to be in great shape. Power was being provided by on base generators and local staff was being treated for blindness. The base had full accommodations available, as well.

The LAX civilian airport, on the other hand, was a bit of a dog's breakfast. There was no power, as that was provided by the civilian grid, and no living staff had been found on site. Sleeping areas were being placed in terminals. The good news was there were many tanker trucks with jet fuel available, and a survey was underway to ensure there was enough to supply a strike mission.

He turned the page and received a wonderful surprise. "Joint Base Lewis-McChord is operational?"

"Yes, sir. A medical team from Seattle got to the base early yesterday and began treating everyone with tubes. The list of their units is appended on the back of the page."

Smith turned the page over, then read aloud, "62nd and 446th Airlift wings. They have C-17s. It's the heavy airlift capability we've been looking for!" His heart skipped a beat. One of his current Hercules transports could carry roughly forty-five thousand pounds of cargo. A C-17 was rated at just under a hundred and seventy thousand. Each C-17 flight equaled four Herc loads. The jet-powered C-17 was much faster as well. *We can do it. Their inability to move lots of cargo was the last remaining obstacle. Barring some unforeseen disaster, we can do this.*

Tyler turned a street corner. "Yes, sir. Several aircraft are already on the way to assist with weapon transport to the forward operating bases. In addition to the transports, there's also a rundown on army units assigned to I Corps. There's four brigades with headquarters, and support units. They've already been warned they may be transported to L.A. later today—pending your approval, of course."

Smith didn't hesitate. "Approved. That's a no-brainer. Get those units moving. I want the L.A. container ports defended. What about the Marines?"

Tyler shook her head. "No word at all. The advance party left for Camp Pendleton, and nothing has been heard since. Shall we send another group?"

Without knowing why the first team didn't report back and with only a day left, they couldn't afford to spare another tube. "No. We'll investigate after the attack, but as long as we have I Corps in place at the container ports, we're in good shape."

Tyler turned into the parking lot for flight ops and parked near the doors. "Your meeting with the squadron COs is in twenty-five minutes. I'll go round up some breakfast for you in the meantime."

"Thank you, Captain."

* * *

President James Calvin sat alone in the large conference room doing paperwork. An army steward had cleaned up after the last briefing, leaving a tray of ice water and glasses. Calvin paused and looked out the window. Beyond the few marching army troops, the trees and blue sky caught his attention. He vowed never to take such sights lightly again. A week of blindness had shown him just how lucky he was to be able to see.

A polite knock sounded at the door.

"Come!"

The door opened to reveal Agent Carter. "Colonel Monk to see you, Mister President."

Calvin waved him in.

Carter retreated, and Colonel Monk entered, carrying a sheaf of stacked paperwork and rolled maps. He began to place them on the table as Carter shut the door. "Good morning, Mister President. We got our first load of tubes on the return flight from Oak Ridge early this morning. I've already detailed parties to venture to several bases. They're waiting on your go-ahead."

Calvin dropped his pen. "Do you have a list?"

Monk rummaged through his papers. "Yes, sir. Here you are. We had four tubes delivered. I'm suggesting we send them to Dover Air Force Base in Delaware, Joint Base Langley-Eustis, Norfolk, and Quantico—all in Virginia."

Calvin indicated a chair opposite him. "Please, sit. Why Dover and Langley-Eustis?"

Monk sat down. "Dover has C-5 heavy lift cargo aircraft, and Langley has the 633rd Air Base Wing, which includes the 1st Fighter wing. We'll need their F-22s to re-establish air coverage on the East Coast."

Calvin put his hand on his chin. "We'll send two tubes to Dover. As soon as we can get an aircraft operational, I want it to go to England to deliver the second pair to Ten Downing Street. We need to get our allies back in the fight, as well. Hold off on Quantico for now. We'll do that with the second shipment. I'd like you to add Little Creek to the list as a high priority. Having a few SEAL teams on hand can't hurt. Same with Coronado, but I suspect you'll need to coordinate that with General Smith, given its location. What about the 82nd and 101st?"

"We have Hercs on the way to both bases. The vice president sent a tube on each flight, along with a small security detachment. A single tube can treat fourteen hundred people per day, so those bases will take at least two to three days before they can get to combat readiness."

"The next time we speak to Doctor Krause, we'll try to get her to send additional tubes to those bases." Calvin reached for a water jug.

"Yes, sir." Monk made a note.

"Any word from General Smith?" Calvin poured himself a glass of water.

Monk lay his pen down. "No, sir, but he would only contact us in case of problems. We're due to speak to him at eleven hundred hours. The vice president said he'd attend that meeting, as well."

Calvin took a sip of water. "Good. Now, to carry on... Where do we hit them first?"

* * *

Linda Krause and Oscar Blake were escorted by one of Lieutenant Ashford's heavily armed soldiers to the East Campus building at the Oak Ridge National Laboratory. She'd initially told the infantryman they didn't need him as they had a campus map, but he'd politely refused. "I have my orders, ma'am. Where you go, I go," was his final answer as he held his rifle in a ready position.

On entry to the building, they were greeted by a short balding man wearing silver-rimmed spectacles and a white lab coat. His glasses reminded her of John Lennon. "Doctor Krause, I'm Ted Innis, Associate Laboratory Director for Neutron Sciences. So nice to meet you. I understand you're responsible for the cure. I have to tell you, there's a lot of people here who want to shake your hand. The conference room is this way, if you please."

Krause stepped after Innis. "Doctor Edmund Wiater in Seattle did the lion's share of the work on the cure. I just conducted the field trials."

"Edmund Wiater? Yes, I know him by reputation. However, you were part of the solution, and there are a lot of grateful people here."

After walking past burnt orange walls, he turned through a pair of open double doors to reveal a large meeting room. A large widescreen projection screen was at the far end on the wall, and a mounted projector hung from the ceiling. The white rectangular table had seating for fourteen people, with additional seating around the periphery of the room. Several coffee decanters and mugs sat on the table beside a conference telephone. Two-sided name cards on the table marked the various assigned seats for the meeting.

Eight people waited inside. They turned as she entered and began to applaud. Innis joined them, and Krause flushed. She tried to wave them down. "Please, please don't. That isn't necessary."

Each smiling person came over in turn, shook her hand, and told her how grateful they were. She was so embarrassed to be singled out that she forgot their introductions almost immediately. She introduced Blake, and the group greeted him no less cordially.

When introductions were done, everyone except Innis sat down. Krause took her place by her name card, and Blake sat down beside her. She noticed her soldier escort standing outside.

Innis said, "Doctor Krause, we understand you want a briefing on the isotope reactors' capacity to produce rhenium-188. I'd like to turn things over to Erin, as she heads up our isotope program."

A young brunette stood up across the table. Her name card said "Erin Rogers". "Good morning, Doctor. I've made up a single slide to illustrate my presentation."

The projector became active, and Krause noticed a man typing on a wireless keyboard. The image that appeared on the screen looked like a series of shark fins, tightly packed in together. The slope was higher on the left and began at "100" and gradually sloped down to the "30" on the right side of the graph. Krause noted that axis of the chart was the half-life[39] value in millicuries.

Rogers, using a laser pointer in her hand, said, "This shows our daily elution of Re-188. Theoretically, our production of rhenium-188 should be eighty percent. In practice, the elution yield is only sixty percent. So for all intents and purposes, if we start with a one-curie[40] tungsten-188 generator, we get a daily yield of six hundred millicuries per day of rhenium-188. Any produced material will be reduced by a factor of point nine eight per day because of half-life decay. As you can see on the chart, the effective time for a hundred millicurie rhenium-188 isotope is only one hundred and twenty days before it falls

---

[39] Half-life is the amount of time required for one half of the atoms in a given amount of radioactive material to disintegrate. For example, the Carbon-14 isotope has a half-life of 5,730 years. If you had a kilo of Carbon-14 today, in 5,730 years you would only have half a kilo remaining.

[40] Curie – a unit of measure for radioactive materials equaling 3.70×10^{10} disintegrations per second. This is the amount of decay seen in one gram of radium-226. It is named after Marie Curie, the Nobel Prize-winning discoverer of radium.

under the thirty millicurie value. Obviously, for more output, you would need multiple tungsten-188 generators."

Krause followed almost everything Rogers had said, but it didn't answer the one question she needed answered. She pointed at the chart. "Given that value, and assuming maximum rhenium-188 production, how many tubes can you create per day?"

"Twelve, at today's production rate," Rogers answered.

Krause stood. "Only twelve? We have millions of blind here in the United States, not to mention the billions worldwide. Twelve a day won't do it. We need many, many more!"

Rogers raised her eyebrows and held up her hand defensively. "I'm sorry if I wasn't clear, but we could increase the output with more tungsten-188 generators. Based on today's output, we can only do twelve; tomorrow, we project twenty-four; the day after, forty-eight. It takes time to set up the tungsten-188 generators to produce them. In a week, we'll be able to put out just over three thousand tubes a day. Our entire staff is busy setting up as many as possible. There are also other facilities in other states that can produce rhenium isotopes. Bring them online, and we're talking close to ten thousand a day."

Krause sat. She hadn't been expecting to hear that large of a number. "Three to ten thousand a day?"

Rogers nodded. "Yes, Doctor. Within a week, as I said."

Krause sat down. "I apologize for my outburst. We need to get to work and set up a distribution system. Lieutenant Ashford mentioned National Guard troops when I landed. Where are they located?"

* * *

General Smith watched the last scheduled pair of F-16s take off from the tarmac at the side of a taxiway. When they lit their afterburners, he felt the deep bass vibration in his chest. They pulled up into the air together and turned west. He watched them become formless dots before vanishing into the distant sky completely.

Sensing movement to his left, he turned to see Captain Tyler pull up beside him in a golf cart. He slid onto the passenger seat, and she drove off smoothly. "Well, that's all of them, Captain. Tomorrow will tell the tale. Let's get back to flight ops."

Tyler handed over a message form, folded in half. "Good news for once."

Smith unfolded and read the brief message. "Two battalions of the 7th Marines and the 1st Tank Battalion from Twentynine Palms are operational. Why didn't we hear about this earlier?"

"When our advance party arrived, a marine sentry shot the radioman. He was the only one who knew the frequencies for making contact. Luckily, he survived, and once he recovered consciousness, he passed on the info. The other members in the advance party healed the troops in the meantime." Tyler said.

Shaking his head, Smith said, "We'll let the marine infantry secure the Long Beach facility and give I Corps responsibility for Los Angeles. We'll keep the marine tank battalion near Downey, California, here where these two major highways cross. They'll be the reserve, ready to support either location. No word from Camp Pendleton though?"

Tyler turned a corner. "No, sir, nothing. We can send Marines from Twentynine Palms over to investigate."

Smith couldn't spare the men, but he needed to know why an entire Marine base was unresponsive. *If the Chinese are there for some reason, then they're in a position to attack our positions from the rear.* "All right. Detail a platoon of Marines from Twentynine Palms to scout Camp Pendleton and report back. If the Chinese are there, we need to know."

"Yes, sir."

Smith checked his watch. The E-6 Mercury needed to be airborne at zero one hundred the next morning to coordinate the battle. That gave him a little over twelve hours, and he needed some rest before the fight began. "Captain, I'll be here for two hours finishing up paperwork. Pick me up at three. I'll want to get some rest before we take off."

"Yes, sir. I'll make sure the mess has sandwiches and drinks for your flight." Tyler pulled into the flight ops parking lot and braked to a gentle stop by the front doors.

"Good idea. Thanks. Carry on." Smith got off the cart and walked into the building.

* * *

President Calvin decided he couldn't hold off going to the toilet any longer. He'd tried to wait until the ever-growing stack of paperwork was reviewed, but nature was calling. Calvin found Agent Carter standing post outside the door of the conference room. The agent turned toward him.

"Need a bathroom break."

Carter indicated the way to the men's room. "This way, Mister President."

The male toilet was only steps away. Carter entered first and scanned the room. He checked the stalls were unoccupied while Calvin moved to a urinal. Calvin heard Carter leave as he stood there.

After washing his hands, Calvin went back to the conference room entrance.

Just as he got to the door, Carter asked, "Mister President, may I have a word?"

"Of course. Come in; shut the door. What can I do for you?" Calvin sat in his chair. He would have offered Carter a seat to be polite, but the agent would refuse while he was on duty.

Carter folded his hands in front of him. "We have several Secret Service offices in and around New York City, about an hour's drive away. I'd like to send Agent Nance there with a tube to supplement the number of agents we have in your detail. Right now, it's just us two, and often there's only one of us. It wasn't so bad in the bunker, but here, there's simply too much ground to cover. The vice president has no detail at all at the moment."

Carter and Nance had stood guard continuously for well over a week without a single complaint. The bags under Carter's eyes told him just how tired the man was. "It's a reasonable request. Talk to Colonel Monk and have him send a detachment with Nance. They need to move into New York City to get the police and fire departments back up and running, regardless. Doctor Krause will have people with tubes moving in there soon, and having emergency services active will help."

Carter smiled and nodded. "Thank you, sir." He began to leave.

"There's one more thing," Calvin said.

"Yes, Mister President?" Carter turned back to face him.

"After things get back to normal, I'd like you to take David Ogden a government check for consulting services. I thought fifty thousand dollars would get him out of that hole in the ground and get his life back on track."

"I'm sure he'd appreciate that, sir. He really pitched in to help us," Carter said, before leaving the room.

Calvin returned to his paperwork. Fifteen minutes later, a knock sounded at the door.

After a brief pause, the door opened, and Keith Hurst strode in with a huge smile, waving a piece of paper in the air. "Report from Doctor Krause. She has Oak Ridge producing tubes. Initial output will be low, but within a week, we'll see three thousand a day coming out of there. She's also identified other facilities that can produce the needed rhenium. I have people on their way to those locations. A flight is coming here tonight with eight tubes. She's sending the other four to Texas."

Calvin smiled. "Good news indeed. We'll need as many as we can get. I'm sending troops to New York City to get emergency services reestablished. We can send half the new tubes there and the others to Boston. Per our discussion with Doctor Krause, we'll use national guard troops for that."

Hurst sat across the table and poured himself a tumbler of ice water. "How goes the war planning with Monk?"

Calvin unrolled a map of the U.S. east coast and swiveled it around so Hurst could see it. He slid his finger down the highway system from Fort Drum in New York State to Washington DC.

"Reconnaissance units from the 10th Mountain Division are moving toward Washington DC, with the rest of the division following. Their brief is to move in quietly—detect enemy strong points, encampments, roadblocks, that sort of thing—and report back. The divisional commander will deploy as he sees fit and then stand by for a 'go' command to assault. His focus will be to get Congress and the remainder of the House leadership back, clear out the government buildings, and return the city back under our control. I don't plan on doing anything until after Smith's attack tomorrow morning. If he succeeds, we can turn our full attention to the occupation forces."

Hurst sat up straight. "*If* he succeeds? You don't sound confident."

Calvin shrugged. "Nothing's certain in war, Keith. The old adage about counting chickens early applies here. We're still weak on the ground. One of the only advantages we have right now is the fact those PLA airborne troops are staying put. If they moved around, they could cause all sorts of havoc. They chose to occupy only strategic bases, and that leaves the rest available to us. They assumed we'd be helpless and wouldn't find a cure. They'll pay for that error."

Hurst took a sip of water. "Yeah, I've been wondering why they're remaining static so long. However, I'm not complaining. It makes the job of attacking them up a lot easier."

Calvin topped up his own water glass. "Monk thinks there are two reasons. First, they're guarding the strategic assets to deny us access, as we previously discussed. Second, because they arrived without mechanized transport, they can't easily get more supplies. They have a lot of mouths to feed. If we can encircle them, we can literally starve them out."

"Does that plan include Washington?" Hurst asked. "It sounds like you're treating that area differently."

Calvin folded his arms. "You're right. DC is a special case. We need to free any members of the House of Representatives and senior government officials. We can't let them keep the government hostage."

"Might make things go smoother if we keep them locked up," Hurst suggested with a wry smile. "Congress has been a huge pain in the ass lately."

Calvin sat forward, flicking an index finger at Hurst. "I know you're kidding, Keith, but don't say anything like that outside of this room. Yes, some are royal pains, but many are our friends."

"True enough." Hurst stood.

"Before you go, Keith. Carter is rounding up a Secret Service detail for you. It'll probably be in place tomorrow."

Hurst looked introspective for a moment. "I suppose I can't avoid that now, can I?"

Calvin shook his head. "Not as long as you hold the office."

"Damn."

* * *

General Secretary Gao gauged the mood in the Politburo's conference room before bringing the meeting to order. Everyone was reserved but still smiling and making and jokes. They were anticipating the convoy that would land the following day. *Excellent. If anyone had doubts, their countenance would be much different.* Gao rapped his knuckles on the polished wooden meeting table, getting their attention. "Comrades, shall we begin?"

Everyone settled in and turned their attention toward Gao.

"Landings are scheduled to commence in fourteen hours. The fleet commander, Rear Admiral Zhao Shouye, reports no issues. The fleet encountered moderately rough weather while transiting south of the Aleutian Islands, but only three dozen men have died on the voyage so far. No American opposition has emerged, nor have any submarines attempted to interdict our force."

Wei Sun gleefully rubbed his hands together and looked around the table. "Then gentlemen, we are set to establish the new eastern provinces."

Bohai Quishan agreed. "Matters have proceeded with excellent results. I must admit, I thought we'd encounter some form of problem, but our preparations and the North Korean misdirection have paid off handsomely. The discipline and effectiveness of our armed services is most commendable."

Shen leaned forward and placed his forearms on the wooden table. "Then we proceed with the landings?"

Gao heard some doubt in Shen's voice. *He has reservations?*

Before Gao could answer, Guoliang Jang did.

"Proceed? Of course we proceed. Why would you doubt our resolve at this stage of the operation?" Jang asked with a semi-mocking laugh.

Shen turned in his swivel chair to face Jang. "My dear comrade, I ask a simple question. There's no need to deride me for it. The Politburo's duty to the party demands we discuss all major decisions before they're made. Else why are we here? I repeat my question. Do we proceed?"

Jang said sharply, "You dare to lecture me on duty—"

"Comrade Jang, Shen is correct. A consensus is needed for all matters brought to Politburo's attention. While the operation has been previously approved, it's prudent to review progress from time to time. I'm sure Comrade Shen meant no insult by it." He looked over at Shen.

"None at all," Shen said calmly.

Jang collapsed back into his chair and nodded stiffly.

Jang is easily insulted and shall remember this supposed slight of Shen's for a long time. Shen has a lot thicker skin, and he's probably already forgotten the exchange. He should be careful. Jang has powerful allies. "Does anyone object to the operation proceeding as briefed?"

Silence surrounded the table.

Gao looked at his watch. "Very well, the landings will proceed. I propose we adjourn and reconvene in twelve hours."

* * *

General Smith's last meeting of the day broke up. As the other officers left flight ops through the doors, Captain Tyler entered, holding several pages of paper. She began to come to attention, but Smith held up a hand. "At ease, Captain. What do you have for me?"

"The report from the Marines sent to investigate Camp Pendleton, sir." She handed it over.

Smith was tired, and after dealing with paperwork all day, he didn't want to read it. He dropped the paperwork on his desk and rubbed his eyes. "Just give me a brief rundown on what they found."

"Yes, sir. Just after the fireworks took effect, seven Pendleton marines who didn't lose their sight decided the end of the world had come and ran the camp as their own dictatorship. They shot several officers, then they refused food and water to the rest unless they followed their instructions. Many of the female marines were badly abused. There's a lot of dead from malnutrition and dehydration. The survivors are in bad shape, and as a result, none of their units will be combat effective for some time."

Smith pulled his hand away from his eyes, disbelieving. Tyler's expression was so serious, though, that it had to be true. "What about the team we sent there?"

"Also shot. The tube they carried was smashed, and I suggest trying to get another there as soon as possible," Tyler said.

"Agreed, make it a priority. The seven marines are in custody?" Smith asked.

"Yes, sir. Four were killed when the marine platoon tasked to investigate moved in and came under fire. Two more were wounded. Only minor casualties in the platoon. What shall we do about this, sir?"

Camp Pendleton was a marine base, and marines from Twentynine Palms were involved in the assault. "We'll leave it with the C.O. of Twentynine Palms. He can assume command of that base in the short term and decide on next steps. This is a marine issue, so we'll let them sort it out. Anything else?"

"The pilot of the E-6 wanted me to tell you the aircraft is serviceable in all respects and ready to go. That's all for now, sir."

Smith nodded and stood. "Thanks. I'm going to go to my quarters. Pick me up there at midnight."

"Want me to drive you?" Tyler asked.

"No, I'll walk. I need the exercise, and it'll let me clear my head. That's all for now, Captain."

"Yes, sir."

July 16th

Chapter Twenty-Eight
Maneuvers

Captain Eric Reid walked through the USS *John Warner* command center and came up behind the sonar station. The sonar displays, which had been relatively blank during deployment to date, were now filled with target tracks. Reid tapped Tolly on the shoulder. "What do you have?"

Tolly pulled the headset earpiece clear of his right ear. "Thundering herd, sir. Multiple large vessels bearing three-zero-eight degrees. Three convergence zones away, so between sixty to eighty nautical miles range. They're throwing off a lot of noise, and I can't determine individual tracks, signatures, or speed, but they're definitely coming our way."

"Designate the convoy as 'Alpha.' Update the tactical plot as needed. Let me know when you have a ship count. If they change course, I need to know immediately. Keep an ear out for escorts—they'll be our first target. Watch for submarines, as well. The Chinese have some capable boats, and they could be hiding in that noise."

"Aye, sir." Tolly replaced his headphone cup over his ear.

Reid stepped around several on-duty crewmembers to get to the navigation table. XO Maddox waited for him. Using a ruler and fine-tip marker, Reid drew the enemy course on the map. The line passed within five nautical miles of the submarine's position. "They're coming. Bearing is three-zero-eight, ship count unconfirmed, and they're sixty to eighty miles away. That puts them here, over the Santa Lucia Escarpment, and that leaves us with a question."

"Which way will they go?" Maddox replied immediately. "Santa Barbara Basin north of the Channel Islands, or the deep water passage via Santa Cruz Basin to our east."

A period of silence passed as Reid studied the chart.

Maddox tapped the chart to indicate the island of San Miguel. "We can make a speed run to the western point of San Miguel and follow them whichever way they go."

Reid shook his head. "Normally, I'd agree, but remember we have the time restricting us. Smith wants us to hit them exactly at six. If we go where you suggest, we'll be early and have to trail them. Last speed report of the convoy was twenty knots. We'd have to go faster to overtake them, and we'd probably be heard if there's a sub in the area."

Another moment of silence passed. Reid finally pointed with the marker he held. "We're in a good position if they maintain course, so we'll stay here for now. If they do take the Santa Barbara Basin, we'll do a speed run between Santa Rosa and Santa Cruz islands to intercept. Either way, our timing holds."

"Affirmative. Shall I call General Quarters?" Maddox adjusted his baseball cap.

"No, not yet. We'll let the crew get breakfast in them first and give Tolly some time to firm up the target tracks. Have the Torpedo Room load four Harpoons in the tubes."

"Yes, sir." Maddox began to walk away.

"XO."

Maddox turned back. "Aye, sir?"

Reid said quietly, "Have them keep a Mark Fifty handy. If we do encounter a sub, I'll want something handy to throw at it."

"Aye, sir."

* * *

General Smith shifted his shoulders to get his seat restraints into a more comfortable position. The E-6 Mercury had just taken off from Hill Air Force Base and was climbing sharply. The navy flight crew seemed determined to get to their operational altitude quickly.

One of the naval communication staff spoke to him over his headset. "General, the encrypted satellite link is established. We have channels open to 4th Fighter Squadron, call sign Fujin, and 421st Fighter Squadron, call sign Widow. Fujin reports twenty-nine serviceable aircraft; Widow has fifteen. POTUS is also connected, call sign Zeus."

Smith keyed his microphone. He double-checked that the stated call signs agreed with his briefing notes for the operation; they did. "Roger, what's our call sign?"

"Caddy, sir."

"Thank you." Smith returned his attention to the screens in front of him. The map displayed was centered just west of Salt Lake City. The map re-centered regularly on the aircraft's position as it moved west. The Pacific coast of the United States was barely visible on the left side of his screen. They would get there in a little under two hours.

There was nothing else displayed on the map at the moment. The F-16s that would take part in the operation would not take off for some time.

The aircraft began flying straight and level.

A voice came over the headset. "This is the pilot. We're now at transit altitude."

Deciding to take advantage of the free time, Smith unlocked his seat restraints. He rose and went back to the small eating area to make coffee and grab a sandwich. When the shooting started, he wouldn't have time for a break.

* * *

Rear Admiral Zhao Shouye stood on the flying bridge of the Luyang-II Missile Destroyer *Lanzhou*. His binoculars were raised to his eyes, and he peered at the shores of the United

States for the first time. The dim coastline was half shrouded in fog and low cloud. At night, he would normally not be able to see it at all, but the rising sun, still well under the distant horizon, faintly backlit the skies and made the coast stand out.

He swung around to view the ships behind him. The large cargo vessels rode the seas magnificently, on their way to deliver a new dawn for these shores. He smiled broadly, reveling in the heady sensation of pride welling in his chest.

The mission had gone exactly as briefed so far. They'd be landing soon, and then the PLA troops would secure footholds on their new territories.

The sudden sound of an overhead helicopter distracted him. He lowered his binoculars to see a Kamov Ka-28 ASW helicopter fly over at low altitude. The convoy had a dozen of them surrounding his fleet, searching for American submarines. The ship he was on, the *Lanzhou*, and the other destroyer, *Haikou*, only had room for one helicopter onboard each. The rest were based from the tops of four container ships. The flat tops of the containers made for an excellent helicopter staging and refueling area.

Captain Hu Ming, commander of the *Lanzhou*, came up beside him. "Admiral, we have no contacts on radar and detect no opposition forces. I intend to turn the fleet and pass north of Santa Cruz Island. This shall—"

"No, Captain," Shouye said calmly. "Taking that route will force us between the shallow and restrictive coastal waters off Anacapa Island. We'll proceed on this course, then turn south of Santa Rosa and transit to our objective via the deep waters north of Santa Barbara."

Ming said nothing, but Shouye recognized his expression. *He does not agree with me. Damn him. I'm the superior officer, and he's a mere captain.* "You have your orders, Captain."

Ming nodded. "Yes, Admiral." He returned to the bridge leaving Shouye alone once more.

Shouye shook his head slowly before returning his binoculars to his eyes to continue scanning the horizon. *Ming has limited experience. I've been embarrassed on many occasions by our comrades in the PLAN submarine force when on exercises, because they use the turbulent coastal waters to their advantage and approach unheard. I shall not make that mistake here.*

Captain Ming obviously does not have the foresight necessary to rise further in rank. His next performance review shall reflect that.

* * *

"Captain, sonar," Reid heard over his headset. He walked over to the sonar station, tapping Tolly on the shoulder.

Tolly pulled aside an earpiece and pointed at his screens. "Sir, I've classified sixteen heavy merchantmen and two destroyer contacts. Destroyers are Luyang class, designated as Alpha 1 and Alpha 2. I have preliminary tracks, positions, and speeds on all vessels. No sub-surface contacts at this time."

"Good. Get the contact information to Chief Holgrim, and he can send it on to General Smith." Reid looked at the plot of the convoy, which was just passing to the west of San Miguel Island. "They didn't turn." *Thank God. That will make our life easier.*

Tolly turned a little more in his seat. "Sorry, sir?"

Reid realized he'd spoken out loud. "Nothing. Get those contacts over to CRSS. Do we have any contacts within ten nautical miles?"

"No, sir," Tolly answered.

"Very well."

Tolly returned his attention back to his screens.

"Pilot, bring the boat up to photonics depth," Reid ordered. To use the satellite communications, they needed to have their mast extended above the surface.

"Bring the boat to photonics depth, pilot aye," came the response from the officer steering the boat.

Reid made his way to the tactical plot table, joining his XO, who was placing the convoy track onto a large-scale chart of the waters off Los Angeles.

Maddox looked up, saw Reid, and returned his attention to the chart. "We're in a good position. The two escorts are positioned to the southeast and northwest of the convoy. If we transit here"—he pointed to a spot to the southwest—"we can hit the escorts simultaneously."

Reid looked at the chart. Maddox's finger was directly over Patton Ridge, an underwater escarpment under several thousand feet of water. "That works for me. I'll want dogleg courses set on each pair of Harpoons. If we can hit their escorts from both sides at the same time, we may confuse them as to how many subs are out here."

"Aye, sir. I'll set it up. What time do we launch?"

Reid picked up a pen and pulled out a reference chart for the UGM-84D Harpoon, listing its flight characteristics. He scribbled a series of calculations. "Flight time is five minutes, thirty-six seconds. To have them arrive exactly at six, we'll need to launch at oh-five fifty-four and twenty-four seconds. Agreed?"

Reid waited while Maddox double-checked his figures. "Yes, sir. I concur. I'll coordinate that with the navigator and make sure we're at the launch point on time."

* * *

Linda Krause worked from the large conference room in the Oak Ridge administration building. The space was overwhelmingly large when she worked alone, but convenient when she needed to meet with multiple people. She looked up at the map of the United States projected on the screen. All states surrounding Tennessee would have advance parties from the Tennessee National Guard in them by now. Their job was to cure National Guard units in those states, brief them how to use the tubes, and then return home to focus on their state's civilian population. The National Guard units in Missouri, Arkansas, Mississippi, Alabama, Georgia, Kentucky, North Carolina, and South Carolina would do the same thing. They were told not to go near any strategic bases for fear of tipping off the Chinese, but otherwise they would each begin healing their respective populaces.

By her rough calculations, there would be tubes in every contiguous state within four days. Not as fast as she would like, but good progress was being made at long last.

Hawaii and Alaska were also on her priority list. The big issue with those two states was the occupying Chinese troops. Some sort of covert mission would be needed, as inbound planes would probably be detected by radar. She would bring that point up with the vice president on their next scheduled call.

Then there was the world. One of the Oak Ridge management team had once worked for FedEx, and he was currently studying how to spread the cure globally. FedEx owned a few hundred aircraft and leased half again that number from other companies. Using them as a delivery vehicle for the tubes, with personnel to train others in their use, made a lot of sense. There was no need for packages until everyone had their sight back.

Following the tube cure, there would be millions of people emaciated, dehydrated, and malnourished. They would all need food, water, and medical care. She also needed to get the power stations operational, the water pumping stations active, and the sewer plants working. A lack of those facilities would produce all sorts of diseases.

The weight of the tasks ahead of her all seemed to press down on her at once. She closed her eyes and sighed deeply. She felt lost, wondering why she'd accepted this position.

She heard the door handle to the conference room being used. Her eyes opened, and Blake strode in with a mug in his hand. He closed the door behind him.

She went to meet him halfway.

"Here, I made you some hot choc—"

She ignored the mug and embraced him, barely holding back tears. "Just hold me, Oscar."

"What's wrong?" he asked as he held her with his free hand.

"There is so much to do! It's too much." She tightened her grip and held him quietly for a few moments.

"Do you know how to eat an elephant?" Blake asked.

She looked up at him, puzzled. "What did you say?"

"How do you eat an elephant?" he asked calmly, reassuringly.

"I don't know." Krause frowned, wondering what he was talking about.

"One bite at a time. You aren't expected to do everything at once, Linda. Just make your plan and let the people around you execute it. We're making progress, finally. People are getting better, the tube production line is ramping up, and soon the country will be healed. You're doing very well from what I've seen so far, and everyone here thinks you're the right person in the job."

She drove her face back into his chest and began to cry softly. She'd be all right in a few minutes, but for the moment, she needed to be in his arms.

* * *

General Smith's E-6 Mercury aircraft took up station in a racetrack oval-shaped position paralleling the west coast of Los Angeles at thirty-five thousand feet. The E-6 was twenty nautical miles inland and cruised at a slow rate to conserve fuel. The navy flight crew stayed well out of the theoretical range of the enemy search radar and kept their own radar off, to avoid detection.

The enemy convoy did have radar active, which could be detected on the aircraft ESM suite. He could see eight individual sets of slow-moving airborne radar operating in and around the fleet. His computer classified them as anti-submarine warfare contacts—or, more simply put, helicopters.

"General, incoming satellite message from the USS *John Warner*," a naval communications technician said over his headset.

Smith rolled his trackball over to the relevant section of his screen and opened the decrypted message, which he read quickly. The course, speed, position, convoy composition, and time of the sighting matched his own data from the aircraft ESM surveillance. Smith plotted the convoy position and direction on his digital map. The computer added a dotted line to show the projected course. He hovered his trackball pointer over that dotted line to see the time the convoy would be at that point, and he slid his pointer along the line until the time equaled zero six hundred.

He clicked to mark the position and sent its coordinates to the communication station on board. He keyed his headset mic. "Send this position to the squadron COs. Tell them to strike those coordinates at oh six hundred. Warn them there are multiple ASW helicopters in the area, and make sure you get an acknowledgement."

"Roger, sir," came the brief response.

Smith leaned back in his chair. That was all he could do. The wheels were in motion, his plan was active, and the rest was up to the USS *John Warner* and the strike force. From that point forward, unless something dramatically unexpected occurred, he would be a spectator only.

* * *

Captain Reid looked up from the tactical plot table and swept his eyes around the Control Center of the USS *John Warner*. Everyone had their heads down, focusing on their jobs. There was little to no conversation beyond what was needed to communicate needed information, and tension filled the air.

He was proud of them. "Weapons officer, what's the status of the torpedo tubes?"

"Sir, tubes one through four have Harpoons loaded. Data link is active on all weapons. Outer doors are closed."

Reid picked up the 1MC. The boat was already at General Quarters, but the crew had to know what was riding on this battle. "This is the captain... We'll be commencing our initial missile attack in a few minutes. Today we fight with no less than the future of our country in the balance. This is not an exercise. Attend to your duties, follow your orders to the best of your ability, and make sure all watertight doors are kept closed. Report any damage to the Control Center immediately. That is all."

Reid hung up the 1MC handset and spoke aloud. "Attention deck party. It's my intention to engage the pair of *Luyang* escort vessels with two Harpoons each. We shall then maneuver closer and engage the remainder of the fleet with ADCAPs." Reid checked the time on a nearby screen. "We'll begin launch procedures in six minutes."

Maddox came up and touched his elbow. He said quietly, "Captain, Wyatt is asking to see you. He says it's important."

Reid considered putting him off but decided he had time, and it would take his mind off things for a short time. "I'll be back in four minutes. XO has the conn."

"Yes, sir, I have the conn," Maddox replied.

Reid left the command center through the rear watertight hatch. The watertight doors were heavy and took considerable effort to move, but he was glad to see someone had recently greased the hinges. That made moving them a lot easier.

To get to the lockout trunk, he had to walk through the crew mess area, then up a set of stairs into crew berthing. This area was typically full of snoring crewmen, but with everyone at their battle stations, the area was deserted.

Two engineer mates were standing guard. One of them carried a well-worn red monkey wrench in his hands. The access door to the lockout trunk was closed.

"They give you any trouble?" Reid asked the senior mate. His name tag read "Farber."

"No, sir, they're as docile as baby lambs. They did ask to see you just before we sealed the hatch for General Quarters," Farber replied.

Reid jutted his chin toward the hatch. "Open it."

Farber handed the wrench off to the other engineer, turned the wheel in the center to release the dogs, and pushed open the access hatch. The circular hatch swung inward.

Wyatt was standing on the inside, waiting. "Good morning, Captain," he said pleasantly.

Reid had no patience for this mutineer. "I don't have a lot of time. What do you want, Wyatt?"

"Sir, we'd all like to ask permission to stand to our duties for the coming battle." Wyatt indicated the two other prisoners who appeared behind him. They both nodded agreement. "We know we're going to face a court-martial for what we did, but we want to defend our country. We'll come back here when done, and we won't be any trouble, sir."

Reid didn't have to think long about their request. "Due to your actions, Wyatt, two members of my crew are unable to stand to *their* duties. You are prisoners and shall remain so until we dock and the judge advocate general reviews the charges against you. Until we do tie up, you shall remain in this space."

He addressed Farber. "Close it up."

Farber pulled the door closed and latched it.

Reid turned toward the two guards. "That hatch remains closed until General Quarters ends. No one save me, the XO, and whoever delivers their food is to have access to them until further notice. Clear?"

"Aye, sir," said both men.

Reid turned on his heel and descended down to the mess. He stopped at the bottom of the stairs, closed his eyes for a moment, and took a deep cleansing breath. He needed to focus on the coming battle, so he dismissed the prisoners from his mind and returned to the command center.

* * *

Colonel "Advil" Harnell of the 4th Fighter Squadron flew a mere hundred feet above the surface of the Pacific Ocean. His five-point ejection harness held him securely in the seat of his F-16. Through his Perspex bubble canopy, he saw Santa Rosa Island directly ahead. He'd have to climb in altitude to get over the island in a few minutes, but for now, the island blocked radar emissions from the enemy and let him close on the convoy unseen. Smith's update on the convoy's position had forced a slight deviation in course, but the attack plan remained unchanged.

He scanned the skies all around him. The single-piece Perspex canopy afforded a wide view around the aircraft. Fang, his wingman, was closest to his wingtip, but two other fighters flew in close proximity.

Harnell had split his remaining twenty-eight F-16 fighters into three flights. He had started the day with twenty-nine, but one had developed a hydraulic failure on the runway and never took off. The lead group of six aircraft was slightly ahead, just barely visible. His own flight of twelve aircraft was followed by the final group of ten fighters.

Fighter pilots multitasked out of necessity. While flying toward Santa Rosa Island, Harnell kept checking the countdown clock on his HUD[41] while he scanned the skies for other aircraft. None were expected, but military intelligence was never taken as gospel in combat. He also double-checked his weapons were configured properly for release—performing all three tasks in under two seconds.

Radio silence was in effect, and everyone knew their responsibilities. He didn't speak and, keeping his eye on the countdown clock, flew closer to Santa Rosa.

---

[41] Heads Up Display

Chapter Twenty-Nine
The Engagement at Patton Ridge

Captain Eric Reid stood before the monitors for the photonics system to watch the Harpoon launch. The USS *John Warner* glided through the water at photonics depth. He'd already launched three successful Harpoons and was watching to make sure the fourth fired correctly.

The photonics mast video camera pointed toward the front of the sub. A sudden explosion of white water erupted as a long cylinder was thrown up from under the surface. A bright plume of white smoke issued from the back of the missile as the rocket booster ignited. The auto-exposure feature in the photonics camera struggled to adjust for the sudden brightness of the motor.

The flight arc of the Harpoon leveled out. Reid zoomed in to follow the missile. The watertight case and rocket booster stage fell away in segments, letting the air-breathing turbojet take over. The Harpoon descended in altitude until it skimmed the surface of the water. After that point, the clean-burning motor left no visible smoke trail, and he lost sight of it. "Chief Holgrim, send my message."

Seconds later, Holgrim confirmed, "Message sent, sir."

Reid stepped away from the photonics station and strode to the tactical plot. "Lower all masts. Pilot, make your depth five hundred feet. Ahead two-thirds. Come to course three-three-zero."

"Make my depth five hundred feet, ahead two-thirds; come to course three-three-zero, pilot aye," responded the helmsman.

"Weapons officer, load ADCAPs in all tubes," Reid said as he passed the weapons station.

"Load ADCAPs in all tubes, aye sir," the weapons officer replied.

By the time he got to the plot table, Commander Maddox had already added the projected courses for the four Harpoon missiles. "First Harpoon will be on target exactly at zero six hundred, Captain. They will hit them as they travel over Patton Ridge here." He pointed at the spot on the chart.

"Good. Hopefully, that should give the Chinese something to think about." Reid tapped the chart, indicating a position near the convoy's projected path. "Once we get here, we'll slow to four knots and scout out the escorts. If they're still a danger, we'll neutralize them, and then turn our attentions to the convoy."

"You're assuming the air force will leave us something to torpedo, Captain?" Maddox asked with good humor.

"Container ships can be up to three hundred and fifty thousand tons displacement. Aircraft can't carry much heavy ordnance, and nukes were ruled out, so I'm sure we'll get a chance." Reid stared at the tactical plot, trying to embed the chart contents into his brain for later use.

Maddox nodded. "I'm going to get coffee? Want some?"

Reid looked up and nodded. "Yeah, thanks."

Maddox left, leaving Reid to study the chart, running various attack scenarios through his mind.

* * *

A naval communications technician spoke to General Smith over his headset. "Message from the USS *John Warner* for you, sir."

"Thank you." Smith opened the message on his computer display. He ignored the header information and focused on the single short paragraph. It read:

Chinese Luyang destroyers positively identified by ESM contact. Successfully launched four Harpoons at escorts. Time of impact: 0600. Maneuvering to engage convoy.

Smith checked his tactical plot. The 4th Fighter Squadron would be striking soon. His anxiety level rose sharply. His whole offensive force was nowhere near as large as he'd wanted.

He closed his eyes for a moment and silently prayed in earnest for the first time in a long time.

* * *

Colonel "Advil" Harnell watched the countdown timer as the last five seconds incremented down, seemingly in slow motion. When the counter reached "00:00:00", he keyed his VHF radio to a frequency that only his squadron would hear. "Fujin flight, execute climb. Buster. Weapons free."

In the right ear of his headset, the two other flight leaders acknowledged, using their nicknames.

"Mayo."

"Ripper."

Harnell yanked back on his control stick and advanced his throttle to full military power. His weight doubled due to the G forces, and he was pressed back into the ejection seat. He climbed sharply in altitude and glanced over both shoulders. He could see the rest of his flight following him.

The increase in altitude would make them detectable on radar, but they needed the additional height for the weapons to launch properly.

Harnell's threat receiver squawked a warning tone as an enemy ship radar swept across his aircraft. He activated electronic countermeasures followed by his own radar system, and began scanning for targets.

* * *

In the Combat Information Center of the PLAN Missile Destroyer *Lanzhou*, Rear Admiral Zhao Shouye smiled to himself, wondering if he could find an American restaurant to dine in that evening. He'd read of the five-star Beverly Hills Hotel and wondered if he could stay there at some point in his trip.

"Multiple airborne contacts bearing zero-two-four degrees, altitude one thousand meters, climbing rapidly! Range three-zero nautical miles; speed nine hundred kilometers per hour!" called out the radar operator, interrupting his daydreaming.

Admiral Shouye spun around, ready to scream at the man. *What does he think he's doing? I haven't authorized any exercises!*

Shouye never got a chance to say anything as Captain Ming ordered, "Sound General Quarters. Signal the *Haikou* and the rest of the convoy of our actions. Activate missile batteries, and fire control radar. Get me a count on the enemy force."

A klaxon sounded throughout the ship, and men began running into the CIC. Hatches were sealed, and red lighting turned on as overhead white lights snapped off. The officers and men in CIC pulled on white fabric hoods and gloves to protect from flash fires.

As the klaxon tone ended, the radar operator said, "I count over a hundred—no, a hundred and twenty high-speed aircraft. They're passing three thousand meters and climbing rapidly. No IFF detected."

"Weapons Officer, attempt to cut through their jamming. You may engage the aircraft with missiles," Ming ordered.

Shouye could take no more. "Captain, I did not receive notification of an exercise."

Ming looked at him with a piercing look. "This is no drill, Admiral. We're under attack."

What? "An attack by over a hundred aircraft? Impossible! The party assured us—"

Ming pointed at the radarscope, and spoke over him. "The Americans are using jammers to create false targets, sir. Our countermeasures will eliminate them in time."

Shouye took a breath to argue that they couldn't possibly be under attack, but the radar operator spoke again. "Two new contacts, bearing two-two-zero degrees, range two-zero nautical miles, speed eight-six-zero kilometers per hour. Flight profile and radar cross section suggests Harpoon anti-ship missiles, Captain."

Ming called out, "Weapons officer, engage incoming Harpoons with the hundred-millimeter gun. Place CIWS[42] in standby."

"Aye, sir."

* * *

Colonel Harnell reached fifteen thousand feet and keyed the squadron channel on his VHF radio while pressing his stick forward to level out. "Mayo flight, Advil. Light 'em up."

"Mayo," came the calm acknowledgement.

Major "Mayo" Sinclair had been put in charge of the lead six aircraft. Each was configured with a pair of HARMs[43]. They homed in on enemy radar signals. Harnell had briefed each pilot to send one HARM missile at each escort ship.

Each pilot confirmed over the radio as he successfully launched his missiles.

"Mayo, magnum."

"Teacup, magnum."

"Grouch, magnum."

---

[42] Close-In Weapons System - A point-defense weapon of limited range, designed to destroy inbound missiles. Typical CIWS designs incorporate radar, computers, and multi-barrel guns that fire rapidly. They are typically the last line of defense against inbound missiles.

[43] High-speed Anti-Radiation Missiles

As they did, Harnell saw a series of white smoke trails heading toward the convoy at high speed.

* * *

The radar operator shouted so loudly that Admiral Shouye jumped in surprise. "Missile detection! Multiple inbounds bearing zero-two-five, speed two-two-zero-zero kilometers per hour. Profile suggests anti-radiation missiles."

Captain Ming shouted, "Weapons officer, inbound missiles are priority target! Engage."

"Aye, sir."

Admiral Shouye felt in a daze. *How can Americans be attacking? The senior admirals of the plan assured me there would be no resistance!* Shouye looked over the shoulder of the radar operator. To the north was a confused mass of dots—the American strike force and their false targets. A dozen dots were moving rapidly toward the center of the screen.

That center point was the ship he was on.

A series of rapid thumps vibrated the ship. Shouye felt them through the soles of his shoes. *Those are our anti-air missiles. Let them attack. Our missiles will stop theirs. Yes, how could it be any other way?*

Dots appeared near the center of the radar screen and moved away rapidly. A notation on the radar screen showed the outbound missiles were traveling at over five thousand kilometers per hour. The dots of the inbound HARM missiles met the dots representing the outbound HHQ9-A missiles at ten nautical miles from the *Lanzhou*. Four dots vanished, but eight dots continued toward the center of the screen.

"Turn off all search and fire control radars. Increase speed to flank, hard to port!" Captain Ming ordered.

Turn off the—? Shouye couldn't believe his ears. Missiles needed radar guidance to hit their targets. With no radar, their HHQ9-A missiles were useless, and he needed those missiles active to protect himself. "Belay that order—keep firing!"

Captain Ming whirled around, screaming, "What are you doing? Those missiles home in on the radar!"

"Keep firing, Captain. We'll soon defeat this—"

"The missiles are within our minimum range, sir," Ming objected. "There is no time for another launch!"

A deep rumbling sounded throughout the ship.

"That's the CIWS. Sound collision! Brace for impact!" Ming screamed.

An explosion rocked the ship to starboard. It was followed almost immediately by a second, directly on top of them, then a third, farther back.

Shouye found himself on his back, looking up at the thick electrical cables near the ceiling. Thick gray smoke roiled in between him and the cables. The red lighting had faded somewhat. *Did someone turn off the lights?* He tried to sit up but couldn't. The wind had been knocked out of his lungs, and he fell back onto the deck. He took a couple of deep breaths and then sat up.

He grabbed the back of a nearby chair and pulled himself off the floor. The smoke caused his eyes a little discomfort, but it was nothing he couldn't handle. His head swam, and he steadied himself with the chair. Several crew members surrounding him still sat in their places. They were not moving.

He looked up and was amazed to see a meter-wide hole in the thick armor plating that surrounded CIC. Daylight streamed into CIC, overriding the few red lights that were still lit. Even dazed, he still remembered his duty. "Captain Ming, damage report."

Hearing no reply, Shouye turned to see Captain Ming impaled on a piece of thick structural steel that had been driven completely through the center of his chest. The left side of his head was missing, and blood completely covered that side of his body.

Shouye screamed and backed away, tripping over more bodies and falling to the deck beside the lower half of a seaman. He vomited and continued screaming as he scrambled away from the dead on his elbows.

* * *

The time had come for Harnell's flight to launch their weapons. "Advil flight, engage. Fang, Igor, Toad, target the escorts. The rest of you, the convoy. Make each shot count."

Harnell's group of ten fighters carried a loadout of AGM-65 Maverick missiles. He selected one of them, and a light flashed on in his cockpit, indicating the gyro had spun up on that weapon. Using his thumb, he moved the infrared television camera on the Maverick's nose to search for a target. He found an escort destroyer with several hot spots indicating fires. It still floated and had to be considered dangerous.

He depressed the track switch, aligned the crosshairs on the TV display in the cockpit with the waterline of the destroyer, and released. The weapon locked on successfully. He pulled the trigger on his flight stick and fired the Maverick. It flew at the target at over a thousand kilometers an hour.

Harnell didn't need to check on the weapon any further. It would correct its own flight until impact, then the hundred and twenty-five-pound shaped-charge warhead would do its job.

"Advil, rifle," he radioed. Others in his flight also made "rifle" calls, meaning they'd had successful Maverick launches.

Mayo's fighters could only carry two HARMs, whereas Harnell had six Mavericks loaded. He selected another.

* * *

Admiral Shouye pulled himself off the floor and away from the bodies. He desperately needed fresh air. He ran out of CIC, turned down a short corridor past several members of a damage control party, and exited onto the side of the ship through a starboard-side hatch.

He grasped the railing and took in deep lungfuls of air to calm himself. The ship had slowed, but was still moving forward. *I survived! No thanks to Ming and his inability to grasp basic tactics. His death was appropriate. I need to take command and make sure nothing like this happens again. Indeed—*

"Keep the hatch closed! We're at General Quarters!" yelled angry voice behind him. Shouye turned in time to see the hatch slam shut and the wheel spin, securing it. He had no idea who had spoken to him.

Irritated he had been addressed in that tone, he reached for the hatch wheel to confront the shouter. Before getting there, he felt a deep vibration through his feet again, but this time accompanied by a deafening *BRRRRRRRRRR* that penetrated his entire body.

He slapped his hands over his ears to protect them from the brutal sound. *That's the CIWS going off.*

Harpoon missiles were a lot slower than the HARMs, and Harpoons had been coming. Shouye twisted around to face the stern. The starboard CIWS was firing at something. He followed the line of tracers and saw a small white dot approach. The tracers met the object three hundred meters from the side of the ship, and it exploded immediately.

Shouye raised his hands in celebration, but metal fragments from the exploded Harpoon struck his side of the ship like a shotgun. As he ducked behind the railing, he saw several pieces of debris strike the CIWS radome. The CIWS weapon barrels pointed straight up and stayed there.

Shouye stood to look at the damage and found his legs shaking. He shook his head to clear it. The damage to the CIWS looked minor, and he vowed to have a crewman look at that weapon immediately. He began to turn back to the hatch when another white dot caught his attention on the horizon.

The CIWS didn't fire this time. He looked at the damaged CIWS then back at the Harpoon. It seemed to be coming straight at him.

Shouye dashed for the hatch.

His hand touched the hatch wheel just as the Harpoon exploded, turning him into a fine red mist.

* * *

Harnell was about to release his third Maverick at the destroyer centered on his cockpit screen when a massive explosion tore through the ship. The vessel heeled over to the port side, paused briefly, and then broke in two pieces. "Fang, Igor, Toad, the closest escort has broken in half and is sinking. Focus on the other."

They all acknowledged by stating their call signs.

Harnell swept the infrared television camera around, looking for the other escort ship. He knew its rough location from his radar but couldn't see it through the haze.

A strained voice came over his headset, "Stoner's hit! SAM got him—he's going down."

Harnell never got a chance to respond. The warning tone indicating weapons lock sounded in his ears. Someone had locked a fire control radar onto his fighter.

As he fired his weapons, his aircraft had gotten so close to the convoy that his jamming was no longer effective. The tone changed to a warbling shriek. A surface-to-air weapon had been fired at him. Checking his Radar Warning Receiver Threat Indicator just under his HUD, he could see the missile was coming from his portside and forward.

Forgetting the Maverick for the moment, Harnell jinked his fighter to port while releasing both chaff and flares to confuse the incoming missile. He searched for the SAM below, considering his options. He had good speed and altitude, which gave him room to maneuver. He could also pull several Gs easily. *There I see it. Fast sucker. I'm only going to get one shot at this.*

Remembering his training, Harnell pulled back hard on the stick, inducing a force equal to eight times the force of gravity. The G-suit around his legs inflated to restrict the amount of blood being pulled into his lower extremities. He grunted from the weight of his own body, which now felt eight times greater.

He released more chaff and flares. Just before the missile reached him, he reversed the turn, hoping to confuse the seeker head. Tunnel vision developed quickly from the pressure—if he kept this up, he would black out. With the alternative being a fiery explosive death, he kept pulling back on the stick.

The SAM missed, barely. It flew so close, he was sure he could have reached out and touched its fins if the canopy hadn't been in the way.

He relaxed his hand on the flight stick, and the heavy G load disappeared. Sweat coated his entire body. Directly in front of him was the destroyer he'd been searching for. He selected, aimed, and fired a Maverick in under three seconds. "Advil, rifle."

"Fang, rifle," he heard over his headset.

A white streak appeared from his right, heading toward the destroyer. He jumped in surprise. Looking over his shoulder, he saw Fang off his wingtip. Incredibly, his wingman had matched his violent maneuvers and remained in position.

Harnell took the opportunity to launch another Maverick at the destroyer.

The squadron radio frequency came to life. "Advil? Bing. Stoner's down, no chute."

In between other "rifle" reports, another voice came over the squadron channel. "Advil? Zephyr. The container ships have troops with shoulder-launched SAMs. I saw at least a dozen launched off one ship alone."

Harnell hit his transmit button. Those were *his* men dying out there. They needed to be warned. "Roger Zephyr. Fujin flight, beware of man-portable SAMs from the container ships."

Someone screamed over the squadron frequency. "I'm hit! I'm—"

A fireball several kilometers away caught his attention, and tumbling debris fell from the sky. Harnell watched a Maverick impact on the waterline of the destroyer with satisfaction. The large hole in the port side let water gush into the ship, and the destroyer already had a slight list.

Further away, container ships had also been hit by multiple Mavericks. His people were landing multiple hits, but the hundred and twenty-five-pound warheads were like bee stings against the huge ships. They needed weapons with a much larger warhead. Fortunately, he had brought some. He turned his jet hard to the left to open the distance up between him and the destroyer. "Ripper, bring in your heavies. Mayo, buddy lase for him."

"Ripper."

"Mayo."

Ripper led the last flight of twelve aircraft. They carried laser-guided GBU-24, two thousand-pound bombs that would make holes the target ships couldn't ignore. Mayo and his jets had no more HARM missiles, but they did have LANTIRN[44] pods attached to their undersides. They would use the lasers on those pods to designate targets for Ripper and his jets.

Harnell checked his fuel state. At his current rate of fuel consumption, he only had enough gas for another six or seven minutes of combat.

While Mayo and Ripper did their jobs, Harnell flew down the length of the convoy to assess the effectiveness of the strike so far. He stayed several nautical miles away from the ships to avoid their SAMs.

Black smoke issued from most container ships, but none had stopped. White frothy bow waves showed the ships were still moving at a rapid pace toward Los Angeles. Harnell spotted a helicopter skimming over the crests of the waves ahead of him. He armed a Sidewinder missile and, hearing the growl of the seeker head locking on, fired it.

"Advil, fox two," he announced as the missile left the aircraft. The heat-seeking Sidewinder, attracted by the hot

---

[44] Low Altitude Navigation and Targeting Infrared for Night. Mounted on F-15, F-16 aircraft, LANTIRN allows a variety of precision guided weapons to be launched in all weather conditions and light levels.

engine exhaust, reached the helicopter and exploded under the rotor blades, blowing them off. The helicopter tumbled and spun heavily into the ocean. "Advil, splash one helicopter."

The squadron frequency came to life as Ripper's pilots dropped their two thousand-pound laser guided bombs.

"Donavan, long rifle."

"Ripper, long rifle."

"Jester, long rifle."

The calls continued until all of them had indicated a guided weapon launch.

Harnell reached the end of the convoy and took the opportunity to reverse course. As he got halfway down the convoy, the bombs began striking their targets. Each bomb had a delay fuse, so they would detonate inside the ships. Harnell saw one bomb impact the ship beside him, directly in the middle of the vessel. The five rows of stacked containers above the point of the explosion were thrown high in the air. The containers landed in the sea and bobbed on the waves.

Hundreds of tracer rounds began issuing in random directions from one floating container. Several secondary explosions were visible on the ship as it turned out of line. *That's a kill,* he thought with a brief smile.

More explosions registered along the convoy as more bombs found their mark.

He saw a RoRo ship hit by a pair of two thousand-pound bombs almost simultaneously. Gouts of flame erupted from the smokestacks, and the upper deck bent upwards. Several secondary explosions came from inside, and dense black smoke came out. Harnell could see dozens of blazing men jumping off the boat deck into the sea several stories below.

Harnell's radar warning receiver chirped as the destroyer's radar swept across him. Surprised the destroyer was still capable of combat, he ordered, "Advil flight, use your last Mavericks and target that last destroyer."

Tracers lanced up into the sky from the destroyer. An aircraft had gotten within range of its CIWS. The F-16 twisted to get away, but tracers intercepted, and it disintegrated. Parts of the dead airframe arced downward and impacted into the sea. The pilot hadn't ejected.

Harnell toggled a Maverick and fired it at the destroyer. "Advil, rifle," he said with grim determination.

Several more pilots called out "rifle" shots as well.

He watched as six other missiles joined his, striking the destroyer on the port side by the waterline in succession. The destroyer heeled and listed heavily to port. The deck touched the surface of the ocean, and the ship capsized. The ship's two massive propellers, now in the open air, slowed to a stop.

A last Maverick blew a hole in the side of the ship. Seawater rushed in, and the hull got lower and lower in the water. With the destroyer no longer a threat, Harnell checked his fuel state; it was time to leave.

Pulling his fighter around until it pointed east, he told his squadron, "Fujin flight, bug out to beta. Repeat. Bug out to beta." He steered toward the coordinates designated as "beta," where the squadron would reform, well away from the convoy.

He keyed his UHF radio to speak to Colonel "Stretch" McConvey of 421 Squadron. "Widow One-One, Fujin One-One. You're clear to engage."

"Widow One-One," came the terse reply. All fifteen jets of 421 Squadron would now engage, each aircraft carrying a pair of GBU-24, two thousand pound laser-guided bombs, to finish off the last of the surviving ships.

Harnell turned his attention to getting back to LAX. He hoped more weapons had arrived by cargo plane, and he could load up for another strike. He didn't think it would be necessary, but he couldn't assume anything with the invasion force.

Besides, even if this convoy was sunk, there were still three airborne divisions on American soil, and that pissed Harnell off to no end.

* * *

Merchant Marine Captain Deng stood on the bridge of his ship, looking out through his binoculars at the carnage surrounding his vessel. He'd been master of the *Feng Mìngyùn* cargo container ship for five years, and he had never seen devastation on this level before. Columns of black smoke rose from several nearby vessels.

His usual cargo run from Qingdao to Yokohama, Japan, was seldom exciting. Indeed, he typically spent most of the transit time reading books. However, on this trip, he hadn't read a single page. Deng dropped his binoculars from his watery eyes. Keeping his composure was becoming a challenge. He had passed dozens of containers floating in the water, with desperate men clinging to them and waving for assistance. Seeing fellow sailors drowning only a hundred feet from his ship brought a lump to his throat. He cast his eyes around the bridge. The bridge crew's faces as they performed their duties showed the same concern and worry he felt.

The law of the sea demanded he stop and render assistance, but PLA Major General Xie stood on the bridge nearby. Po's leather pistol holster was still unsnapped. The general had undone it earlier as a threat when Deng had tried to stop his ship to assist the men in the water. Xie had made it quite clear that the ship was to make it to port as quickly as possible. According to Po, anyone who disobeyed "the will of the party" would be shot.

Of further concern, Deng's ship had taken two small missile hits, opening holes in the hull at the waterline on his port side.

The bridge phone rang. Glad for the distraction, Deng grabbed it. "Bridge, Captain."

The voice on the other end was breathing hard and quickly said, "Chief Engineer Huang, Captain. We've sealed watertight doors on both affected compartments open to the sea. Pumps are working but cannot keep up with the inflow. The ship's speed is driving water into the hull faster than we can pump it out. We need to slow down and counterflood to bring the port side of the ship up above the waterline. Then the pumps can clear the compartments, and we can get in there to fix the holes. We can do nothing at twenty knots!"

Deng didn't even consider asking Xie for permission to slow the ship. "We cannot slow. We shall be in port in five hours and shall conduct repairs at that time."

Huang answered curtly, "If we lose any more watertight compartments, we'll be on the bottom long belong before that!"

"Do your best, Chief Engineer. We shall maintain speed until we get to port." Deng had to tear the phone from his ear as Huang slammed his phone in response. Shaking his head in empathy, Deng hung up the handset.

A PLA private that Xie used as a messenger ran into the bridge. He stopped by Po, braced and saluted. "Comrade General, a second flight of aircraft approaches. Major Hu reports they are F-16 fighters and asks permission to fire on them."

"Permission granted," said Xie. His accent revealed him as from the Sichuan region.

The private saluted and ran out the way he came.

Deng returned his binoculars to his eyes. From his vantage point on the bridge near the rear of the ship, he had an unobstructed view of the containers before him. Along the tops of the metal boxes, several dozen pairs of men stood with shoulder-fired QianWei 18 anti-air missiles. Each firing team wore black goggles to protect themselves from the solid rocket motor when it ignited. Xie claimed they had killed eight fighter-bombers already, but Deng doubted that boast. He'd only seen one fighter crash into the sea, and that was well outside the five-kilometer effective range of the QianWei 18s.

A flurry of activity caught his attention near the bow. Three missile teams fired in the same direction. Using his binoculars, Deng followed the smoke trail. A rapidly moving black dot, high in the sky, caught his attention. It seemed to be heading directly for him. As it got closer, the shape of a bomb was unmistakable. "Sound collision!"

A klaxon reverberated throughout the vessel. Everyone grabbed a railing or otherwise braced themselves. Deng put his head down and waited for his own death.

Deng felt the low vibration of impact. He tensed up, closed his eyes, and waited for the inevitable explosion.

After two seconds, he opened his eyes. Nothing had happened. "Get me a report on the damage!" he ordered while standing.

The soldiers on the containers fired off several more missiles, immediately reloaded their launchers, then began jumping up and down in excitement. Deng looked in the direction that they were pointing and saw an F-16 on fire as it entered the sea.

A parachute floated down from a thousand feet in the air. Deng heard rifle shots and walked out of the bridge onto the portside fly bridge. By the ship's railing below, he saw a line of PLA soldiers shooting at the descending pilot. A soldier ran over to them and placed the barrel of a long machine gun on the rail. He squeezed off several long bursts toward the pilot.

Multiple rounds impacted the sea. The pilot entered the water and was covered by the canopy of his parachute. The soldiers kept firing as the ship passed.

Slowly, the canopy disappeared under the waves until there was nothing but open ocean. Someone below him yelled, and the firing ceased.

The bridge phone rang, and Deng moved to it in a hurry. He picked up the handset. "Bridge, Captain."

"Chief Engineer Huang. A bomb passed all the way through the hull without exploding. We were lucky—it appears to have been a dud. There's a fifty-centimeter hole between the two main engine mounts, and we're taking on water, but the pumps are able to keep up. Two hours to repair."

"Carry on, Huang." Deng hung up, breathed out hard, and closed his eyes to thank his ancestors. They'd been lucky. A large bomb going off between the main engines would have caused catastrophic damage.

A loud distant explosion caused him to open his eyes. Three nautical miles away, large chunks of a container ship's hull arced away from a huge fireball. *They're doomed.*

Deng scanned the horizon. He saw only two other vessels still underway besides his own ship. Both had heavy smoke issuing from them. He turned toward Po. "General, it's my intention to break convoy formation and make my own way to port as best speed. With only a few surviving ships and no naval escorts, staying in formation makes no sense."

Xie looked out over the ocean silently for a moment before facing Deng again. "I concur. Proceed to the closest dock, at best speed."

Deng grabbed the dual handles of the nearby engine order telegraph and moved the arrow until it pointed at "Full Ahead" on both engines. A bell sounded. Five seconds later, an engineer below acknowledged the order, and the bell sounded a second time.

The vibration from the engines soon increased, as the ship accelerated to full speed.

* * *

The USS *John Warner* had reached the convoy's projected location and slowed to increase sonar effectiveness. Captain Reid looked over at Tolly, who was working to update the plots for the convoy. Tolly was hunched over his console, minutely adjusting his controls. Reid didn't bother him; Tolly would report when he had something.

Reid had no idea how well his Harpoon attack had gone. For the moment, he didn't think about it. Right now he had a convoy to attack.

"Conn, sonar. All convoy tracks have been updated," Tolly called out.

"Thank you," Reid said as he walked over to the plot table. From the tactical plot display, he could see a number of ships had disappeared, including the two destroyer escorts. Only five container ships and one RoRo were left. That was good news. Now he just needed to sink them.

A few ships were on a course to the ports of Los Angeles and Long Beach. He needed to take care of those first, then he could double back and sink the stragglers.

Reid turned to the pilot station. "Pilot, come to course—"

Tolly's voice came over Reid's headset, interrupting him. "Conn, sonar. Transient, definitely sub-surface, bearing zero-two-four. Designating contact Sierra Two."

Reid hurried to the sonar station. He met the XO's eyes as he passed him. Maddox looked concerned. He had a right to be. An enemy submarine in the area changed things. They needed to take it out before engaging the convoy.

Tolly had his headset cup pulled back when he got there. "Someone just dropped a heavy piece of machinery, skipper. Heard it plain as day. Definitely a sub. No more than a nautical mile range. His depth is between two to four hundred feet."

Reid slapped Tolly on the shoulder. "Well done." He grabbed the handset for the 1MC and announced to the entire crew, "Rig for ultra-quiet." They couldn't risk being heard by the enemy.

The sub was already at battle stations, but he did have a problem. There were four ADCAPs loaded in the torpedo tubes. He could use one against the enemy sub, but the six hundred and fifty-pound explosive warhead was overkill. The Mark 50 lightweight torpedo had a smaller shaped-charged warhead and would work more effectively, but he didn't have one loaded. Reid made his way back to the tactical plot table. "Weapons officer, load a Mark Fifty in tube one."

"Load Mark Fifty in tube one, aye," responded the weapons officer.

"Pilot, make your depth four hundred feet. Reduce speed to four knots and come to course zero-four-five."

"Depth four hundred feet, speed four knots, course zero-four-five, pilot aye."

"Sonar, conn. Report Sierra Two information as it develops."

"Conn, sonar, aye," Tolly replied.

By turning toward the source of the transient noise, Reid hoped to firm up the enemy sub's location without giving away his own position. Now he had to be patient. That was tough, for he knew the convoy ships were making a break for the ports—but if he sped after them, the Chinese sub would hear him, and then he'd be the hunted. He had to kill that sub first.

Reid studied the tactical plot map. He calculated he had three hours to kill the sub before the eastbound ships were beyond his reach. He made eye contact with Maddox. "Get down to the Torpedo Room." He didn't say why and didn't have to. Maddox moved off in a hurry.

The attempted mutiny had cost him three Torpedo Room crew, and loading operations would be slower as a result. He hoped Maddox could inspire them to load faster.

Tolly said softly over Reid's headset, "Conn, sonar. I'm getting something on the towed array. Suggest we come to zero-two-zero to firm it up."

Reid didn't hesitate. "Pilot, come to course zero-two-zero."

"Course zero-two-zero, pilot aye."

Reid leaned forward, placing his knuckles on the tactical plot table. Waiting was the hardest part of his job.

A minute later, the weapons officer said, "Mark Fifty loaded in tube one. Tubes ready in all respects, outer doors are closed."

"Thank you." Reid checked his watch. They'd made decent time swapping out the torpedoes. He returned his knuckles to the table. He couldn't do anything else until the course, depth, and speed of the enemy submarine had been established.

Chapter Thirty
Ripples in the Pond

General Smith stretched as best as he could within the tight seat restraints on the E-6. Overall, he was happy with the attack. There had been losses among the two F-16 squadrons, including Colonel "Stretch" McConvey of 421 Squadron, who had been hit by at least two surface-to-air missiles while on a bomb run. His parachute had been seen by other pilots.

He watched those surviving ships on his radar screen. Three helicopter targets were visible, as well. After the destroyers had been confirmed as sunk, he had the navy crew turn on the aircraft radar. As long as he stayed clear of the man-portable surface-to-air missiles, they were perfectly safe. Four of the large vessels were dead in the water. Only two continued to move toward the docks. One was on course to Los Angeles and the other to Long Beach. Smith hoped Captain Reid could intercept at least one with his submarine. If not, the marine and army units would be getting a fight.

Smith decided he needed to update the president and keyed his microphone on the encrypted satellite link. "Zeus, this is Caddy."

Immediately President Calvin's voice answered, "Caddy, Zeus. Go ahead."

Smith condensed the multiple reports he had received into simple terms. "Only six vessels remain. Four are dead in the water; two are on route to L.A. and Long Beach. Our submarine assets should be intercepting them as we speak."

"What were our losses?"

"Nine F-16s were shot down, five returned to base damaged," Smith summarized.

Calvin paused then asked, "Can we do anything for the pilots who bailed out?"

"With no Coast Guard or naval search and rescue assets active, I doubt it, sir. If they made it into the water, they have survival training, and the Channel Islands are nearby." Smith tried to sound positive, but realistically, the water was cold, and chances of survival were slim without someone to assist them.

"How long can you remain on station?"

Smith clicked a button and brought up a series of numbers displaying the aircraft fuel state, which the navigator kept updated. "Four hours, sir."

"Keep me updated."

"Yes, sir. Caddy out." Smith clicked his controls until the radar image returned, with the current position of the two moving ships. He had to warn the marine and army units of the incoming threat, so he activated his microphone. Captain Reid would do his best to keep the ships from reaching land, but in combat, he couldn't take anything for granted.

* * *

Captain Reid's head snapped up from the tactical plot table when Tolly said, "Conn, sonar. Sierra Two, broadband contact, bearing zero-three-five, speed twelve knots, depth four-five-zero feet, range eight-zero-zero. The Q-70 computer identifies Sierra Two as a type zero-niner-five class sub. I concur with that assessment, skipper."

The Type 095 subs were the newest the Chinese military had. Reid had been briefed that they only had two in service. Their full capabilities were unknown, but it was a nuclear attack submarine of a foreign power. They were within U.S.

territorial waters and therefore were a viable target in his eyes. "Sonar, conn. Good work. Attention, deck party. I intend to engage submerged contact, Sierra Two. Weapons officer, report tube status."

"Tubes ready in all respects, outer doors are closed," answered Lieutenant Palas, the weapon officer.

Reid nodded to himself. "Firing point procedures, Sierra Two. Covert launch, tube one primary, tube two backup. Open outer door on tube one."

Palas said, "Tube one, outer door open."

Petty Officer Graham manned the fire control console. "Weapon ready."

Reid glanced over at the fire control console. He saw nothing untoward that would stop him from firing. "Final bearing and shoot."

Graham called out, "Set."

Palas commanded, "Shoot."

Graham raised a small plastic cover and pressed the switch below. "Fire tube one."

There was no traditional loud rush of compressed air announcing the launch. Reid had ordered a covert launch and the torpedo swam out of the torpedo tube under its own power. This allowed it to be a lot quieter than normal.

Palas said, "Torpedo course zero-four-two, run to enable."

Now Reid just had to wait as the torpedo swam closer. Several tense moments passed. No one spoke.

Palas called out, "Torpedo is at the enable point. Recommend applying TELCOM for system solution."

Reid saw no reason to override the weapons officer's recommendation and said, "Apply TELCOM."

Palas said, "TELCOM applied. Terminal homing."

"Conn, sonar. Sierra Two's cavitating," Tolly reported.

Cavitation meant the propeller of the enemy sub was turning very quickly, generating lots of noise. He'd heard the inbound torpedo and was trying to run. He also might fire back. "Increase torpedo speed to maximum. Weapon officer, launch countermeasures."

Graham said, "Torpedo speed to maximum, aye."

Palas said, "Countermeasures launched."

Twenty tense seconds passed. No one said anything.

Graham called, "Loss of wire."

The hull vibrated suddenly.

"Conn, sonar. Explosion at zero-four-seven degrees… I have breakup noises at zero-four-eight degrees."

Reid felt a surge of pride in his boat and crew. He picked up the 1MC handset and made an announcement to the entire boat. "Attention. This is the captain. We've just sunk a type zero-niner-five Chinese SSN. Secure from ultra-quiet. That is all."

As Reid hung up the 1MC handset, he saw smiles and backslaps throughout the command center. "Pilot, engines ahead full. Come to course zero-two-zero." *Time to go after those other ships.*

"Engines ahead full. Come to course zero-two-zero, pilot aye."

* * *

Captain Deng was convinced he'd make it to port. Through his binoculars, he could plainly see the stacked containers on the docks of Long Beach. His crew already stood by on the starboard side, ready to descend to the dock and tie her up. He had reduced speed, overriding Xie's initial objection. Deng had reasoned with him, and even Xie had seen the logic in slowing the vessel, which weighed well over forty-six thousand tons without cargo.

He dropped his binoculars to his chest and looked at the beautiful weather. His ship glided past several other offshore ships at anchor. The waters were calm, and there was no wind to speak of. The docking and subsequent troop landing would be conducted in the best possible conditions.

* * *

Lieutenant Colonel Jesse Morton, USMC, studied the inbound container ship through his binoculars. Morton lay flat on the roof of the Southeast Recovery Building. The height let him see almost every area of the Long Beach Container Terminal.

The red Chinese flag flying from the mast caught his attention and offended him deeply, that they would dare try to invade. The large ship was coming into Pier T, just as he had predicted. Several dozen enemy soldiers stood on the tops of the ship's containers. Many carried surface-to-air missiles on their shoulders, which were no threat to him and his men, but they were a concern, because he was going to depend on friendly air support soon. Morton was the commanding officer of the 2nd Battalion, 7th Marine Regiment. He, along with the 3rd Battalion, had been tasked with holding this position. Normally, they would have been commanded by a general, but no one had been able to find General Scott, who had vanished after everyone went blind. As senior officer, Morton had taken command of the marines.

He slowly lowered the binoculars. Surrounding him were his headquarters staff. He turned to one of his radiomen, Sergeant Bilkins, and held out his hand for the handset. Bilkins handed it over.

Morton held it to his ear and pressed the transmit button to talk to the commanding officer of the 3rd Battalion. "Destiny Actual, this is Rampart Actual, over."

After a brief pause, Morton heard, "Rampart Actual, Destiny Actual, over."

Morton looked up at the incoming ship. "Destiny, he's coming into Pier T at the end of Navy Way. Get your marines in place to defend the access bridges. That's a natural bottleneck and the only way out. If we can hold them there, then they're screwed. Are your snipers set? Over."

"Rampart, roger sir. Snipers are good to go. Over."

"Destiny, wait until we open up, then give 'em hell. Have them take out as many of their anti-air troops and officers as possible. Other than that, no one gets over those bridges, over."

"Rampart, roger. Over and out."

Morton handed the handset back and turned to face Second Lieutenant Williams, his forward air controller. "Williams, make sure you have the coordinates to Navy Way ready to go. As soon as you see a significant force on the dock, get 'claw' to nail 'em."

"Yes, sir."

* * *

"Sir, we are at photonics depth," the pilot stated.

"Sonar, conn. Report all contacts within ten nautical miles," Captain Reid ordered.

"Conn, sonar. One contact, Alpha Seven, heavy merchantman, bearing two-four-seven, range three thousand, speed twenty-two knots."

Captain Reid took two steps to get to the photonics station. "Raise photonics mast."

A hiss of hydraulics sounded for a few seconds, and an image appeared on the flat-panel display. Using the hand control, Reid rotated the camera system a full three hundred and sixty degrees, even after spotting his target ship, to avoid surprises.

Once he completed a full revolution he returned the photonics camera to his target. Behind the ship, he could see a port with several stacks of containers and many tall red cranes. The ship was dangerously close to docking. Reid centered the crosshairs on the ship and pressed a stud on the photonics controls. Above him, an infrared laser found the range to the ship. "Bearing mark, range mark. Angle on the bow, zero-four-zero."

XO Maddox came up beside him. "Big son of a bitch. Close to fifty thousand tons, I'd say. Two ADCAPs?"

Reid nodded. "Yes, we need to make sure he doesn't get ashore." Reid turned on the tracking mode. From that point forward, the photonics camera would automatically track the target ship. "Attention, deck party. I intend to engage surface contact, Alpha Seven. Weapons officer, report tube status."

"All tubes ready in all respects, outer doors are closed," Lieutenant Palas reported.

"Firing point procedures, Alpha Seven…"

Reid ran through the standard engagement procedures for a surface contact and launched two ADCAP torpedoes. He left the photonics camera up and made sure the video was being recorded. Waiting for the weapon impact was the hardest part of the attack.

An explosive eruption on the starboard side of the ship tossed water up and well over its tall superstructure. The second explosion, soon after, rocked the massive ship. Several containers were thrown off the vessel.

Reid zoomed into the ship. Hundreds of people emerged from the containers and raced around the deck. *Just like kicking an anthill.*

The ship began to settle deeper into the water. It listed to the starboard side until water began coming over the rail. More containers fell into the sea in a domino effect.

The ship was doomed. Reid wanted to document the entire sinking, but couldn't take the time. There were other enemy ships to take care of. Reid picked up the 1MC. "This is the captain. We've just sunk the Chinese container ship *Zhan Feng.* That is all." Reid hung up the 1MC and turned toward the navigation table. "Navigator, I need a course to intercept contact Alpha Five heading to Long Beach."

* * *

Captain Deng slipped the container vessel *Feng Mìngyùn* against the concrete dock. The two met with no more force than a tender kiss. From his position on the starboard fly bridge, he watched his crew drop down the sea stairs onto the dock itself and then scrambled to grab the thick hawser lines to secure the ship to the dock. Fifty armed soldiers descended down the sea stairs soon after, not waiting for the vessel to be completely tied up. They spread out around the dock area, looking for any opposition, but Deng saw none from his high vantage spot. Deng took his walkie-talkie and began giving orders to his crew. "Chang, take the—"

A half-dozen soldiers on top of the containers, wielding surface-to-air missiles, fell.

Deng stopped talking in surprise. Multiple loud rifle shots followed soon after. He turned to find which direction they had come from, and something like a lightning bolt hit him in the chest. He fell back, dropping the walkie-talkie.

As he landed on the metal deck, he saw the hand-held radio skitter across the deck then fall overboard. He touched his chest with an open hand then looked at his palm.

It was covered in blood.

He heard multiple weapons fire, coming from the starboard side of the ship.

Deng couldn't move. He had never felt so weak. He saw General Xie run out onto the fly bridge. He glanced down at Deng, obviously horrified, but instead of helping him, he turned on his heel and returned inside in a hurry.

A bullet, obviously aimed at Po, struck the bulkhead where the general had just been standing. It left a deep crater, and several layers of white paint fractured.

It was the last thing Captain Deng saw before his eyes closed of their own accord. He heard several violent explosions as he died.

* * *

At his current location, Lieutenant Colonel Jesse Morton, USMC, had his view of the ship and pier blocked by a tall line of containers. "I can't see anything from here. We're moving closer to the action, people, down to the vehicles. Let's go."

The headquarters staff members packed up their equipment in seconds and ran for the stairs. Morton felt pleased his planning had paid off. He had assumed any inbound ship would dock at the first available space and deployed his troops accordingly. They had parked the ship in the center of his planned ambush.

As he ran down the flights of stairs, he smiled. *Now the slanty-eyed S.O.Bs will pay.*

Three armored Humvees waited at the bottom of the steps to transport him and his staff. Gunners, standing in cutouts in the roof, manned .50 caliber machine guns.

Morton jumped in the passenger seat, and the Humvee began moving forward before he had the door closed.

Sergeant Bilkins called to him from the backseat, "Sir, Major Valentine reports minimal resistance and is asking permission to advance."

Morton whipped around. "Negative. All units are to hold in place and defend only."

"Yes, sir," Bilkins replied.

Morton turned back to face the road. *Valentine's an idiot. This battle's just begun. We don't have that many troops, and we'll lose fewer people if we defend in place.* "Driver, get me to Terminal Island."

"Yes, sir."

The Humvees traveled down the seaside freeway at speed. Morton couldn't see any of the action from this point, but the sounds of mortar and machine gun fire reached him. The marine defenders were giving them hell.

* * *

General Xie ducked in reaction to the light machine gun fire raking the bridge of the *Feng Mìngyùn*. He screamed for a messenger as several explosions sounded along the length of the ship. *Mortars? There are defending troops on the shore.*

A nervous private first class appeared at his elbow. "Comrade General!"

"Senior Colonel Zhuge is to form an initial line on the dock. Then, supported by machine guns from the ship, he's to advance to contact and press forward aggressively. The remainder of his assault force will follow close behind and support where needed. The party tells us this area is sparsely defended. I want this facility secured as fast as possible. Wipe out any defenders!"

"Sir!" The private first class ran down the internal staircase leading to the deck below.

With the volume of fire striking the ship, they were sitting ducks. Getting troops off the ship to engage the attackers was the only sensible route to take.

Xie followed, bending over to minimize the chance of being hit by anything lethal. The machine gun fire hitting the bridge area forced him to crawl the last few meters. Once in the stairwell, he stood up, then descended a level to the radio room.

Xie turned through the hatch to find a half-dozen communication technicians from his division. They'd taken over the space. The senior technician came up to him and braced to attention. "Comrade General."

"I need to send a message to Lieutenant General Yuan," Xie stated.

"Comrade General, we've had no contact with General Yuan's ship since the second wave of air attacks."

If General Yuan was sunk or unable to communicate, then Xie needed to go to the next highest level of command. "Message to General Dezhi at PLA, General Staff Headquarters."

The technician grabbed a message form and pen from a nearby desk. He scribbled hurriedly on the form then looked at Po. "Comrade General, I'm ready to take your message."

Xie paused. *With Yuan out of the picture, my words will be seen at the highest level of the PLA. This is an opportunity for me to be noticed, and I need to ensure it's seen in a positive light. The defenders are throwing up a commendable effort, but the party said the area would be easily taken. I can't contradict that opinion without consequences. Nor do I want to mention the ship losses. My first communication with the general staff needs to be confident and positive. Let others report the losses.*

Xie dictated a brief message. "Send that out immediately, highest priority."

"Yes, Comrade General."

He turned on his heel and went back into the corridor, down two more levels, and toward the hatch out onto the main deck. Ahead of him, he saw several soldiers supervised by a chief sergeant, class 4. All had QBZ-95 assault rifles. The soldiers shot around the corner of the steel door, using it for cover. "Chief Sergeant, I need to get past and see Senior Colonel Zhuge."

The sergeant turned, initially looking annoyed, but his look and attitude changed immediately upon seeing Po. "Comrade General, I wouldn't recommend that route. The open area beyond this door is covered by enemy machine guns, and several men have been shot by snipers already. We're also taking sporadic mortar fire."

A bullet ricocheted off the nearby superstructure to reinforce the sergeant's assessment.

Xie looked out the hatch. Through the hatch to the left was a railing about a meter high. Directly ahead was a space of five meters with no cover. Directly ahead, an open container door held more soldiers firing back. Two still, bloody bodies lay in the open.

Xie needed to cross. He steeled himself. "Give me covering fire, Chief Sergeant. I'm going across."

"Yes, sir!" The chief sergeant yelled across to the soldiers opposite. "Prepare to give covering fire for the general! Ready... *Now!*"

Xie ran out of the hatch as fast as he could. The troops around him fired toward the enemy defenders. In two steps, Xie was halfway across.

A huge explosion directly to Xie's right blew him up and sideways. His upper left thigh struck the railing as he went over. He was aware of falling and the splash of landing in water, but little else.

He lost consciousness knowing he was sinking in the sea but unable to do anything about it.

* * *

From his new vantage point on Terminal Island, Lieutenant Colonel Jesse Morton, USMC, watched as his mortars came into play. They raked the ship from bow to stern, limiting the movement aboard the enemy flagged vessel. He could see most of the Navy Way road and the two key bridges that lay side by side. One bridge had rail lines, and the other a single-lane road. Those were the only places the Chinese could cross onto the mainland from Pier T without a long swim.

The dock area was concrete and perfectly flat. The only cover was to the north of the bridges, and marines were dug in there. Any attacker would have to endure withering crossfire to get across those bridges.

Morton opened his mouth to ask for an update when he heard a shrill whistle blow in the distance.

A mass of hundreds of Chinese troops came into view, screaming and running flat-out for the bridges. Medium and light machine gun fire lanced out from the marine lines. Tracer bullets disappeared into the Chinese and Morton saw bodies fall by the score. A marine mortar began dropping rounds into the attackers and bodies exploded upwards, many landing in the water, but the Chinese still surged forward. There were so many troops that, even with heavy losses, they still advanced.

Morton had heard tales of Korean War troops facing wave after wave of seemingly endless Chinese attackers, but the sight of it in person was something he would never forget. A pair of Humvee-mounted .50 caliber machine guns behind him added their heavy rounds to the slaughter.

Unbelievably, Chinese troops reached the bridges and began to cross, but now the narrow passages gave the defenders the advantage. Marine machine guns could fire directly down those bridges. Numerous bodies fell from both bridges into the water. No one made it past the midway point alive.

Two sharp blows of a whistle sounded. All the surviving Chinese soldiers fell to the ground, took cover, and began returning fire. Several light machine guns began raking marine positions. *They're crawling forward, using their own wounded and dead as cover. They'll try to reduce the defenses and then try to rush forward again.*

A few marine defenders fell to Chinese fire.

Morton whipped around and faced his forward air controller. "Williams, get 'claw' on target immediately."

"Yes, sir." Williams picked up his map and radio handset.

Morton turned to Sergeant Bilkins, "We have inbound aircraft. Make sure the snipers keep the anti-air troops suppressed."

"Yes, sir." Bilkins replied.

* * *

PLA Senior Colonel Zhuge observed the scene before the bridges from his forward command post, located in the door of an empty container. Whoever had chosen this landing zone was an idiot. Only one way off the dock, and that was a natural choke point.

Still, even in the face of heavy fire, his troops had made it to the bridges and were still advancing, albeit by inches at a time. Opposition was heavy, but he still had the advantage of thousands of troops and ample supplies on the ship. It was only a matter of time before they broke through.

"Assemble the reserve units and be ready to rush forward in support when a breakthrough is made. We take no prisoners," he ordered an enlisted runner.

"Yes, Comrade Senior Colonel."

* * *

Captain Sarah "Ducks" Margolis eased the flight controls to port and advanced the dual engine throttles to military power. She flipped the master arm switch to "ON" and prepared for combat. She commanded a flight of six Fairchild Republic A-10C Thunderbolts. Her aircraft, along with five others, had just finished maintenance at Hill Air Force Base and had been destined to return home when the blindness struck. As the aircraft were from all over the country, and she was the senior A-10 pilot, she'd been given command of the flight. She was posted to the 74th Fighter Squadron, so Margolis used their call sign, "Claw."

Margolis had spent over a week being blind in the base gymnasium. She had no idea if her brothers and parents were alive, but the Chinese would pay for what they did to her, at least. "Claw Two, Three, and Four—you're with me. You're cleared hot, and we attack as briefed. Claw Five and Six hold back in reserve," she said into her helmet microphone.

Her flight members acknowledged in turn. Margolis pressed the switch and lowered her seat several inches. From personal experience in Afghanistan, she knew taking ground fire was a serious possibility. With her seat lowered, the titanium armor around the cockpit would protect her.

She reduced altitude to only five hundred feet. With her engines at military power, the world below whizzed by. Margolis selected the weapons on her wing pylons, and her displays changed automatically to deliver that ordinance.

Margolis saw the tall cranes of the container port from a fair distance away and nudged her pedals to line up for her run. She selected the impact point based on the coordinates given to her by the marine forward air controller on the ground. The other A-10Cs would attack from different directions and altitudes to confuse the enemy.

The onboard computer beeped to indicate a lock. All she had to do was stay on course, and the computer would automatically launch the weapons.

Several columns of dark smoke came from a container ship dead ahead, telling Margolis she was heading in the right direction. The ship advanced quickly, and she kept her eyes on the countdown. *Three... Two... One...*

The ejector racks released the four CBU-59B Rockeye II cluster bombs perfectly. "Claw One, pigs away."

Margolis yanked back and to the left on her flight stick while applying maximum left rudder. She released flares and chaff behind her to confuse any missiles. She saw the numerous explosions in her wake. "Claw One, splash."

Her aircraft turned over the water. She kept it in a long bank to see the attacks of her wingmen. They hit other areas of the dock. Each dropped four CBU-59B bombs, which meant twenty-eight hundred exploding sub-munitions were being dropped by each aircraft. Delivered onto a flat concrete surface with nowhere to hide, she imagined it akin to a scythe cutting through tall wheat. *Welcome to the United States, you sons of bitches!*

* * *

Lieutenant Colonel Morton, even though he was over a kilometer from the impact zone, cringed and ducked instinctively as the cluster bombs went off over the area south of the bridges. The noise and sight of the explosions was horrific even from his position.

As the breeze blew the black smoke away, he saw little movement in the target area, and no more weapons fire came from the pile of bodies.

"Sir, Major Valentine is requesting permission to advance again," Sergeant Bilkins said from behind him.

Morton turned on Bilkins, snarling, "Dammit, tell him to hold in place until further orders." He turned back to view the carnage. That ship could potentially hold a lot more men. Having his marines rush forward would place them in the same flat, open killing ground without cover. Then the Chinese would have the advantage and be able to cut them down.

The goal of this mission was to neutralize the Chinese invasion. They were effectively bottled up and could be worn down. Morton saw no reason to risk his marines' lives for no good reason other than "glory." At least, not when the future of his country was on the line.

* * *

Margolis watched Claw Four deliver his ordinance perpendicular to the docked Chinese vessel. General Smith had briefed her that the container ships were being used as troop transports. She looked at the stacks of different containers and decided she could do more. "Claw Five and Six, cleared hot for pigs. Claw Two, Three, and Four cleared hot for guns. Everyone target the containers on the ship."

As the individual acknowledgements came over the radio, Margolis activated her GAU-8A Avenger 30mm cannon. She lined up her crosshairs on the containers themselves. Four thousand feet out, she squeezed the trigger on her flight stick. The airframe vibrated as the weapon sent armor-piercing incendiaries and high-explosive incendiary rounds into the container stacks. She used her rudders to shift the impact point of the rounds left and right, to cover more area.

Designed to kill tanks, the armor-penetrating rounds would easily pass through the sidewalls of the containers, shredding anything unfortunate enough to get in their way.

Margolis pulled up sharply to avoid another A-10C coming in from another direction. As she passed over the ship, she fired off more chaff and flares, just in case anyone got cute with an anti-air missile.

* * *

Senior Colonel Zhuge staggered to his feet and wiped blood from under his nose. The wave of destruction caused by the dropped cluster bombs had barely missed him, but he'd felt the nearby concussion of thousands of exploding rounds. He ignored the nosebleed as a minor nuisance. He needed to keep the momentum going to press back the defenders.

Turning to his radioman he said, "Radio Major—"

The soldier no longer had a face and lay still. Zhuge flipped the man over to get at his back-mounted radio. The jagged hole in the case told him the radio was useless.

There's still hope. I need to gather men for a follow-on attack. There are ten thousand more troops on board. I shall use all of them in one massive push to get across the bridges. I must get back to the ship.

Zhuge checked around the door of the container he occupied. Some of the thick black smoke still persisted from the bombing run. Deciding to use that to his advantage, he ran toward the sea stairs of the ship.

One of the infernal aircraft flew overhead, a mass of smoke and flames coming from its nose. The bullets tore into the container stacks with a deafening roar.

He got halfway to the sea stairs before two massive explosions on the ocean side of the ship stopped him in his tracks. Columns of water shot up several hundred feet, and the ship lurched so hard to starboard that several of the top containers fell off, smashing into the dock's concrete surface. The ship settled back to an even keel before listing quickly to port. Men—his men—scrambled all over the ship to get clear. Few made it off the vessel.

Zhuge began walking toward the ship as the massive hull settled deeper in the water. As he got closer, the starboard side of the ship tilted up, to the point that it broke the thick hawsers securing it to the dock. Desperate men, trying to jump from the ship, fell out of sight into the wide space between the hull and the pier.

His steps faltered as the reality of what he was seeing sunk in. The ship was sinking. There would be no more men, no further offensive...

A bullet exploded out of his chest. Zhuge fell to his knees and remained there. Looking down, he saw the blood bubble on his chest as he tried to breathe. As he bled out, he watched the *Feng Mìngyùn* sink to the shallow bottom at a forty-five degree angle.

Aware he had failed, Zhuge began to weep softly as darkness overwhelmed him.

* * *

Captain Reid watched the display at the photonics station in awe. Several containers tumbled off the deck and into the sea. An A-10 flew over the doomed vessel, banking hard at the last minute. The two ADCAPs he had fired at the docked Chinese ship had done their job. The vessel was no longer a threat. Reid grabbed the 1MC handset. "Attention. This is the captain. We have just sunk the forty-five thousand-ton cargo container vessel *Feng Mìngyùn*. That is all."

Reid hung up the 1MC and turned to the navigator. "I need a course to take us back to the surviving Chinese ships that are dead in the water."

"Aye, Captain."

Reid turned to the CRSS station, which was on the opposite side of the Control Center, and said for the entire compartment to hear, "Chief Holgrim. Send an update to General Smith and let him know we sank the *Feng Mìngyùn* with a pair of ADCAPSs. We don't want the air force taking any credit for our kill."

Holgrim and the surrounding crewmen in the command center laughed out loud. "Roger, skipper."

* * *

Above and back from the coast, General Smith flew in the E-6 Mercury. Apart from an initial report of first contact from the marines, nothing else had been heard. He felt anxious over the lack of news. He checked the time. They could only stay on station for another hour at most. *What the hell is going on down there?*

"Incoming message from the USS *John Warner*, General," announced a naval communications technician over his headset. He quickly selected the message, skipped through the header info, and read the main text.

> *Both surviving container ships heading to port have been sunk. No further threat to mainland detected at this time.*

*Four damaged CHICOM vessels remain adrift in
vicinity of Channel Islands; returning to engage at this time.*

What felt like a weight of thousand pounds lifted from Smith's shoulders. He needed to confirm this message with Lieutenant Colonel Morton and make sure the marines concurred with Reid's assessment, but the content of the message was exactly what he wanted to see.

And after checking with Morton, he needed to update the president.

* * *

General Secretary Gao called for an emergency politburo meeting. Most politburo members were in their offices, so even though it was two in the morning, they were able to respond quickly to his summons.

Gao had been the first to arrive and sat in his usual place at the head of the table. As they came into the meeting chamber, he looked over each man. All had stated they supported him, but he knew a few felt differently in private. Regardless, they would all have to be watched.

The doors of the meeting room closed as the last member, Shen, arrived.

Gao called the meeting to order as Shen sat down. "I have a message from the invasion force and wished you to hear it."

He picked up the message form he had been handed twenty minutes earlier. He shook the page once to get it to stand up and read verbatim:

*Initial invasion landings conducted successfully.
Minor opposition encountered. They shall be
brushed aside for the glory of the party.*

"The message is signed Major General Xie," Gao concluded.

There was silence in the room.

Quishan spoke first. "Who is Major General Xie? I've not heard his name before."

Gao placed the message on the table. "I asked the same question. Xie is an army corps commander. If General Yuan was incapacitated, Xie would take over."

More silence.

Shen frowned and leaned forward. "The message is optimistic, certainly. However, there is little detail."

Gao placed his forearms on the table. "I have asked for clarification as to the location of the landings, type of resistance, casualties suffered, etc. I'm sure that information will be forthcoming. However, I wanted to pass along the information I did have."

"Thank you, Comrade General Secretary, for your consideration," said Wei Sun.

"We shall reconvene when we have more information." Gao dismissed them.

As the men left the room, he noticed no elation. The men acted as if they were at a state funeral. Instead of scoffing at them, Gao found he shared their dark mood, and he hoped future news was positive.

* * *

Upon landing back at Hill Air Force Base, General Smith unstrapped himself. He bounded down the portable stairs as several of the navy aircrew slapped his back and shook his hand. The smiling crew displayed an overwhelming sense of relief.

A golf cart awaited him at the foot of the stairs, but an unknown male officer stood nearby.

He saluted, saying, "General, I'm Second Lieutenant Kramer. Captain Tyler asked me to pick you up and deliver you to your quarters."

Smith returned the salute and slip onto the bench seat. Kramer jumped behind the wheel.

"Where is she?" Smith asked.

"I don't know, sir. Captain Tyler simply said she needed me to drive you, as she had other matters to attend to."

The cart began moving forward. Morton had confirmed the marines were mopping up the last of the opposition on the docks. The president had been thrilled upon hearing the news. After several hours of flying, he needed a shower and to change out of his flight suit back into a regular uniform.

Kramer dropped him off outside the Mountain View Inn. Smith alit from the cart.

"Shall I wait, sir?" Kramer asked.

"No, thank you. I'll walk back to flight ops. After being strapped in a seat for eight hours, I need to stretch my legs."

"Very good, General." Kramer pulled away.

Smith walked upstairs, retrieved his room key from his flight suit, and opened his door. He tossed his key onto the nearby side table and slammed the door closed. As he entered his bedroom, he began unzipping his flight suit.

He stopped on the threshold. Captain Tyler sat up in his bed with a sheet just barely covering her breasts. She looked to be naked underneath.

She patted the bed beside her, smiling at him. "'To the victor belong the spoils.' Come over here and let me spoil you."

Smith stood there, his fingers on his flight suit zipper. She wanted him, obviously, and he had always been attracted to her.

The sight of her black skin against the white sheets was all the convincing he needed. He stepped toward the bed, unzipping the rest of the way.

July 17th

Chapter Thirty-One
An Eye for an Eye

President James Calvin brought the morning brief to order exactly at six a.m. In the conference room were Vice President Hurst, Colonel Monk, the commanding officers of all base units, three secret service agents, and several support staff. Through the windows, Calvin could see bright sunshine, and a gentle breeze tickled the ends of visible trees outside of the headquarters building.

"Colonel Monk, please proceed," Calvin stated.

"Yes, Mister President." Colonel Monk stood and unrolled a large laminated map of the United States he'd produced from beside his chair. Neighboring officers helped him hold it down by placing empty water glasses on the corners. He pointed to Los Angeles. "To begin, General Smith reports all Chinese ships have been sunk through a combination of efforts from air force and naval units. The few PLA troops that did land in Long Beach were contained, and several hundred prisoners were taken. They are being held on site until their disposition can be arranged."

Calvin asked, "What were our casualties?"

"Sir, the marines report thirty-seven KIA and ninety-three wounded. Aircraft losses are unchanged from yesterday's brief. I'll have a full list of casualties to you by noon." Monk sat down.

Calvin made a note to write personal letters to the families of those marines and pilots who'd lost their lives. "Thank you. Continue."

Monk drew a circle around Washington DC with red wax pencil. "Tenth Mountain began their offensive in DC two hours ago. They started after jamming enemy communications. Their first assault took the Chinese airborne troops by surprise, and they were able to destroy their main supply dump. They're making steady progress in spite of stiff resistance. The 10th Mountain commanding officer estimates two to three days of combat to retake the city. The 1st Fighter Wing out of Langley-Eustis should be supporting the offensive with thousand-pound bombs later this morning.

"Other military units are slowly becoming available. They'll be used against other occupied bases as soon as they are able to conduct operations."

"Thank you," Calvin said.

Monk sat down.

Calvin looked to his right. "Keith, where do we stand on tube distribution?"

Hurst stood and pointed at Seattle on Monk's map. "Washington State, especially the city of Seattle, is in excellent shape. The majority of the surviving population has been cured. Communications and power stations are coming back online, and life is returning to normal. According to Doctor Krause in Oak Ridge, production of the tubes is ramping up faster than estimated. All states surrounding Tennessee have National Guard units cured or in the process of being cured. She estimates they'll have tubes in all contiguous states within three days."

Calvin sighed in relief. "That's good news."

Hurst shook his head and glanced down. "It is, but initial estimates of civilian casualties are running between thirty to fifty percent at this time."

Calvin made some quick calculations on his notepad. "So you're saying we've lost between ninety to a hundred and fifty million people? What about the shelters we ordered set up?"

"The losses would have been much higher without them, sir. The shelters were mostly in cities. Many people, especially in rural areas, didn't go to them, electing to stay home or with family. When they ran out of supplies, malnutrition combined with dehydration and disease took its toll."

Calvin clenched his pen in his fist. He had been expecting some deaths, but up to *half* the population? That was horrific. *A hundred and fifty million people dead, and that's just in this country. What's the loss worldwide? A billion? More?*

No one said anything for some time. Calvin realized he had to move on to other business. "What about the United Kingdom?"

"Tubes were delivered to Number Ten late yesterday evening. Prime Minister Gladstone has asked to speak to you in two hours' time. I suspect he'll be asking for radioactive material to build their own until they can get their reactors operational."

"Coordinate with Doctor Krause and see what she can do to assist. We're now in a race to save the population of the world, and we shall do whatever we can to save as many lives as possible."

"Yes, Mister President," Hurst replied.

* * *

Captain Reid conducted his daily walkthrough accompanied by Chief of the Boat Duggan, as usual. Smiles greeted him in every compartment as he worked his way forward from the rear of the boat.

On entering the torpedo compartment, he realized the men were quiet and, if anything, morose.

Chief Petty Officer Marquez saw him and came over. "Good morning, skipper."

"Morning, chief. Why the long faces?" Reid asked.

Marquez said softly, "Sir, the men feel like they let you down. A lot of them agreed with Wyatt when he started shooting off his mouth, but now they realize that you were right in defending the coast and their families. They're, well, sir, ashamed of themselves that they didn't trust you."

Reid nodded and called out, "Everyone, gather around." He waited while the crew assembled. "Chief Duggan and I wanted to thank each and every one of you for your service on this patrol. We're the first U.S. submarine since 1945 to sink a ship in combat. In the space of eight hours, we sank a half-billion tons of transports and a pair of modern escort destroyers. That's something a hundred German U-Boats needed a month to accomplish in World War Two. Your fast response in loading a Mark 50 resulted in the sinking of a Chinese nuclear attack boat."

Reid looked around. His men were looking better, more optimistic. "I hope to take every last man here on our next deployment. You're now all combat veterans who've proven themselves under fire, and I'll be honored to serve with you again."

Reid stuck out his hand to the nearest torpedo man. He hadn't planned that, it just happened. They shook hands, and Reid kept going until he'd shaken hands with everyone from the torpedo room save Chief Marquez.

Reid turned to see Marquez wiping his watery eyes.

"Thank you for those words, Captain," Marquez stammered.

Reid shook his hand. "You have one last duty, Chief Marquez."

"Sir?" Marquez asked in a broken voice.

"I'll expect to see a broom on our mast[45] when we sail into port. Make sure you track one down."

The chief's chest swelled. "Yes, sir. You can count on it, Captain."

Several crewmen in the Torpedo Room slapped each other on the backs. Any shadow of negativity had vanished.

---

[45] A naval tradition. The broom on a submarine mast indicates a "clean sweep" to indicate all enemies have been swept from the seas.

* * *

Larry Vinson and his communications equipment had been relegated to a small office in the basement of the base headquarters building. He'd been told it was for his own protection in case bombs fell, but he knew the military just wanted the space close to the president for themselves. Even in the midst of a global blindness pandemic, inter-service rivalries still occurred.

He'd been offended initially but decided it was probably for the best in the long run. Air force communications technicians had moved in to "assist him," but he recognized they were trying to take over the systems and edge him out. A quiet word with the vice president had stopped him from being excluded completely, but they were now effectively running the communications, and he had little to do. He still maintained the clandestine back door into the Chinese network, as he had not advertised that fact to anyone but the president and vice president. No one else on base knew about that little secret.

Vinson had just checked in with Noel and passed on some information for General Smith. Afterwards, the two men had caught up. Vinson was replacing the handset after that call when the president and vice president of the United States walked into his room without knocking.

He stood from behind his small desk only to be waved back down by Calvin. Hurst closed the door on two Secret Service agents who stood post outside, and the two men pulled up chairs.

James Calvin said, "Mister Vinson, we need to ask you to do something for us."

Vinson finished hanging up the handset. "Yes, sir?"

Calvin took a deep breath. "Up to half of our civilian population have died, or will die. A higher percentage globally will not survive, as we simply can't get the cure to them fast enough. The Chinese have damned billions of people to a slow and lingering death. Even if we can cure the world, as we recover, China can press its advantage on multiple fronts to emerge as the dominant power for some time. We can't allow that."

"Yes, sir?" Vinson had a suspicion what was coming next.

"We need to rebalance the scales." Calvin described what he wanted.

* * *

General Smith looked around the flight ops building for Captain Tyler. He found her outside near the golf cart, talking to a male lieutenant.

"Good morning," Smith said as he approached.

Tyler saluted. "General, this is Lieutenant Bell. He'll be taking over all aide duties from me immediately. I've reviewed his record, and I think you'll find him to be a solid resource you can rely on."

"I'm looking forward to my new duties as your aide, General," Bell said with enthusiasm.

Smith frowned. "Lieutenant, if you would wait inside, please? I'd like a word with Captain Tyler."

"Yes, sir!" He saluted and then retreated inside.

When Bell was well out of earshot, Smith faced her. "Is something wrong?"

"I can't be your lover and work for you. It isn't professional, and we could both be charged with misconduct. Bell is a good choice. Besides, I'm resigning my position as soon as I can. I'm simply not cut out to wear the uniform."

He took a step closer to her, forcing her to tilt her head back to continue to look into his eyes. "Are you just leaving the job, or me as well?"

She paused. "I'd only planned on taking off the uniform."

"Good," he replied immediately, and she smiled. "Now, before you quit, you should know Noel just spoke to Vinson. Your parents are safe and sound. Your father slept through the fireworks, and he's not only been taking care of your mother, but he also brought in several neighbors. There's a transport aircraft leaving for New York within the hour." Smith produced some folded papers from his uniform shirt pocket. He handed them over to her. "I can't give you leave, as that was cancelled indefinitely by presidential order, so here's your duty travel orders to New York state. You're going to assess the impact of the blindness in the region of Severance, New York, for the next week. Report back here when you're done."

She looked at the papers in her hand with obvious disbelief. "I can see my parents?"

"Yes. There'll be a tube for your use on board the transport as well. Use it wisely, Captain."

She grabbed him without warning. Wrapping her arms around his neck, she broke down in tears. "I can't think of a better gift. Thank you, Alvin."

He hugged her quickly and nudged her back. She had been right earlier; it wouldn't be appropriate to have his aide holding him. "You'd better get going, Captain. Take the golf cart."

She braced to attention and saluted, tears in her eyes. "Yes, sir. Thank you, sir."

* * *

General Secretary Gao called for another late-night meeting at ten p.m. Contrary to his usual custom, he was the last of the seven to arrive, and he was several minutes late. He carried a series of message forms in his hands.

Gao sat down and said without preamble, "Comrades, I came directly from the communications center." As he went through each point, he tossed the respective message form onto the table before him. "The information coming out of the United States is fragmentary and incomplete. Nothing more has been received from Major General Xie, despite numerous attempts to contact him. A fragmentary message was received from airborne forces in Washington DC. The contents were garbled and unreadable. The rest of the airborne forces in the U.S. have checked in, reporting nothing untoward." He tossed the last page onto the desk.

Wei Sun pounded the table with a closed fist. "This is unforgivable. We must impress on our force commanders the need to report to us in both a timely and accurate manner. Even if we have to shoot a few to inspire the rest!"

Guoliang Jang spoke in a calm voice from the opposite side of the table. "May I suggest we utilize our reconnaissance satellites to take images of the Los Angeles and Long Beach Ports to gain information?"

Gao sighed. "I've tasked them to do just that along with Washington DC and Colorado. However, I'm told the launching of the blindness warheads set back our own surveillance program maintenance schedule, and several of our spy satellites are low on maneuvering fuel. It will take four hours to shift them into the right orbits."

Wei Sun pounded the table with his palm. "I shall investigate this failure and—"

The double doors to the conference room burst open, and the head of Gao's personal protection detail, Tung He, entered. Behind him, two suit-wearing men followed, carrying stubby automatic weapons. "Comrade General Secretary, the city is under attack. For your safety, you must come with us to the bunker immediately."

"Attack? What are you talking about, He?" Gao and the other politburo members stood.

"We're not sure, Comrade General Secretary. We can see what may be bombing on the horizon," he replied.

"Show me, immediately!" Gao demanded, heading for the door. The rest fell in step behind him.

He led them out onto the seventh-floor balcony and pointed into the distant sky. "There, strange lights, on the horizon."

Many people below him were also pointing up.

Gao strained his eyes but saw nothing. "I see noth—"

The entire sky lit up as if it were day. The illumination undulated in the air, shimmering, shifting the colors of everything around him. Reds became blue. Blues became green. Greens faded to black.

Gao screamed and tried to cover his eyes with his forearm and elbow. He already knew it was too late. "*Noooo!*"

Tung He came up beside Gao. "Comrade General Secretary, are you harmed? Comrade General Secretary?"

Gao pulled his arm away from his eyes. The secret of the blindness warhead had been held very tightly. Even his own protection detail hadn't known of its existence.

Gao collapsed to his knees, panic overwhelming him. Someone had deployed their own blindness warheads on China. He would be blind within a day, and there was no cure, no hope.

Tung He reached down to help him up. "Comrade General Secretary, are you injured? Let me take you to the bunker and have your physician examine you."

As soon as he was on his feet, Gao knew he could never live as a blind man. Those who were not affected by the blindness would take his position and his power, and he would eventually be liquidated. He would not face being helpless and dependent on others. He *could* not face that. Gao straight-armed Tung He away from him and threw himself over the railing. The ground rushed up, and he closed his eyes.

He never made a sound until he struck the concrete sidewalk seven floors below.

Author's Afterword

During my time in the Air Force, part of my daily duties included refueling anti-submarine maritime patrol aircraft, specifically, P-3s. One summer day, while on the flight line doing just that, I breathed in what I considered to be a minor amount of fumes from JP-4 aviation fuel. Within a few minutes, I could no longer see out of my left eye, and the vision in my right was spotted, fuzzy, and fading quickly. All I could see through my left eye was a milky white color, with the odd isolated spot of color.

At the base hospital, I received oxygen, and within twenty minutes, my sight returned. I had maintained some vision in my right eye throughout the incident, but I came very close to losing that as well. The memory of that event stuck with me.

Years later, during a Canada Day fireworks celebration in St. Andrews, New Brunswick, I had the opportunity to SCUBA dive in shallow water directly under the wharf where the pyrotechnics were being ignited. I turned off my dive lights and let the colors of the explosions above be my only illumination. The colored lights appeared quite different under the water due to the diffractive nature of seawater. There was no sound underwater, and the pulsing lights looked strange and alien.

The inspiration for *Twinkle* came from a combination of those experiences.

In my science fiction novels, I try to place the science first and fiction second. Doctor Helena Reinardy, PhD, a Postdoctoral Scientist and Doctor Andrea Bodnar, PhD, Associate Scientist—both of the Bermuda Institute of Oceanic Sciences (BIOS)—assisted me in keeping the science behind the blindness warheads and cure solidly based in reality.

Exposure to UV light does not cause retinoblastoma. While UV light can damage the eye's tissues over time, causing cataracts, pterygium, and photokeratitis (snow blindness), I found no definitive link connecting UV light to any cancerous growth in the eye. That was an invention of mine (and why this book is in the science fiction genre). A good pair of UV-filtering sunglasses will keep your eyes healthy in the long term.

Isotope radiation is indeed used to treat cancer, but takes weeks and multiple exposures. I had to both dramatically shorten that time line and oversimplify the process to make the story progress in a timely fashion.

My gratitude to my Alpha readers: Jim Gleason, Marcus Cooper, Christina Azharian and Janice Chase for their early feedback and comments on this manuscript.

Thanks go to Jeff Shelton and numerous unnamed members of the research and production staff at the Oak Ridge National Laboratory in Tennessee for providing me with in-depth information on rhenium-188 and its production. It played a huge role in forming the backbone of the novel and kept it scientifically plausible. The half-life of rhenium-188 is only 16.94 days, so the material degrades quite quickly. It is used in many different applications and has emerged as a consistent, and reasonably safe, treatment for cancer.

The initial draft of *Twinkle* began with an alien invader using blinding warheads from orbit. After three chapters, it became obvious the premise wasn't working, and while trying to work through the issues, I watched twenty minutes of cable news concerning the shooting of unarmed protestors in Biru, Tibet, by Chinese soldiers. Soon after, I changed the aggressors to human beings, and the story jumped onto the page. Humanity abuses their fellows far worse than anything an alien species could imagine. On a daily basis, we are exposed to open warfare, ethnic cleansing, child soldiers, drone strikes, dictatorships, gun violence, piracy, domestic surveillance, coups, terrorism, chemical and biological weapons—and there is more we don't know about. For those who doubt the communist Chinese military/government would act in such an atrocious manner as represented in this novel, I ask you pick up a pertinent newspaper and read some history books.

The Chinese communist government has shown a brutal hand to those unable to defend themselves. After the establishment of the People's Republic of China in 1949, there followed the Korean War, the invasion of Tibet, the Cultural Revolution, numerous Spratly Island confrontations, Tiananmen Square, and many other more recent incidents. Even today, unbridled political repression, imprisonment, and draconian punishment of their own citizens continue. My portrayal is rather tame in comparison.

If Carl Waverly did type a tweet inside China to announce a global fireworks display, it would have been filtered and deleted automatically, as Twitter traffic is blocked (as is Facebook) on the "Great Firewall of China." Indeed, "free speech" inside the People's Republic of China is as fictional as this novel.

In Tibet alone, an estimated one million people have died since the Chinese invaded. The actual number is probably higher, but Chinese officials do not release such information publicly. The Chinese government has imported seven and a half million Chinese citizens into Tibet, resulting in the native six and a half million Tibetans being outnumbered in their own country. Unemployment and inflation for Tibetans is rampant. Numerous UN Resolutions (1353, 1723, and 2079) and multiple international condemnations of the Chinese human rights abuses in Tibet have been dismissed, vetoed, or simply ignored by the Chinese communist government through the years. At one point, only twelve of the three thousand Buddhist monasteries in Tibet survived destruction. Many were used for target practice by PLA artillery units. With the Chinese control of all media in the country, the Tibetans have suffered in metaphorical silence for decades.

This is not purely a Chinese issue, however. "Civilization" has supposedly been around for over four thousand years, but we are not maturing as a species. If anything, we're sliding backwards. It seems as if every good act in this world is met by three bad ones. As this world metaphorically shrinks in size, I suspect this to get worse over time. I do hope I'm wrong, for all our sakes.

The information presented about NORAD, military units, their call signs, command structures, plus all information dealing with presidential security along with the various "sites" referenced were taken from public information sources, news stories, and various other reputable references. Obviously, some of that information is closely guarded and changes without notice. I also had to amend a few things to make the story progress coherently. Everything presented in the above areas is, to the best of my knowledge, accurate at the time of writing. That being said, I did take a few liberties in order to make the story flow better. Those "in the know" will recognize what I'm referring to.

Writers typically get critiqued for inaccurately writing about the military. Militaries operate in secret, for obvious reasons. Much of what I did in the military thirty years ago is still classified, as an example. Firsthand, accurate information is hard to come by. I did receive assistance from several former serving members of the U.S. Air Force and Navy, who shall remain nameless at their request. I certainly have not disclosed any information that has not already been published elsewhere.

The USS *John Warner* (SSN-785) is one of twelve *Virginia*-class submarines purchased by the U.S. Navy. It had a keel-laying ceremony in March of 2013 and is under construction as I write these words. It is due to be delivered to the U.S. Navy in 2015.

Astute readers will have noticed that I shortened the ranks of the PLAAF. Typically the words *Kong Jun* (literally "Air Force") are placed in front of all Chinese Air Force ranks to differentiate them from the PLA ranks. The correct rank for a Lieutenant General would therefore be, "Air Force Lieutenant General." As this was cumbersome to write and would be confusing to some, I chose to omit it.

If you see anything you feel is factually incorrect, please contact me via my website, and I'll be happy to address it.

Twinkle was not an easy novel to research. I typically spend one to two weeks investigating various facts before writing a novel. The depth of *Twinkle* required three solid months of my time before a single word was written.

Ronald Perron supplied a list of all U.S. squadron call signs, which I relied on heavily. Through correspondence he was also kind enough to give me advice on their application.

The Mount Weather Emergency Operations Center (Site MW) opened in 1959 near Bluemont, Virginia, and remained secret until December 1974 when TWA Flight 514 crashed into the side of the mountain. The site is today maintained by FEMA and designed to support Continuity of Government plans. In times of crisis, senior civilian leaders and military personnel would be located there.

Fort McNair (Site E) became the place where Congress would assemble during an emergency after the west wing of the Greenbrier hotel in West Virginia was exposed as having a secret bunker under it. The Greenbrier does host tours of the former congressional bunker. Fort McNair does not.

The Raven Rock Mountain Complex (RRMC or Site R) was the "undisclosed location" that Vice President Dick

Cheney used during the 9/11 crisis. It is located in Pennsylvania, ten kilometers northeast of Camp David. In a national emergency, it would host the sixteen U.S. intelligence services and the Joint Chiefs of Staff. It is colloquially known as the "backup Pentagon."

The bunker described in Pottstown, PA, does exist. I came across a reference of a homeless man living in this Cold War-era bunker while conducting initial research into this novel. It's a two-level concrete structure completely below ground near the Pottstown Memorial Medical Center, and it belonged to AT&T as part of the Long Lines communication network that crossed the United States. This bunker was one of many that would have provided cross-country communications in the aftermath of a nuclear attack. Some adept searching online will result in above- and below-ground photos along with an architectural layout of the bunker, if interested. I used those references to flesh out my descriptions.

The Pottstown bunker is located at 40°14'30.89?N, 75°36'40.07?W.

It should be mentioned that this is private property and does have active (and reportedly very loud) alarms.

In July 1958, from thirty to three hundred miles around Washington, DC, there were ninety bunkers and backup facilities designed to operate the U.S. government in times of crisis. Another three hundred relocation sites existed across the United States for regional and field offices of various government agencies. No one knows how many are in operation today.

The U.S. Navy keeps its secrets close to its chest, and I could find few recent "official" U.S. references to sonar or submarine operations published since 1954. Ironically, my best source of information came from Russian websites and journals, which openly publish extensive papers on sonar propagation, convergence zones, and even military application of those technologies. I used those references where official U.S. Navy sources proved inadequate. I credit their use of

English-captioned pictures rather than my limited and underused Russian language skills.

In addition to SSN- and SSBN-type submarines, the U.S. Navy operates four SSGN-class boats (Submersible Self-propelled Guided Nuclear). They remained unmentioned to keep confusion to a minimum.

An excellent starting place to learn more about obscure Cold War communications infrastructure may be found here:

http://coldwar-c4i.net

The title of "Duke of Clarence" has been established five times since its first inception in 1362. The third and certainly most colorful Duke of Clarence was executed for treason in 1478. He died by being drowned in a barrel of Malmsey wine. The title has not been used in the United Kingdom since 1892, when Prince Albert Victor of Wales, the son of King Edward VII, died of pneumonia, leaving no heirs. In theory, a ruling monarch of the United Kingdom can reinstate this title at any time. I used this title in relation to the character of Denise Cartwright to avoid confusion with any active royal lineage.

AIS (Automatic Identification System) tracks ships and is used to identify and track vessels around the world. The system works through a digital exchange of information with other ships, shore stations, and satellites. Anyone can see real-time locations of ships in any part of the world at the following web site:

http://www.marinetraffic.com/ais/

The last ship to be torpedoed and sunk in combat by a U.S. Navy submarine was Japanese Coastal Defense Vessel No. 47 on August 14, 1945. The USS *Torsk* (SS-423) was on her second patrol under the command of Commander Bafford E. Lewellen. The Japanese ship was attacked with an acoustic

Mark 27 torpedo and sank at 35°41'N, 134°38'E. The order to cease offensive operations was sent out on August 15, 1945. The USS *Torsk* still survives and is docked at the Baltimore Maritime Museum.

The paragraph above took me a week of searching to discover. Several of my posts on Navy forums went unanswered, and I finally received an e-mail from Charles R. Hinman, who sent a detailed response to my inquiry. Thank you, sir. His web site is:

http://www.oneternalpatrol.com/

Vinson's tapping into a computer network through a VPN is based on an actual event.

At one point in my career, I was working for a large organization as their IT manager. A major accounting firm talked a company vice president into doing an IT audit, telling him they would use state-of-the-art methods to validate and improve our security. He agreed, and two weeks later, half a dozen accountants descended on our offices. They plugged their laptops into my network and began doing a security survey. One of them activated a VPN package to check his corporate e-mail, and I was surprised to see a new domain appear on my workstation. It had the same domain name as the accounting firm. I clicked it to find I could access over eleven hundred computers, servers, and other associated nodes listed from their branch offices worldwide. They used a simplistic naming system, in which their CEO's laptop was called "CEOLAPTOP," their payroll server was called "PAYROLL," etc. When I clicked on their "HR_FILES" server, I found a subdirectory of almost a thousand folders with people's names. I recognized it as a staff listing, as the six accountants doing the audit each had a folder. All this information was accessible to me without a username or password. In fact, of the ten or so servers I checked, none— including their payroll server, accounts, HR, or file servers (individually named "MOSCOW," "LONDON," and "NEWYORK," etc.)—had any protections whatsoever. It was an egregious lack of even the simplest of security measures. Anyone with evil intent and a delete key could have done a lot of damage in a very short period.

Later in the week, after they had presented their audit findings (my network passed with flying colors), I handed over printed screenshots of their own internal network layout and a two-page list of suggestions on how to improve their own security. To the best of my knowledge, we never received a bill for their audit, but I did get an unsolicited phone call weeks later asking if I'd be interested in working for the same accounting company, "in an IT security capacity."

After some discussion, I said no. To my credit, I didn't begin laughing until after I'd hung up. Don't get me wrong, I love a professional challenge, and the money they offered was decent, but some problems are so huge the only sane option is to walk away.

Thank you for supporting my work! I hope you enjoyed my latest novel. Please feel free to leave a review where you purchased this book to let other readers know what you think. For up-to-date information on this book and other projects, please check out my website:

http://sjparkinson.com

Novels by SJ Parkinson

The Legionnaire: Origins
The Legionnaire: Mask of the Pharaoh
The Legionnaire: Vendetta of Shadows

Predation
Twinkle

Available in electronic reader and paperback formats.

More coming soon…

Made in the USA
Charleston, SC
09 November 2014